THE CLINIC

"Doctor Lambert," Joanna said, "you offered me a career as a marital counselor. I understand the need for surrogate partners, and I was willing to do my best, but. . . ." Joanna looked away. "It is extraordinarily difficult for me."

Lambert knew he had to quell her objections quickly. She was the key to so much.

He might even say that she was the key to everything.

The Clinic

Charlotte Mallory

TOR

A TOM DOHERTY ASSOCIATES BOOK
Distributed by Pinnacle Books, New York

(title of book) THE CLINIC

Copyright © 1981 by Cnarlotte Mallory

A Tor Book

First printing, October, 1981

ISBN: 0-523-48017-2

Cover illustration by Frank Marchesano

Printed in the United States of America

Distributed by Pinnacle Books, 1430 Broadway, New York, N.Y. 10018

THE CLINIC

1

It amused Dr. Dawson Lambert to think he had once considered asking Joanna Caldwell to wear contact lenses. Her eyes were blue, large and arresting, but she covered them with huge oval lenses which seemed to fill half her face and make her look like some kind of blonde, Nordic owl. But now, as she sat across the desk from him, her head bent forward slightly as she read the file folder, he realized the glasses made her look studious and professional, even scholarly. A very nice touch, indeed.

Appearances were not everything, he knew, but how a person looked surely was important. He had a highly developed sense of himself and the impression he made, handsome but kindly, friendly but dignified, authoritative yet fatherly, a man who could make a woman's heart beat faster while inspiring confidence and trust at the same time.

It was all carefully arranged, beginning with his selection of conservative three-piece suits to accentuate his tall, lanky figure. He was fifty-seven but had a full head of thick hair, for which he was grateful. It was gray, almost white, with a dark fringe around his ears. He wore it just long enough and had it cut so it looked a trifle unruly and boyish. He affected a white brush mustache to lend authority and applied the sunlamp each morning to enhance an appearance of ruddy good health and deepen the laugh wrinkles around his eyes. He knew the importance of eyes. Indeed he did. His were a gift, a remarkable deep blue-violet under heavy, artificially darkened brows. Years ago he had learned the value of eye contact, focusing directly, unblinkingly on another person, a slight smile of intense interest on his lips. He had practiced until he could hold the pose an extraordinarily long time.

He had parlayed his appearance into a thriving practice in, first, obstetrics, then gynecology. As luck and his own interests would have it, he became increasingly interested in treating sexual problems. His book *In Search of Eros* had become a best seller. After a year on talk shows and the lecture circuit, he had opened the Center for Human Potential here in Westport, Connecticut. It was a whole lot more fun than giving pelvic exams and taking pap smears. And he was in the process of making a fortune. Masters and Johnson could have their scholarship and science. He'd take the money, thank you.

His thoughts came back to Joanna Caldwell. Yes, appearance counted, and those big glasses were the right touch. Her hair style helped, too. She combed her straw-colored hair straight back from her face and tied it behind her ears. With that severe hair and those big glasses she looked every inch the proper psychologist. He smiled inwardly—well, almost. What she really looked like was the sexpot of the western world—blonde; blue eyes; smooth, puffy, magnetic lips and soft translucent skin that seemed to demand to be touched. He glanced down from her face, searching for her breasts beneath the white medical coat. He couldn't see them, the way she sat, but it didn't matter. He knew they were there, so high and pointy he would have sworn she had been to the plastic man if he didn't know better. God, she sure looked sexy. But she was right to play it down. To have her too obviously a sexpot would be bad for business.

He felt a touch of envy. He had recruited her, trained her and brought her along to be the best in the business. The folder she was reading was proof of that. But he had never touched her. Nor would he, no matter how much the thought appealed to him. She was a valuable asset. One untoward move from him and he'd lose her. She trusted him, and right now trust was the coin of the realm.

She looked up from the folder, disbelief on her face. "Brad Dillon—the actor?"

He smiled. "You're surprised?"

She looked down at the folder again and read the medical report sent from a Beverly Hills psychiatrist. Brad Dillon, America's newest he-man, heartthrob and sex symbol, was a premature ejaculator of a chronic and debilitating nature. Severe personal and psychological problems had resulted. Treatment was requested. Still looking at the folder, she said, "I guess I am."

He spoke quietly and with authority, his voice deep and well modulated. "You shouldn't be. The macho types often have sex problems—chiefly, I think, because too much is expected of them. Dillon has had a big buildup as both an Adonis and some sort of sexual freak. The moment he started to believe it, he was in trouble. Does that make sense to you?"

She raised her head to listen to him. "Yes."

"It's seen in actresses a lot, too. I call it the Marilyn Monroe syndrome. The image is divorced from reality. Unreal expectations lead to disappointments, then to worry about performance and finally to serious sexual dysfunction—and we have a new patient at the Center for Human Potential."

She listened, but she had heard it all before, many

times. "Is he married?"

"As you might guess from that report, no. Nor does he have a girlfriend who might be suitable. As you can imagine, this is all going to be very hush-hush. Can't have his image tarnished. I know I can count on your discretion."

She was shocked. "Me? I'm to—"

"Yes. I can't think of anyone more qualified."

"But—"

"The similarities between Brad Dillon and your ex-husband must be obvious, Joanna. Judd Forbes was a big football star, he-man, body beautiful, that sort of thing. He was under the same sort of pressure I suspect Dillon has. You handled your husband's problem extremely well. You should do the same for Dillon."

He remembered the first time he had seen her and Forbes together. She was so gorgeous, blonde, all eyes, and that figure. No wonder Forbes kept getting his rocks off early. But he was such a fool. Fearless Forbes, star halfback, vain as a peacock and nothing but a jock.

"My husband and I are divorced, Dr. Lambert. I couldn't have been too successful."

"But you were, Joanna. Judd Forbes came in here with a serious sexual dysfunction. You took instruction, you followed the course of treatment to perfection, you worked with him. And you cured him. Am I not right?"

Images flicked through her mind, she and Judd in their bedroom, dutifully performing the exercises. "Yes." She smiled wanly. "The operation was a success, but unfortunately the patient died."

"Joanna, his sexual problem was only a symptom. I warned you of that, if you'll remember. He was grossly immature and had serious problems of self-image. He'll never make a successful marriage until he grows up. I know it takes two to make a divorce, but in your case I know your only fault was in selecting a poor husband."

She sighed. His words comforted her and they were probably right. Her marriage to Judd Forbes had been all show and glitter, no substance, the cheerleader and the football jock, female beauty and male handsomeness personified. They made the perfect couple. So everyone said. But everyone didn't go to bed with Judd Forbes—at least not then. He was a disaster and on advice they had come here to the Center for treatment. He hadn't wanted to. He couldn't admit any physical weakness. She had insisted and had worked with him and cured him. He had learned to perform like a man. And that had made divorce inevitable. He couldn't have anyone know of his weakness. He couldn't be constantly reminded by her presence. And there were all those chicks out there for him now to enjoy.

She heard Lambert speaking. "You were so very good with your husband, so patient and understanding. That's why I asked you to come to work here. I have never regretted it for an instant. I hope you haven't."

She had. "Dr. Lambert, I was hoping that when I finished with Wofford, I could work more with the married patients, do more counseling."

Most people referred to the Center were husband and wife seeking cures for impotence, frigidity or some other sexual dysfunction. During an intense two-week period, the couple received counseling and detailed instruction, then were sent off to hotel rooms to practice, returning to the Center each day for evaluation of their progress and more instruction. Lambert had told Joanna he was recruiting her for this work, but from the first he knew she would make a damn near perfect surrogate partner. The Center accepted unmarried male patients. They needed someone to help them cure their disorders. They needed a surrogate partner.

Selecting Joanna Caldwell for this work, he knew,

was an act of pure genius on his part. She was neither a whore nor a hard, brassy, sex-starved divorcee eager for a fast tumble—the usual public images of a surrogate partner. Joanna Marie Caldwell, daughter of a Pentecostal preacher from Zanesville, Ohio—the Bible Belt, no less—was pure, unadulterated, walking, talking male fantasy, the sweet, sexy-looking girl next door who did it simply to please. But that's not all that made her so good. *She didn't want to do it*, and Lambert's genius had been his recognition of that. Her religious training, the Sunday school classes, the choir singing, the hellfire and brimstone, the worry about the Seventh Commandment—all had etched her. In her case, appearances were most deceiving. She looked like she would do it—did she ever, and men could tell she'd be good at it—could they ever, but she didn't, wouldn't, couldn't be made to. A whole lot of Judd Forbes' problem was he had been driven wild with lust for her, all that necking and petting, but she would not give in to him until just before the wedding.

From the outset, Lambert had sensed that if he handled her right, she would be merely immense—shy, reserved, embarrassed, doing it not because she wanted to but because she ought to—and oh, so sexily. "Joanna," he had said, "can you understand there are men out there, men not unlike your husband, who desperately need help, suffering men, alone, humiliated, being destroyed by their sexual inadequacies? They are caught in a terrible bind, Joanna. Because of their dysfunction they are either never married or divorced. Are they to be denied a cure because they have no wives to help them?" It had been surprisingly easy. Since she had majored in psychology in college, Lambert did not find it too difficult to appeal to her both as a professional in the field and as a caring, compassionate human being.

Now, about a year later, he again fastened his most sincere, penetrating gaze upon her, then spoke. "I understand how you feel, Joanna, and I want you into marital counseling, too. But Brad Dillon needs help. He's in a very exposed position. There is fear of eventual suicide." Lambert spoke with great earnestness. "Will you take him as your patient?"

He saw her look down at her hands and bite her lower lip. He knew he'd won. Dawson Lambert was exceedingly confident of his ability to persuade women to do what he wanted. It was his specialty.

She sighed. "All right, if you wish me to."

"I know it's difficult for you, Joanna, and I thank you."

She looked up at him, determination showing in her eyes. "And then I want to do counseling."

"Of course." He smiled in reassurance.

"When is Dillon scheduled?"

He hesitated. The rock and the hard place had just arrived. "He's coming Monday, Joanna."

"Monday! This is Friday, Dr. Lambert. I already have Jerry Wofford."

"I know."

"Am I to drop him?"

He had been expecting this, dreading it in fact. In less than a year, Joanna Caldwell had become perhaps the best surrogate partner in the business. She was being asked for, and he could command an extremely high fee for her. Wofford was paying ten grand for two weeks of treatment, twice the usual fee. Dillon was shelling out twenty. After him, the sky would be the limit for the celebrated ministrations of Joanna Caldwell. Dillon was paying the high price partly because he was a celebrity, but also because he posed a problem. He could come only during the next two weeks. He was booked solid. It was then or never. Joanna already had Wofford. Dillon would mean two patients at one time for her. To convince her to do this was a problem he would have to finesse most delicately.

"Where are you with Wofford?"

Joanna still found it difficult to speak of these matters, but she knew it was expected of her and that her attitude was silly and immature. As matter of factly as possible, she said, "He is erective rather easily now and has also experienced erective return. I plan to start intromission and containment today."

Images flicked through his mind, but he squelched them to maintain a mask of professionalism. "You feel a second week is necessary."

"You must know it is."

He smiled. "I do, of course, but you can't blame me for hoping it might be otherwise."

"Wofford is a most difficult case, Doctor. He is an extremely sensitive person. That's a whole lot of his problem, as you know. If treatment were interrupted it would be most traumatic for him. He'd feel rejected. Everything we've gained would be lost—probably permanently. I don't think we can let that happen."

"Of course. You must continue with Wofford."

He leaned back in his swivel chair, hands clasped behind his head, seemingly deep in thought. Actually it was a pose and he held it for a well-timed interval. Then he moved effortlessly into another pose, his arms outstretched, his palms flat on the desk, looking at her intently. He was turning on his charm full force.

"The problem is, Joanna, Brad Dillon is a big star, a hot property, as they say. He's booked solid for movies, his TV show and personal appearances. The next two weeks are the only free time he has for the next year, maybe two or three years."

He said no more, but continued to enmesh her with

his eyes. This was all much used technique with him. He didn't insist or beg. He merely stated facts in such a way the person could not refuse. Rarely was anyone, particularly females, selfish enough to tell him no.

Joanna was not very resistant to him. From the first moment she'd met him over a year ago with Judd, she had come under his persuasive spell. There were times when she couldn't believe she had ever been talked into doing what she did. She knew Lambert had caught her right after her divorce, when she was depressed, full of guilt and uncertain what she was going to do with her life. She had been lost and empty. He had offered direction and an anchor.

And there was more, she knew. As long as she could remember, there had been a dominant male in her life. Her father, oh yes, her father, born again, so severe, dealing in fear and guilt, demanding the proper behavior from the preacher's daughter. She did what was expected of her. Oh, how many times had she faked God's Call to lead the congregation to the altar at Sunday night services? Then there was Mr. Cullen, the high-school teacher. *You're a bright girl, Joanna. You can do anything, be anything you want. You owe yourself the chance. Go to college.* Ohio State. Scott Hodding, graduate fellow in psychology. *You're very intelligent, Joanna, but you're so naive. You need experience to develop your potential.* She soon discovered the experience he had in mind. Judd Forbes. He'd led her into athletics, for which she was grateful. She enjoyed sports. Marriage? Marriage to a football star, first draft pick of the New York Giants? Why not? What else was there to do?

But of them all, Dr. Dawson Lambert had been the greatest influence. She looked at him, the gray hair, the comfortable cherubic wrinkles around those strange, compelling eyes, the full sensitive mouth. He was an extremely handsome, distinguished looking man, author, lecturer, physician, director of the Center for Human Potential in Westport, Connecticut. Who was she to quarrel with him?

"You want me to take two patients at once?" she said. It was both a statement of fact and a question.

He hesitated, seeming to stammer. "Joanna, I—"

"I said how difficult Wofford is."

She let the statement hang there, watching distress rise on Lambert's face.

Finally he spoke. "Joanna, I know how difficult it is for you. Believe me, I know how much you give of yourself and what it takes out of you. It is precisely because you are such a caring, giving person that you are so good at what you do. I don't want to overuse you and cause you problems. But—" He hesitated, seemingly agonized. "Joanna, I'm hoping that—" Again he paused. "The overlap will be only a few days, no more than a week. You'll be in preliminary treatment with Dillon at first. Then you should be finished with Wofford." He tried to smile. "Does that seem possible to you?"

She looked down at her lap, sighing deeply, then raised her head and gazed at him. "Dr. Lambert, I've been meaning to talk to you about something. Perhaps now is the time."

"Yes."

She looked away from him. His eyes always seemed to unnerve her. "I came to work here, Doctor, because I thought I was going to do marital counseling. You talked to me about the great need for sex therapy in marriage, and from my own marriage I certainly knew that to be true. You offered me an opportunity for a career in this field. You would train me and—"

"Haven't I trained you?"

"Yes, you have. I've learned a lot." She pursed her lips. This was all difficult to say. "I'd been here—how long? Three, four months? You gave me an unmarried male patient, a. . .a premature ejaculator."

"I remember. Eller, wasn't it?"

"Yes." She looked at him, then away again. "Doctor, I understood then and I do now, the need for surrogate partners. These men are in an impossible situation. They need help. But, doctor, it was extra-ordinarily difficult for me—being naked. . .in bed . . .doing these things with a. . .a virtual stranger. I've never been that sort of person. I wasn't brought up that way. I—"

"Believe me, Joanna, I understand, truly I do. I think I know you better than you know yourself. But I needed someone to work with Eller. You had had experience with your husband, with premature ejaculation. And you did a marvelous job with Eller. You cured him. Believe me, I know how hard it was for you. I'll always be grateful to you for your efforts—so will Eller."

"You don't understand what I'm trying to say. After Eller there was Stang, then Pritchard, then—Doctor, I can't remember their names. I don't even want to." She looked at him now, her indignation making her bolder. "Do you realize, Dr. Lambert, for weeks now I've had one patient after another? I spend some part of almost every day in bed with a man. I don't do any counseling any more. It's been going on for weeks—months really."

Distress registered on his face. "I know, I know."

"It's not supposed to be this way, is it, Doctor? Masters and Johnson used surrogate partners. But they were all volunteers, carefully screened."

"Is that what you want, Joanna? To work in an

office somewhere, or maybe as a waitress, and volunteer? I thought you wanted to become a professional in the field."

"The point is not that they volunteered. My concern is—Doctor, Masters and Johnson used their surrogates maybe once a year—perhaps not that often. I'm with a male patient *every day*. Now you want me to have *two* a day."

He sucked in air deeply and let it out in a long sigh of acute distress.

"It doesn't seem right to me, Doctor. What is going on?"

The question just hung there while he went into his repertoire of poses, leaning back in his chair as though deep in thought, then leaning forward over his desk to affix his most persuasive gaze on her. "I understand how you feel, Joanna. And you are right, of course. You are being used as a surrogate too often, much too often. We have a problem." He smiled. "I think it's called success. Our success ratio with patients here at the Center is well over ninety percent. Word has gotten around. Every day the mail brings new requests for treatment. Everyone of them seems to be desperate. Perhaps I'm at fault for not saying no more often."

He now had his hands flat on the table. The way he looked at her he was the living embodiment of sincerity and earnestness. "Our patient ratio to staff is too high, Joanna. I know that. Everyone here is being overworked. But it is merely temporary. I'm taking steps to increase the staff. I'm trying right now—have been for some time, actually—to recruit another surrogate. As you can imagine, the *right* person, someone who possesses the qualities that make you so very good, is difficult to find. But I've narrowed the ~rch to one or two people. I'll make a choice very soon." He smiled his warmest at her. "Can you bear with me only a little while longer? Believe me, I know how much I ask, but I really have no choice just now."

She looked at the folder in her lap, biting her lip, knowing she had lost. Always it was so. He apparently could convince her to do anything. "I guess you want me to keep this folder then."

"I promise you, Joanna. When you finish with Dillon, I'll move you over into counseling. All right?"

She looked up at him, smiling wanly. "Yes, thank you." She sighed deeply. "I'll manage somehow. I always do."

He rose quickly from his desk and came around to her. Very fatherly, he put his arm around her shoulders, feeling the delicacy of them. "I know it's hard for you, very hard. And that's why you are so very good."

She looked up at him. "Am I, Dr. Lambert? Sometimes I feel I'm just a glorified—"

"Don't say the word. Don't even think it. You may not have a medical degree, Joanna, but you practice medicine as surely as—as a surgeon. Wofford and Dillon are *patients*, Joanna, ill men, suffering serious impairment of sexual function. They are miserable, unhappy. In treating their illness, you are helping them toward full productive lives. If that isn't the practice of medicine, I don't know what is."

It was something she told herself over and over.

She smiled. "I know it—at least most of the time. "You're good to reassure me. I feel better already." She glanced at her watch and sighed. "I'd better go. It's almost time for Wofford."

2

The center for Human Potential was housed in a new building of poured concrete nestled among birches and maples on a Westport hilltop. When approached from the front it was windowless, but many of the rooms and offices, including Joanna's, had windows to the rear overlooking a woodsy scene.

The building had been cleverly designed. There were often a good many people in the building, but traffic flow was such that hardly anyone was seen. Developing human potential seemed to involve a great deal of privacy and confidentiality. Joanna's suite was on the second floor, tucked off to the rear. Her name was on the door as a staff psychologist, but no one on the staff except Lambert knew the form her counseling took. She suspected there were other surrogate partners on the staff. She never asked or speculated. She didn't want to know.

Her door opened on a small and rather typical office, with desk, swivel chair, typewriter, telephone, dictating machine, file cabinet, coffee pot. Joanna had only a few minutes before Wofford was due and this was important time for her. She needed a few minutes to think about him, his problems and to prime herself to deal with him.

The pertinent facts about Jerry Wofford were implanted in Joanna's mind. He was forty-two years old, five seven and a half in his elevator shoes and a hundred thirty-five pounds. But his lack of physical stature was not his real problem. He was the son of strict Hasidic Jews from Brooklyn, New York, who not only taught him that sex before marriage was a sin, but also did everything they could to prevent him from discovering sex at all. He did not date girls until he was twenty, and even then only girls from as restricted a background as his. He never masturbated, having been falsely accused of it by his rabbi father and severely threatened with the direst consequences. He had had one nocturnal emission. His mother found the evidence on his bedsheet, upbraided him ummercifully and whacked him with a stick.

But the seeds of rebellion were in him. To his parents' consternation, he abandoned rabbinical studies and at age twenty-four borrowed money to open a fabric shop in Manhattan. He had a good head for business, and by the time he was thirty, he owned a string of shops and a substantial bank account. At age thirty-four, he completed his rebellion, or so he thought, by marrying a gentile, an attractive fashion model a head taller than himself. He had charmed her because he was honest and sincere, spent lavishly on her and didn't try to get her into bed. That was the first time that had ever happened to her.

He was impotent on their wedding night and remained so for some months until the marriage was annulled. Thereafter, he attempted several affairs, remaining consistently impotent. He sought help from psychiatrists, the last of whom referred him to the Center for Human Potential. Since he was unmarried and indeed had stopped seeing any woman, a surrogate partner was assigned, and he became Joanna's patient.

Since he had never ejaculated, indeed rarely achieved an erection, Wofford was classified as a primary impotent. Lambert warned her these were the most difficult cases with a high rate of failure. Often the guilt and fears taught in childhood were too deepseated ever

to be amended. The best she could do was try, Lambert
said, and spent a lot of time instructing her in how to
treat this her first case of primary impotence.

Joanna considered Jerry Wofford a challenge and
worked harder and longer with him than any patient
since her ex-husband. She was with him three and four
hours a day, and he was emotionally and physically
exhausting to her. For the first couple of days that week
she had done nothing but sit and talk with him, trying to
break down his fears and rigidity. He was in terror of
being humiliated and quite understandably reluctant to
put himself in a position of being hurt yet again by a
woman. Joanna had worked very hard to convince him
that she was his friend, a person who wanted to help
him, and not in any way a threat. She had high regard
for him, whatever he did or did not do, and nothing
would change her attitude toward him. On Wednesday,
she managed to get some of his clothes off and engage in
some physical touching. They had gone a bit further
yesterday. She worried that it was perhaps too far. How
would he react today? Would he show up at all?

She glanced at her watch. He should be coming any
minute. She rose from her desk and opened a small
closet in the corner of her office. There was a full-length
mirror on the inside of the door and she used it to untie
and brush her hair, fluffing it up around her head and
molding it into soft waves to her shoulders. Then she
removed her glasses and put them in her purse. This
played havoc with her far vision, but she was all right up
close. Eventually, she would get a headache, but she
knew the big lenses acted as a shield between her and
Wofford, and she couldn't have that. She then applied a
generous layer of bright lipstick and dabbed herself with
Charley perfume. Next, she slid off her earth shoes and
stepped into white pumps with three-inch heels. Lastly
she removed her medical coat and hung it in the closet.

She examined herself in the mirror. The blue summer shell and white chino skirt were too tight and obvious, she knew, and the heels and lipstick were ridiculous. But all this was part of the treatment. Anything to turn on Jerry Wofford. It had taken a half hour to get him to admit he found heels, lipstick, perfume and tight sweaters sexually stimulating.

It was the first time she'd worn the heels with him, and when he rapped gently and she opened the door, she found herself a half foot taller than he. For a moment, she thought the shoes a mistake. Being taller might intimidate him. But she saw the pupils of his eyes widen as he looked at her. He must like tall women.

"You look very nice," he said.

She smiled at him. "Thank you—and so do you." There was truth to the statement. He was shorter, darker and far more hirsute than she liked, but in all, he was not the worst looking of men. He was clean, well mannered and nattily dressed. He was thoughtful, sensitive and intelligent. He certainly would have no trouble attracting girls, if only he knew what to do with them after he got them. Never had. Forty-two years old and he'd never made it with a woman. Forty-two. Seventeen years older than she. A passage from Masters and Johnson came to her mind. They always assigned surrogates who were about the same age as the patient. The men wanted younger surrogates, but Masters and Johnson argued patients were likely to marry women their own age. What was she doing with a man almost old enough to be her father?

She took his hand and led him through the small office into what was formally called the "treatment room." By any other name it was a bedroom, done in warm, tasteful blends of tan and brown. There was a queen-sized bed, already turned down invitingly, nightstands, chairs, a bureau with a tray of whiskey bottles and glasses, lamps, but no mirrors. She had removed them, not wanting Wofford to have any quick glimpse of himself to damage his self-image. There was a small bath with a shower off to the side.

She closed the door behind her and leaned against it, her hands still on the knob, and smiled at him. For an instant, the hopelessness of the situation thrust into her. She was twenty-five years old, and he was older, wiser and far more experienced. He was intelligent, informed and sophisticated, well-to-do, successful in business, admired and respected by his friends, and accomplished in all ways except the one that matters most to a man. He was no child, nor was he sick. There could be no phony, cheery, bedside manner with him. He came equipped with a normal amount of justifiable pride, and he had radar for any sort of condescension or ridicule. And just his presence in this room was a blow to his pride, proof he was not a real man. It would be better were he crippled or paralyzed. People could more easily accept and understand his problem then.

She felt she was in a hopeless situation. She was to help him accomplish what he could not do for himself. She was somehow to undo decades of parental mistakes. Yet do it all so as to leave him his pride. It was all clearly hopeless. What on earth was she doing here?

Her smile broadened and she reached out both her hands for his. They were cool and dry. Thank God. She hated clammy hands. "How are you today, Jerry?"

"I'm fine, Joanna, I—"

Again she smiled. "I don't think so. I can tell you're nervous." Slowly she spread her fingers and entwined hers with his. It was a deliberate act to increase the area of skin contact and encourage familarity.

He tried to force a smile. "Yes, I guess I am."

She squeezed his hand. "Don't be. C'mon, let's sit and talk a moment." She led him to the bed and sat beside him, holding his hands, touching his knee with hers. "Now what's bothering you?" She saw him look at her shyly and saw how difficult it was for him to speak. Suddenly she was overwhelmed with compassion for this suffering man. What a ghastly, humiliating experience for him. "Jer, can I tell you something?"

"Sure."

"This isn't very easy for me, either."

He looked at her, very seriously, very intently. "Why do you do it?"

"Because you're a nice person. Because you deserve some happiness. Because you need help—the sort of help I think I can give you. If there was anyone else to do it, I'd happily let them. There isn't, is there?"

"I'm afraid not."

She smiled and squeezed his hands. "So you're stuck with me, then. Can you bear it?"

"I'll try," and his responding smile was genuine and boyish.

"Good. We're stuck with each other. You know, Jer, our sitting here, talking honestly, is the most important thing we'll ever do together. We've got to talk, as frankly as we can, without shame or sham, hiding nothing, holding nothing back. What's bothering you, Jerry?"

"Nothing much, really. I just didn't sleep well last night."

"Why not?" She saw embarrassment creep into his face. "C'mon, tell me."

"I kept thinking about you and. . .and. . ."

She waited for him to go on, then prompted him. "And what, Jer? What did you think about me? None of this'll work if we have secrets."

"Don't you know? Do you have to force me to say it?"

She smiled and shook her head. "I guess I do, 'cause I

really don't know. If I've done something to offend you, I want to know about it.''

He laughed. "I guess you really don't know. A man sees a girl and thinks how beautiful she is. He just naturally assumes she knows it, too. It comes as a surprise to find out she doesn't know it."

"I'm beautiful?"

"The most beautiful and desirable woman I've ever known." His voice became soft, dry. "And that's why I couldn't sleep. I kept thinking about you and all the things we did yesterday." She felt him tremble. "It was so wonderful. The things you did to me—and let me do to you. I—"

"I didn't let you, Jerry. I wanted you to."

He sighed deeply, trying to control himself. "That's what I mean. I—Lord, I wanted you. I was very excited all night."

She was genuinely pleased. "That's wonderful, Jerry."

"Is it?"

"Oh yes. Wasn't it pleasant to have sexy thoughts in bed?"

"I guess so."

"Did you have an erection?"

He seemed stunned by the question. "Do you have to ask that?"

"Yes." She was serious. "It's what we're here for, Jer."

"Yes, I did."

"A good one? A real hard one?"

"Yes."

"Like you had with me yesterday?"

"Yes."

"How long did it last?"

"It seemed like all night. That's why I couldn't sleep."

She smiled at him affectionately, genuinely happy for him. "Such good news, Jerry. We're making progress. I'm happy for you, for both of us."

"I know I'm going to make it today. I just know I am."

She shook her head. "Oh no you're not. I'm not even going to let you try."

"Why? I want to. I need to."

"No."

"Joanna, I know I can now. I want to try."

"Jer, let me explain something, very seriously, okay? I don't want you *trying*. I want you *doing*. Your problem is that you've thought about it so much, wanted to so much, and worried way, way too much about not being able to do it. Instead of enjoying it and doing it, you're trying and worrying. Am I right?"

"I suppose."

"Okay. I'll tell you exactly what's going to happen. With a little luck, you'll come to want me so badly that when it finally happens, you'll be taken by surprise." She laughed. "You do like surprises, don't you?"

"Yes."

"Meanwhile, let's just have fun, enjoy ourselves. Don't make any promises. Don't expect anything. Above all, don't *try*. Just enjoy. You don't have to prove anything to me and you don't have to prove anything to yourself. Understand?"

"Yes."

"Are you sure, Jer? It's terribly important that you be under no pressure to perform. I'm not pressuring you. Please don't pressure yourself."

"I won't."

"Good." She smiled and stood up in front of him. "Do you want to undress me like you did yesterday?"

She saw the excitement in his eyes as he hesitantly reached his trembling hands toward her.

3

Joanne did not like her job, but she truly believed it was one which had to be done. Men like Jerry Wofford legitimately suffered and someone had to help them. Much of the time she was able to maintain a clinical attitude toward her task. But occasionally her veneer of professionalism wore thin and cracked.

Thus, as his fingers clasped the hem of the thin blue shell to raise it, she reached out and took his hands to stop him. It was in part an involuntary gesture, a sort of last reaching out for rescue, much as a drowning person reaches out vainly to be saved. This wasn't her. She didn't want this. In allowing it to happen she was somehow being violated, not just a violation of her body, but the ultimate violation of herself as a person. She felt in some little understood way she was becoming truly lost as a human being.

She saw him looking at her, intense, mystified. She smiled. "It unzips down the back." She turned away from him and felt his fingers fumbling at the nape of her neck, then the gentle ripping as the zipper parted. "Slowly, Jer, make it last, savor it." If she couldn't cure his impotence, she could at least teach him better seduction techniques. "Enjoy the anticipation. It's half the fun." At last the shell gave way and she felt the cool, air-conditioned air against her skin.

She folded her arms across her chest and held the front of the garment to herself. "Kiss my back," she whispered. "I like it."

She felt his hands at her waist, his breath warm, his lips moist against her skin. She shivered. "That's so nice, Jer."

In a moment she slid the shell from her shoulders and arms and turned to face him as he sat on the edge of the bed. As a surrogate partner, she had learned a lot about men. In sexual heat, they feel able to impregnate and service anything by sheer, overpowering need, will and strength. But she now knew the very different truth. Despite his bluster, sex is a fragile process for a man. Oh sure, when aroused, he is a bull, but what arouses him is imagery. The discovery had surprised, then amused her, and she wondered how many women knew the male secret. She had lain in that bed with men she hardly knew and really didn't like, yet she had been turned on and become orgasmic with them. Contrary to the public notion, it was the male who needed the soft lights, music and romance. The striptease had to be a male invention.

She saw him staring and knew she was right. Ordinarily she didn't wear a bra. They were uncomfortable and she didn't need one, at least not yet in her life. But she had visited the lingerie shop last evening. "Do you like my new bra?"

He nodded. "Very much."

She thought he would. It was a stage bra and rather uncomfortable, thin, flimsy, with just a hint of nipple peaking through the white lace. It pushed her in and up, creating rounded tops and a deep valley. "I bought it just for you. I thought you might find it attractive."

"I do. It's lovely."

"Exciting to you?"

She already knew the answer. "Very."

She smiled. "I've another surprise for you."

"Yes."

She laughed. "You're going to have to find it." Again a light laugh. "I doubt if it'll be hard."

As his hand reached for the fastener on her skirt, she again had an impulse to stop him, but controlled it this time. As the skirt whispered to the floor, she said, "You like?"

She saw the expression on his face. It was the closest he had come to pure lust. "I guess I can tell you do."

"It's *very* sexy." His voice was barely audible.

She tried to laugh lightly, but it came out too high pitched with a timbre of nervousness. "Would you believe? This is the first time I've ever worn stockings and a garter belt. I had to go buy them last evening."

"Just because I liked them?"

"Of course."

"I'll pay you."

Over my dead body. "Don't be silly. I should have bought them long ago." She looked down at herself, the high heels making her legs longer and slimmer, the stretched stockings, far sheerer and smoother than pantyhose, the taut elastic over the tantalizing stretch of bare thighs. A wave of self-revulsion swept her. She looked like a tart. She was being a whore. She felt her skin crawl and goose bumps rise. She knew it wasn't from cold.

She fought against her sinking feeling. "Very strange," she said, trying to make her voice light. "Sort of like a harness." She turned in front of him, as much to avoid his eyes as to flirt. "But I guess it looks sort of nice, doesn't it?"

She was facing him again. His eyes were fixed on her naked skin above the stockings, then he looked up at her. "Very nice, Joanna. You're lovely."

God! *I can't. I won't*. She smiled. "One of us has too many clothes on, and I don't think it's me." She pulled him to his feet and helped him off with his suit jacket, then with fumbling fingers undid his tie. *What does a whore do that I don't*? Her fingers were shaking, making the unbuttoning of his shirt difficult. There were so many buttons, too many. Finally she finished the last, undid his cuffs and pulled the tail out of his pants. She slid the shirt from his shoulders.

He wore no undershirt. His arms, shoulders, chest, even his back were covered with a mat of heavy, black hair. It extended so high toward his neck he had to cut and shave it to keep it from creeping out his collar. She hated the hair. He looked like an ape. But she smiled and ran her fingers over his chest. *Just like a whore*. "My," she said, forcing a smile, "you sure are the hairy chested man."

It didn't come out funny, and she saw the hurt look in his eyes. This was going badly. She was heading for disaster. She broadened her smile and took his hand. "C'mon, let's have a drink. We're being much too serious about all this. Besides, I doubt if you want me out of this getup just yet."

She tried to have a party, parading around the room in her heels, gartered stockings, panties and phony bra. She went to the refrigerator in her office for ice, stopping a moment out of his sight to lean against the desk. She took deep breaths, trying to relax and get hold of herself. She forced a smile and reentered the treatment room. "Did girls wear this when you were young, the heels, stockings, garters and all?"

"Yes."

"Is that why you like them so much?"

He hesitated. "I suppose so, yes."

She handed him the bucket of ice. "I have an idea

those ladies knew what they were up to.''

They had a highball and started a second. She talked with him and tried to be gay and flirtatious, but inwardly fear and desperation mounted. Maybe she should call this off. In her mood today, she could make him worse, much worse. No. There were only two weeks for the treatment. Each day was important.

She had intended the party to be intimate, fun. It would relax him, make him more sociable, teach him how to be natural with women. It wasn't working. She was as uptight as he. She smiled at him over the top of her glass. Then she saw the sunlight filtered through the fiberglass drapes. It was a nice day outside, June, warm, soft breezes, the best time of the year. She should be out on the tennis court, at the pool, not cooped up in here, doing. . . .

She had planned to remove her bra during the party, tease him, provoke him to another level of desire. Now she couldn't. If only he'd touch her in some way, say something, do something. She was a responsive woman. She knew she was. But she needed help. All her other patients had been premature ejaculators, overeager. She had had to hold them back. This was the first man she'd needed to tease to arousal. It was so damnably premeditated and she felt like a slut. Nor could she believe she was really doing it. She had held out so long. There were times in high school, certainly in college when she felt she was the only one who didn't do it. Look at her now, parading around in her underwear with a man she hardly knew.

It's your job. You're well paid. This sort of thing happened naturally between husbands and wives. They love each other. They want to help one another. She didn't love Jerry Wofford, not at all. She was a surrogate partner. *Stop it! Somebody has to do it.*

She set down her glass, reached behind her back and unhooked her bra. She saw him look at her breasts. She had great breasts. She knew she did, high, pointy, firm. She could feel her nipples hardening, flowering, the baubles growing at the ends that reached toward him. Shame stabbed at her. She didn't want this. All she'd ever wanted was marriage and fidelity. That was the whole reason for Judd Forbes, that and escape from home. How had she stooped to this?

She saw Wofford look up into her eyes. His expression was serious as he spoke. "This is terribly difficult for you, isn't it?"

She gasped. He did understand. He had reached out to help her. Her eyes filled with tears, and she spoke softly. "Yes, but it'll be worth it if I can make you well. I really want to, you know." His compassion for her had triggered hers for him.

"Yes, I do know. You are extremely generous."

She bit her lip to keep from crying, then forced a smile. She reached out, took his hand and brought it to her breast. "Or would you rather roll down these crazy stockings first?"

The hardest, most demanding and totally wearing part of Joanna's task was being aroused herself. She didn't fake it. It was vital to his treatment that he discover how to give pleasure, how to create passion, and be stirred himself by witnessing another's enjoyment. As Masters and Johnson put it, he had to learn "to give to get." The central problem of the impotent male is that he wends his way through the sexual experience as an observer. He is interested, even fascinated, but not truly a participant who abandons himself to enjoyment. Joanna had to get him to discard the observer. One way, as she had told him, was to get him so aroused he could think of nothing else than his own release. Another way was to absorb him in what was happening to her. There could be no faking it, as she set out this June afternoon to accomplish both goals at the same time.

As the last of her clothes came off and for a long time after both were naked, she took his hands in hers and guided his fingers in the caresses that turned her on. She helped him lightly trace the outline of her face, down her temples, across her eyes, gently over her lips, sending shivers of sensation through her until she had to bite at his fingers involuntarily. She guided his hands across her shoulders and through her armpits and down to her breasts and led him as he cupped and lifted and stroked and pressed and squeezed and kneaded them, and, removing his hands, guided his mouth to her breasts and, gasping under the onslaught of what she was causing to have done to herself, said, "A little harder. . .a little more, yes, yes. . .now bite the nipple gently. . .yes, not too hard. . .fine. . .oh yes, yes." Holding his head she trembled.

They sat facing each other on the bed, her back against pillows at the head, their legs spread and intertwined. Again she took his hands and guided his fingers over the silky flesh and around the lubricated orifices, showing him where to touch her and how to pinch and tease her most sensitive places until she was panting, gasping, nearly choking with passion. She managed to speak, "Oh, God, Jer. . .so wonderful. . .harder . . .there. . .oh, God. . . ." And through her moans and beneath her half closed eyelids, she saw that he, too, was aroused, his mouth open, breath short, his erection proud. And she had not even touched him.

Her body cried out for entry, for fulfillment, for hard driving force to climax, but she forced herself to take his hands away. "Now you. . .show me." Timorously, he took her hands as she had his and guided them to himself. She squeezed his hard, pulsating penis. "Like this?"

"Yes."

"Is that too hard? Does it hurt?"

"No."

"Show me, guide me," she said. "I don't know what pleases you. I want to please you."

He was inexpert. As she kneaded and stroked, pinched and rubbed with little guidance from him, it occurred to her that he probably didn't know himself, so restricted had his whole life been. So she asked, "Is this nice? Shall I do it harder? Does it hurt? Does this feel good?" until she learned from him the movements, the places, the ways to touch him that reduced him to paroxysms of trembling.

She took her hands away, looked at him and smiled. "I think we need a drink, don't you?"

He seemed stunned. "Please. . .no."

She looked down at his rapidly shriveling penis and patted it. "You did well, now you get a rest."

"Please, I—"

She smiled at him. "It's part of the treatment, Jer. I want you to learn you can not only get an erection, you can also get it back."

"Is that what you're doing?"

"Yes." She clasped his limp organ in both her hands. "You don't really want a drink, do you?" She lifted his testicles and gently stroked beneath and felt an instant hardening. She tenderly circumnavigated the coronal ridge and felt his whole body jerk in reactive spasms. Once, twice, a third time. He was as iron. She put her hands on his shoulders and gently pushed him down on his back, while she rose to her knees above him. "Put

your legs together," she whispered. He did, and she
straddled him, hands still on his shoulders, her knees
beside his chest, and settled comfortably atop his loins.
It was the female superior position, prescribed for cases
such as his. She was dominant, in control. With her
right hand, she found his erection hard against her
pubes. She caressed the coronal ridge again and felt his
spasms beneath her and heard him moan. "My
breasts," she said. "I like it." In a moment his
trembling hands sent shivers coursing through her. Then
she raised her pelvis and swept his glans between her
vulva, once, twice, over her clitoris, then she gently sat
down on him. It felt heavenly, so needed, so filling, and
she trembled with the effort to fight back her own overwhelming thrust for orgasm. She tried to concentrate on
him, what she was doing to him. The advantage of this
position was the ease of intromission. Few males are
adept at finding the vagina. Many an erection has been
lost in the futility of trying to find the place to put it.
She was pleased to have crossed this hurdle with him.

She opened her eyes and saw the amazement, desire,
disbelief in his face. She smiled. "Nice, isn't it?"

"Oh, God, Joanna, I. . .I never. . .knew. . . ."

"You do now. Just relax and enjoy."

She was careful not to move at all, just to contain
him, hold him, squeezing him a little with her vaginal
muscles. But she could feel her overwhelming need for
orgasm tearing at her. She fought against it. If she came
on too strong now, she'd ruin everything. "You feel so
good, Jerry. Do you like being inside me?"

"Yes." The word was more air than sound.

She held him inside a moment, then lifted herself up
and off of him.

"No, please, I. . . ."

She waited a moment until his erection began to fade

in the cooler air. Quickly she stroked him again and took him back inside. Twice more she did it, the last time even letting him deteriorate all the way to the flaccid state before arousing him again. The last time she took him, she felt him start to hump into her. "No. Just lie there and enjoy." Both hands on his shoulders, her breasts filling his hands, she began to move a little on him, forward and backward, never more than an inch and very slowly. Her own need was so great she was tempted. Maybe he could make it. But the risk of his failure was too great. She had come too far with him to lose him now.

She stopped her movement, held him a moment longer, then smiled down at him. "I'll see you on Monday, Jer."

"Oh, please, I know I can."

She laughed and pulled off of him. "I'm sure you can, too, but we've got all next week."

Frantically he begged, "Please, Joanna, please."

"No." She scrambled off the bed. "And no masturbating and no other women."

After he had dressed and left, she took a long, hot shower, put on a terrycloth robe, for she was suddenly shivering, and made herself a strong highball. She felt bone weary, angry, frustrated and extremely depressed. A little corner of her cortex told her she'd feel better if she masturbated, but she couldn't. She knew it would be too degrading. There would be nothing left of her if she did. She tried to think of Wofford. It had been a good session. He was going to make it. Then she remembered Lambert's words, "If this isn't the practice of medicine, I don't know what is." As she began to dress to go home, she told herself she hoped he was right.

4

Dawson Lambert was also working late at the office. He had been accepting fewer patients lately, partly for reasons of time, but also because he wasn't as young as he used to be and there was no point in kidding himself.

Laura McGovern lay atop him in the lateral position, still panting from the exertions of her orgasm, sighing from the pleasure. He patted her back, dipping his hand down to fondle her derriere. "If this were school and I handed out grades," he said softly, "you'd get an A-plus."

She sighed deeply, lending a particularly breathy quality to her deep contralto voice. "It was so wonderful, Dawson."

"I'm so very glad for you."

She shuddered from remembered pleasure, then raised her head to look at him. "And you? What grade do you get?"

He laughed lightly. "Teacher doesn't get graded, but it was very nice for me, too, Laura. In fact, exceptional." It was the truth. He hadn't really thought about going himself, then to his surprise, he had, her frantic thrusting propelling him into ejaculation right after her. It had been powerful and prolonged, something which rarely happened to him anymore. "I'm not the one who counts."

"I know. It's all supposed to be for me. But it was awfully nice that you came. It makes me feel like. . .like a real woman, a total woman." She sighed happily. "It's so wonderful."

"You most definitely are a real woman, my dear." He patted her behind. "Shall we get up now?"

She protested a little but dutifully rose from him and padded into the bathroom. Wide awake and extremely relaxed—he had indeed had a splendid ejaculation—he lay back against the pillow.

Sessions such as this were an extremely important part of his income. He normally had two, occasionally three a week, invariably with rich, bored and exceedingly frustrated widows and divorcees. He selected only those with the highest Dun & Bradstreet rating, charged them five thousand for the usual two weeks of intensive treatment, then kept them in "private consultations" for as long as a year—in one notable instance two years. Since the women paid five hundred dollars a week as "outpatients"—one fat and thoroughly unappealing woman had paid seven fifty—he did rather well financially. In fact, the splendid balance in his checkbook made an often onerous task much easier. Some of his patients were dogs.

Laura McGovern was perhaps his finest achievement. He had met her socially shortly after he came to Westport to open the Center. She was program chairman for a local women's club and had invited him to talk to the ladies. One thing led to another and she had become a member of his advisory board, performing the extremely valuable function of making the Center socially acceptable in the Town of Westport. For this he was grateful.

What people didn't know was that she had also

become his patient. She was a recent widow, blessedly rescued from a miserable twenty-year marriage. Ralph McGovern was, as near as Lambert could determine, a philandering rake. He had married Laura for her money, of which she had gobs, and she had married him because he was handsome and willing. She simply was not favored physically and had a poor self-image which Ralph McGovern proceeded to make worse. He blamed her for his succession of affairs. If she wasn't frigid and such a poor wife to him, he wouldn't have to seek sexual release elsewhere. The fact she had bought this ridiculous argument for so many years suggested to Lambert that Laura McGovern was indeed easily persuaded, if not downright gullible.

Lambert had quickly discovered that Laura's frigidity was merely a product of tragic mishandling. All she needed was a little sensitive treatment, intelligent foreplay and the right position. The so-called "missionary" position, with the man on top, was a disaster for her, as for many women. But her husband had insisted on it as the only and best way, leaving her a suffering, frustrated and allegedly frigid woman. Lambert had simply put her on top in the lateral position. He lay on his back, legs apart. She mounted him, her legs astraddle his right leg. This gave her freedom of movement and enabled her to bring the right degree of pressure on her clitoris. She had come quickly the first time they tried it, then lay there in his arms weeping with pleasure, relief and remorse for the lost years.

Acting on an inspired impulse, Lambert had not charged for her treatment, saying that she did so much for his community relations the least he could do was offer her "professional courtesy." Her joy at discovering her sexuality at age fifty-two, together with his insistence she was vital to the success of the Center—he "didn't know what he'd do without her"—made her generous. She eagerly paid for "badly needed" equipment which was never purchased, and financed studies which were not performed. She even set up a fund for nonexistent charity patients. Thus, with one thing and another, Lambert was into her for over two hundred grand, far more than he would have made by charging her a fee.

That was only the beginning. Laura McGovern was a well of money which could be made to flow with little more than a tumble in bed and some intelligent flattery. Little effort was required to "ask her help" or "seek her advice" on some matter concerning the Center for Human Potential. She was thrilled to be not only sexually relieved but made to feel important and needed in life. If her phone calls and visits were a nuisance to him, her checkbook certainly was not.

As he lay there relaxed in bed listening to her in the shower—she was even singing—he smiled. This bitch was about to make him an extremely wealthy man. Some weeks before, after a most satisfying "treatment," he had talked to her confidentially and expansively about his "life's dream."

"What is that, Dawson?"

He had stroked her sagging breast and said, "To open a second Center on the West Coast. It's so needed, Laura. The whole way of life in California, the unreal expectations, the licentious atmosphere, is creating sexual problems wholesale. Right now, over a quarter, almost a third of our patients come from California. And at great expense, I might add. If we had a Center on the West Coast, why we'd be able to help a great many more people." What he really wanted to say was that "it would be a gold mine." He didn't, because

Laura McGovern preferred the loftier plane of helping mankind. She was a do-gooder.

"I think you're right, Dawson."

"I know I am. The need is there. One of these days I'll be able to meet it." He sighed. "We're starting to show a profit here. Perhaps in a few years, I'll be able to—"

"How much money would it take?"

"Oh, a great deal, of course—but I think a million or so would get it started. The rest could be borrowed."

It had been so easy. A million dollars had not shocked her. He knew it wouldn't and thus did not suggest more.

"I might be able to help you, Dawson. I've never known what to do with my money. It should be used to help people, don't you think?"

So easy. It would only be a loan. She would be investing in the Center as a full, financial partner. And it would bear her name. She would help run it, too. And she would share in the profits. After a couple of years, she should get a handsome return on her investment.

"I think it's a marvelous idea, Dawson. I'm most enthusiastic."

Nothing had been decided. No commitment had been made. But he knew he had her hooked for a million. That would be only the beginning. With cost overruns, design changes, new features and such, he ought to be able to get a lot more than that out of her—and he stood to make a bundle in kickbacks from architects, contractors and equipment manufacturers. The only question in his mind was how many millions he could get Laura McGovern to cough up.

They had several discussions about the project. He had his architect draw up a schematic sketch for a suitable structure, and they talked about possible sites. He was leaning toward the Palm Springs area. But what did she think about Beverly Hills? Perhaps they could buy an estate there and remodel it.

These discussions had been interrupted for several weeks. Chances were, he now realized, he had made a tactical error in suggesting to Laura that she have plastic surgery. No need any more for a woman to look her age. Her enthusiasm had surprised him, and she had gone almost at once to the West Coast and the plastic man. It had cost a bundle—in part because he had demanded a kickback for the referral—but when she returned even Lambert had been amazed. He almost didn't know her. Not only were her nose and eyes and wrinkles fixed, but her whole figure as well. He had given her breasts, a nice set of buns, removed an unsightly fat pad of longstanding duration and tightened her skin here and there. The transformation was completed with sessions at Vic Tanny to tone up her muscles and visits to the beauty shop, where she had been transformed into a redhead, expert in fixing herself up to look her best.

Lambert had been effusive in his praise. She looked ten, even fifteen years younger, and her whole personality had changed from a defeated, mousey matron to a vibrant, exciting woman. Admittedly, this made it easier for him to "treat" her now nonexistent sexual dysfunction. But he paid a penalty, he quickly sensed, in that she was no longer nearly as emotionally dependent upon him as she had been. She came to see him less often. She began to give parties, circulate more. He knew she was even going out on dates. This concerned him, but not now, not as she padded from the bathroom toward the bed. He marveled again at the plastic man's art. Laura McGovern had been transformed from—hell, she wasn't bad looking at all.

She sat on the edge of the bed and smiled down at

him. "That was a very satisfactory treatment, doctor."

And he smiled. "Yes, wasn't it?"

She reached down and patted his flaccid penis. "I'm going to miss it, Dawson. I'm certain of that."

"What d'you mean?"

"This is the last time, Dawson. It has to be. You have to help me stick to my resolve." She gave his organ a squeeze. "It won't be easy, believe me."

"I still don't understand."

"A miracle has happened, Dawson. I'm so happy. I know you will be, too—for me." She paused, her face beaming. "I'm going to be married."

He sat up in bed. "You're kidding."

She laughed. Laura had a generous, full-chested laugh which she used frequently now that she had become a more confident and happier woman. "If you'd said that a year ago, I'd have been destroyed. Now I think it's funny—and that, I think, is the measure of how much you've done for me." Again she laughed. "Why is it so shocking that someone wants to marry me?"

Lambert caught himself just in time. "Don't be silly. I'm not shocked by that. You're a beautiful woman. But—but, I'm just. . .surprised, that's all. I didn't know you had a. . .a. . .serious boyfriend."

More laughter flooded out of her chest. "That'll teach you to take a woman for granted, Dawson. All this time I had hopes for you—" She smiled. "I'm afraid you've missed your chance."

Inwardly he seethed, but he masked it behind a smile. "I never took you for granted, Laura. I just didn't think you were interested in marriage."

"Nor I. But. . .I was asked. It seemed the thing to do." Another burst of laughter. "Really, it's quite sudden. I'm surprised myself."

Carefully he said, "Who's the lucky man?"

"Someone you know. Charles Randall."

Not that sonofabitch. Charles Randall, neurosurgeon with a practice in Stamford, was the stuffed shirt of the Western world, a somber, serious prude. Member of the AMA ethics committee, he was a sanctimonious wart on a hog's hindend. Lambert remembered his open attack on him at a county medical society meeting. "Do you really believe there is a need for sex therapy, Doctor? And how do you construe it to be the practice of medicine?" The prick.

"Don't you approve, Dawson?"

He put on his most professional face. "Of course I do, Laura. He's a grand fellow." Damning with faint praise is what it was called.

She smiled. "But. There is a but, isn't there?"

He sighed, using the time to try to think. "It's just—well, you know, you have a lot of money and—"

Her laughter interrupted him. "How like you to worry about me. But you shouldn't. I'm no babe in the woods. Charles is loaded himself. You know that."

Yes, damnit, he knew it. Neurosurgery was the richest medical specialty and Randall had a thriving practice in one of the poshest areas in the country. A back-and-right-leg-pain man. Spinal discs. He should have gone into that. Pelvic exams and pap smears never brought in that kind of money. "Of course. That's true."

She reached up and patted his cheek. "Dawson, can't you wish me happiness?"

She wanted his approval. Couldn't do a thing without it. But she wasn't about to get it. Never. But take it slow. Just make her uneasy. He smiled. "Certainly." He consciously made his voice a little cold, distant. "I wish you every happiness."

She stood up, looking at him, her eyes questioning. Then she began to dress.

"Have you and Randall—"

"Gone to bed?"

"Yes."

She had pulled on her panties and just now fastened her bra, glancing at him as she did so. "No. Not until we're married."

"Good heavens, Laura, why not? What's wrong with this fiance of yours?"

"There's nothing wrong with Charles. He's a dear." She laughed, but a bit nervously. "And I get him very excited. I know we'll be fine. But he wants to wait till we're married. He thinks of me as a virtuous widow, a contrast to the other women he's known. He's got me on a bit of a pedestal—which is sort of nice these days. I'll wait."

"Do you think you ought to, Laura? I mean—are you sure?"

She laughed. "After our performance just now, have you any doubts? I'm a fully functioning woman—thanks to you. I know I'll be fine with Charles."

"Of course you will. That's what the treatment is all about." There was nothing else for him to say. She had buttoned her blouse and was preparing to put on her pants. "You'll be breaking off your association with us here, I imagine."

"Why should I? I may not be as active as I've been, but I hope you'll keep me on the advisory board."

"Of course. Don't know what we'd do without you." The pants were on now. She was stepping into her flats. "But you'll be discarding our plans for the West Coast Center."

She looked at him. "I don't see why I should. It's a

good investment. I'll speak to Charles about it.''

Fat chance! Charles Randall would approve her investment in another doctor's project about as fast as he'd approve an outbreak of the plague. He could hear Randall now: "Invest in a sex clinic? Are you out of your mind, Laura?" The man was a prude. No doubt about it.

She was leaning over him. "I've got to dash, Dawson."

She kissed him lightly on the lips. "Yes."

"You are a love. Will I see you tomorrow?"

His mind was already on other things. "Tomorrow?"

"Yes, my tennis party. You will come, won't you?"

Tennis? Again he forced his mind back to her. "Oh, I'm sorry, I can't. I have to go to New York."

"Too bad, we'll miss you. I've already invited Joanna Caldwell from here. I hear she's a fabulous tennis player."

"Joanna? Oh yes, she's quite good."

Laura was moving toward the door. "I must run, really I must." She stopped, her hand on the knob. "You are happy for me, aren't you Dawson?"

He forced a smile. "Of course. Why wouldn't I be?"

She stood there a moment, looking at him, wanting to say something. Instead, she shrugged and went out the door. He rose from the bed, snugged on his pants and in bare feet exited the treatment room into his adjoining office. He leaned over his desk, pushed a button on his console, listening to the whine of the motor as it opened a small bar in the wall behind him. He quickly poured himself three fingers of Scotch and swilled it down neat.

The bitch. How could she do this to him? Aloud he mimicked her in falsetto voice. "I'm going to marry a stinking prude, Dawson. Aren't you happy for me?" He then uttered a string of swear words and four-letter vulgarities—all most uncharacteristic of him and a symptom of his anger. Laura McGovern thought she was going to louse him up, did she? The biggest deal of his life and she was going to foul it up by marrying that overblown bluenose. "Do you really think there's a need for sex therapy, doctor?" The sonofabitch. Now he was going to marry Laura McGovern. Oh no he wasn't. It just wasn't going to happen.

He poured himself another drink, but this time only swallowed from it. This marriage was as good as dead. Laura McGovern couldn't take a shit without asking him. Who did she think she was to decide to marry that self-righteous, holier-than-thou creep? He'd stop it. Laura McGovern wasn't going to marry anyone.

When he raised the glass this time, he drained it, another string of obscenities entering his mind. But accompanying them, little recognized and quickly squelched, was a warning. Let her go. Find another fish to fry. No, goddammit. Laura McGovern was the best thing that had ever come along. He had invested too much time and effort in her to let her get away now.

5

Hank Kraft would not ordinarily have gone to Laura McGovern's tennis party. Tennis was hardly his game; indeed, he wasn't much of an athlete at all. Besides, he suspected Laura was matchmaking again, and the thought of her trying to fix him up was a little more than he could bear. But he went because of his son. Timmy needed to get out of Manhattan. A Saturday afternoon in Westport, some swimming and maybe a hamburger on the way home would be just what the boy needed. Maybe it wouldn't be too bad for his old man either.

Laura McGovern was technically his stepmother. Ralph McGovern had been his father, but Hank had hardly known him. The divorce had occurred when he was a toddler and his mother married Samuel Kraft who had adopted him, Ralph McGovern being supremely eager to escape financial responsibility. Hank had grown up only dimly aware he had a real father in Westport, Connecticut, and wholly unconcerned about him.

Laura, childless and extremely unhappy in her marriage, had encouraged some contact with the long lost son. After college, Hank visited his father. The two of them had nothing in common, including mutual affection, but Laura doted on Hank. For his part, he found her merely tolerable, but he visited the

McGoverns occasionally, principally as a source of free
meals and a little booze while he was in art school in
New York. After McGovern's death and the breakup of
his own marriage, some contact had continued. But
Hank was determined to strike a happy medium
between not unnecessarily hurting her feelings—after
all, what harm had she ever done him?—and keeping
her at arm's length.

Hank arrived about noon. Laura greeted him with
what he considered a much too intimate hug and fussed
over Timmy as though he were her flesh-and-blood
grandson. Hank was a bit annoyed at her insistence that
Timmy call her grandma. That left him with three
grandmas. Oh, well, Timmy was smart enough both to
ask about it and to understand the explanation he'd be
forced to give him someday. Hank was also singularly
unimpressed with the "new" Laura. He'd liked her
better drab and unhappy. He admitted the plastic
surgeon had done a helluva job, but he couldn't forget
the old Laura. This new one was too hyper for him. Nor
was he impressed with Charles Randall, her new
boyfriend. He struck Hank as dull, boring and a stuffed
shirt. Hank was just about to dwell on the negative
aspects of a day in the country when he was introduced
to his doubles partner, a pretty blonde who wore
outsized glasses.

Joanna hadn't wanted to go to Laura McGovern's
tennis party, either. They were for boozing and making
out. Tennis was incidental. Besides, it made her nervous
being around Laura, who knew she worked at the
Center. She knew her as a staff psychologist. What else
did she know? But Lambert had said someone from the
Center really ought to go and, as the best tennis player
on the staff, she was elected.

Joanna had gone to bed early, she slept poorly and

awoke crabby. She had enough self-realism to know what she really needed. Since that was out as far as she was concerned—a busman's holiday she hardly wanted—she knew the next best thing was some vigorous exercise. She loved tennis. It was an important outlet for her tensions and she played with energy and skill. A few whacks at the ball and she knew she would begin to unwind. She went to the party, hoping for a couple of good sets. Failing in that she'd at least get in a swim.

Joanna was astounded at the metamorphosis of Laura McGovern. Almost before her eyes, Laura had changed from a defeated, unhappy middle-aged woman into someone younger, far prettier and positively vivacious. Joanna suspected Dawson Lambert had something to do with it. She had heard him speak of the advantages of cosmetic surgery for older women. "Why be defeated by age when you no longer have to?" he asked. Seeing Laura, so changed, so glamorous in her white pants suit, so terribly happy with her new fiance, Joanna concluded Lambert's was a good question indeed.

"You look divine," was the greeting Joanna received.

"You're the one who's divine, Laura. I've never seen you so radiant. And you are happy, aren't you?"

Laura hugged her again. "I am, Joanna, I am. Dr. Lambert has helped me so much."

"I'm glad. Did he suggest your cosmetic surgery?"

"He did. Arranged the whole thing." She smiled. "Am I ever glad I took his advice. Can't believe my mirror."

"Believe, believe. You're just lovely."

Doctor Charles Randall came up to greet Joanna. He seemed a bit somber and stuffy to her, but otherwise a handsome man with a good head of dark hair. He was a few years younger than Laura—the real Laura, that is—but why shouldn't she marry a younger man? Joanna couldn't help but wonder, though, if Laura had told him her real age. She smiled at them both. "So you two are getting married?"

Charles grinned broadly, his arm around Laura's shoulder. "Indeed we are."

"Have you set the date?"

"We plan for September," he said, "but sometimes I think I can't wait that long."

"Then why are you running off to San Francisco?"

"I'm not running off. It's an important medical meeting. I'm to read a paper. You know that."

Laura patted his cheek. "Of course I know it. I'm only teasing."

Joanna and Hank were introduced to each other and summarily declared partners for the tennis tourney. Joanna forced a smile and said something in greeting, but inwardly she seethed with disappointment. She could tell he couldn't play. Even his tennis shoes were new. He was big and heavy boned, and the way he walked and held himself, she knew he was awkward. With his thick auburn hair, green eyes and masses of freckles, he looked like a large, economy-sized Charlie Brown. She suddenly realized how seldom she read the funny pages and how little she cared for cartoons.

Hank's first reaction was one of good fortune. She was very pretty with shoulder-length blonde hair tied behind her head with an orange scarf, immense blue eyes that were probably myopic behind those big glasses, and a lovely mouth, narrow in width with a lot of bright pink skin turned out to form appealing lips. It was a pretty face, but he sensed it would not photograph well. Too much flesh in the cheeks, the whole face a bit too round. He wondered how old she was. She would probably always look young, appealingly cuddly and childlike, at least for many years.

They headed for the court in silence—he decided she must be shy—and immediately his enthusiasm for her disappeared. She was a jock, he could tell, and had come to play. He saw the way she held the racket, got her arm back and turned her body to take a well-practiced swing, and got up on her toes to bound and bounce after the ball. In her tiny white skirt and cotton shirt, she provided an arresting jiggle, but he knew he was in the deepest trouble. His game stank compared to hers, and he could tell she was gritting her teeth in frustration.

He was merely perceptive in that. She tried to make up for him, but he missed so many shots and was out of position so often it was hopeless. They were eliminated quickly from the tournament. She had hardly broken a sweat.

As they walked off the court, he knew he had to say something. He was going to tell her he was sorry for playing badly, then thought better of it. What the hell, it was only a game. "I was planning to take lessons from Jimmy Connors," he said, no hint of a smile on his face, "but he declared me too good already. Said he didn't need any more competition."

It flew like an anvil. She stopped, turned, looked at him in disgust and stalked off. He stared after her a moment and shrugged. So much for Laura McGovern's matchmaking.

Joanna was in a state and knew it, but she was unable to stop herself. She was enraged. She wanted to scream obscenities, throw things, even burst into tears. How could he play so badly? He didn't even try. Any fool could have done better. If he couldn't play, what did he even get on the court for? He was an ill-mannered bore, forcing himself in where he didn't belong, just to keep others from having their fun. And comparing himself to Jimmy Connors. What a conceited idiot. He couldn't even lace Jimmy Connors' shoes. God! Men! Every one of them a fool, an idiot, a weakling, looking to be mothered, wetnursed, coddled, babied, then told how grand he is and isn't it simply marvelous that the world is honored by his presence. Men! Oh how she hated them, their damned precious egos, their useless cocks, their feeding off women then treating them like second-class citizens. If she never saw a man again, it would be too soon.

As she ranted, the observer hidden in the left cerebral cortex of her brain remained aware of how irrational she was. She had been rude to this guy, whatever his name was. He had done nothing except not play tennis very well. She was taking out on him her anger and frustration at others and the situation she had gotten herself into. By the time she reached the pool, the cortex had gotten through to the irrational Joanna enough to make her realize she was angry at herself for being so rude in public to— She remembered. His name had been Hank.

Joanna had worn her swimsuit under her tennis outfit, intending to cool off with a swim after what she imagined would be several hard, free-swinging sets of tennis. Now, she stripped off her whites and dove into the pool. She began to swim laps, flat out as hard as she could go. The water felt wonderful, and as her muscles began to heat up and her breath shorten, she could feel the tension leaving her. Her pace slackened, but she pushed herself as long and as far as she could. She drove herself one final lap and stood up at the shallow end of the pool, water streaming from her face and hair, her lungs heaving to suck in air.

In a moment she became aware of a little boy sitting

at the edge of the pool, his feet dangling in the water. He was perhaps six or so and the most beautiful child she had ever seen, with a great deal of black, curly hair and immense brown eyes shielded by lush double lashes. There was a pensive look on his face, and he was looking intently at her, not her face, but her body. It disconcerted her and she looked down at herself. This was not her most concealing bikini, but still. . . . He *was* just a child. "Hello," she said finally.

He raised his head. Such depth in his eyes, she thought. Then he spoke, his voice childish. Somehow she felt relieved to know he was a child after all. "Could you teach me to do that?"

"What?"

"Swim. I'd like to be able to swim like that."

Hank had been too long without a woman and her jiggle had been too enticing for him to put her entirely out of his mind. But the whole tennis scene had been unpleasant. He wasn't concerned an iota that his tennis was lousy, nor did he care what she thought of him. But she might have accepted his self-deprecating joke, however weak it was, as an apology. A little sense of humor wouldn't hurt her. But apparently she suffered from a severe shortage of both humor and the milk of human kindness. Well built and nice to look at, but about as much fun as a Barbie doll. He shrugged away any hopes for her or indeed any real interest in her and went in search of the bar.

He found it set up under a shade tree near the house and made himself a sour mash and water. He sipped the drink, watched a little tennis and had a desultory conversation with a couple of other guests. In a few minutes, he decided he ought to check out Timmy at the pool. Hank worried that his son couldn't swim. He wanted to teach him, but he wasn't much of a swimmer himself. In fact, he rather hated the water. Still, Timmy should learn. If he learned as a child, he'd enjoy swimming.

He saw him with Joanna. They were bosom buddies—literally. She stood nipple deep in the water teaching Timmy to swim. Her milky mounds rising above the blue bikini top stabbed at his loins, and when Timmy lurched for her and put his arms around her neck to hold on, it wounded him. Smart kid. Sure can pick 'em. He heard them both laugh, then he turned and walked away. Neither had seen him.

Two drinks and a highly bored hour later, he returned to the pool. The two of them sat at a poolside table, improving their tans while playing gin rummy. He heard them laughing and talking. Well, at least his son was having a good time this day. He started to turn away.

"Daddy, Daddy, guess what?"

He turned back to see Timmy running toward him. "I can't imagine."

"I can swim. I learned. Joanna taught me."

"That's great, Tim." He said it matter of factly without a trace of phony enthusiasm.

"Lemme show you."

The boy took his hand and began pulling him toward the pool. In a moment Timmy broke away, ran ahead and jumped into the water. He began to swim across the width. He was inexpert, but he was swimming.

"So you're Timmy's father."

He turned to look at her behind him, squinting a little in the sun. "I fear I can't do any more about that than I can my lousy tennis game." He saw her smile. It was a nice smile, bright in the sun.

"I had that coming. Will it help if I tell you I was going to take lessons from Amy Vanderbilt on good manners, but she said mine couldn't improve?"

So she did have a sense of humor. He laughed and

started to say something about hoping Tim hadn't been an annoyance.

"Daddy, Daddy, watch me."

He turned back to the pool. "I am, son. You're doing fine." He watched his son thrash toward him across the pool.

"You're amazing," she said. "I used to be a lifeguard at a children's pool. I think you're the first parent I've met who didn't warn their kids to be careful or not swim too far."

"That's amazing?"

"I think so."

"I suppose maybe it is. But don't give me too much credit. I make a conscious effort to hold down the number of no's, warnings and negatives."

"That's a good idea."

He smiled. "Besides, if he's old enough to pick up girls at the pool, he doesn't need any advice from me."

She laughed. "He is a charmer." She motioned to a seat beside her. "Won't you join us?"

He looked back at Timmy, who was happily occupied for the moment, then sat opposite her. "I thank you for teaching him to swim. I've wanted to do it, but never got around to it."

"They learn quickly when they're young. Besides, he's a darling boy and I've enjoyed his company."

"I imagine he's talked your leg off."

"Oh, not too much. I learned his name is Timmy Kraft and he is six and-a-half and going into the first grade this fall. He lives with his father on East Eighty-Fifth Street in Manhattan. His mother also lives in New York, but not with him and his daddy."

"We're divorced."

"I learned his daddy is an artist and works at home and—"

"Artist is a bit grand for it. I'm more of a drawer,

actually a free lance illustrator."

"I didn't connect him with you." She smiled. "In my awe at your stupendous tennis prowess I forgot your last name."

"Kraft."

She guffawed. And despite his attempts to keep a straight face, he had to join her. Finally she was able to speak. "Are you always this funny?"

He started to suggest she ought to stick around to find out, but thought better of it. "I don't know. I doubt it."

Timmy was trying to climb out of the pool and having a difficult time. Joanna got up to go to him. Hank stopped her. "Let him do it himself. Don't baby him."

She looked at him sharply, then sat back down. But when Timmy climbed out and padded over to them, she took a towel and began to dry him vigorously. Hank watched her breasts jiggle as she moved her arms.

"This is not called babying," she said. "This is called drying off."

"Sure beats a puddle."

When Timmy wanted to resume their gin game and she agreed, Hank offered to fetch drinks, gin and tonic for her, coke for his son. As he returned with theirs and a fresh one for himself, he heard her laughing and squealing. "Your son is a wicked gin player."

"I should have warned you. Hope you don't lose too much."

"Did you teach him to play?"

"He did," Timmy said, "but I beat him most of the time."

Hank sat down and watched. Lord, but she was a beautiful, animated, sexy looking dame. But he consciously put brakes on his lust. Slow and easy. Besides, he didn't need any complications in his life right now.

She smiled at him from time to time. He wasn't handsome, certainly, but very nice, sort of relaxed and loose. She remembered her early antagonism toward him.

"Do you like Charlie Brown, Timmy?"

"Sure, do you?"

She smiled, then looked at her cards. "I do believe I have a gin on you for once."

After awhile she saw Hank whisper in his son's ear. The boy brightened and quickly said, "Would you like to have dinner with us, Joanna?"

Hank laughed. "You blew it, kid. You were supposed to ask her to have dinner with you."

"And you were to chaperone?"

He smiled. "Something like that. I'm not sure the kid's to be trusted."

She stood up. "Do you swim as well as you play tennis?"

"Better. Mark Spitz was going to teach me, but—"

She was laughing as she dove into the pool. He joined her along with Timmy. While she lapped the pool, he thrashed around, mostly playing with Timmy. He really did swim badly, but somehow it didn't matter to her. And the observer in her cerebral cortex noted that she was suddenly very relaxed. She hadn't laughed so much in a long time. It felt good to laugh.

6

They had a logistics problem, two cars, clothes to be changed in two different places. Hank made a game of it, pretending it was an unsolvable problem and suggesting ludicrous solutions. Timmy laughed himself silly and Joanna joined in the fun.

Hank and Timmy changed at Laura's, said goodbye to her, then met Joanna outside to go to her apartment. Timmy rode with her in her Karman Ghia, part of her settlement with Judd Forbes, while Hank followed alone in his five-year-old Pinto. She led the way, through Saugatuck, over the bridge toward the beach and past the Longshore Country Club, owned by the Town of Westport. Not far from Compo Beach, she pulled off the road and parked before a block of two-story garden apartments. He didn't know Westport very well, but it figured these new apartments located this close to the water didn't come cheap. Then there was her sports car. He quickly figured he was financially outclassed.

He didn't alight from his car, but waited till she came over to him. She had put on her tennis whites and carried her racket. The outline of her wet bikini through the cotton made an appealing sight. Timmy was beside her.

"Come on up." He surprised her by suggesting he

could wait in the car. It was not shyness or social unease, she decided, nor did he seem to be playing games with her. "Timmy wants to see my place, and I suspect we'll need a chaperone." She smiled. "Besides, chaperones get a free drink."

"Done."

It was a small, modern apartment on the second floor, with a rather large living-dining room and a small kitchen. He gathered there was a single bedroom and bath toward the back. There was a splendid view of Long Island Sound, and he saw sailboats racing the setting sun. The place was sparsely furnished, a small sofa and a couple of chairs, all unmatched and turned to give a view of the Sound, a coffee table, TV, bookcases and a few other pieces. "I furnished it in Goodwill modern," she said, then bent to pick up some plates and cups from the coffee table. "Last night's dinner, this morning's breakfast. Housekeeping is a major interest of mine." He said nothing. She found some cartoons on the tube to amuse Timmy, then showed Hank the liquor and glasses in the kitchen before leaving for the bedroom. He soon heard the shower.

He made a pair of bourbons and set hers aside. Then, carrying his own, he again checked out the view. Eventually, he began to peruse her book shelves. A variety of college texts, a few Book-of-the-Month Club novels and a significant collection of self-help and psychology books. Almost involuntarily, his mind started to figure what these books told him about her, then he abruptly stopped the process with a shrug. For reasons he could not begin to fathom, he knew he didn't want to figure her out. Joanna Caldwell was a girl to be taken just as she came.

He heard the shower turn off. He went to the bedroom door and hollered that her drink was ready. "I'll be right there,'' he heard, and moments later she appeared, hair wet, her body wrapped in a white towel, smiling, protesting her thirst. He was about to suggest the towel had to be one of the more appealing and neglected items of fashion. Then he thought better of it, but was unable to comprehend why he bit back his words.

She did not dawdle getting ready and soon appeared in a cool and reasonably modest sundress held up by tiny straps. "I didn't know what to wear because your son didn't tell me where he's taking me."

"He figured you could wear anything to McDonald's."

She really believed him until he drove past McDonald's. "Where're you going?"

"I figured if I drove around long enough I'd stumble on a place with decent seafood."

She laughed. "I've got to learn when you're kidding."

"I'm not sure I know myself."

"Turn right."

She led them to the Whaler's Inn, and they arrived before dark, early enough to get a seat by the window overlooking the Sound. The water came up close and Timmy was fascinated by the ducks and geese. The ordering of drinks then dinner took some time.

"I got one tired kid. I think that means you showed him a good time."

"No, he showed me. He's a beautiful child, Hank." She smiled at Timmy as he looked up, knowing he was being talked about. "Those lashes and brown eyes are enough to make a girl weep with envy. Does he favor his mother?"

"He sure doesn't me. He hasn't a freckle in sight. His mother's Italian. I guess I should say of Italian descent.'' He saw the expectant look in her eyes. ''How do I happen to be raising him?''

''I'm not prying.''

''I know. I get asked a lot. Actually, it's more common than you think for fathers to have the kids. Been happening a lot lately. Vicki has a good job in the fashion business. Her career's important to her. I work at home. It's easier for me to look after him. She does her part, weekends, anytime I really need help. Vicki's no ogre. She's a good mother.''

''And you, I suspect, are a superior father.''

''Maybe. We'll see what prison he ends up in.''

She asked about his work. ''Actually I do anything that makes a nickel and am damn glad to have it. I illustrate a couple of children's books a year, which I really like to do. Mostly I pay the rent with an occasional commercial job and a book jacket or two. I've even been known to sell a cartoon, though that isn't so easy any more.''

''What would you like to do?''

''You should always listen to my son.''

''Be an artist?''

He smiled. ''Pretty nice ducks out there, aren't they?''

''You don't want to talk about it?''

''Maybe I'll get to show you sometime. Then you'll know.''

Their food came and they began to eat. She watched him with Timmy, the relaxed way he had with him. He was very much his father, yet, something else. Then she knew: his friend. There was an easy acceptance between them, as if the generations had welded to make a new one. There seemed to be an absence of tension between them. She couldn't recall ever having seen a parent and child so relaxed with each other.

Hank found out Timmy could go out back to feed the ducks. So the boy happily went off, leaving Hank and Joanna alone over coffee and brandy.

"Can I ask you something?"

"Sure."

"How did your wife ever let you get away?"

He laughed. "I'm on my good behavior. Actually, it's a very modern, very dreary tale. Vicki and I married too young. She discovered a great big wonderful world out there which she had missed. She wanted her share. By the time I grew up enough to realize I wanted her to have a career—that I could admire her independence and success, I'd lost her. My fault really. My loss."

"Women's lib."

"For want of a better name. Actually, it has worked out for the best. We get along better now than when we were married." He smiled. "I told you it was a familiar story."

Suddenly the silence between them became awkward. She picked up her brandy snifter and rimmed it with lipstick while he watched Timmy with the ducks out the window. "Do you realize you haven't asked a single question about me?"

"Yes."

"Why not?"

"I figured you'd tell me what you want me to know." He hesitated, picking up a spoon and stirring his already cold coffee. "There's another reason, I guess." He smiled, the sort of boyish grin which was becoming familiar to her. "Actually, I'm quite a nosy guy. I've a highly developed curiosity. When I'm out with a girl, excuse me, woman, I usually want to know all about her ancestry, upbringing, aspirations, everything." Again he hesitated, seeming to concentrate on the spoon revolving in the cup. "I can't begin to explain how or why it is so, but I have no questions of you. It is enough for me just to be with you.''

She gasped and felt her eyes moisten. "Oh, wow," she said softly. "Please, God, don't let that be a line."

He looked up at her and grinned. "Kinda elaborate, wasn't it? I'll have to remember it for future use."

And she smiled back. "It's a good one, all right. Get 'em every time."

"I mean it, Joanna."

"I know." She again rimmed her brandy glass. "I'm twenty-five. I was born and raised in Zanesville, Ohio. I graduated from Ohio State University, majoring in psychology. I was on the swimming team, but not quite good enough for the tennis team. I was a varsity cheer-leader. I'm divorced from Judd Forbes."

"The New York football player."

"Yes." He said no more and the silence stretched between them. "You're not going to ask how he let a marvel like me get away?"

"Nope."

She smiled. "Lord, but you're a wonder."

Timmy returned, babbling about the ducks and what funny feet they have. The check was ordered and paid and they arose to leave.

"Good evening, Joanna."

The voice came from behind her and she reacted with surprise, then shock as she recognized it. Slowly, her eyes wide, her mouth open a bit, she turned to face Jerry Wofford. It was the first time she had ever encountered one of her patients in public. It was not supposed to happen and it had never occurred to her that it could. She recalled that Wofford was supposed to be in New York. She spoke to him nervously. Her surprise made her stare at him a moment longer, then she turned to the waiting Hank. "Shall we go?"

The restaurant was now crowded and the entrance way clogged with waiting diners, so it took some effort for them to make their way outside. Joanna talked to herself. So she had run into Jerry Wofford. It was no big deal. He had probably decided to stay in Westport for the weekend. Lots of people vacationed in Westport. And he had to eat somewhere. Whaler's was a famous restaurant.

In the car Hank said, "That fellow upset you?"

She smiled. "No, I'm fine. Just someone I know. I was surprised to see him in Westport, that's all." When he asked nothing further about it, she was grateful. It would have been natural if he had inquired where he was from, how she knew him. She would have said from work. And he would have asked where she worked. She looked at him as he started the car and smiled again. Such a wonderful grant of freedom he gave by simply not asking questions.

He drove along the beach road, returning the same way. It was for him an exercise in prolonging the evening. When he parked in front of her apartment, she asked him to come up.

He glanced at Timmy in the back seat. "I'm afraid my buddy has passed out on chlorinated pool water and ducks. I better take him home."

"Back to New York?"

"Yes."

She had the strongest impulse to protest that it was too early, barely ten o'clock, to plead with him to stay with her if only for a little while. Instead she said, "You're welcome, you know."

"Thank you."

There was silence between them and he reached out and took her hand. It was cool and soft and he felt that curious, indescribable sense of aliveness and sensitivity which occurs when two bodies are reaching out to unite.

"It's been a nice day," he said. "It's not an easy one to end."

Again she wanted to urge, to coax. Instead she placed her other hand atop his and said only, "Yes."

He looked at her a moment, made an expression of resignation, then took his hand away. "I hope to see you again."

"I do, too."

She reached for the handle and opened the door. Then both she and Hank burst out laughing as a voice from the backseat said, "I have to go to the bathroom."

She leaned against the doorway to the kitchen as Hank made them both a drink. When a sleepy Timmy emerged from the bathroom, she took his hand and led him to the sofa, tucking him in beneath an afghan. She came back to her place at the doorway and whispered, "Hope you don't mind. He's so sleepy—and I don't want you to go yet."

"I'll have to speak to him about his responsibilities as a chaperone."

Nothing was said as he finished making the highballs. He returned the tray of ice to the freezer, then picked up the two glasses and handed one to her.

"It's sorta nice."

"What?"

"Not having questions asked, being a mystery woman." She saw him nod, but he said nothing, only swallowed from his drink. "I feel you've offered me total acceptance. I've never had that happen before—to be accepted just as I am."

"It isn't hard, you know. You're a very beautiful woman."

"Even with my glasses?"

"Yes." He again swallowed from his drink. "This is

a new experience for me, too."

"What?"

"To ask no questions, to not want to know or care, to offer someone unconditional positive regard."

"You know Carl Rogers?"

He smiled. "You're not the only one who reads psychology."

He looked down at her as she leaned against the doorjamb. He heard the refrigerator shut off behind him, the ticking of a clock somewhere in the distance. For the first time he noticed her perfume, delicate, feminine, not too strong.

He bent and kissed her lips, tenderly, barely making contact, marveling at their softness. He felt her eager acceptance of him as, their mouths joined, his nose smearing her glasses, she slowly rose on tiptoes toward him, her arms outstretched above his, her drink still in her right hand. Then, suddenly, impulsively, as though from a spasm, she clutched at him, and, almost unnoticed, he felt a little of her drink spill down his back as her passion erupted through her mouth.

Her lovemaking stunned him, quick, almost painful, savage in its intensity, so a product of need. Yes, she seemed to need it so. For his part, he believed he had never known anyone whose body thrilled him so, whose skin seemed so sensitized to his touch, who possessed such expertness in driving him wild with hand and mouth and quick, pouncing movements of her body.

The light from the living room made soft illumination in the bedroom. And, for just an instant, as his body came down atop hers, Joanna was aware of his shoulders shadowing her eyes. She cried out from the pleasure of having a man submerge her body with his. As she raised her pelvis and guided him into her, she thought how wonderful it was to have him be on top, taking charge of her. Then as he filled her, she became almost instantly climactic, her orgasm thundering into her, shattering in its intensity, leaving her writhing and gasping, helpless, caught up in an onslaught of elemental forces, inundated by her own pent-up desire and its release. It seemed to go on the longest time, then return as she felt him thrusting and thrusting into her, so wonderfully powerful, demanding, commanding what her own flesh cried out to receive, to give, to share.

They lay in each other's arms, winded, but not exhausted. Then he went into the kitchen and returned with their drinks. He sat on the edge of the bed beside her, but they still did not speak. In time their hands found each other's bodies and both felt the rise of their passions again. This was the first time in her life, she realized, she had been with a whole man, a man capable of filling his own needs and hers at the same time. As their mouths and bodies came together and she felt him again commanding her flesh, she realized how very healing it was. She was being healed, made well, made into a whole person. Then a word learned at the Center flitted through her mind. Multi-orgasmic. She had never known she had the capacity.

He left her before dawn, saying he hoped she'd understand but he didn't think he was prepared just then to cope with having Timmy wander in and find them in bed. He picked up his son and carried him, still asleep, out to the car and headed for New York. It was daylight when he arrived home, not having slept a wink that night.

7

Joanna awoke hard, sleep tugging at her, repeatedly pulling her down into semiconsciousness amid unremembered dreams. Some mysterious part of her brain, monitoring all that affected her body, kept trying to throw the awake switch, but it would not stay on. The brain registered the amount of sleep she had had, the degree of relaxation of her muscles, the light through the windows, the warmer temperature of the room because the sun was higher in the sky, and much more. The cortex rejected the monitored information, reasoning that the alarm clock would go off when it was time to get up. She drifted down into sleep again, how long she could not know. Then she was shocked awake, turned her head, opened an eye and looked at the clock. Twenty after ten. Lord God, she had overslept. She would be late for work. Not this day of all days.

In one movement, she rolled out of bed and stood up, then bent to examine the traitorous clock. She had failed to pull the alarm release. How could she be so stupid? She padded into the bathroom and turned on the shower, then sat to relieve a full bladder while she affixed a shower cap to her hair. No time for the dryer this morning. Quickly she lathered and rinsed her body, then turned the shower off, generously applied Alpha-Keri lotion to every bit of her skin, and rinsed that off.

70

The softness of her skin was no accident.

The whole shower didn't take five minutes. She dried herself, reached for the stick deodorant, then padded back into the bedroom, the air suddenly cool to her skin. From a dresser drawer she selected briefs and put them on, then went to a vanity and sat down before a large mirror to commence the task of fixing her hair and face. It was all familiar, much practiced and therefore largely unconscious. But this Monday morning on which she had to hurry, she suddenly stopped and looked in the mirror, seeing not the image, but the person, a pretty girl, both arms raised as she brushed shining straw-colored hair, a girl with naked, flowered breasts. And suddenly Joanna knew. She saw the lips purse, the mouth firm with determination. She knew what she must do. The doubt and indecision of yesterday was ended.

She had slept late on Sunday, too, nearly till noon after a night of love. Her first act had been to reach out with her hand, discovering the emptiness of her double bed and feeling a sense of disappointment and loss. She lay there a time, her eyes closed, remembering him, herself, them. She smiled, at least inwardly, in part from remembered pleasure, oh yes that, but mostly from sudden self-knowledge. Here she was, Joanna Caldwell, twenty-five years old, divorcee, alleged expert in treating the sexual disorders of men—she avoided the words *surrogate partner*—lying in bed, languid with love, yet reaching out vainly for more. She had been married to Judd Forbes, supposedly the cocksman of the Western world, and had, however secretly, for whatever high-minded purpose, taken to bed a succession of men, more than she wanted, certainly, more than she counted. She refused ever to keep score. But not until now, this night—she still thought of it as night—had she been with a real man. Her inward smile broadened, almost into a laugh. All of this alleged experience, all these men, all her undoubted expertise, and this was the first night she had ever been loved, really loved, turned on, fulfilled, satiated yet hungering for more. Amazing. Simply amazing. Twenty-five years old, divorcee, surrogate partner (she could now think the words) for the Center for Human Potential in Westport, Connecticut, and she had just discovered what girls of sixteen must know: what it is to be thoroughly made love to. Hilarious. And she did laugh out loud. Just has to be a joke.

She had opened her eyes then, just to make certain he was gone. She remembered. Hank had left in the middle of the night, saying he had to take Timmy home. Said something about difficult explanations. Why? My God, why, in this day and age? They could have been together now, all day, another night. It wouldn't have been impossible to explain to a four-year-old. Was her life to be run by and for a mere child? Then she sighed. Hank had been right, of course. Even young children know of mothers and fathers. It would be hard to explain, a precedent, a gross difficulty for a bachelor father. He had asked her, she remembered, to understand. Yes, she understood.

She had gotten up and showered, returning to the bedroom, quite naked, arms raised as she squeezed her hair dry in a towel. She had looked down at the bed—God! Lord God! First came recognition, then realization, finally something terribly akin to horror. The skin at the back of her neck pricked. Her breath came hard. The stains on the sheet, yellowish, surrealistically random, Hank's semen and sperm, oozed from within her body. She remembered feeling the dampness during the night. It came as all one thought, recognition triggering remembrance, then realization and horror. How many times had she seen similar sheets, stained with other men's semen and sperm? Oh God, Lord God, he could never love her if he knew.

The problem had been with her all day, a great mental wrestling match between reality and hope, rationalization and unrelenting truth. The phone rang in the afternoon. She was asked to make a fourth in mixed doubles on a private court. That had provided her only escape from her mental quagmire. Hank Kraft, nor no man like him, could want a woman as used as she. Some man, surely. Whores find husbands. They are supposedly turned on by having a whore for a wife. Not Hank Kraft. Not any man like him. Are you sure? He said nothing. He asked no questions. Said he didn't want to know. *It is enough just to be with you. Please, God, don't let that be a line.* He offered unconditional positive regard. Carl Rogers. He wouldn't care what she did for a living. Oh-h-h, yes he would. You better believe he would. But he could forgive, forget. It wouldn't matter to him. Oh yes it would matter, matter everything, and don't kid yourself. Above all, don't kid yourself. He could forgive. I know he could. Okay, maybe, but could you? Can you forgive yourself right now? *Goddammit.* He need never know. He hasn't asked, I need never tell him. Now that *is* a laugh. People always know. Everyone always finds out everything. I could lie. Oh yes, lie—and a long, happy, contented life of lies to you. I could quit now, this day, never doing it with another man. I could—oh God, that wouldn't help, would it? It's too late, much too late, isn't it? But I want him or someone like him. Am I to be denied happiness? What is to become of me?

This Monday morning, having overslept, rushed, she

looked at the person in the mirror, saw the bare, flowered breasts, now slightly blurred because she had not yet put on her glasses, and she knew. Hank Kraft was hopeless for her. It was best not to see him again. She had expected him to call all day yesterday and was strangely disappointed that he had not. But he would, tonight probably. She would be cool, distant. Hank Kraft was an impossibility, the Mt. Everest of men. She resumed brushing her hair, curling the ends out into a flip. She watched in the mirror, then spoke aloud in affirmation of her new determination. "You're a working girl, remember." Her hands stilled and her eyes widened as the full realization of the meaning of what she had just said struck her.

She arrived at Lambert's office about eleven-thirty, nearly a half hour late, having stopped at her office to don a clean white coat and make a phone call. She asked Jenny, the receptionist, to try to get Jerry Wofford and tell him his appointment was set back to four-thirty. If she could not locate him, under no circumstances was she to let him come to her office before that time. As she hung up the phone, she had insight into her situation. Two in one day. God forbid. It was impossible.

She took a quick look at herself in the mirror then rushed, even running some in her high heels, to Lambert's office. A little short of breath, she made her apologies. Lambert arose from behind his desk. His first thought was disappointment and irritation. Why had she worn the blasted medical coat? He wanted to show off his pride and joy. He wanted Brad Dillon to see what he was getting for his twenty grand. But he only smiled, assured her that her tardiness was no problem and executed the introduction, Brad Dillon, Joanna Caldwell.

She saw his smile and bobbing head and was conscious of her reciprocation.

"You'll be working with Miss Caldwell, Mr. Dillon."

She forced herself to look at the actor, levelly, unblinking, measuring his reaction to her. She applied her trick. With a man don't look at his mouth. Look at his eyes. If the pupils enlarge, he likes what he sees. Brad Dillon liked what he saw.

She was motioned to take a seat and the men resumed theirs.

"As I was saying, Brad, the Center for Human Potential has been open for only three years, but I think the fact you have come all the way from Hollywood, from Beverly Hills, indicates the reputation we have earned in that short period of time."

Joanna had heard it all before, many times, the concise, punchy history of the institution, its aims, record of success, the high caliber of the staff, the excellent treatment facilities. *Treatment.* It always amazed Joanna that Lambert could give this spiel without ever mentioning the word sex. To the uninformed, it sounded for all the world like the Center for Human Potential dealt with problems of tropical fish or maybe world hunger, or at the most was dedicated to the eradication of lumbago.

She glanced again at the famous Brad Dillon as he looked at Lambert. The face was surely familiar from the tube, movies and myriad magazine covers. And in profile it was a handsome face, phenomenal really, blonde hair, elegantly coiffed so as to be curly on top and combed straight back above his ears. A "careless" lock fell halfway down his forehead—his trademark, much imitated by both men and women. Yes, a handsome face, no doubt about it, rugged, masculine, with a pronounced brow and extremely strong chin. The nose was perhaps a trifle small for a purist, but that mouth was simply gorgeous, wide, with a firm upper lip and a full turned out, pouty lower lip that could spread into a boyish grin.

All familiar from the tube, yet he seemed different somehow in the flesh. He was smaller, skinnier than he appeared on the small screen. Then she remembered reading that video enlarges everyone. Most performers have to be super thin to appear normal on television. And his coloring was more vivid. Clearly, she needed the color fidelity on her set checked. His eyes were a deeper blue than on the screen and his skin tone so pinkish-brown it was almost a salmon color. For a moment she thought he was wearing makeup. No, she decided, it was merely lots of California sun. And he looked younger than he ought to. A visual image of the number of his medical record flitted across her mind: twenty-nine. He looked more like twenty-two.

Brad Dillon had burst on the show biz scene four years previously, in a low-budget, most unpromising TV sitcom called "Mr. America." Fred Silverman, desperate to reverse the slide of NBC, had come up with another piece of crass commercialism, full of jiggles and bun shots. "Mr. America" was sort of a poor man's imitation of "Happy Days," but with a twist aimed to cash in on an alleged fad for body building. Silverman had wanted to get Arnold Schwarzenegger for the part, but he was above it. Brad Dillion, a total unknown—actually it was his first acting role—had been chosen. Initially, Dillon was just a foil for the other characters. He was supposed to stand there, show his profile and flex his muscles. The comedy, what there was of it, was to come from other actors, a couple of puny looking pals and various teenage nymphs who drooled over Dillon. He was supposed to be irresistible

to women. His pals called him "piranha," and were forever getting him to attract girls so they could have the
leftovers. The smitten maidens called him "The
Incredible Hunk" or simply "gorgeous." One English
girl in the plot called him "dishy."

Startled NBC executives were delighted to discover
"Mr. America" was a hit, largely because of Brad
Dillon. He caught on with the public and no one could
explain him any more than they could Farrah Fawcett-
Majors. He absolutely could not act. But he was handsome, photographed well, something. The public liked
him and a massive publicity campaign was cranked up
to make them like him still more. His part was enlarged
in the show. As originally conceived, he was just
supposed to stand there and be beautiful but dumb. He
had almost no lines. But there was something camp
about his performance. Probably unintentionally, he
was satirizing himself and all other handsome, vain
men. To everyone's surprise, it was discovered he had a
talent for rendering the comedic quip. What the writers
did next was give him a heart of gold. In one episode he
was in the process of seducing a young, awed but
frightened girl. At the last moment he changed his mind
and took her home, quite virginal. Before the original
thirteen shows were over, Brad Dillon was a star.
Quickly, he made a couple of movies, both similar to
"Mr. America," and he was a hit at the box office, too.
In four years, his carefully orchestrated success had not
diminished. Wherever he went, he was surrounded by
screaming teenage girls. His appearances on talk shows,
commercials and such enhanced his image as an
incredibly handsome but basically decent boy next door
who couldn't help it if he was irresistible to women.

Joanna wondered how much of all this was true.
What was he really like? A little in dismay she realized

she'd probably find out. She glanced at his face again. Well, she couldn't complain that he wasn't good looking. Suddenly she realized that beautiful mouth of his had parted to reveal brilliant teeth. He was smiling at her, a most self-assured smile, full of confidence of its effect on her. Nervously she smiled back and looked away. Why on earth was she nervous? From the far periphery of her vision she realized his face was still turned toward her. My God, was that a smirk on his face?

She forced her attention back to Lambert, listening. "During your stay here, Brad, you will be working with Miss Caldwell—Joanna. She is one of our very best therapists—thoroughly knowledgeable about your type of disorder. I believe you will find her entirely helpful."

She glanced at Dillon. He was smiling at her. No, it was more like a leer. "I'm sure we'll get along just fine."

"Good. I will of course be receiving regular reports on your progress and advising Joanna on your treatment. But, let me urge you to feel free to discuss any question or problem with me at any time. My office is always open to you."

Again the strange, leering smile. "I'm sure she and I will have no trouble, none at all."

What on earth was going on? This Dillon acted like a man on the make, not a patient suffering from chronic premature ejaculation.

"There is another matter on which I wish to reassure you, that of confidentiality. A great deal of effort and no small expense went into designing this building to offer a maximum of privacy." He smiled. "How many people have you seen since you entered the building, Brad, other than Joanna and myself?"

She glanced at Dillon. He said nothing, yet the point had registered on him.

"Because I realize your celebrity status poses special risks for you and you require complete privacy, I'm giving you this plastic card." He handed it across the desk to Dillon. "This will enable you to use my private parking garage beneath the building. Just drive around to the rear and you'll see it." He handed another object to the actor. "And here is the key to my private entrance. I'll show you the passage that leads to Miss Caldwell's office. You will not need to see anyone else unless you wish to."

"Thank you, Doc."

"There's more. Because I realize we live in the age of news leaks and the exposé—and celebrities such as yourself are especially vulnerable—I have taken special pains to protect our records—from everyone." He pointed to a console beside his desk, smiling. "We live in an age of electronics. Might as well take advantage of it." He leaned forward ready to press a button. "If you'll look to the rear of my office, I'll show you."

Joanna saw Dillon's head turn. She did, too. All this was new to her. Instantly, mahogany paneling slid aside to reval a bank of filing cabinets. "That, Brad, is the entire system for this whole building. I keep it myself. Not even my secretary has access to it. I give out files only on a need-to-know basis. I might point out to you, also, that this room locks automatically. The doors can be opened only from the inside or by a key which I alone possess." He laughed. "Not even the cleaning woman comes in here unless I'm present."

He waited until Dillon was again facing him. "I realize such security may seem excessive, but, you see, I can guarantee confidentiality to our patients."

Joanna saw Dillon glance at her. She was uncertain what the look meant, but Lambert was quick to interpret it. "You may be certain of Miss Caldwell's complete discretion, Brad—and my own. No one will

know of your visit here unless you yourself tell them.
Does all this seem satisfactory to you?''

Dillon looked at him and nodded, then turned to
Joanna and smiled. ''I'm gonna like it here just fine,
Doc, just fine.''

''Then everything's settled.'' Lambert stood up.
''I've arranged for a small lunch in my private dining
room. Shall we go in?'' With a quick movement of his
hand, he pushed another button. At once a panel to the
left of the desk opened to reveal a small, sundrenched
room beyond. She saw a table set for three, and through
the windows the familiar woodsy scene beyond.
Lambert was chuckling. ''I'm afraid I'm a kid at heart.
I get such a kick out of secret doorways.'' He motioned
to Dillon. ''Why don't you go on in? I think you'll find
the makings of a drink there.''

Joanna was dumbfounded. She had been there almost
a year and hadn't known any of this—a private dining
room, private files, private garage, private entrance,
private passage to her office. Of course, there was no
such passage, but it sounded good.

She hung back a moment to speak to Lambert. ''Are
you coming to lunch with us?'' she asked, her voice little
more than a whisper.

''Yes, I think it's best.''

Joanna didn't. This wasn't the way it was supposed to
be at all. Ordinarily, she and a new patient went through
a get-acquainted process before beginning treatment.
They would go to lunch, maybe dinner, even the
theater, just the two of them, talking, finding common
interests. It was vital to breaking down barriers of
shyness. The patient had to come to like her, to find out
she was genuine, in no way a threat to him, sincerely
interested in helping him cure his problem. In short, he
had to come to trust her. She didn't just hop into bed

with these guys like a whore or a pickup on a one-night
stand. A three-way lunch attended by Lambert hardly
qualified as an intimate tête-à-tête encouraging trust.
She shrugged, nodding acceptance. Who was she to
argue with the great Dr. Lambert.

"And please take off your coat, Joanna. It's—it's a
little too formal, I think."

She stared at him a moment, then removed her white
coat and placed it on the back of a chair. She had worn
attire more suitable for Wofford, a thin blouse, blue in
color, a narrow skirt, also blue, slit up the leg. When she
entered the dining room, she saw the expression on
Dillon's face change.

8

Walking back to her office with him, Joanna had a sense of foreboding. Nothing was going as it should. The lunch had been a disaster, and she had gotten nowhere with Dillon. At this very moment, they should be talking amiably, at least somewhat comfortable with each other. But nothing was being said. She was choked with nervousness, unable to think of anything to say to him. And she had not an iota of an idea what was going on in his mind.

She simply could not figure him out. Other patients had come to the Center nervous, defeated. Their very presence in the building was a grossly humiliating admission of sexual inadequacy. She had reached out to all these men in sympathy, determined to reassure them of their essential worth as men. Her ministrations were aimed not so much at curing sexual dysfunction as rebuilding their shattered egos. She had always known this.

But in no way did she know this with Brad Dillon. Nothing in his manner conveyed nervousness or defeat. If there was any sense of humiliation in him, she simply could not find it. It was all unbelievable. He had come on to her, like someone at a cocktail party or a singles bar. He was loose, relaxed, supremely confident of his attractiveness and her undoubted interest in him. He simply knew, apparently without a shred of doubt, that he was handsome, possessed a great body, and irresistible to women. He had a manner—Joanna suspected it was practiced—of fixing his gaze upon her quite unblinking and smiling at her in an intensely intimate way, as though not only was she the only woman in the world at that moment, but also the most desirable. It clearly was intended to ensnare her, like a force shield on *Star Trek*. And it worked. Damn him, it worked.

She couldn't figure it out. Here was this immensely attractive man, and here was the Center for Human Potential. The two just didn't go together. He was a thoroughly sexy, self-assured man. What was he doing in a sex clinic? It couldn't be, not when he acted like he did. He was supposed to be there for treatment. He was not supposed to be there for making out. But, by God, that was the impression he gave her. Who was helping whom? What on earth was she supposed to accomplish for him?

Midway through the soup, she had reminded herself he was an actor. He played roles for a living. He was used to meeting the public. Beautiful women are a dime a dozen in Hollywood. On his public appearances he probably beat them off with a stick. Yes, she could understand. He knew how to handle himself around women and in public, but that understanding did not help her a bit in getting close to him. She didn't have a chance. Lambert kept asking him if he knew so-and-so in Hollywood or at NBC and querying him about the mechanics of TV or the movie business. They were just two guys having a nice friendly lunch. She felt useless, the paid companion whose turn came later. The way Dillon looked at her left no doubt of that.

She unlocked the door to her office and they entered.

She hung up her coat, which she had been carrying, and her purse, then sat at her desk, motioning him to a chair beside it, facing her. She didn't know what to do but plunge ahead in the usual manner. She reached in a drawer and pulled out his file, then picked up a ball point pen. It was customary to begin with a history of the patient, thus gradually getting him talking with ever increasing intimacy about his sexual difficulties. It was a method of breaking down barriers to communication.

"You're a very beautiful girl, you know."

She looked up at him. He was smiling at her, leering actually. "Thank you," she said and nodded acceptance of the compliment. As an afterthought she added, "You're not bad yourself." It was a mistake. He accepted the compliment not only as the ungarnished truth, but as his due. It was to him inevitable that she should both think it and say it. She knew all this was a disaster, nothing less. She looked down at the file. "We need some preliminary information. You are Brad Dillon, actor. You are twenty-nine years old."

"Say that softly. I'm supposedly younger. Do I look it?"

She glanced up at him, hesitated, then returned to the file. "On November 12 last, you conferred with a Dr. Lester B. Edgerton in Beverly Hills, who recommended you to us."

"And here I am."

She maintained her gaze on the file, but saw not a word of it. This was impossible. He was acting as though this were fun and games. He was being anything but a patient, she hardly as a therapist. What was she to do? Her training, her experience had never prepared her for an attitude such as his. She sighed. She pursed her lips in determination. Might as well get to it.

"All right, Brad, do you want to tell me about your

problem?'' She looked at him soberly. It was her most professional manner. She waited, but he said nothing, just returning her gaze. She could read nothing in it. "I'm here to do all I can to help you, Brad. I want to—very much. I hope you realize that.''

He said nothing. Except for an involuntary eyeblink, he might have been a wax figure.

She was unnerved by his silence, but went on ahead. "I know this is difficult for you, Brad. It is hard for anyone to admit to any sort of. . .of physical problem.'' She tried the psychological technique known as modeling. "I know it's hard for me. I came here first as a patient. It was very difficult. Believe me, Brad, I know and I sympathize.'' She smiled her best. "But when we are sick we go to a doctor—or should. I came to understand that my sexual problems were just a form of illness. I came here to the Center for help. I'm very glad I did. I want you to be glad you came, too.''

Still he said nothing. She saw no hint of a reaction.

"If I am to help you, Brad, we must communicate.'' She smiled. "Oh, that's an awful word, isn't it? Talk is so much better. We must talk, Brad. It is the most important thing we'll ever do in your treatment.'' Again she paused. Nothing. She tried a new tack. "When did your problem first begin to occur?''

"I have no problem.'' The words came out of him matter of factly. His mouth just opened and the words came out. His eyes, his face showed no reaction to the utterance.

"I see.'' She looked down at the file, then back at him. "It says here that you have a problem with premature ejaculation. Isn't that what you went to see Dr. Edgerton about?''

His gaze remained level with hers. He was surely an expert on the uses of eye contact. But for the first time she saw a hint of change in him. What was it? Wariness, fear maybe? She knew she was getting through to him. It was confirmed when he looked away, crossed his legs and knocked an imaginary fleck off his pantleg.

"Yes, I did go see this doc in Beverly Hills. I guess his name was Edgerton." He kept his head tilted down slightly, but looked at her sideways. "I was having a problem then. I was getting my rocks off too early. But no more. I got over it."

She nodded, smiled a little. "I see. That's very nice. I'm glad for you."

He made another swipe at the invisible speck of lint. "It never really was a problem." He raised his head, suddenly confident again, and smiled at her. "Just a matter of technique. Gotta have technique, right?"

"In large measure that's what we teach here, techniques to surmount problems."

His smile turned into a come-on. "I'll bet you're a good teacher."

She ignored it. "If you no longer have a problem, Mr. Dillon, why are you here?" She waited for an answer. It never came. "Why are you sitting in that chair, Mr. Dillon?" Again she waited. It was all wrong, she knew, to antagonize a patient. But she didn't know what else to do. Surely unusual cases require unusual means. "I have no doubt you spent money to come here. Why, Mr. Dillon? You owe me at least an explanation."

He hesitated for a time, but finally spoke. "It's simple. I'll tell you. I know you'll keep it to yourself. I meet a lot of chicks—er, women. Nice looking women. I can have my pick." He laughed. "Believe me, I got no trouble finding dames. All I want, any shape or size, more than I want." His amusement faded. "There was this one broad—I'm sorry to use bad language, but that's what she was, a broad—damn her. She started telling around what a lousy lay I was, gettin' my rocks off so early I didn't do nothin' for her. That kinda talk is dynamite for me. Understand?''

He looked at her. She nodded only imperceptibly.

"Well, it cost Derek, my agent, the producers of my show a bundle to shut the bitch up. That's all she was after anyway. Little money grubber was all she was.''

She waited for him to continue. When he didn't, she said, "I don't understand. Why are you here?''

Again he hesitated. "Don't you see? Derek—there are others, but mostly him—they don't like paying out money to dames. They're afraid I'll—well, my reputation will get tarnished. I keep telling them I'm all right now. I got this new technique. But, Derek. . .the others, they want to be sure.''

Again he didn't finish. "Then you are here to ascertain that you don't have any problems. Is that correct?''

She saw him grinning at her and was dumbfounded. What on earth was she to do next? "Let me get this straight, Mr. Dillon—''

"Brad, please.''

"I'm sorry, Brad. You had a history of premature ejaculation, right?''

"If that means getting your rocks off early, that's right.''

"That's what it means. Then you learned to control your ejaculations?''

She saw the hesitation. "Well-l, not—okay, I guess you can say that. I learned how to do it.''

"How to do what?''

"Good God, you ought to know. You're in this business, aren't you?''

"Sometimes I wonder why." And she knew she had never spoken truer words.

I told you, I learned a better way of doin' it.''

"Having intercourse?"

"What else?"

She shook her head. It was like conversing with a child. Patience was an unrivaled virtue. "Okay, what I need to know is this new method. Tell me about it.''

"Why don't I show you?"

She saw his smile broaden, the come on in his eyes. He meant it. He rose from the chair beside her desk, went to the door to her treatment room and opened it. "Isn't this where we're supposed to do it?"

It was all unbelievable. "Mr. Dillon, I don't know what you expected when you came here, but I assure you I'm—"

"Come off it, Joanna. You're a surrogate partner. This is what you do, isn't it? Why all this phony, shrinking violet act? Let's get with it.'' He walked into the room, pushed on the bed with both hands to test it. "Nice. It'll do.''

From her chair at her desk, eyes wide with disbelief, she watched him start to unbutton his silk body shirt.

"Come on, Joanna. Let's get to it.''

She went, and later she would try to fathom why. Pride, she guessed. She could hardly call up Dr. Lambert and holler for help. She was supposed to deal with these problems, help these patients. And that meant having sex with them. She could hardly complain because the sex was not on her terms.

He had removed his shirt and was tossing it on the bed. There was no doubt his upper body was beautiful, broad shoulders, deeply muscled. He seemed hairless and his skin was the same salmon color as his face. It was familiar, of course, much seen on the TV show, but again he seemed smaller, less massive than on the screen.

"You like?"

She shook her head with dismay. She couldn't believe this was happening. "What's not to like?"

"Nothin'." He reached out, took her shoulders and kissed her. She didn't want to. It happened too fast for her to protest.

It was quite a kiss, really, his mouth open, soft, moving. Brad Dillon was an adept kisser. But she couldn't take him seriously. In the back of her mind a thought formed. Wait till I tell the girls in the beauty parlor about this. It was a joke, of course. She would never tell anyone, couldn't, wouldn't want to. But there was an unreal cast to his whole seduction scene.

She felt his breath quicken against her cheek. Lord, he was quick. A girl didn't have a chance, even if she wanted a chance. She felt his hand at her breast, squeezing, testing, then inside her blouse, searching out her bare skin. She made no effort to stop him. All this had to lead somewhere. Nor did she protest when he stood back from her and quickly removed her blouse and the phony bra she had worn for Jerry Wofford. She had hardly expected this sort of activity so soon with Dillon.

"You got great boobs, baby. Really something else."

He removed her glasses and threw them on the bed. Then he pulled her to him and again devoured her lips. She wanted to be very clinical about it, and she was. She had had lots of experience with premies. After all, she had been married to Judd Forbes, a premature ejaculator if there ever was one. All her patients until Wofford had been premies. It was the other disorder she understood and knew how to treat. And she saw all the signs in Dillon. They had hardly started and he was already in full heat, way ahead of her.

It could not be said he was ineffective. Being clinical

did not mean being detached. His use of mouth and tongue was adroit. When he moved away from her and rubbed his hand over her breasts, pinching and rubbing her nipples, sensation coursed through her. When he knelt in front of her and took her nipples in his mouth, one, then the other, rubbing his smooth handsome face over and over and around them, she wanted him never to stop. Indeed, she held his head and moved her breasts to heighten her pleasure. When she felt him fumbling with her skirt, she wished he would hurry. Confronted by the stockings and garter belt worn for Wofford, he seemed stymied. She sat on the edge of the bed and removed them, while he took off his already bulging pants. They were skin tight and almost as big a production as her stockings.

When at last the garter belt was unhooked and thrown aside, the last stocking unrolled and pulled from her foot, she turned to face him and gasped. She had never seen anything like it. He had extremely narrow hips and a truly scrawny fanny, but thrusting from between his legs was the most massive penis she had ever seen. She did not know one could be so large. Nor did it seem to her there was any opening in a woman's body big enough to accept it.

"You like?"

She stared at it in fascination. Unreal, that's what it was. Again, the amusement center of her brain formed a thought. That face, that body and all the equipment. It just wasn't fair to other men. But she did not laugh or smile. She didn't dare and she had no time. He was at her again, mouth to mouth, hand to breast, and that unreal organ pushing her thighs apart. She felt all. She reacted. She wanted him—quite badly. But the clinical in her now understood. Among men in a shower room or wherever, that penis made him special. He was the main bull, the leader of the pride of lions, the big ram who got the pick of the ewes. To have expected defeat and humiliation from him was ridiculous. He knew what he had.

She also knew he was a premie. He was so hot he could go in a second. She reached down with her hand to clasp him, but he moved away from her and pushed her down across the bed sideways. As one movement, he knelt, spread her thighs and thrust his head between them. She felt a momentary groping and parting, then the delicious sweetness of hot lips and tongue upon her. So this was his new technique. Cunnilingus. Get the girl so ready, she would come almost as soon as he entered her. Either that or satisfy her orally, so she was glad to have him be quick.

She lay there and relaxed and simply enjoyed, the sensations, the circling tongue, the nibbling lips, the tormenting suction that produced the slow, splendid rise of her tensions until the entry of that immense penis, which once had appalled her, now seemed a commanding need. She wanted it. She wanted to be entered, filled, fulfilled. Anything for release.

She pushed her head away. "Now," she said. Her voice was more air than sound.

She bent her knees and spread her legs as he rose above her, his hand wielding what for all the world seemed to her to be the Excalibar of heaven, stabbing at her, once, twice, a third time in search of its welcoming sheath. He could not find it. And if the truth were known, she truly did make it difficult.

She reached down with both hands to guide him into her.

"No," he cried. "Don't touch."

She disobeyed him. One firm movement was all it took, and his ejaculate splattered over her abdomen.

Even as he came, unable to stop himself, his face screwed up with pain as much as pleasure, and he moaned, "Why did you do that? I told you not to."

In a moment he stood above her, anger, suffering on his face, one hand still on a shrinking penis. The proud sword became a dagger, now a pocket knife.

She rolled off the foot of the bed and stood before him, her passion still flaring. She trembled both from unrequited desire and the effort to control her rage at him. She turned, went to the bathroom and got her terrycloth robe from the hook. Putting it on and fastening the belt, she twice gulped air to gain control of herself. Then she went back to where he sat on the edge of the bed, his head in his hands.

She forced her voice to be calm. "Brad, it doesn't have to be this way. Premature ejaculation is easy to cure. I've done it several times, including my own husband."

He held his face in his hands a moment longer, then turned to look at her. She saw the anguish in that handsome face.

"I coulda made it, I know I coulda. I told you not to touch me. Why did you?"

"No, Brad, you would never have made it. You would have gone the second you entered me. I would never have had a chance and you know it."

"But I would have—"

"Yes, but what fun is that? A woman wants to be more than a seminal receptacle. She has her own needs."

"I would have taken care of you."

"I've no doubt, but who wants it that way? They don't call it intercourse for nothing. *Inter*, between two people. She wants to touch you, explore you, have the pleasure of turning you on. It isn't a one-way street, Brad."

He turned away from her then, putting his head back between his hands. She glanced at her watch. God, five after four. Wofford was due at four-thirty. She had to get him out of here.

"I can't spend any more time with you today. You're going to have to leave. I'm sorry."

She waited for him to move, to speak, to do something, her impatience rising, turning to panic. She was just about to open her mouth to speak again when she heard his words muffled by his hands.

"What time shall I come tomorrow?"

"One o'clock."

He was standing, reaching for his pants as she entered the shower. When she emerged, he was gone.

9

She sat on the edge of the bed and began to slide the stocking over her foot and up her extended left leg. The nylon was stretched out, anything but snug, and when she stood up to fasten the garter, she saw the sheer fabric bagging around her leg. She undid the garter and cinched the stocking up tighter, then twisted around to look at the back of her leg. Ghastly. Couldn't be helped. She'd have to remember to bring extra stockings tomorrow—either that or not wear them until she dressed for Wofford.

Hurrying, she pulled on the other stocking, as tight as she could, and looked down at her legs. She sensed they looked bad, but what was she going to do? She had no time to mess with them. quickly she stepped into her pumps, feeling her body equilibrium change, then picked up the bra and harnessed herself into it. She had slipped on the blouse and picked up her skirt when worry about the stockings again nagged at her. She looked down at herself. God! Still carrying the skirt, she strode into her office and examined her legs in the closet mirror. Awful. Ghastly. The bagging knees, the tops sagging around the garters. She looked like a frump. A scene from a forgotten movie came to mind, a French whore in black stockings and garter belt in bed with a man. She now understood. Whores leave stockings on so they won't be baggy for the next customer. She shivered. Couldn't help it. Quickly, she bent and removed the stockings and the garter belt, tossing them into the bottom of the closet. Jerry Wofford was just going to have to do without that little turn on today.

Now barelegged, she stepped into her skirt and fastened it to her waist, standing up straight as she momentarily examined herself in the mirror. Yes, better. She reached for her purse and got out her makeup. She had her bottle of liquid makeup in hand when, beyond the mirror, she glimpsed the treatment room through the open door. God, the bed. It looked like an army had slept in it.

Changing the linen, remaking the bed was something that just happened. It wasn't her job. A cleaning woman came in at night and did it. All Joanna knew was that the place was spotless in the morning, bed made, ashtrays wiped, glasses clean. She didn't want to know who did it. Indeed, she purposely avoided knowing. Somehow, she always imagined the cleaning woman to be a black from Norwalk, fat with an immense bosom, who worked at night to put her undeserving son through college so he could be a doctor. She would be a virtuous woman, God-fearing, church-going. She would shout "Amen" at the minister's every word. What must she think about this unmade bed every night? What must she figure went on in this den of iniquity? Sodom and Gomorrah indeed. Joanna never wanted to meet her. She didn't want to have to explain anything. She didn't want to see the disapproval in the black woman's eyes.

Joanna ran into the other room. The bed had to be remade, and quickly. But she had no sheets. Where were the sheets kept? God! There was no time. Quickly she smoothed out the bottom sheet, pulled it tight and

tucked it in firmly beneath the mattress. She started to
pull up the top sheet and coverlet when she
remembered. Stains. Frantically she searched for them.
None. Thank God, none. Hurriedly she stretched up the
covers and folded them back, then fluffed the pillows
and smoothed them out. Not good, but it would have to
do. Then on impulse she turned over the pillows. Yes,
that was better.

Another quick dash and she was back before the
mirror, bending close to it to improve her focus. She had
opened and was just about to apply liquid makeup when
she realized it was silly. It would be off in a few minutes.
She tried to put the cap back on the bottle quickly, but it
wouldn't go on right. Fumbling, almost frantic, she
swore at the lid, then set the bottle uncapped on the
shelf in the closet. Hurrying as fast as she could, she
found and opened her compact and dabbed her face
with powder, smoothing it so it disappeared. Not good,
but at least the shine was gone. Then she brushed
shadow on her eyelids and reached for the eyeliner
pencil, wetting it. But as her fingers approached her
eyes, she knew it was impossible. Her hand was shaking
too much. She settled for broad strokes to darken her
brows, then flecked mascara generously to her lashes,
lengthening, curving and darkening them. She looked at
the result and shook her head. Have to do. Lipstick last.
But when she opened the tube and brought the bright
red cylinder to her lips, her hand shook so bad she
feared smearing it. Lord, Joanna, stop it. She lowered
her arm, shook it to relax it, and breathed deeply, once,
twice. Then she was able to do her lips.

She surveyed the result in the mirror with disapproval, shrugged, shut the closet door, then sagged
into her swivel chair at the desk. She closed her eyes,
trying to relax. It didn't help. She could feel the tension

popping and snapping within her. She was on edge, jumpy, her nerves raw. It felt like two steel files were being rubbed together inside her. And she knew the cause. Damn Brad Dillon. Damn him.

There was no time for this. She opened her eyes and put on her glasses. That helped. Her eyes were tired. Four thirty-five. Wofford was already waiting. Shouldn't keep him waiting, but she needed a moment more. Had to take it. She picked up Dillon's folder and put it in her file drawer, retrieving Wofford's at the same time. She opened it on the top of her desk and read her handwritten notes of Friday, forcing herself to try to relax as she did so. The words she had scrawled leaped out at her. "Nocturnal fantasies with erection. . .erective easily. . .erective return on several occasions. . .intromission and containment with return. . . ." She remembered. Images of Friday came to her. It had been a good session. She had made good progress with him. Yes. She had been sure he was going to make it. She was helping him. She wanted to. Yes, Jerry Wofford had suffered enough. Never in his whole life had he made it with a woman. Primary impotence. He needed help. He needed her. Yes, she wanted to help him. She picked up the phone, dialed a single digit and told Jenny to send Wofford on up.

He came and she greeted him. He wore dark slacks and shoes, a light seersucker jacket, shirt and tie. "You look nice," she said.

"So do you."

She laughed. "Thank you, but I know better. I've had a hectic day, terrible in fact. I feel absolutely thrown together." She saw his smile, a suggestion her self-disparagement was unnecessary and unbelievable. A nice man Jerry, thoughtful, considerate. He deserved happiness. "I'm sorry to have set you back till four-thirty. Hope it hasn't put you out."

"No. I was in New York at the store. Lots to do I'm afraid. I could use the extra time."

"Then it's all right if we make it four-thirty all this week?"

"Yes, better actually. I'll get more work done."

"Fine. It's settled then." There was a pause, awkward, just standing there between them, a barrier. She could tell he was nervous. And why shouldn't he be? She smiled. "I don't know about you, Jer, but I could use a drink the worst way." She opened the door to the treatment room.

"Sounds good to me."

"You pour, I'll bring the ice."

She drank the first one too fast. It hit her head, dizzying her slightly, but it calmed her jangled nerves and she welcomed that. She made a second while he was still on his first.

"I've never seen you wearing glasses before."

She had forgotten to remove them. She quickly did so now. "I try to wear them as little as possible, but I'm afraid I'm as myopic as an owl—if owls are myopic." She laughed.

"I think owls are farsighted."

"I should be an owl."

She smiled at him. The drink, the banter, something was relaxing her.

"You needn't have taken them off. They look nice."

"It's better this way." She raised her glass and took another swallow.

"Was that your son you were with?"

"My son? I don't have a son." Then she remembered, Saturday night at the restaurant. Hank, tennis, Charlie Brown, a shoulder blotting out the light. It seemed an eon ago, but she involuntarily smiled, remembering Timmy. "That was my friend Timmy. Isn't he darling?"

"Yes, very cute boy. I thought perhaps he was—"

"I have no children, Jer. He's the son of my friend." She started to say Hank's name, but thought better of it. Her personal life was no business of Jerry Wofford.

He was an empathetic man. "I didn't mean to pry."

"You weren't. It's all right." She hesitated. Something had to be said. "I-I hope I wasn't rude or anything. I was. . .well, a little surprised to see you." She forced a smile. "I thought of you as being in New York."

He cleared his throat and raised his glass toward his lips as he spoke. "I should have been, I know. But it was too nice out here in the country, I decided to indulge myself."

She sensed he was lying, but let it go. "Yes, the city is insufferable in the summer."

She took a large swallow from her glass, almost draining it, and set it down. She took his and set it beside hers, then took his hand and led him to the bed, sitting beside him, holding his hand in both of hers. "Now to business. How was your weekend?"

"Fine."

"Nice dreams? Pleasant thoughts?"

"Yes."

"What thoughts?" She saw the pained look in his eyes. Such talk remained grossly difficult for him. "Come on, Jer. You have to tell me. What did you think after Friday?"

He hesitated a moment longer, then spoke, his voice dry and strained. "I couldn't forget it all weekend. I still can't."

She smiled. "That's wonderful, Jerry, isn't it?"

"I could hardly wait for today. . .now. . .you."

She squeezed his hand. "Good, I'm glad—and I'm glad you're here, too. Did you have erections?"

He blinked. "Yes." Then he laughed, the genuineness of it almost erasing his nervousness. "Damn near all the time."

She joined his laughter. "Good. I've an idea, Mr. Wofford, that you are going to become a celebrated Don Juan. I sure hope so." She saw his smile, shy, boyish. She stood up. "Before we begin, is there anything you want to say, ask, do?"

He hesitated. "Yes, there is, if you don't mind."

She sat back down beside him, looking at him, expectant. She saw his hesitation, but waited it out.

"May I kiss you? I never have, you know."

The question surprised her. It was true. She never had kissed him, never wanted to, never thought about it. In milliseconds, the synapses of her brain reacted and half-forgotten information reached her cortex. Whores never kiss their customers. She knew why. A kiss, even at its most casual, is a sign of affection. A kiss freely given is far more powerful than a dozen orgasms. She looked at him. Jerry Wofford wanted affection, not just sex. She couldn't refuse. She'd lose him if she did. Slowly she leaned her face toward him.

He was the second man to kiss her that day.

He was inexpert. The poor man apparently knew nothing. "Open your mouth a little," she whispered. He did and the kiss improved, gradually at first, then radically. She felt the smooth trickle of saliva at one corner of her mouth.

She pushed him down on the bed, following him with her mouth, her hands clutching his face. She felt his arms around her, her breasts hard against his chest. She deepened the kiss and felt his body stiffen at the same time passion arced through hers. She surprised herself.

It couldn't be. Then she knew. Damn Brad Dillon.

Abruptly, she broke off the kiss, panting a little, also trembling, as she raised her face from his. "Clothes may make the man," she whispered, "but not just at this moment."

The process of undressing cooled her off for a moment, but she sensed she was in trouble. She tried to be clinical. Brad Dillon with his damn cunnilingus and premature ejaculation had aroused her, almost to the point of orgasm, then nothing had happened. She was like tinder. She would have to be careful, watch herself, keep control.

It was not at all easy. She sat against the head of the bed as before, facing him, their legs spread, intertwined. She took his hands and guided them to her, hesitantly, fearfully, her rational mind negative about this course of action while her body cried affirmation. Her skin leaped to his touch and she knew she was in a highly sensitized state. His fingers, warm, smooth, sent delicate shivers through her, like the first drops of rain on a window, welling up, enlarging, then coursing down the surface. She was not guiding him, she suddenly realized. She was following. An intelligent man, he had learned, remembered. He knew all the secret places and ways to touch her to turn her on.

"I've done nothing but think of you," he whispered, "doing this. . .having you."

Clearly it was true, and Friday's experience, enhanced by a weekend of re-experience, showed in the talent of his hands. She moaned, stiffened, leaned her back against the pillows to steady herself against her trembling, and her hands involuntarily left his. She felt only the hand at her breasts, kneading, stroking, the fingers of the other hand at her mons, caressing the vulva, entering, spreading the major labium, separating the minor labium, sliding over her clitoris, rising along its shaft, each movement, taught by her, learned by him, an unspeakable luxury of sensation.

Through hooded eyes she saw him leaning toward her. "No," she moaned. But she was too late or it was too weak a protest, for his mouth was on hers. That act of affection, the kiss, surely the least of all that was being done to her, had an exponential effect on her tensions. She seemed unable to breathe. Trembling gave way to spasms. She seemed unable to control her muscles.

To stop him, she reached out and clasped him, large and hard in her hand. She wanted to tear at it, twist it, somehow hurt him, anything to stop this pleasure-pain she was allowing to have inflicted on herself. But the clinical in her knew she should not. Instead, she gently probed the meatus and with the lubricant found there circled and recircled the coronal ridge until she felt the jerks and spasms of his body and heard him gasp and the movements of his hands on her were stilled.

She pushed him away from her, flat on his back on the bed, legs apart, but hers inside his, and she began to inflict her own expert torment on him, plying his most sensitive places. She saw him stiffen, arch his back, throw back his head, his eyes squint shut, and she heard the sounds burst from him, half gasps, part moans.

"Don't. . ." he said, ". . .stop."

"Which," she whispered, "Stop or don't stop."

With difficulty the words came out, "I. . .don't know."

She took away a hand and touched his leg. He understood and pushed against the head of the bed with his feet, sliding himself toward the foot. She scrambled up his legs and sat on his loins. Again she circled and recircled his coronal ridge, then in a mere whisper of a

second she raised her pelvis and took him inside.
Intromission. Containment.

It was all a huge mistake. He was so big, so hard, so
filling. Her body shook with the pleasure of it and
seemed to cry out for orgasm. But she fought against it.
Containment, containment. Just hold him. Let him feel
the sensation, get used to it. She had done it many times
with many men, even with him. To steady herself, somehow control her urge to move against him, she leaned
forward and put her hands on his shoulders. She opened
her eyes, looking down at him. She saw him, eyes open,
wonder in them. Contain, contain, she said to herself,
steady, steady, it will pass in a moment. A new
sensation buffeted her. He had reached up, filled his
hands with her breasts and was stroking her nipples.
Her eyes closed. She could not keep them open. She
tried to think, to stop him, but she could not. She had
no right to. It was she who had taught him to do that.
She felt him hump into her, once, twice. A low, gutteral
moan escaped her and then she was lost, savagely
thrusting with her hips, back and forth, driving,
plummeting for orgasm. As it thundered into her, she
was aware he had gone soft, come out, but at that
moment, arching her back, all she cared about was
raking herself again and again over his pelvis,
prolonging the spasms which racked her.

Finally she stopped. Her hands against his chest, she
leaned on her extended arms a moment, struggling for
breath, for orientation in her mind. She tried to open
her eyes, but couldn't because of the effort of
swallowing what seemed to be a lump in her throat.
Then, in a moment, she was all right and opened her
eyes. She saw his, wide with wonder, looking at her. She
blinked, swallowed again and looked away from him,
then slowly straightened her back and slid back down

his legs. She took his flaccid penis in her hand, caressed it, rubbed, stroked, everything she knew. But she could not arouse him. Bitter tears scalded her eyes and she closed them. Disaster. Absolute disaster. She had ruined everything with her damned, selfish thrusting. She had set him back, almost to the beginning. Another failure for him. God, how could she?

"Oh, Joanna, that was so wonderful." There was softness to his voice, awe. "To have done that to you, to finally please a woman, to see her. . .her. . . . Oh, God, Joanna, I loved it."

She looked at him and saw he meant it, every word. She shook her head at him, sadly, forlornly, and bit her lip.

"It was nice for you, wasn't it? Real nice?"

She continued to shake her head, but incongrously the word "yes" was said, almost inaudibly. She crawled off him then and off the bed, padding into the bathroom for her robe. When she returned, he was sitting in the middle of the bed. He had no robe, but he had covered his legs and loins with the sheet.

"I mean it, Joanna. You must know what it means to me to have finally, at long last, made a woman come like that, to have pleased her, to have pleasured her, to have seen it all, been a witness to the giving of such pleasure. I can only repeat—the wonder of it all. You have made me very happy, Joanna."

She listened, making no effort to stop him, and again she knew he meant it. Her only reaction was to again bite at the inner surface of her lip.

She turned away then and went over to look out the window, toward the woods. Near sunset. A dying day. She'd been cooped up in this room the whole day.

She longed to tell him, to turn around and scream at him that he was a fool. He had done nothing. It had been she who had had the stupid orgasm, she alone. He had nothing to do with it. She could have masturbated to the same effect. She could have used a cucumber, even a goddamned zucchini squash. She could have sat in a washing machine. He was useless.

But she could say none of it. A word of it, even the conveyance of empathetic, non-verbal thought would merely compound the disaster which had already occurred.

"Don't you believe I enjoyed it, Joanna?"

She turned to face him. "Certainly, I believe you enjoyed it, Jerry. And I enjoyed it, too. I guess I needed it and I thank you." She saw him beaming. If he had a tail he would have wagged it. "But that's not the way it's supposed to be."

"What d'you mean?"

How should she say it? Her mind contained conflicting versions of the same words. She elected to just open her mouth and let the right hemisphere of the brain, the intuitive part, wing it alone. "You didn't go, Jerry. I wanted you to."

"I know, but it doesn't matter."

"But it does. That's what you're here for. Believe me, Jerry, I don't have any trouble with orgasms. I can have one just about anytime." She saw the hurt in his eyes and quickly sought to dispel it. "Do you remember my telling you about the observer in you, the fellow who is watching all the time?"

"Yes."

"That's what happened to you just now. You were so busy observing me you forgot to participate yourself. That's why you lost your erection."

He looked down at his hands. "I'm sorry."

She railed at herself. *Don't make it worse than it is, you idiot.* Quickly, she went across the room, leaned over the bed and lifted his face with her hand. She forced a smile. "But it was sort of nice, wasn't it? We'll get it tomorrow, won't we?"

"Sure." His smile as he said it was genuine.

After he had gone and she had showered, she sat bundled in her robe on the foot of the bed, watching the purple twilight pass. She was relaxed. The orgasm had done that. But she was bone weary and extremely depressed, depressed over what she was doing to herself and to these men. The whole day had been a disaster. She had absolutely humiliated Brad Dillon, and in the worst possible way it could be done to a man. And Jerry Wofford. Hopefully she had only set him back. She'd be lucky if she hadn't ruined any chance he might have had for a cure to his impotence. She had no idea what to do next with him. What was she doing with these men? What possessed her to think she could play doctor and undertake the treatment of male sexual inadequacies? Madness on her part, utter madness.

She got up and went to the buffet, pouring herself a bourbon. As she raised it to her lips and swallowed, she sensed her two drinks earlier were probably at fault. They had hit her, hard. She hadn't been able to control herself with Wofford, and she had always known how to hold off before. Yeah, the booze. She wouldn't make that mistake again. She looked out at the deepening dusk. Must be after eight o'clock. She'd been here the whole damn day. Too much. Too much for her, too much for any woman. She couldn't handle it. Might as well admit it before she did any more damage to these men and to herself. Damn, double damn. How had she gotten herself into this mess?

She raised the glass again and swallowed, her mind gradually sinking into despondency. For the first time in a long time, she thought of her father, the Reverend

Luther Caldwell. If he could see her now. He'd been beside himself when, legally of age at eighteen, she went off to that heathen college in Columbus, cut her hair, took to lipstick, rouge, nail polish, mini-skirts and bikinis. He hated her marriage to the unchurched Judd Forbes and railed at her divorce. What would he say now? Then she shrugged, pursed her lips. Might as well get dressed and go home—home in Westport. The abyss between here and Ohio was too wide, too deep ever to be crossed again.

As she dressed, she recognized it was the third time that day she had put on the same clothes. Ridiculous. Something had to be done. Either bring fresh clothes here or—yes, she had to get out of this bind she was in, this double bind. Indeed, a double bind. It was by then nearly dark in the treatment room and she switched on the light, looking around to see if she had left anything. She saw the tousled bed and shook her head at it in dismay. She had left nothing. Her drink. She went over, picked it up and drained it. Out the window, she saw a bright spot on the ground below. In a moment she realized it came from her own windows. Dark outside. Been here the whole day. Bitterly, her mind added: just a working girl. Then she saw another rectangle of light to her left. Someone else still working. From the location she guessed the light came from Lambert's office. If he was in she had to talk to him. Something had to be settled and the sooner the better. She turned and strode toward her office and the phone.

10

Dawson Lambert stood behind his desk, head bent forward slightly, nervously poking at his desk blotter with the tip of a letter opener as he listened to the voice on the phone.

"Dawson, can't you be pleased I'm marrying Charles?"

He gritted his teeth. The bitch. Knifes him in the back, then wants to be reassured he's enjoying it. But this was only a flash of annoyance on his part. Actually he was pleased to receive her call. He had been expecting it. "I am, Laura. I'm extremely happy for you."

He heard her sigh over the phone. "No, you're not Dawson. I could tell Friday you were upset. I can hear it in your voice now."

He could read her voice, too, and what he heard made him smile in triumph. Laura McGovern was halfway a manic-depressive. She had been on a prolonged high ever since the plastic man. She had been going to parties. She got herself engaged to that creep Randall. But the inevitable low had now set in. If he handled her right, she'd never marry Randall. She'd never marry anyone. "I don't know what you hear in my voice, Laura. I've had a hard day. It's nearly nine. I'm tired. That's all you hear." Yes, deny it, but distantly, a little chill to the voice.

Long pause on the line. "Dawson, why can't you be happy for me?"

He smiled. *Why can't I indeed*? "I am. I've said I am. I don't know what more to do, Laura."

There was another long pause, then he heard her voice, weak, whining. My, she was depressed. She sounded ready for the strait jacket and the shock box. "I haven't had much happiness in my life, Dawson. I wasn't born pretty. I don't know how to be bright and witty and charming. All I've had is Daddy's money—and it won't buy happiness."

The hell it won't.

"I tried to buy it, Dawson. I really did. I went out and bought Ralph McGovern—and that was twenty years of hell. You know that, don't you, Dawson?"

"Yes, I know."

"Is it wrong of me to want happiness now?"

She sounded like a puppy, a female puppy, a bitch. If she had a tail, she'd be wagging it right now. "I thought you *were* happy, Laura. You look like a new woman. You certainly act like one. I've heard you laugh so much lately. You're getting to parties. You've come out of your shell. You're engaged to be married. I don't understand what your problem is."

Yes, he had said that right, perfect, uttering all the right words, but without any feeling. The silence on the line told him he was getting to her. "You're my problem, Dawson. I want your approval."

He smiled. "Then you have it, Laura. I've told you over and over."

"I don't believe you. You. . .you say all the right words, but. . .but I can tell you don't mean them."

He almost laughed out loud. Yes, it was working. Like all neurotics, Laura McGovern had radar for the slightest variance in attitudes toward herself. "Really,

Laura, you're a big girl now. What does it matter what I think?''

"It matters everything, Dawson. I was nothing till I met you. You're the one who has made me happy, taught me to be a woman. I owe everything to you. I want your approval."

"And you have it, my dear."

The silence on the line was so prolonged he might have thought she had hung up except there was no dial tone. "Why are you being so beastly to me, Dawson?"

Yes, he had her now. She was ready for it. He relieved himself of an exaggerated sigh. "All right, Laura. You are too perceptive. I knew I couldn't fool you." He paused, cleared his throat, made a false start, very nearly stammering. "Look, Laura—what I'm trying to say—" He laughed, seemingly nervous. "You put me in a difficult position. I'm both your friend and your physician. I want nothing but your happiness. But I can't go around casting aspersions." He laughed. "You know how it is. When a woman's in love, she wears rose-colored glasses."

"Are you saying something's wrong with Charles?"

Heavens no. He's just a sanctimonious prig. "Of course not. I'm sure he's a marvelous fellow."

"But you are saying something, Dawson." He heard the urgency in her voice.

"I'm just saying, as your friend—be careful. You've had one unhappy marriage, Laura. I'd hate to see you have a second."

"I know. I worry about that, too."

"Do you really know him, Laura—I mean really *know*—*everything* about him? Sometimes in courtship a man appears one way and—"

"What are you trying to tell me, Dawson?"

He saw the light flashing for another line. Who could be calling at this hour? "Laura, I'm concerned that you and he haven't had sex. A grown man just doesn't act that way. It's unnatural. I'm worried there is something wrong with him. . .that he's not right for you.''

He heard her laughter on the line and it unnerved him. ''Is *that* what's bothering you, Dawson?''

The flashing light on the second line unsettled him. He couldn't think. ''I'm sorry, Laura. I've another call. Let me put you on hold a moment.'' He pushed the red button, saw it light, then pushed line two. ''Dr. Lambert here.'' It was Joanna Caldwell. She was sorry, but she just had to talk to him. ''Of course, Joanna, but I'm on another call. Let me put you on hold a minute. I'll get right back to you.'' Without waiting for her approval, he executed the buttons and Laura was back on the line.

Suddenly, he couldn't remember where he was in his conversation with her. Damn Joanna. Why did she have to call and ruin his train of thought. ''Where were we, Laura?''

''You were just telling me to have sex with Charles.''

Her voice disconcerted him. It was louder, lighter, bright with laughter. ''Yes, it worries me that—''

Her laughter, deep, throaty, cascaded over him. ''Oh, you are a dear, Dawson, worrying about me so. You make me feel terrible for having lied to you.''

''Lied?''

''I was just protecting my privacy, Dawson—Charles', too. I don't have to tell you *everything*, do I?''

''You mean?''

''Of course, silly. We've done it lots of times, and it was simply splendid. You needn't worry about Charles. He's very much a man. Quite demanding really.''

Lambert's rage ripped through him like cold fire, and he trembled with the effort to control it. ''I see.''

''I didn't really lie to you, Dawson. Charles and I

know everything is fine with us. So, we're waiting now till our wedding night, saving it up. We want it to be really special—sort of like newlyweds. Isn't that marvelous?"

Lambert's rage filled his mind. *The sanctimonious sonofabitch. Holier than thou about sex clinics. All the while he's ripping off a piece on the side. Fucking bastard.*

"But you're so sweet and dear to worry about me, Dawson."

All he wanted to do was jerk the phone out and throw it. But he couldn't. His voice glacial, he said, "That's what friends are for."

"And you are a friend, the best of all possible friends. I knew if I called you, talked to you, everything would be all right. You'd make me feel better."

Shaking, unable to control it, his knuckles white as he gripped the phone, he only knew he had to get rid of her. "I've got to go, Laura. It's late. I'm terribly tired."

"Of course you are, you dear. But I want to tell you what a love you are to worry about me."

"Yes, Laura, but I really must go. Good night."

He hung up without waiting for another word from her. The bitch. The she-bitch. His mind racing, he stalked across the room to his bar and poured himself a heavy whiskey, raising the glass and swallowing. Where had it gone wrong? He had her. She was putty in his hands. He had her all but talked out of that goddamned marriage. Then he'd lost her. How had it happened? Then he remembered. The phone call from Joanna Caldwell. It interrupted him. He'd bungled his chance. He glanced over at the phone. The red light. She was still on hold. What did she want at this hour?

Carrying his glass, he went back to the phone, lifted the receiver, then hesitated a moment before pushing the hold button, swallowing, taking a deep breath, trying to get hold of himself. "I'm sorry, Joanna. I was tied up longer than I thought. What's up?"

He listened to her a moment. Dillon. Wofford. A bad day. He did not so much hear the words she uttered as he did the timbre to her voice. She was upset, on the edge of hysteria. He interrupted. "Where are you now, Joanna?" He listened. "Still at the office. My God, it's almost nine o'clock. You shouldn't still be here." She spoke and he replied, "Yes, I know I'm still here, but that's different." Best to divert her. "Man's work is never done. You know that." He listened to the words pouring out of her. She had made a mess of Dillon. Wofford was a disaster. She was no good, ruining everything. "That's ridiculous, Joanna. You're—" She was extremely upset. She had to talk to him. Right now. She was coming to his office. "No you're not, Joanna." Best to be firm with her, fatherly. "I know you're upset. I can hear you. You needn't tell me. But it is pointless to try to talk about it tonight." He listened. She had to talk to him. "No you don't, dear. What you have to do is leave this office immediately, get something to eat and go to bed." He heard her protest. "Believe me, Joanna, I know what I'm talking about. Nothing can ever be settled when a person is as upset as you." Again her voice, an appeal. She was begging him. He could hear the tears in her voice. "Joanna, listen to me. You need food. Have you eaten since lunch? . . .Well then. Get a steak or something. And a bottle of wine. That'll relax you. Your problems won't seem so serious. Believe me." He listened. Her determination had dissolved. She guessed he was right. "I know I'm right. A good night's sleep and everything will be different. . .of course, I'm going to help you. Haven't I always? But tomorrow. Believe me, tomorrow is better. Let me look at my schedule." With a forefinger he flipped the page of his desk calendar. "Joanna? Eleven tomorrow. I'm free.

We'll have lunch. Just the two of us. We'll talk out all these problems. All right?'' He heard her reluctant acquiescence. "Fine, Joanna, and goodnight. And do what I say, dinner, wine, sleep.'' She agreed. "Byebye, dear.''

He held the receiver away from his ear, looking at it, shaking his head. His mouth, obeying his brain, silently formed a string of obscenities. Women. Might as well live in a zoo.

More slowly now, he went back to his bar and poured another Scotch. His chat with Joanna Caldwell served to divert his anger. So Laura McGovern was going to marry that prick Randall. Over his dead body. He lifted the glass, filled his mouth, then slowly swallowed it, letting the action relax him. He repeated this a couple more times, his mind returning to the calm calculation which was more characteristic of him. Then he smiled. Yes, there was more than one way to kill a goose—or break up a marriage.

He returned to his desk and flipped open his address book. No home address. He thought about dialing information, then thought better of it. Probably unlisted anyway. Abruptly, he picked up the phone and dialed.

"Dr. Randall's office.''

"Is this his answering service?''

"Yes.''

"This is Dr. Dawson Lambert. Is it possible to reach him? At his home, perhaps?''

"I can give you his number, Doctor, but I know he's not there. He's in San Francisco at a medical convention.''

"I see.''

"He'll be checking in. I can give him a message.''

"Just tell him I called.''

As he hung up the phone, he was again swearing.

Nothing was going right.

Forty miles away another phone was being hung up in Manhattan apartment. It was the fifth time Hank Kraft had tried to reach Joanna Caldwell that evening. No luck. Nothing to do but keep trying. He just had to talk to her—whether or not that was the thing he ought to do.

"Daddy?"

Timmy's voice from the bedroom. "Go to sleep."

"Daddy?"

It was a nightly ritual. There just had to be a couple of questions at the end of the day. And he really didn't mind. Didn't know what to do about it anyway. He went to stand in the doorway to his son's bedroom. "What?"

"Who you calling?"

The kid had ears like an elephant. "Joanna."

"Why you calling her?"

"To tell her we had a nice time Saturday, thank her." It was mostly the truth. "Now go to sleep."

"Yes, she was nice. I liked her."

"Good. Go to sleep."

"Did you like her?"

"She was all right. Go to sleep."

He turned from the doorway and crossed the room to stand over his drawing board. He was working on a book jacket for a science fiction novel. A bosomy girl, bodice in disarray, was about to be attacked by a claw emanating from a bald-headed green man with eyes the shape of pullet eggs. Hank shook his head. Art, no. Rent money, yes. He sat on the edge of his stool, picked up a pencil, then reached up and adjusted a lamp to bring greater intensity of light on his creation.

Ordinarily the light was pretty good in the daytime. It was a corner apartment on the fourth floor, which is one reason he'd taken it—that and the fairly reasonable rent. His drawing board was in the far corner of what passed as a living room. The corner windows offered fair light in the daytime. The rest of the room was sparsely furnished, couch, chair, coffee and end table, all mismatched; TV, a large shelf of books. A chrome and formica dinette set was at the far end. The apartment had once been a railroad flat, a long hall with rooms off each side. The remodeling had improved on it, combining two or three small rooms to make the long, rectangular living-dining room. A wall separated it from his bedroom. Off the foyer was a small room for Timmy, a tiny bath and diminutive kitchen. Not much, but home.

He raised his head and looked at the phone on the end table, as though it could solve his problem. Why was he compelled to phone her? He honestly did not want to get involved with her. He most certainly did not want marriage—not for a long time, if ever again. Nor did he covet any sort of live-in arrangement. This apartment was too small. He had no money for a girlfriend. And there was Timmy. He didn't want to see the confusion in his son's eyes, the hurt. He didn't want explanations. He didn't want to be on the defensive with him. Things were fine now. The two of them were getting along great. Almost a couple guys baching it. Let it be. Leave well enough alone. Don't complicate your life. Don't call Joanna Caldwell.

But he had, or tried to, repeatedly. It had started yesterday afternoon. That's when he discovered she had an unlisted number. Why would she have an unlisted number, a young, attractive girl like her? Probably had had some obscene phone calls. He tried to persuade the phone supervisor it was an emergency. Used his best line. She phoned Joanna to give his number. No answer at Joanna's end. He thought maybe Laura McGovern would have Joanna's number. He tried all afternoon and evening to get Laura. Out, out, constantly out.

Finally, he'd gotten Laura this morning. Yeah, she had Joanna's number. He dialed it. No answer. He could visualize the empty apartment with the big window overlooking the Sound, the phone echoing again and again in the vacant rooms.

Why did he have to talk to her? He was far from certain he knew the answer. She had gotten to him, obviously. He glanced down at the egg-eyed monster, his work, his rent money. Precious little he'd done on it today. Didn't seem to be able to think of anything but Joanna Caldwell. Under his breath he swore. Why? What was there about her? Good in bed. Was that it? Was he captured by a good lay? Yeah, she had been good. No doubt of that. Her skin, how soft it was, her figure. He shook his head. She sure was something else. And she had been so damned adept, so giving, yet demanding. Couldn't get enough. Wanted it, wanted it, and knew what to do to get more from him. Whatever his record was, he'd broken it. He'd always thought Vicki the best in bed. He smiled, remembering the old radio joke. For the best in bread eat whatever. The announcer had said breast in bed. Whatever had busted up Vicki and him, it wasn't sex. That had been good. But Joanna was better by a factor of ten. Make it a hundred. Or was he just horny and sex starved? No, she had been good, too good. Question: how on earth had a girl from Zanesville, Ohio, varisty cheerleader for Ohio State University gotten so good in the sack? Said she was married to Judd Forbes. Big ladies man. Maybe that was it. But, shit, Forbes'd let her go, hadn't he?

Sex. Is that why he was phoning her? Just want another lay? No. He wanted to tell her the opposite. If he'd driven off with Timmy at ten o'clock like he intended, if there had been no sex, he'd still want to call her. He wanted to tell her that. She'd gotten to him. There was something about her—God knows what, the still waters running deep within her, the easy banter, her care and concern with Timmy. He'd seen others with him. All wrong, too motherly, too childish, too saccharine. Nobody, except Vicki of course, handled his son right, or at least the way he wanted him handled. Joanna had. Instinctively, no prompting. Hell, she didn't even know he was his kid, and there she was teaching him to swim, playing gin, having fun. He'd liked that.

Then he knew. He wanted to tell her she wasn't a one-night stand to him. He wasn't going to fall in love with her. He wasn't going to get involved, by God, no, he wasn't, but he wanted her to know she hadn't just been a tumble in the hay. He liked her. He had really enjoyed the day. He appreciated her being nice to Timmy. Yes, that's why he wanted to talk to her. And what the hell kind of a reason was that? She needed his approval? Bull. He needed *her* approval. He needed to have her know he wasn't a guy for one night stands. Christ, what a sap he was.

To stop the mental fencing—*touché, touché*—he went to the phone and dialed her number. He heard it ring, twice, four times, then as he was about to hang up—she was never going to be in—he heard, "Hello."

"Did I wake you up? You sound sleepy."

"No, I wasn't sleeping. Who is this?"

"Hank. Hank Kraft." He waited for some reaction, some burst of enthusiasm—oh, Hank, how are you, so good of you to call. Nothing. Silence on the line, awkward, needing to be filled. "I tried to call you yesterday. But I didn't have your phone number. You're unlisted."

Finally a word. "Yes."

"I called Laura McGovern. She gave me your number. Hope it's all right." Why say that? They'd slept together. Surely it was all right to use the damn telephone.

"No, it's all right."

Nothing more. She offered not a word. Joanna Caldwell might be great in bed, but she was lousy on the telephone. "Tim asked me to tell you what a great time he had Saturday." That would get her.

"Who?"

"Tim. My son. Remember?"

"Oh, Timmy, sure."

Nothing more, no "how is he," no "What a marvelous kid," no "give him my love," no "be sure to keep up his swimming." Nothing. He would have a fine time telling the kid about this conversation. He hadn't made as much of an impression as he thought.

"Are you all right, Joanna? You sound strange."

Long pause. "I'm just tired, Hank. I had a ghastly day."

Doing what? Working the blacksmith shop? Sand-hogging an East River tunnel? He had no idea what she did. That had been charming Saturday. Now it wasn't. "I'm sorry."

"I just got home. I've got to get something to eat and go to bed. I'm sorry."

"Sure. It's all right."

"Thank you—and thank you for calling."

"Sure."

The phone clicked dead without even a goodbye. Slowly he lowered his own phone to its cradle. Figure that, would you? He had talked to more warmhearted polar bears. Figure that. Just figure it. Wow, too much. Two days of worrying about her for that. He shrugged and went back to his drawing of the green monster. It suddenly took on greater importance in his life.

11

"Doctor Lambert, we have an impossible situation. In attempting to treat two men, I am harming both."

Joanna's words, rehearsed all evening and refined during the morning, were uttered emphatically, expressing the determination she felt. However much she wanted to, however much she felt she had a right to, she would not complain. She would not speak of *her* difficulties. Nothing would smack of self pity. No, she would raise her arguments to the loftier plane of good medicine. As a doctor, he could not fail to react to the need to do what was best for the patient. In her mental fantasy, she had come to expect him to agree with her, perhaps a little reluctantly, then seek her advice. Which patient should she drop? She wanted to say both. But that was asking too much. She would say Dillon.

She waited for him to speak. He sat behind his desk, backlighted by the windows of his office. She was sure he had to see the determination she felt.

"I gather you had difficulties yesterday."

"Yes."

"Tell me about it."

She sucked in her breath. Yes, he'd want to know what happened. "All right. Dillon first." She hesitated, then a rehearsed sentence came to her. "Doctor, isn't it axiomatic in medicine that you can't treat a patient who doesn't want to be treated?''

She saw him turn down the corners of his mouth, an expression of doubt. "I don't know if it is axiomatic. Patient cooperation is necessary, of course—the will to live, that sort of thing. But I'm sure many patients have been cured despite themselves. What are you driving at?''

"Dillon insisted he had no problem. . .no sexual inadequacy.''

"He did?'' She saw his eyebrows raise in surprise.

"Yes, he said he had a problem in the past. I believe he spoke of it as a *former* problem. But he had gotten over it, learned a new method, he said.''

"That can't be so, Joanna. Before you came into my office he and I had quite a chat. He explained his problem. Seemed quite eager to improve his performance.''

"Well he wasn't that way with me. He came on very strong. Acted like God's gift to women. Believe me, Doctor, that's the way it was.''

"I believe you, of course, I just don't understand it.''

"Nor I. I've never seen a patient act like him. He wasn't here to get well. He was here to prove how good he was.''

He leaned back in his swivel chair, actually thinking this time, not posing. Finally, he leaned forward and spoke to Joanna. "I think I know what happened. He was one way with me, worried, wanting help. But when he saw you, he turned macho, came on strong, man and woman, that sort of thing.''

"Perhaps you're right, doctor. But whatever the reason, it doesn't matter. The whole situation is impossible.''

"I doubt that. Tell me what happened.''

She didn't want to tell him, but she had no choice.

This was the Center for Human Potential. He was the director. "Dillon insisted on showing me his. . .his new technique."

She hesitated so long he finally prompted her. "Go on."

She bit at her lip. Only the realization she was being silly, actually making a fool of herself, drove her on. "His technique is to perform cunnilingus, postponing entry until the woman is nearly orgasmic."

A mental image travelled across Lambert's mind, arousing him a little. "Quite common," he said. "Anything is tried to hurry the partner to orgasm or delay his ejaculation. All quite desperate, really. Was he successful?"

"He ejaculated prior to entry." She said it matter-of-factly, but her voice was low, strained.

"There you have it. The man clearly does have a problem, obviously a serious one."

"But what good does it do if he doesn't think so?"

He laughed. "I'm sure he thinks so. How could he help? What was his reaction to his. . .his debacle?"

She hesitated, but only briefly. "It was very humiliating for him, Doctor. And that's why—"

"Of course it was humiliating. Why wouldn't it be. Seems to me you handled him beautifully."

"But that's just it, doctor, I didn't." She now sensed this conversation was not going as she wanted, and urgency crept into her voice. "Brad Dillon is a successful man, a TV and movie star, quite the sex symbol. He has his pride. Indeed, he is, well, arrogant. It was very humiliating for him. I don't see how—"

"Joanna, Joanna, listen to me." He leaned forward, elbows on the desk, narrowing the distance between them. "I told you before. It is these macho types, the big sex symbols who often have the most difficulties.

You did fine with him. I'm sure you did." He saw doubt rise on her face. "And don't worry about humiliating him. Probably the best thing for him. A little humility will do him good. I, too, got the impression of a young man rather stuck on himself. Yes, you did fine."

"I didn't, doctor, I didn't."

"All men who come here are in a state of humiliation. After all, they can't perform adequately the most basic male function. Whatever success they may have in life is nothing, if they can't be adequate sexual partners. You know that. It is precisely because you do know it and are such a caring person that you are so very good at what you do. Believe me, Joanna, I know what I'm talking about." He saw he was silencing her, winning. "The man's humiliation is necessary before any treatment can begin. As you suggest, he must know he needs treatment before he can accept it. You did precisely the right thing with Dillon. I suspect treatment will now proceed as it is supposed to."

She sat there, averting her eyes. Again, he was talking her into something she didn't want to do. She felt helpless, frustrated.

He hesitated a moment, looking at her downturned head, sensing her discomfort. Deliberately, he softened his voice, adding a tone of fatherliness. It was important that he not badger her. She had to believe he was on her side. "What happened with Wofford? Did you have a problem with him?"

She sighed deeply, then slowly raised her head and spoke. But she did not look at Lambert, but away, somewhere past him. "Jerry Wofford is a very nice man, intelligent, sensitive." In her peripheral vision, she saw him nod agreement. "I have worked very hard with him."

"I know that."

"I thought I was making—he was making, great progress. He was. . .had been easily erective. He had learned. . ." She sighed, again deeply, her shoulders rising and falling from the effort. "He had learned to give pleasure, respond to it, and to enjoy receiving and respond to that. I felt he was beginning to stop trying for an erection, for performance. He was beginning to simply do it. He seemed to no longer be observing, analyzing. He was performing."

Now her gaze met Lambert's. She saw him nodding in agreement, urging her to continue. Again she sighed and looked down at her hands. "I was making progress and I goofed that, too." She paused. Why did she have to say these things? Sex is a private act. But she knew she did. This was a sex clinic, the Center for Human Potential, devoted to education, frankness, openness about the most private act. Again she sighed. "During intromission I. . .I was unable to control myself. I. . .I—" Her mouth seemed dry and she swallowed. "I became orgasmic. I couldn't seem to help it. During my. . .my thrusting, he. . .he lost his erection."

His mental image of what must have gone on between this gorgeous creature and that creep Wofford thoroughly aroused him, but all he said was "yes."

"It was a total failure for him. And the last thing he needed, of course, was *another* failure. I simply set him way back in his treatment."

"Was he upset?"

She hesitated, looking up at him. "I don't know. I'm not sure. He believed he had created my orgasm. He reacted with pride to that. He used the word wonder in speaking of it. I probably erred in suggesting to him that the whole episode was a failure. Do you see what I mean, doctor? In trying to treat two men, I'm simply harming both."

He leaned further over his desk, clasping his hands in front of himself and leaning over them. "Joanna, let's be rational, all right? What you really feel guilty about is that you were orgasmic with Wofford. My dear, stop it. You are a normal, healthy girl. You couldn't help yourself."

"But I could have, I should have. I had a couple drinks and—"

"Listen to me. I gather the cunnilingus with Dillon led to no release of your tensions. Is that correct?" He looked at her. No answer. "Is that right, Joanna?" He saw her nod. "Okay. You were in a high state of sexual tension after Dillon. When you had intromission with Wofford. . . My dear, of course you became orgasmic. You could do nothing else. Just stop blaming yourself."

"But the effect on Wofford. Another failure. I've set him back. I may have ruined any chance with him."

"Nonsense. Failures occur in all treatments. You're trying too hard, expecting too much. Wofford will be fine, and if he isn't, so be it. You will have done your best. Remember my telling you primary impotence is the most difficult male problem. Failure rate is at least fifty per cent. No person, most especially a surrogate partner, can be expected to offset deepseated childhood teachings and a lifetime of problems. Don't take him so seriously."

He saw her look at him, her eyes wide. He had surprised her. The plain fact was that he didn't give a damn about Dillon, Wofford or any of the others. He didn't care if their sex problems improved. They could worsen for all he cared. What was important—he thought of it as keeping his mind on the main chance—was the treatment. Get 'em in here and get their money.

"I surprise you, Joanna. I've told you again and

again, you are so very good at what you do because you care so much. And that is as it should be. I want you to try, to care about these unhappy men. I certainly do. But please, dear, leave room for perspective. Don't get upset by every little failure, every setback in treatment." He smiled broadly at her. "Take the long view of things. In the long view you will realize what a splendid job you're doing and how very much I appreciate it."

She looked at him, the smiling face, the confidence exuding from it. "Doctor, I want to drop Dillon. I can't take two patients at once. It is too much." She saw him frown, open his mouth. Suddenly she didn't want to hear any more silken words from him. "Doctor Lambert, I was a basket case last night. I was too weary, too torn apart emotionally, too utterly despondent even to cry. I can't take it, Doctor. I can't go through it night after night." She hesitated, then plunged in her ultimate weapon. "If you cared about me as a person, Dr. Lambert, you would not ask this of me."

He leaned back in his chair a moment, looking away from her, deep in thought. Yeah, he cared about her all right. She was the best damn surrogate partner in the business, potentially worth a fortune to him. He didn't want to lose her. The problem was how to handle her. Damn. Women. Sometimes he swore he'd. . . . He forced that thought out of his mind and swiveled his chair to look at her.

"Of course, I care about you, Joanna. You must know that. Why if I had a daughter, I would ask no more than that she be like you."

"You'd let your daughter be a surrogate partner?"

Damn her. Goddamn her. "I might—if she wanted to, if—"

"I don't want to, doctor. I want to counsel married couples. I've had enough. I've paid my dues. I want—"

"What you want, Joanna, can't be." He said it

firmly, testily. Then as an afterthought, a sop to her feelings, he added the word, "—just now." He knew what he was about to say was a risk. He had to take it. "Joanna, I have no choice. And therefore you have no choice. You must continue with Dillon."

"And Wofford?"

He saw the anger, defiance in her. It was the rock and the hard place. She just might quit on him and walk out of the room. "Unless you are prepared to leave him at this juncture."

He saw her anger. "Then you are ordering me to continue with both?"

He sighed. "I dislike the word order. I'm telling you there is no choice in the matter." Again a sigh. "Joanna, I understand yesterday was difficult. Truly, I don't blame you for being upset. Dillon was difficult, but surely he will be more cooperative today."

"And the sun will rise in the west, too."

"Scoff if you wish, Joanna. But I cannot help but feel you are being excessively negative. You are—how else can I put it but frankly?—enjoying a bit of self-pity." He saw her react to the word. "Feeling sorry for one's self, one's job, believing one's self put upon and abused is a normal reaction, probably therapeutic, but like everything else it can be carried to excess."

His words stabbed at her. They hurt terribly. Tears welled into her eyes. "God, Doctor, I'm not doing that. You don't know what yesterday was like. In the evening I received a call from—" Then the tears did come out, many of them, and she hated herself the more for being a tearful woman, acting so unprofessional.

He came around the desk and stood beside her, his hand on her shoulder. He knew he'd won. Joanna Caldwell was not going to quit. She was going to do as she was told.

He let her cry. It was the best thing for her. Then he

handed her his clean linen handkerchief and let her cry some more. "I think you'll be all right now, Joanna. You did the right thing in talking to me. That's what I'm here for, to help you, advise you. We are a team, you and I. Just proceed with your work. Do the best you can. I've no doubt that will be more than enough."

In a moment she controlled herself, dabbed her eyes dry and stood up. He suggested they go to lunch, but she refused, saying she couldn't eat, which was true. Back in her office, she sat at her desk, feeling weary, drained, empty. She had failed with him as she knew she would. Why had she brought a change of clothes if she hadn't known she was going to fail?

She got up from the desk, entered the treatment room and stood looking out the window at the coveted sunshine and fresh air. Her mind remained vacant for a time, her feelings healing, her ragged nerves somehow repairing. Yes, she was a working girl. She needed the job. She indeed had no choice, not today at least. And he was probably right. She was feeling sorry for herself—a little at least. She could have worse jobs. The money was good. Six hundred a week. And the hours couldn't be beat. Didn't have to be at work till eleven. Yes, she could do worse. She could be trapped in a miserable marriage to Judd Forbes. So she was still expected to produce sex on demand. But at least she had variety. And she had her independence, some free will. What was she complaining about?

Her mind returned to Lambert. *You did the right thing with Dillon.* No she hadn't. Not with Wofford either. Lambert could tell her how great she was doing, but that didn't make it so. She knew she wasn't. There was no point in kidding herself. And if she was going to be a surrogate partner, she might as well do it right. No sense in harming these men. She needed more information, more training—a whole lot more than Lambert had given her. Ignorance was not bliss, that was for sure.

Feeling a new determination, she went into her office, sat in her chair and swiveled over to her bookcase. She got out her notes from her training sessions with Lambert and re-read those. Then she studied Lambert's book, re-reading the chapters on premature ejaculation and primary impotence. Finally, she reached for Masters and Johnson, *Human Sexual Inadequacy*.

When she spread the book atop her desk, it opened on a business card she had used as a bookmark. She picked it up and read. JULIA W. QUENNELL, PH. D. Underneath were the words "Sex Therapist." Joanna looked at the card, puzzled. Then she remembered. A lecture last winter in New York. Julia Quennell had talked about sexual problems, the need for therapy. Very knowledgeable, and nice. She had seemed decent, outgoing, not at all embarrassed by what she did. She had talked to her briefly after the meeting, told her that she worked for the Center for Human Potential, but not what she did there. No way would she do that.

Again Joanna looked at the card. She had seemed very approachable. Not young. Late forties, maybe. The business card seemed to take on life in her hand. Maybe if she talked to her. Maybe if—

Joanna dropped the card on her desk. She wouldn't want to. How do you know? She might. Heavens knows you need to talk to someone.

She dialed the number on the card. A secretary answered. Mrs. Quennell was with a patient. Joanna left her name and number.

12

Brad Dillon didn't come till one-forty, after she had given up on him, uttering no explanation or apology. Even as she opened the door she saw the arrogance in him. And more, insolence. There was a mocking laughter in his eyes and his lips were twisted into a permanent state of defiance. *God*! He seemed so grossly immature, a handsome, muscular dreamboat, chronologically a man who was giving a positively virtuoso exhibition of terminal adolescence.

She motioned to the seat next to her desk, itself a way to maintain distance from him. With anyone else, she would have gone into the treatment room to encourage intimacy. "Mr. Dillon—"

"Can't I be Brad?"

It was not an encouragement to familiarity, but mockery. He was laughing at her. "Of course, I'm sorry. Brad. I would like to ask you to do me a favor before we begin."

"Sure. Always like to do favors—for my friends."

"Good. I'd like you to understand I don't really give a damn—" Her use of even that mild swear word was so uncharacteristic of her that had he known her better he could have measured just how much she seethed with anger. "—whether I am able to help you or not. I also don't give a damn whether you ever learn to perform like a man. What I do care about is myself and my time—an attitude of I-me-mine which I expect you can endorse. With you, I'm out for the Big I. Understand?'' She paused. She saw the twisted mouth had straightened. She was having an effect. "I have a prescribed amount of time to work with you and, believe me, buster, I have an idea you are going to need every second of it. My favor is this. Be on time from now on. On second thought, consider it a favor to yourself.''

She looked away from him, down at his open file on her desk. She could feel the anger sparking through her. Lord, what was happening to her? Never had she told off a patient like this.

"Aye, aye, teach.''

She glanced back at him in time to see him lowering his hand, having rendered a phony salute. The mockery had again returned to his face. "Good," she said. "So nice to get off to a good start." She looked down at the file, forcing her mind on what she had to say to him. Without looking at him, she began. "Premature ejaculation, which believe me is your problem, is the most common of all sexual inadequacies among males. Dr. Lambert believes premature ejaculation affects virtually all men at least some of the time and a great many men all the time. He estimates it is a discomforting disorder for at least half and probably more of the married couples in the United States. Among young, never married or unmarried males, premature ejaculation is epidemic in Dr. Lambert's opinion.''

She turned to look at him. The lips had returned to normal. At least he was listening to her. "Premature ejaculation is easily treated among cooperating adults.'' She emphasized the word "cooperating." "Here at the Center we have a nearly one hundred percent success ratio with the dysfunction. You have been wise to come here. I believe we can help you." She paused, but merely as punctuation, signalling she was going on to another subject. "Doctor Lambert believes—"

"Question. May I ask a question?"

"Of course. Any time you wish." She started to say how important communication was in the treatment, but thought better of it.

"Why? Why is it such a big deal if I get my rocks off early or late? Why all the fuss?"

She shook her head in disbelief. And even more amazing than the question was his apparent sincerity in asking it. "You really are an old-fashioned fellow, aren't you?"

"What d'you mean?"

"In times gone by—really not long ago, so I'm told—sexual intercourse consisted almost entirely of male pleasure. 'Getting his rocks off,' as you put it, selfishly enjoying his own pleasure and maybe begetting an offspring, preferably male, was the object of sexual congress. I never have believed that myself, but this attitude is much written about. The woman was not to derive pleasure from sex, other than maybe a little warmth and closeness. She was to endure, a seminal vessel for male needs. Oh yes, she was to derive pleasure from the knowledge she had been a good wife, meeting the needs of her husband." Her smile was pure sarcasm. "You really are an old-fashioned guy, Mr. Dillon."

He wasn't and she had hit him hard.

"You go right ahead, Brad, getting your rocks off anytime you can. But I assure you you'll have lots of different partners. Times have changed and few women are going to put up with it very long. You see, my friend, word has gotten around among the *weaker* sex. They have heard about orgasms, multiple orgasms even, passion, pleasure. They have an idea this sex thing isn't just a male perogative. They have a certain expectation of performance, *male* performance which leads to *female* performance."

"All right, all right, I get the message."

"Good." She couldn't believe herself. Not even in her worst moments with Judd Forbes had she been so destructively sarcastic. What was happening to her? "As I was about to say, Dr. Lambert believes premature ejaculation is a phenomenon peculiar to the United States or perhaps Western cultures. Certainly Oriental men take pride in their ability to hold off ejaculation. There are cultures where men hold off ejaculation until their female partners have had several orgasms. That may surprise you, but it's true." She saw intense interest in his face.

"It does surprise me."

"I thought it might. Clearly, the male, any male has the capacity to restrain, measure out for maximum effect his ejaculatory activity. The question is: why is this ability so rarely found in our society? Dr. Lambert believes its roots lie in our puritannical attitudes towards sex. Our sex education is abyssmal. Young men are simply not told the value of ejaculatory control. Indeed, until recently sexologists didn't even know it was possible. And it isn't just young men. Young women are still beleaguered by the old ideas of purely male pleasure. Get at it and get it over with."

She saw he was listening to her, for his expression changed. And she wondered why she was being so pedantic with him, but she couldn't seem to help it.

"Dr. Lambert believes early experience conditions a male for quick ejaculation. Masturbation is still frowned on in much of our society. Boys, young men, do it hastily, secretly, guiltily, seeking only a quick release. Many men have their first sexual intercourse with a prostitute. Time is money to her. She constantly urges the man to do it quickly so she can get on to the next customer. Nor do the experiences of dating help the situation. Among young, dating couples having premarital intercourse, the emphasis, unfortunately, is also on speed. The girl only wants him to hurry up and finish before her parents come home, before the police come around checking the parking lot or whatever. In such conditions, ejaculatory control is an unwanted luxury.'' She paused. She already knew the answer, but she asked anyway. "Is any of this getting through to you?"

He nodded. "Yes. I know where you're at."

"Good, then you'll understand when I say I understand what a difficult problem premature ejaculation is. An aroused, passionate woman needs about a half minute, perhaps a full minute of containment to reach orgasm. The premature ejaculator finds it extremely difficult to give her that much time of rapid thrusting. In his efforts to hold off, the male takes desperate measures. He tries to distract himself, thinking about anything and everything except his partner, what he is doing, and what he is feeling. He thinks about his work, the office, problems with the car, the unpaid bills, anything so as not to enjoy what should be one of the most pleasant activities in his day. Some men resort to physical pain as a distraction, biting their lip, pinching themselves. Again, anything for distraction. Then there are devices such as you attempted yesterday, manual manipulation of the woman, cunnilingus. Just get her so ready she'll go quickly, hopefully as soon as he does."

She saw a tinge of color darken the tanned skin of his face. He looked away. The poor dear was embarrassed. Unconsciously she picked up a pencil from her desk and began to revolve it within her fingertips. "Treatment of premature ejaculation involves retraining. It's that simple. I am, with your cooperation, going to endeavor to teach you to hold off, to control your ejaculation until what is deemed the appropriate time in intercourse.''

"How do you do that?"

She hesitated. Lord, she disliked him. This was the first time, she realized, she'd ever really disliked a patient. The problem had never come up, but she'd always assumed Lambert would never inflict on her someone she patently disliked. It wasn't fair. It wasn't right. Then she shrugged, at least inwardly. It was her job. Lambert had made that most clear.

Determination showed on her face as she slid back her chair and stood up. "Come," she said and walked into the treatment room. Again she hesitated, looking at him. Quite coldly, like a doctor beginning an examination, the taxman auditing a return, she said, "If you'll remove your clothes, we'll get started." And she began to unbutton her blouse.

She turned her back to him to undress, placing her blouse, slacks and briefs on a chair. She bent to remove her shoes and footlets. As she did, she was shocked to feel his hips against her buttocks, then his arms at her sides, his hands cradling her pendulous breasts. Abruptly she stood up. "Take your hands off me."

She saw him grinning. "Aw, c'mon, you know you like it. It's what you want."

She moved away from him. "Let's get it straight up front, Mr. Dillon. I don't want it and I don't want you. Above all I don't want it with you. I happen to dislike you. No, I think I detest you, your conceit, your arrogance, your insolence. I'm just doing the job I'm paid to do, which is cure your stupid premature ejaculation. In the process, I'll do the touching. You keep your hands to yourself. And above all stop coming on to me like you're God's gift to women. You're not, most especially to me. Do you have any questions?''

She saw he was stunned, speechless. Apparently it was a new experience for him. Indeed, it was new to her to tell off a man, especially a patient.

''All right. Now that we understand each other, I want you to lay flat on your back in the middle of the bed with your legs apart.'' She watched him. ''No, the other way. Put your head at the foot.''

When he was in place, she climbed on the bed, stepped over him and sat between his legs, her back resting against the headboard. Her legs were atop his. ''Scoot down, closer to me.'' He did. ''You can bend your knees. That's right. Come a little closer. Fine.''

She was at that moment sitting between his bent knees. His hips were between her outspread legs, and his genitals were within easy reach. And so she did, lifting his flaccid penis with her left hand, then his testicles with her right. She heard him gasp with surprise and felt his body stiffen, his erection commence. ''Just relax,'' she said. ''I'm not going to hurt you.''

''Oh, baby,'' he breathed, ''you ain't hurtin' none.''

Gently, she caressed him, feeling him jump and lurch at her touch, and within seconds he was fully erect and hard, so immense her fingers would not go all the way around the base of it. The sheer size of it boggled her mind.

''You really do like it, don't you, baby? I knew you did.''

She took her hand away. ''God, you're insufferable. One of these days you're going to OD on conceit. Mr. Dillon, your penis is nothing special.''

''That's what you think.''

''Not to me, it isn't. I hate it and I hate you. I'm just

doing my job. Now lie back there and do as I tell you."

"Yes, ma'm."

She shook her head, again lamenting the impossibility of being here, in this bed, naked with this impossible man. A nunnery suddenly began to have attractions for her. But dutifully, she clasped his shrinking organ again, fondling it back into full erection, though being careful not to stroke him into ejaculation.

"All right. What you're going to do is learn to maintain an erection without ejaculating."

"Could you use another word. I hate that one."

"No. This is not a brothel. We don't deal in vulgarity here." Her hands still on him—she could feel the heat of the blood trapped there—she said, "I'm going to arouse you—"

"Baby, you already done that."

She shook her head in disgust. For two cents she'd get up and leave him. But she stayed. "—and I'm going to propel you toward ejaculation."

"I can hardly wait."

"Look, Dillon, this is not fun and games. If you're not taking this seriously, if you're not going to cooperate, I've lots better things to do with my time, believe me."

"Okay, okay, you're going to make me come."

"No, I'm not. That's exactly what I don't want you to do. The male, when stimulated, reaches a point when he no longer can hold off. There is a point when ejaculation becomes inevitable. I want you to tell me before you reach that point. Do you understand? *Before*. Say stop, now, whatever word you want, but you must cooperate and tell me before you reach the point when you cannot stop. Do you understand?"

"Yeah, I guess so."

She caressed him, running her finger tips gently over

the glans, around the coronal ridge, over the meatus, gaining a responsive jerk from him. She could feel the heat of him, the throbbing in his penis. Then, she moved her hand down the shaft and back. Just once, and she heard him gasp. A moan escaped him. My God, he was coming already. Quickly, she moved her hand up to the glans and squeezed him hard, her forefinger and middle finger on either side of the coronal ridge, her thumb hard against the fenulum on the underside of the penis. She could feel him pulsing and squeezed harder, indeed as hard as she could. He moaned and covered his face with his hands, but only a few drops of semen came out the end. She held him tightly a few seconds until he relaxed. "I thought I told you to tell me when you were coming."

"I didn't know. Wow, that was something else. It felt like I went, but nothing came out, did it?"

"No. In all it was pretty good for the first time." It was the truth.

It was also the truth that despite him, despite hating what she was doing, she was excited by it. And she disliked herself for that.

His penis receded, but only part way.

"Wow, that's something else."

She made no reply. And in a moment she clasped him again and began stroking him toward erection again. When it was achieved, she said, "Please try to tell me sooner this time." She stroked him, once, twice, very gently, then more aggressively one time. When she felt him harden, she immediately moved back to his glans and squeezed him as before.

"What're you doing?"

"I'm squeezing you. By doing it in this manner, thumb in this spot, on the underside, in the crevice between the coronal ridge, fingers around the barrel, it will stop the impulse toward ejaculation." Even as she said it, she released him and saw the erection diminish slightly.

"But why?"

"You will learn to feel when ejaculation is coming. When you recognize that it is going to happen you will be able to exert control over it. I want you to try, all right?"

"Whatever you say."

Again she aroused him to full hardness and stroked him. "Now?" she asked.

"I think so. I'm not sure."

She squeezed him anyway, until his erection softened.

"Wow, this is great fun," he said. "I'm coming to this hospital more often."

"I'm glad *you're* having fun. I'm not. Please try to tell me what I want to know."

Again she propelled him to erection. "Now?"

"No."

She looked at him. He seemed to be trying.

"A little more. . . Again. . .oh God, now!"

Quickly she squeezed him, so hard this time her hand ached. He had an internal orgasm, but again only a little semen escaped.

"Wow," he said in a moment. "I don't know whether I like this or not."

"I told you to tell me sooner."

"I know, and I'm sorry. I'm trying, really I am. It isn't as easy as it looks. I never tried this before. Didn't know it was possible."

"I assure you it is. And if you'll try to cooperate with me, you'll learn to do it for yourself."

He laughed. "But I sure will miss you, baby."

She swore under her breath, but dutifully clasped him again. After she had squeezed him this time, she pushed herself up and stepped off the bed. "That's enough for today, Mr. Dillon."

"You can't quit."

"I'm afraid I can and I am."

"But what about me. I'm dying. You gotta finish."

"I have finished." She went to the bathroom, got her robe and put it on. As she came back to the bed, she said, "There's the bathroom. Relieve yourself if you want. I'm not about to."

He sat on the edge of the bed, staring at her malevolently. She stared back. Her only movement was to arch an eyebrow. She had gotten even. Ordinarily, she did relieve her patients. But not this one. Dillon was a creep. And she was only doing her job. Masturbation was not part of it.

"I think I could come to hate you."

"I don't have to think about it." She turned and walked toward her office. "Get dressed. Session's over." She closed the door for punctuation. Thus, she didn't know whether he used the bathroom or not.

When he came out a few minutes later, she was writing her notes on the session. She turned to look at him. He was dressed.

"You don't like me, do you?"

She stared at him a moment. "You're prescient, Mr. Dillon."

"What's that mean?"

"It means—" She wasn't sure of the exact meaning. "It means you're smart. You figure things out."

"Okay, I didn't do much in school. Why don't you like me?"

She hesitated, measuring her anger. It was all new to her. Never had she felt this way toward a patient. Sympathy, understanding, kindness were what she dealt in normally. Brad Dillon encouraged no such feelings.

"You don't listen very well, Mr. Dillon. I already told you. You are conceited, arrogant and insolent, qualities I can do without. Somewhere you got the notion, perhaps because of your outlandish penis, that you are God's gift to women. You aren't. Believe me, you aren't. Penis size has nothing to do with it. It may make you a big deal in the locker room, but it is of no particular appeal to women. It is what you do with it that counts. And you, my friend, don't do very much." She saw his face redden, his mouth harden in anger. "I don't mean to be unkind, but you asked me. That's the way I feel."

He glared at her. She was not sure he wouldn't hit her. Then his mouth opened. "If you dislike me so much, why did you do all that just now?"

"Because it's my job. You paid your money. You're entitled to our services."

He stared at her a long moment, then turned and reached for the doorknob to leave. When the door was open, he looked back at her. "You're some broad. That's for sure." And he left.

She couldn't tell whether it was a compliment or not. She stared after him a moment, then shrugged and went back to her notes.

13

Joanna had more time to dress and prepare for Wofford. Thus, she was in a better state of mind when he arrived, as usual, clean and natty. She really didn't know what to expect of him, but in her determination to somehow succeed with him, she had gone all out, wearing what she knew was a ridiculously sexy outfit. She had put on stockings, garters and the high heels, all of which she knew he liked, and a tight straight skirt with a slit up the side. With it she wore a tank top, mostly straps, nearly backless and so thin her nipples decorated the front. She saw him react when he entered. The garment had been no mistake.

They sat on the side of the bed which she had remade with fresh linen, and she held his hands, feeling the tenseness in him. She smiled. "I think we have to talk, don't we?" Terribly ill at ease, extremely uptight, he said nothing. Her smile broadened and she squeezed his fingers. "I said we have to talk, don't we?" Still a silence. "C'mon, Jer. What's bothering you?"

Finally, he spoke, his voice low, a little halting. "I don't understand, Joanna. Why was it so wrong for me to have enjoyed making you come. . .have an orgasm with me?"

She bit her lip, uncertain what to say. "Of course it wasn't wrong, Jerry. It's just that—"

"That had never happened for me, you know."

"I know, but—"

"It meant a lot to me, more than you can ever know, to have finally pleased a woman. I felt ten feet tall. But then you. . . ."

She understood in time. Her orgasm had given him his first success. She shouldn't in any way take it away from him. She smiled. "You think I didn't like it? If I gave you that impression I'm sorry." She squeezed his hands till her knuckles and his went white. "It was wonderful, Jerry, so very wonderful, and I enjoyed it immensely. And I thank you for it."

She saw him beaming, a softness and wonder entering his eyes. And suddenly she had greater insight into him. "You really are something else, Jerry Wofford."

"Wat d'you mean?"

She hesitated, framing her words carefully. It wasn't hard, for she meant every word. "You really are a nice person, Jer. In these days when everyone is out for themselves, you—well, you're merely incredible. You're a giver. In a world of takers, you're a *giver*." She saw him looking at her seriously, mouth open, eyes intent on her face. "I mean it. You're a wonder. When you meet the right girl, you're going to make a simply grand husband. Some girl is going to be so-o-o lucky to find you."

He looked away from her then. "I like you Joanna, very much. You're one of the nicest people I've ever met."

His words surprised her and she felt a momentary prickle of her skin at the back of her neck. If she had taken time to think, she would have recognized the sensation as a reaction to danger. But she was so intent on keeping and enhancing this moment of closeness with him. "And I like you, Jer."

He looked up at her then and smiled, wanly, boyishly. "Do you?"

"Of course I do."

"I thought you must. I told myself you couldn't do what you do with me if you didn't have at least some affection for me."

Then, too late, she realized the danger signals. It was a gross mistake for a surrogate partner and a patient ever to become emotionally involved. She was tempted to tell him that, to emphasize theirs was a doctor-patient relationship. But she couldn't. She had to succeed with Jerry. She had invested too much of herself in him to lose him now. And she sensed she would if she even hinted at her real feelings. "Of course I like you. I'm very fond of you." She put as much feeling into the words as she could, then changed the subject. "About yesterday, I don't want you to think you didn't please me. You did. . .very much. But, Jerry, I want to please you. I really do. Can you believe that?"

"Yes."

"It was no good for me without you. It's never any good for a woman unless she pleases her man, just as it shouldn't be any good for him unless he pleases her. We use the word intercourse —*inter*—between, between two people, a mutual giving and taking, a sharing of sensation and intimacy, each helping the other." She paused, looking to see the effect of her words.

"I know."

"You can't just lie there and watch me. . .any woman. I understand, because you are a giving person, that brings you enjoyment. But it's unfair, selfish of you. Really it is. You have to offer her the same gift of enjoyment. You have to allow her to please you."

"You did please me, Joanna, so much."

"Oh Lord, Jer, you don't—"

"Yes I do. I understand and I'll try." Then he remembered that was the wrong word. "No, I won't try—I'll just do it. I want to."

She patted his head. "Good," she said and stood up, seeing him look at her tank top. She waited till his gaze returned to her eyes. "I wore it just for you. Is it too. . .too, you know?"

"No, I like it—very much."

She laughed. "But you wouldn't be caught dead walking down the street with me." Before he could protest, she pulled him to his feet. "You better take it off."

"I'm not sure I want to."

But he did, almost immediately devouring her breasts in his mouth. She could tell he was in a high state of sexual excitement. Good. She did nothing to discourage him.

When both were undressed, they enflamed each other in familiar ways. She marveled at his expertise and told him so. She mounted him, on her knees, in the female superior position. And with intromission she again shuddered from the pleasure of it. But she knew she was in control of herself.

"Does that feel good, Jer?"

"Oh yes." The words were mostly sigh.

"How good? Tell me."

He rolled his head from side to side, suggesting he couldn't express it. Finally the word, "Wonderful," came out, mostly air.

He was like iron and she moved forward and back on him, just a little, hardly an inch, and very slowly. "And that?"

"Oh yes, yes."

She moved her hips a little further forward and back, though still very slowly. "And that?"

"Yes, oh yes."

She did it again, twice, a third time, but very slowly. "You feel so good, Jer. So hard, so big. I love it." And it was the truth. "Does it feel good to you, being in me?"

"Oh God, Joanna, so wonderful."

She maintained her movement, increasing the length, but as slowly as she could. "Don't talk. Just enjoy. . .enjoy. . .enjoy."

Again and again, steadily, but ever so slowly, she lengthened and maintained the forward and backward movement of her pelvis. She ached for more, harder thrusts, but she kept her mind solely on him and what he was doing. She saw his eyes half open, desire, pleasure in them. "It's so wonderful, isn't it?" His sigh, the forced closing of his eyes was her answer. Again and again she moved on him, slightly harder and faster, and when she felt him hump into her, demanding more, she made no effort to stop him. She could feel him, harder, swelling inside her and she constricted her vaginal muscles around him as faster, harder, he humped into her. She watched. His body stiffened, his hands moved involuntarily against her breasts, his practiced movements now wild, strong. His breath quickened to a pant. Yes, he was going to make it. Oh God, wonderful God, he was going to make it.

With quick, hard, savage movements, back and forth, she forced it out of him. His face went red. She thought he would burst. Then his head went back and a terrible moan escaped him as she felt him arch his hips into her, almost lifting her off her knees, then the quick pulse of his penis just before the hot splatter flooded her insides. Frantically, herself wild with pleasure, she moved again and again on him, forcing more out, listening to him moan and watching as he covered his face with his hands. "God, God," he gasped.

When he was finished and their movements had stopped and he lay spent beneath her and he had opened hooded eyes, she smiled down at him, believing she was happier than she had ever been in her life. "Congratulations, Mr. Wofford," she whispered.

"Oh, Joanna, I—"

She put a finger across his lips to silence him. "Sh-h, don't say anything. You don't need to."

He had softened and come out and she could feel his semen flowing from her. She longed to clean herself, but she knew this moment was important. She lay down beside him, on her side, her head on his shoulder. She felt his arm around her, his hand down her back.

"You didn't?"

"No."

"But—"

"No buts. I lost you yesterday, remember? I didn't want to today. All right?"

She saw him nod acquiescence.

"Joanna, I love you."

The words stunned her and her body stiffened from the shock of them.

"I can't help it. I love you."

She didn't know what to say. She couldn't reciprocate, and she shouldn't, not even in a lie. But she couldn't hurt him, risk losing him again.

"I've never been able to do it with anyone else. It took you—only you."

That gave her something to say. "I'm just the lucky girl it happened with. There'll be lots of them from now on."

"No, no, I could never."

She raised her head so she could look down at him. Smiling, she said, "That's what they all say."

"Don't make fun of me, Joanna."

"I'm not making fun of you. That's the last thing I'd ever do. Can't you understand how happy I am, how tickled I am for you." She sat up then and pummeled his chest. "You made it, my friend. God, you made it. I could burst from pride and happiness."

He beamed at her, pure happiness on his face, too.

"You're cured, Jer, cured, well, a fully functioning man. You can do it with anyone now. You can marry, have a family. I'll bet you'll make a wonderful father."

Still he beamed. "I dunno. Are you sure?"

"Of course I'm sure. Trust me."

She scampered off the bed then. In the bathroom she swiped at the rivulet on her leg and put on her robe. She came back to stand over him. He still lay on his back, looking up at the ceiling. The sour, musty odor of semen was in the room.

He turned his head toward her. "Can we go somewhere and celebrate?"

Oh, Lord!

"I'd like to take you out to dinner. It's a cause for celebration, don't you think?"

Her expression was sober as she looked at him. He couldn't want to. He was supposed to know he wasn't to get emotionally involved with her. Hadn't Lambert talked to him about that? She forced a smile. "I'd like to Jerry, but I can't. I'm sorry. It's my night for tennis with the girls." It was a lie, but she was desperate. Her smile broadened. "Tell you what? I'll buy you a drink here. Will that do?" She saw the expression on his face. She hadn't hurt him. He was accepting it. "You take a quick shower while I make the drinks. Okay?" As she moved toward the liquor bottles, she saw him begin to roll off the bed.

At almost that precise moment, Dawson Lambert was

nearing the end of his consultation with Helen Wexler. An interesting case. She was forty-two, but didn't look it. Blonde. Out of a bottle but still blonde. Well-coiffed, made-up and manicured. Trim figure. Nice boobs. Well-dressed. Obviously monied. She could have just about any man she wanted. Trouble was she didn't want any—or did she?

Helen Wexler married in her mid-twenties. She was virginal and her husband, obviously smashed from the wedding reception, took her roughly, breaking an apparently thick hymen, causing her great pain and making her bleed. Traumatized, she hated but endured overtures from her husband thereafter. Divorce followed. In the years thereafter, she made a career in interior design, but did not remarry. There were several men, but each time she approached sexual intercourse, she broke and ran. Her shrink had referred her to the Center for Human Potential.

Yesterday, her first, he had given her a physical exam to see if she had anything physically wrong with her. She didn't. It was all in her head. Late on Tuesday afternoon, he was showing her video tapes surreptitiously taken at the Center of couples in the act of various forms of sexual congress. While the tape ran, he kept watching her face, and he was vastly amused. Poor Mrs. Wexler. She was shocked. He glanced at the screen. A woman was going down on a man. Actually it was Janet Bolton and himself, only his face didn't show and who was to know it was he? Maybe Mrs. Wexler would find out and identify him. He doubted it.

He flicked off the TV set. In his most professional voice he said, "I showed you these, Helen, not to shock you or even to titillate you. I'm simply trying to suggest to you that sex can be—in fact is for nearly all women. . .a pleasurable experience. There is nothing dirty about it. There is no pain associated with it. Did it look to you as though any of these women were not enjoying themselves?''

"No.''

"I'm sorry. I didn't hear you.'' He had, but he wanted to make her look at him.

She did. "I said, no. They seemed to be. . .enjoying themselves.''

"Did they look forced? Put upon in any way? Were they suffering?''

"No.''

He smiled at her. "It can be that way for you, Helen. It ought to be. It will be.''

She looked away from him, down at her hands. "What's wrong with me, doctor?''

"If you'll look at me, I'll tell you.'' She did and he gave her his most dazzling smile. "Nothing, my dear, nothing at all. You are merely a victim of tragic mishandling. You need only what the psychologists call reconditioning. There's a famous experiment in which a rat was put in a cage. A whistle would blow, a light went on, the floor slid away and the rat dropped on a grid which gave him a nasty shock. The rat ran around wildly, finally jumping over a low wall into a part of the cage where he was not shocked. It didn't take very long for the rat to learn to jump as soon as he heard the whistle. Even after the wires were disconnected, the rat still jumped when he heard the whistle.'' Lambert smiled. "You're that rat, Helen. Someone whistles at you—and you are whistle bait—and you jump the wall. You don't wait around to find out the whistle might lead to something pleasant. Do you understand?''

She smiled. "Yes, I do, of course.''

"What we have to do is retrain you not to jump the wall, don't we?'' Out of the corner of his eye, he saw the light on his phone begin to blink. Who could be calling?

He'd had all calls stopped. Then he remembered. All but one. "Will you excuse me, Helen. I have an important call. I'll take it in my office." Quickly, he flicked on the TV set. "You watch these again and try to think more kindly about them. I'll be back in a minute."

Quickly he retreated to his office and crossed to the phone. "Lambert here."

"This is Charles Randall. I'm returning your call."

"Oh yes. Where are you? Not in Frisco I hope."

"Yes. My answering service said you'd called. I thought it might be important."

"Oh dear, that's too bad. I didn't expect you to call cross country."

"That's all right. What can I do for you?"

Lambert laughed. "Nothing really. I didn't have your home phone, and I wanted to call to congratulate you."

"Congratulate me?"

"Yes, on your forthcoming marriage—to Laura McGovern. Fine girl. Real fine girl."

Randall seemed flustered. "Oh yes. Well, thank you, thank you very much. I think a lot of Laura."

Lambert smiled. Indeed, he was hardpressed to suppress a giggle. "And well you should, Randall. There's none better than Laura. Believe you me."

There came a pause on the line. "You know Laura?"

"Of course. She's on my board here."

"Oh yes. . .of course. I guess I knew that."

"And she's been my patient for some time." Now he did laugh. "I can assure you everything is in working order, Randall." The silence on the line went on so long, Lambert felt justified in asking, "Are you there, Randall?"

"Yes. I suppose she would go to you for gynecology."

"Yes—and other things." Again he laughed. It could not possibly have sounded more knowing. "Look Randall, I'm with a patient, and there's no sense in enriching Ma Bell. Just wanted to say congrats. Buy you a drink when I see you." He said goodbye and hung up without ever hearing another word from Randall.

He stood there a moment, smiling broadly, shaking with the effort to suppress his glee. That should fix the sonofabitch. Then, wiping away the grin, he returned to his treatment of Helen Wexler.

Joanna's elation over her success with Wofford quickly gave way to depression. Part of it was simply a normal rebound from a high, she knew, and much was her own unrequited sexual tensions. But she was also upset by this new development with Wofford. He was becoming emotionally involved. His saying he loved her had unnerved her. She had found a way to avoid a reply, but how often could she? She wouldn't hurt him and there was no point in lying. Damn, double damn.

She made the two drinks, then stood looking out at the deepening twilight. From the bathroom she heard the sound of humming, the water shut off. Perhaps it was just a moment of happiness, a thoughtless expression of pleasure. Heaven knows the man had waited long enough for it. Yes, she'd have to hope that was it.

She deliberately kept her back to him, but in the reflection in the window she saw him dressing. She looked away even from that. The moment was too intimate. She wished she'd gone to her office to wait until he was dressed. Yes, she should have done that.

"You know, the funniest thing has been happening at the stores. I figured that when I came up here, you know, took so much time off, everything would fall apart. Actually, business has never been better. Everything's as smooth as silk." He laughed. "I think there's a message there for me somewhere."

How very like a man, she thought. His sexual tensions relieved, he's happy as can be, humming, singing, greatly invigorated. The first thing he thinks about is his work. This knowledge gave her a sinking feeling. This was all too intimate, too much like marriage. Damn, she should have gone to her office.

The reflection showed him dressed, putting on his tie. She turned, picked up the drink she'd made for him and reached it out toward him. Quickly, holding his half-tied tie, he bounded over to get it. "Just what I need." Lord, he had the jollies.

He finished the tie and folded down his collar, then picked up the drink. "To you, to us," he said.

God, no. Never. "To your success, long awaited, much deserved. May it never leave you."

He raised his glass to hers. "That's nice, Joanna, very nice." They each took a swallow. "Sure I can't take you to dinner?"

"No, I can't, I'm sorry." She forced a smile.

She sensed a change in him. He was more confident and relaxed. The defeated, fearful man who had been coming to her for over a week seemed nowhere in sight. Good. That was what all this was about.

She tried to divert him, asking about his stores, the fabric business and such. Rather too quickly, she drained her glass, set it down and refused his offer to fix another one. "I guess you must need to get going if you're to play tennis."

"Yes," she said, "I better had."

He chugalugged his drink, set it down, then strode purposely across ther room and snugged on his jacket. He came back to where she stood by the window and faced her. "I cannot begin to thank you enough, Joanna."

She smiled. "Don't even try. It was all *your* doing."

"Hardly. I just wish I'd met you years ago." Then he bent over and kissed her.

It was a light kiss, little more than a peck, but utterly outrageous to her. It connoted an intimacy she did not feel, an affection between them which did not exist, nor should exist. But she could say nothing. She couldn't hurt him now and ruin all she had worked for. He placed his hands on her shoulders and bent to kiss her again. She wanted to turn her cheek, but again she couldn't. It was more than a peck. She wanted to protest, but it was lost in an even greater outrage. As he raised his face from hers, he slid her robe off her shoulders, exposing her breasts. She had been naked with him every day. She had been physically intimate with him. But nothing they had done was as intimate as this. His action was a wholly untoward invasion of her privacy as a person. It said *possession*. And her anger flared.

"Forgive me, Joanna, but there is no one as lovely as you."

Quickly she covered herself with her garment and stepped back.

"Well, better be going so you can get to your tennis game." Abruptly he turned toward the door, apparently unaware of her anger. "I'll see you tomorrow."

She started to form the word "yes," but the sound was never made before he was gone.

In a deep funk, she showered, dressed and went home. She made herself a sandwich, but only nibbled about a quarter of it. She tried to watch some TV to distract herself, but that wouldn't work. By ten she was in bed. She thought of taking a sleeping pill, but didn't. She hated pills. To her surprise she fell asleep quickly.

14

Joanna arose shortly after daylight full of energy. She donned her running togs and jogged to Compo Beach. She twice ran its full length in a series of windsprints, then back to her apartment, standing in the doorway, winded, but feeling good.

She made breakfast of toast and orange juice, then in a fit of domesticity washed an unreal collection of dishes and cleaned the whole apartment. She even collected her things for the laundry and dry cleaners. Finally, she pampered herself, showering, putting a lightener on her hair, giving her legs and underarms a wax job, painting her finger and toe nails.

It was therapy, a whole morning of it, and she arrived at her office shortly before one o'clock, more able, she felt, to cope with whatever disaster this day would bring.

When she let Brad Dillon in, he carried a large sack in one arm, and a broad smile on his face. "I come bearing gifts," he said. "Close your eyes."

She was still hostile to him, ready to bristle at his slightest word or action, but she obeyed and in a moment felt something round and soft in her right hand. Before she could identify it, he said, "You may look now."

It was a roll of plain white toilet paper. She looked up at him.

"I've been so shitty to you, I thought maybe you could use this." His smile broadened into a laugh and, despite herself, she had to join him. "Close your eyes again. There's more." She saw him reaching into the sack as she again obeyed. A thin cylindrical stick was in her hand. She opened her eyes to see a child's toy tomahawk.

"I thought maybe you and I could bury that," he said. "Look, I even brought the ground." And from the bag he pulled a child's bucket half full of sand. He placed it on the desk in front of her. "Can we?"

She had to laugh.

"Good." He clasped her hand holding the tomahawk and plunged the plastic blade into the sand. "All wars and hostilities between Joanna Caldwell and Brad Dillon are now and forever ended." He laughed and she laughed, then he leaned toward her. "The above parties shall now kiss and make up."

She placed her hands against his chest to stop him. "No way."

"I was afraid that might be too much to hope for. Really, Joanna, I have been shitty to you and I'm sorry."

She looked at him quizzically. "What led to this?"

"I don't know. You, I suppose. I really am not such a bad guy—however difficult it may be to convince you of that. My mother loves me."

"She is undoubtedly the only one."

"Touché. I have it coming. I just realized yesterday, last night really, how very difficult what you do must be. It occurred to dumb ol' me I could make it a little easier for you."

Despite herself, Joanna felt her eyes moisten.

"I do appreciate what you're trying to do for me—really, Joanna. I know I need it. I want to have it work. Okay?"

She nodded. She hadn't expected any of this from him. Suddenly she was too surprised, too relieved, too glad for his change of heart to speak.

"Besides, you're such a knockout, can't fight with a gorgeous number like you."

She saw him smiling. "I figured it was a snow job."

"A regular blizzard."

In bed, in the training position, his hips between her legs, he said, "I have a question. Do I have to ask the girl to squeeze me everytime I get going too quick. I'll find that a bit—well, you know—"

"Embarrassing? Damage your masculinity?"

"Why not?"

"I don't know what to tell you. Hopefully, before you leave here you'll have learned to recognize impending ejaculation—"

"Disaster you mean?"

"An apt word. The aim is for you to recognize the feeling and learn to control it yourself. But chances are you won't be a hundred percent successful with it for a long time, maybe never. A little retraining with the squeeze technique may be in order for a long time. Ordinarily you'd be doing this with your wife. It would be a normal part of the process. But you don't—"

"Have a wife—thank God. Look, how about I take you along? You could stand there and whenever—"

She had to laugh, the idea was so ridiculous.

"You could be my full time squeezer."

She took him in both her hands and felt him jump at her touch.

"It pays well, you know."

"Thanks, but no thanks."

The training went far better than it had the previous day. He was more cooperative and she could tell he was gaining control, allowing longer intervals between the times he needed squeezing. She asked him if he was getting it and he said he was.

They took one rest period in which he sat up and they talked. "How'd you get started doing this sort of thing?" he asked.

"Oh, I came here with my husband. He had the same problem as you. He was worse if anything. I worked with him and cured him."

When she didn't go on, he said, "Then what happened?"

She sighed. "My husband is—or was Judd Forbes. Know him?"

"The football player. Sure, I know him—or of him. Who doesn't?"

"I cured him so well he—let's just say we're divorced."

"And you came to work here?"

"Something like that. I was depressed, at loose ends. Dr. Lambert offered me—talked to me." She sighed. "Here I am."

"Do you like doing this?"

"No."

"Then why do you do it?"

"You didn't let me finish. I like helping men who have no chance for help, for happiness. It's rewarding, when it works."

He looked at her for a long moment. "You really are a nice lady."

She stared back at him, unblinking, and unconsciously bit her lip. Then she pushed him back down. "Back to work."

Repeatedly she aroused him close to ejaculation, squeezing him back each time. Finally, with quick, firm, demanding jerks, she let him come into a towel, ignoring his frantic protests that he couldn't hold off. A startling amount welled out of him, surprising and indeed arousing her.

"Why didn't you stop me?"

"Session's over, that's why." She wadded up the towel and threw it toward the bathroom.

"But you. . .yesterday, you—"

"That was thanks for the tomahawk." She was smiling as she said it.

Her session with Wofford also went well. Sitting atop him in the female superior position, she again propelled him into orgasm, noting that he went easier this time, quicker. When he protested because she was not orgasmic with him, she said it was better that way and promised to join him the next day. She tried that evening to cheer herself with the knowledge of her success with Wofford. Her first case of primary impotence and she was curing him. But she remained tired and depressed, retiring early.

On the next day, Thursday, both sessions were again productive. Dillon exhibited growing ejaculatory control and confidence in his ability to restrain himself. And she felt more comfortable with him. He seemed to have fully discarded his conceit and insolence with her, and at one point she said, "I'm a little surprised. Beneath all that handsomeness and body beautiful is a real, live person, quite likable really."

He looked at her through slitted eyes, scratched at his chin and with an actor's superb timing said, "I knew you'd have use for that roll of toilet paper."

She laughed. "I mean it. I didn't think you could be so nice."

"I know you mean it, but that doesn't make it easier for me to hear. I said I was sorry. What do you want me to do?"

She understood. "And I'm sorry too. Okay?"

During the break in the training session, he asked if the liquor bottles were only for decoration. She said hardly and they got up and had a drink together. Both were naked and she saw him looking at her. "You're embarrassing me, you know," she said. "I'd better put on my robe."

"No, don't, please." He raised his gaze to meet hers. "You're very beautiful, Joanna, really special."

Her voice low, soft, she said, "Thank you, but you're still embarrassing me."

"I mean it. It's no line. Half the girls in tinsel town would trade their souls for your figure."

She glared at him, pursing her lips in mock disapproval of him. "I'm about to change the subject. How do you like being a big star, a celebrity?"

He swallowed from his glass. "You want the party line or the truth?"

"Truth—always."

"I guess I like the *idea* of it—the money, being recognized, asked for autographs, feeling successful, knowing you're somebody when neither you nor anyone else ever thought you would be."

"There's a but, isn't there?"

"Yes. But— It's hard work, really hard work. Long hours. That's not the problem. I've so little time for myself. My idea of unparalleled luxury is to put my feet up, turn on the boob tube and listen to my beard grow." He saw her laugh. "I mean it. Doesn't happen often. I feel a lot of pressure, to keep these muscles up, to be on, to do what is expected of me. You have no idea how many people depend on me, I mean really depend on me for their living, manager, agent, publicity agent, hairdresser, coaches, the cast and crew of the show. That's by no means a whole list. I feel like a property, indeed that's what I'm called, a property, a thing, go here, do that, meet this columnist, go on this talk show, go out with this girl. And so on and so on. It's very easy to lose yourself in it all."

She was moved, by the honesty of his words, the insight into himself he was giving.

"Can you believe I can't remember the last time I stood with a girl, with anyone, talking this way? It's been a long time. And I thank you."

"There's nothing to thank me for."

"Oh yes. You made me realize what a really shitty, overbearing person I had become. Brad Dillon, big, phony star. I didn't like myself very much. I may go back to being that, probably will, knowing me, but just for this little while, I'm being sorta me. I thank you again."

"I hope you stay you."

He looked down, a little awkwardly, working his bare toes. "Did you know my real name is Ronnie Sadowski?" He looked back at her. "I'm a nice Polish boy. And you *will* keep that to yourself."

She nodded, then on impulse, consumed by the intimacy of his words, she stood on tiptoe and brushed his cheek with her lips. "I promise not to tell any bad jokes, either," she whispered. She knew, sensed his desire to grab her, pull her to him. Indeed, his hands moved toward her slightly. But he restrained himself. She believed she was glad for that.

She smiled. "Shall we go back to work?"

"It may be work for you. I got another name."

"I won't ask."

She saw he already had an erection as they climbed back on the bed.

When Wofford came at four-thirty, she saw immediately his greater confidence and masculinity, and she again realized that in curing sexual inadequacy she was building a man's ego. She felt her job really was worthwhile.

"Jerry," she said, "your two weeks are up tomorrow."

"I'll regret that."

"No you won't. You'll go out, meet people, begin to date again. Very soon, I promise, you'll meet a nice girl whom you'll like and who'll most definitely like you for the attractive man you are."

He nearly blushed. "We'll see about that."

"In any event, Jer, I think that today and tomorrow we should practice for the future. I'd like you to pretend I'm a girl you've met. We've talked, got acquainted." She smiled. "Nature has taken its course and you are at her apartment or yours, wherever. Can you try that, pretend I'm a girl you're fond of and want to go to bed with?"

"Yes," he said, his voice husky. "It won't be pretending."

Something inside her screamed at him, but she let it go. Only two more days. Then he'd be gone.

He was clumsy, yet adroit enough. He became aroused too quickly, and she had to tell him to slow down a little, give the girl a chance. His embraces were strangely difficult for her, his deep kisses something she didn't want, and when he undressed her and caressed her, she had to fight a tendency to recoil from his touch. How strange. When she did it, provoking him, it had been all right. But this pretense of seduction was difficult and she didn't know why. She knew she was sexy. And Wofford did arouse her. But not enough. She mostly pretended.

The seduction scene fell apart when they were in bed, for he clearly didn't know what to do. His first thought was to be on top, the missionary position. She took over then, told him to lie on his back and played with him till he achieved a full erection. She mounted him in the female superior position until she knew he was going to make it, then she quickly slid into the lateral position, atop, yet to the side of him, her right leg between his, her left leg crooked over his right, their pelvises joined. It was considered the ideal position, giving full freedom of movement to both of them without her weight in anyway interfering with his breathing. He came easily and most satisfactorily. She surprised herself by not coming. He had felt good. She knew she wanted it, but she couldn't. She was too conscious of him and his need for success, too worried about his growing involvement with her to abandon herself to the process. Any chance of her making it was lost when, near his climax, he said he loved her.

She tried to be matter-of-fact afterwards, telling him not to worry about her. She promised to be orgasmic with him tomorrow, the last day. He said he couldn't bear to think of tomorrow. She ignored the remark, repeating the advantages of the lateral position and recommending he try it with his other partners. He said he had no other partners. She told him not to be silly. He would, lots of them.

When he left she stood in the darkening room, shoulders slumped, feeling defeated, utterly depressed. She knew what was wrong with her. Her last orgasm had come Monday with Wofford. This was Thursday. Tuesday, Wednesday, Thursday, three days spent—God, hours with two different men, each day, playing with them, taking them inside, being aroused, tormented, almost coming. God, what a way to live, horrible, utterly horrible.

She undid the tie to her robe and let it fall open. Slowly, hesitantly, not really wanting to, she strode to the bed and sat on the foot. She sighed, closed her eyes, then raised her hands to her breasts, kneading them, running her fingers over the nipples, making them hard. Slowly she fell back on the bed and lowered her hands between her thighs, the heavy fluids deposited by Wofford making her fingers slippery between the labia, over the clitoral shaft. Her breath quickened as she abandoned herself to herself. Her eyes opened a little, mere slits, and a vision of another darkened room entered her mind, a shoulder blotting out the light, a heavy body atop her, entering her, filling her. "Oh Hank, Hank, I need you so. Please, I want you, need you."

The movements of her hands stopped abruptly and she sat up. No good. She couldn't. She stood up, slipping out of the robe as she did so, and showered, prolonging it, turning on the water full force, letting it bite into her skin. When she emerged and had dried herself, she leaned against the doorjamb of the steaming room, her eyes closed, trying to quell the jagged grating of her nerves. There had to be another way to live. There was. She thought of Hank. Could it be? Was she wrong? Shouldn't she give him a chance—herself? No. It could never be. She opened her eyes, unconsciously firming her mouth. Not Hank Kraft, not Joanna Caldwell. The Brad Dillons, the Jerry Woffords were her lot in life.

She dressed and went home. It was after dark and she was weary, extremely frustrated, wholly depressed. She told herself she ought to think seriously about quitting this impossible job and finding something to do with the rest of her life. She might go back to school, get a master's, even a doctorate in psychology. But the truth was she was unable to think clearly about anything. That was her whole trouble, wasn't it? She never had been able to think, to plan. She had spent her whole life just reacting, racing from one disaster to another, home, to school, to marriage to Judd Forbes, to. . .to that Godawful bed, to a succession of men. Images of Dillon, Wofford, a succession of hair, slimy cocks flitted across her mind. God, Joanna, will you stop it and go to bed?

The doorbell rang. Who could it be? She glanced at her watch. Ten after nine. Who came at this hour? She opened the door and was appalled to see Wofford there, smiling broadly, a large sack in his left hand, a bottle of wine in his right. "If I can't get you to go out to dinner with me, I decided to bring the dinner to you. Hope you like Chinese."

She was shocked speechless, mouth open, eyes wide, momentarily paralyzed with surprise. Thus, when he pushed against the door for entry, she involuntarily moved back. When she recovered, it was too late. He was already inside her apartment. She saw him looking at her front. She still had on that ridiculous tank top.

"What are you doing here?"

Still he grinned. "I told you, dinner. I got sweet and sour—"

"Please. This is my apartment. You have no right."

"I should have phoned, I know, but you're unlisted and. . . ."

The day, the week, her impossible situation, her fatigue, frustration, gross depression, all conspired against her at that moment. Wofford, there, that silly, stupid grin, that sack of Chinese food, a bottle of wine held by the neck. It was too much, all too much. She felt torn apart, cleaved in two, sundered. Her emotions, spraying over already jagged nerves, erupted into open warfare until she didn't know whether to give in to anger, a fit of hysterical laughter, or tears.

Anger won. "How did you find out where I live? You're not supposed. . ." Then she knew. "Have you been *following* me?"

Her voice had raised in pitch and volume and he now

realized she was angry. His smile faded. "I'm not going to harm you, Joanna. God, never that. I just thought we could eat together, talk."

"Have you been following me?" Her voice cracked under the excess of air.

"Joanna, please. You can't expect—"

"*Have you*?"

He sighed. "I wouldn't call it following. I'm in—interested in you. You must know that." In his distress, he began to stammer. "I-I like the b-b-beach, too." He stopped and breathed deeply, trying to control his speech. "It's nice in the early morning. I saw you there and. . . ."

She raised her hands, as fists, wanting to strike out at him. But she did not, could not. Instead, she closed her eyes, letting out a long, low sound, mostly a growl. Again she sucked in air and let the raging animal in her escape through her lungs. "God," she said finally, through clenched teeth. "What a disaster." She turned her back to him, struggling for some kind of self-control.

He didn't know what to say. None of this was expected. In a small voice, nearly a whine, he said, "Can I set my package down?"

She wheeled on him, voice strident. "No you may not. You may take it and leave this instant. This is *my* house. I *live* here. I give you several hours a day. You have no *right* to follow me, come here, *invade* my home and expect *more* from me." Her rage was at floodtide now. "This is an intolerable invasion of my privacy. I won't have it. Do you hear me, I won't have it? It isn't fair. Oh God, it isn't fair." And then she knew the tears would come in a second. That she didn't want.

She was saved by the telephone. Quickly, grateful for something to distract her, she went to the kitchen doorway and answered the wall phone. "Yes."

"This is Hank Kraft."

Oh God, Hank Kraft. Instantly, she reached out to him. *Hank. Hank.* He was all things great and wonderful at that moment, sanity, strength, maturity, reasonableness, rescue. Then she remembered, as if from a great distance. She wasn't to talk to him. She was to be cool, distant. In her confusion, agitation, she could only stand there, breathing heavily.

"Are you there, Joanna?"

She wanted him—there with her. Oh God, how she needed him—now, this minute. Why did she have to be distant? Why couldn't she just say to him—come, now, save me.

She closed her mouth and swallowed hard, trying to control her breathing. "No, I'm all right."

There was a long pause on the line, one she had no capacity to fill. She opened her eyes. There, still by the front door, was Jerry Wofford, in his blue blazer, clutching his bag of Chinese food and bottle of red wine. It was awful. Life was an imponderable mess.

"Okay, Joanna, I get the message. I thought, when I called Monday night, it was—well, Monday night. You said you were tired, had a bad day. I thought I'd try again. That'll teach me to think. More of the same, isn't it? You're sending me a message. And I'm getting it all right."

She heard the anger, bitterness in his voice. She reached out to stop it. She couldn't bear it, not now. "Hank, please, I—"

"It's all right, Joanna, I understand. But there's something I have to tell you. It's been bothering me all week. I'm not going to be any good till I get it off my chest."

"Hank, I—"

"You weren't just a one-night stand to me. I liked you. I cared about you. I'd have felt the same if I'd left at ten o'clock. I intended to—should have. I didn't need to go up to your place."

His words were like physical blows to her, blows to her midsection, taking her breath away. And they hurt. She could not hold back the tears. Eyes smarting, voice choking, high pitched, she could only say, half moan, part whine, "Please, Hank, oh God-d. . ."

"I understand, really I do. It didn't mean that much to you. That sort of thing happens. Okay, so be it."

She couldn't speak. She couldn't tell him. No words would come out.

"But I gotta tell you. At the risk of being a damn fool, I gotta tell you. Being with you meant a lot—oh, what the hell, I already said it. You weren't a one-night stand to me."

Tears welled out of her, running down her cheeks. "Please, please, I—"

"If I'm upsetting you, I'm sorry, but—"

She could take no more. Slowly she lowered the phone from her ear, and with both hands hung it back on its hook. She stood there immobile, except for the tears and an occasional sob.

"What's the matter, Joanna?"

She looked at Wofford, now watery, swimming through burning eyes. "Please go, Jerry. I'll—I'll see you tomorrow."

He set down his bag and bottle in the Morris chair, the only stuffed furniture in the room other than the couch. "No, I'm not going to leave you upset like this. You need someone."

"God, please, just go. I don't need—"

"Joanna, I know now I shouldn't have come. You're right. I have invaded your privacy. But is it so wrong for

me to like you? You said I'd find a girl. You're right,
only I already have. Is it so wrong for me to try to see
you, court you?''

"Please, Jerry. I can't think just now." Her
desperation had entered her voice.

"You have to care something about me. You must, or
you couldn't have done the things you. . .we did. It
can't have been just—oh, I don't know. There has to be
some feeling between us. Is it wrong for me to want my
chance with you, to try to see what might become of
us?''

She closed her eyes and tilted her head back, trying to
gulp in air. She wanted to scream, to throw things, to
surrender to a first class temper tantrum. But this had
never been permitted in her whole life, and it was
impossible for her now. Besides, she was too tired. She
didn't have the strength for it. She leaned against doorjamb to the kitchen, resting her cheek against the cool,
enameled wood. Slowly, with great difficulty, she
managed to say, "Jerry, you're a decent man, a
generous man, a kindly man. I believe all that is true.
And if it is, will you please, just this once, have mercy
on me and leave—now. Please. I'll talk about it
tomorrow, but, Jerry, please, leave.''

He stared at her a moment. Then, being decent,
generous and kind, he picked up his bag of Chinese
food and bottle of wine and left.

15

By the time Dillon arrived the next afternoon, Joanna considered herself in fair shape. She had taken a barbituate, sleeping late, awakening groggy. But she came out of it, running on the beach and treating herself to a little therapeutic pampering. At the office she talked to Lambert by phone. How was she getting along with Dillon? At least someone was concerned about her. "Better, Doctor. He's being cooperative, very nice, really." She thought about telling him about Wofford, but had no chance to.

"Goo-o-d." The word could not possibly have been said more expansively. "I told you it would work out. You should listen to me more often." His chuckle kept the words from being supercilious. "Is he making progress?"

"Yes, quite good I think." She did not offer details of the treatment, nor did he ask. She was experienced with premature ejaculators. Supervision was not required.

"And this is your last day with Wofford?"

"Yes."

"Things will be easier for you then. Joanna, I want you to know I appreciate how difficult this week has been for you. And I appreciate your willingness to help out in a pinch. Not everyone will, you know."

"Yes."

"I was going to surprise you, but I can't resist telling you there will be a little something extra in your next check. Just my way of saying thanks."

That news, his words did cheer her.

When Brad Dillon entered, he looked at her quizzically a couple of times. Finally he said, "You look tired."

She smiled, a little wanly. "TGIF. Been a hard week."

"My fault?"

She patted his hand. "No, not especially. Shall we get started?"

"Why don't you take the day off? Give yourself a break."

"No, can't. Each day is important. There are only ten, you know." She smiled. "If you'd come with your wife or girlfriend, you'd be able to work all weekend. That I refuse to do. So we need each day. But thanks for thinking of me. It's nice."

"We Polish boys are all nice—and we are all drinkers. C'mon, I'm making."

She went along, but was careful to merely sip it. With Wofford coming, she wanted to be in complete control of herself.

"I find myself thinking a lot about you, Joanna."

Inwardly, she bristled. Not another one. "That hardly qualifies as profound thought."

"I wonder about what you do here. How long are you going to stay a. . .a—"

"Surrogate partner. Not long, I hope. I want to go back to school."

"For what?"

"Psych. Get my master's, maybe a Ph.D., hang out a shingle. I really don't know."

"When is this going to take place?"

She saw him lift his drink. She did likewise. "I dunno. Money's a problem."

"What about your ex—Judd Forbes."

She smiled. "Huh-uh. I got a Karmann Ghia out of it. The well is dry." She sat her glass down to control her consumption. "I'm saving a little money. I'll get there soon. Are you ready now?"

"Ever think about show biz?"

"Think what about it?"

"A beautiful girl like you could make it. People have started with less."

She laughed. "No way. I really don't photograph well. I've a tin ear and two left feet."

"I doubt that."

"Go ahead and doubt, but no, Brad, I've no ambitions to be a movie star or any other kind of star. I couldn't take the rat race, the pressure. I'm trying to simplify my life, not complicate it." To signal the end of the conversation, she began unbuttoning her blouse.

The training session went well. She could tell he was gaining control, despite her energetic stroking of him. She told him so.

"Is this it? Is this all we do?"

"No, not hardly. Next week we'll start intromission and containment."

"What's that?"

She smiled. "Don't worry, you'll like it." She glanced at his engorged penis. "I'm not sure I will, but I guarantee you will."

"But what is it. Talk English."

On impulse she told him to scoot down on the bed and put his legs together. She moved up his legs in the female superior position, stroked him, then squeezed him back again. When she had aroused him again, she raised her pelvis to take him inside. Immediately she winced with pain, then cried out. He was too big, stretching, hurting her. She forced a little, then pulled off him. "You're too big," she said, "and I'm dry. You'll have to help me."

"Help you what?"

She forced his legs apart and sat down between them again, her back against the headboard. "C'mere. Sit facing me. Give me your hands." She took them, placing her hands on the back. "This shouldn't have to be part of the treatment. You get a dividend."

Slowly at first, then with increased momentum, she showed him all the ways to touch her to turn her on.

Wonder in his voice, he said, "You're something, Joanna, really you are."

She was panting, already finding it hard to speak. "Each woman is different. You should. . .let all your girls show you what. . .to do, where. Saves time. . .better. . . ."

In a minute she felt herself tremble and gasp. "Lie down again," she said. She scampered up his legs, raised her pelvis and took him inside. "Oh Lord," she gasped. He was so big, she felt filled to bursting. "It's not. . .possible." She trembled, but, hands on his shoulders, she managed to hold herself steady. "God, Brad, you're so *big*." Then she remembered. "Can you hold off?"

She saw him struggling. "I'm not sure."

Quickly she pulled off of him and with her right hand squeezed him down. "Is that better?"

"I guess so." He was breathing heavily.

She sat on his thighs a minute, letting him rest. "That's called intromission."

"Is that what you mean? Why didn't you say so?"

"I did say so." She took him in her hands again, and

began to arouse him anew, her fingers arcing the
immense glans and its coronal ridge. She felt him jerk
and shake. "You really are too big, Brad. Girls must
hate you."

"I guess so. Wow, Joanna, I—"

She squeezed him back again. "I can see why you
have trouble holding off. As big as you are, the
sensation must be unbearable when you are inside."

"You're telling me."

In a moment she again raised herself, taking him
inside. This time it was pure pleasure for her and she
moaned from the sensation. She felt the desire to move
her hips, thrust for orgasm, but she did not. "This is
called containment. I just hold you, not moving at all."

"You better not, believe me."

"I won't. You just enjoy it, feel it."

He sighed. "I do, I do."

"Try to get used to it. Try to accept the sensation and
control your ejaculation. If you can't make it, say so.
I'll squeeze you."

She looked down at him and saw the open mouth,
squinted eyes, the disordered breathing. He had to be
suffering. She sure was. Never had she been so filled up.
God, the sensation.

He exhaled in a "whew" sound. "Wow, oh wow,
Joanna, you—"

She understood, coming off him and squeezing him
just in time. He moaned with the paroxysm of an
internal orgasm and some ejaculate escaped. From a
distance, half-heard amid his gasps came another
sound. "Wow," he said, finally. "I'm not sure I'll
survive the treatment, doctor."

She smiled down at him. "Oh, I've an idea you will."
Again, she heard the sound. The door. Somebody
rapping. It was locked. Whoever it was would go away.

She clasped him again, moving her hand over the now lubricated surface, stroking him back to hardness. Again she heard the rapping. Again she ignored it, raising her pelvis, taking him inside, gasping at the pleasure of it. But the rapping was too insistent. "I better see who it is," she said. She pulled free of him, scrambled off the bed and ran to the bathroom for her robe, quickly putting it on, tying the belt. To Brad she said, "I'll be right back. Don't go away."

"Who can move?"

She closed the door to the treatment room, then opened the exterior one, ready to protest the intrusion. It was Jerry Wofford. Again he had surprised her. She glanced at her watch. Three twenty. "You're not due 'til four-thirty."

"I know, but I have to talk to you. I can't bear having you mad at me."

"I'm not mad, Jerry. It's just—"

"You are, too. I know it and I have to talk to you—this minute."

He was pushing against the door, trying to come in. It took all her strength to hold the door half closed against him. "Jerry, listen to me. I want to talk to you, too—and I will. At four-thirty. Come back then." She tried to close the door, but with sudden strength he pushed hard against it, forcing her back, entering the office.

She struggled for control. She had to remain calm. "How did you get by Jenny, the receptionist?"

"She wasn't there. I came on up. I have to talk to you."

"Can't you understand, Jerry? Not right now. I'm busy."

He was an intelligent man, and understanding came all at once. He saw her robe, her bare feet. His eyes widened. "You're with someone else."

She saw the expression on his face, disbelief, shock, even horror. "Jerry. . ." But the word was not enough to stop him. He opened the door to the treatment room and saw Brad Dillon. He lay where he had been, on his back, quite naked, his penis still half erect.

Wofford's face, his whole body seemed to crumble as he looked at Dillon. His eyes closed. His mouth went slack and his jaw dropped. His shoulders sagged as though from a great weight. Slowly he closed the door on what he had seen.

"Jerry. . .you shouldn't have come till—"

"My God, Joanna, how could you?" He said it repeatedly. "How could you? How *could* you?" It was a litany for the suffering.

"Sit down here," she said. And he was unable to resist as she pushed him into her swivel chair. "I'll be back in a minute. You wait."

Agitated, desperate, she went back into the treatment room. Dillon, embarrassed, had sat up and covered himself with a sheet. "Who was that?"

"Someone. It doesn't matter. Brad, I have to ask you to go now."

"Another customer?"

She reacted as though he had hit her. "God, Brad, don't—"

"I'm sorry, really sorry. He's another patient?"

"Yes. I've had two this week—you and him." She shuddered. "Now you know why I'm such a mess. It's been to much. I'm about to explode."

"I understand. I'll get dressed and leave." He rolled off the bed and reached for his pants.

"Thanks, Brad. I'll see you Monday, all right?"

"Sure."

"Are you upset with me, too?"

He was zipping his pants. He stopped, looked at her and smiled reassuringly. "No. I just want to know if you are going to be okay with this guy. Is he trouble?"

"No, I can handle him."

When she had passed Brad out through her office, she turned back to face Wofford, a sinking fear tugging at her bowels.

"Who is that? He looks familiar."

She did not reply.

"I asked who that was."

She heard the quiver in his voice. He was on the far edge of hysteria. As calmly as she could, she said, "Jerry, it really is none of your business." She saw him glaring at her, breathing heavily. Again forcing her voice to be level, she said, "You really shouldn't have come early."

"Oh, you're damn right I shouldn't have. God, Joanna, how could you? I cared about you. I thought you. . .we. . . Goddammit, Joanna, I was falling in love with you."

"I know that. And you shouldn't have. I never wanted it. I never encouraged it."

He was on his feet now, gesturing wildly. "You did so, damn you. What you did. . .what we did. . .in that room, in that very bed where that other sonofabitch was lying. Oh God, Joanna, how could you do this to me?"

She sighed, deeply, letting the air escape between compressed lips. "Jerry, listen to me. I am a surrogate partner. I help men with their sexual inadequacies. You are not the first man I've helped, nor will you be the last."

"I suppose that's what you were doing in there just now."

"Of course. You can't think anything else."

"I'll think whatever I damn well please."

She saw his anger flaring, overriding what little control he had. Again she tried to calm him. "Jerry, I'm sorry you mistook my—my kindness for. . .for something more. It is common for patients to become attached to their doctors, nurses, those who help them. You'll get over your feeling about me."

"You're goddamn right I will. You know what you are?"

It was coming now. Inwardly she tried to brace for it.

"You're nothin but a goddamned whore. That's what you are, a lousy, fucking whore."

She had braced, but the blow, delivered in anger, was too strong.

"I'll say this for you. You sure are a high-priced one. I paid ten thousand dollars for you. Ten grand I earned myself. Can't even declare it a medical deduction or a business expense. Ten grand right out of my pocket. And what do I get? I get to share you with a bunch of other fucking pigs. God, what a sucker I am. Gerald Wofford, sucker of the year. They ought to put me on the cover of Time magazine."

She was crumbling, her whole facade of calmness breaking away, letting out her own roiling waters of self-loathing.

"Ten thousand bucks, and I even have to share you with some other bastard. And I get seconds to boot. Jesus Christ, have I been had."

Slowly, to avoid falling, she collapsed into her chair and bent over, covered her ears with her hands to blot out the words. But she could still hear.

"Ten thousand bucks and you weren't even any good." He was wild now, striking out, saying anything to hurt her. "You stink, that's what you do. You stink like shit. You look lousy, you are lousy, you're nothing but a cheap fucking trick. I've seen better on street corners—*colored black.*" Wild, frenzied, he was not quite finished. "You she-bitch. You fucking she-bitch. To think I liked you. God, you make my flesh crawl. You're *dirty* and you made me dirty."

He was gone then, his tirade finished, leaving Joanna alone to somehow survive in a silent room. She sat there a long time, numb with pain and fatigue. But in time, her brain, surely stubborn, began to function. All systems were monitored. Decision was reached. She needed help. She dialed Lambert's number. No answer. She dialed Jenny at the switchboard.

"He's gone, Joanna. He had a speaking engagement in New York."

New York.

16

There was doubtlessly a sequence, but for Hank Kraft, walking home in a deepening twilight, it all happened as one, hearing his name, noticing the little Karmann Ghia with Connecticut plates at the curb, seeing Joanna, standing in the open door of the driver's side, facing him, mouth open, hand raised to signal him. His hesitation was only fleeting, virtually non-existent, then he was there and she was in his arms, her face against his chest, her arms around his waist.

He felt rather than heard her crying, the spasmodic shaking of her body held tight against him. She raised her head to look at him, and he heard her choked words delivered amid sobs. "I. . .shouldn't. . .have. . . come. . . . I tried. . .not to." He silenced her with his mouth, tasting first the saltiness of her tears. Then, as before, he felt her passion erupt through her mouth, and standing there in Eighty-Fifth Street inside an open door of a ridiculously small car, he felt himself being assaulted with desire as he held her, embraced her, kissed those moving lips. A taxi beeped, then a second. Someone hollered something about the street. He pulled away from her, stepped back and slammed the car door. Then, his arm around her shoulder, he entered his building, unlocked the door and ran her full speed up four flights to his apartment.

They stood inside the doorway, not bothering to turn on lights, winded. She tried to say something, but he silenced her with his lips and, panting, struggling for breath, they smothered each other's faces with kisses. But only for a moment. He picked her up, so light, and carried her into his bed. There was frantic fumbling with unwanted clothes, then her nakedness, soft, warm, sensitized, clinging, slid next to him. He felt her trembling and knew she was crying again or maybe still crying. "No," he heard, "you. . .don't. . .want me. . ." But he did, drowning her mouth, engorging his hands with her soft flesh, coming atop her, hearing her sobs, feeling her arms clutching at him as he entered her. Again he had such a sense of her need, great need, as she came so quickly, so shatteringly, almost spastically before he had hardly moved. He felt her wrap her legs around his and ride with him, clutching him, sounds, half moans, half sobs escaping her, until when his own eruption came he again felt her gasping and writhing beneath him.

He rolled to his side, facing her, and still panting, they held each other close. He stroked her back, her hips, her hair, then wiped away the tears which were still coming out of her. "I'm sorry," he heard her say, the words still distorted. "I've. . .no right to. . .to do this. . .to you."

"I'm the one who should apologize," he said. Then he laughed. "I don't even think I've said hi." In the blinking light from the neon sign across the street he saw her wan smile. "Hi," he said. "There are greetings and then there are greetings." He moved to get up.

"No, please. Don't leave me."

"I'll be right back. You need a drink."

Naked, he went into the windowless kitchen and turned on the light, quickly pouring two generous highballs of bourbon. When he turned to go back to the bedroom she was there, in the doorway, looking at him. She was unutterably lovely to him, a peculiar softness to her nakedness, a languid intimacy of lingering passion. But in her tear-stained face he saw tension, strain, and in her eyes, unhappiness, a hint of desperation.

"I like a girl who can't wait for her drink." He handed it to her and she took it.

"I've no right to do this to you, Hank." Her voice was nearly normal, but when she finished he heard the quick, soblike sucking in of breath.

He smiled. "You're right. Terrible thing for you to do."

"I mean it, Hank. I'm a mess. I shouldn't have come here. I should stay away. I'm no good for you."

"Yes, clearly you are a terrible person."

"I tried to call you, but there was no answer. I shouldn't have come. I've been waiting a long time."

"I had to deliver some work downtown. One thing led to another. I had a couple drinks with an art director. I'm sorry. I could have been here sooner."

He went to her, turning off the light with his left hand, then putting it around her shoulder, pulling her against him, holding her.

"Where's Timmy?"

"At his mother's. I'll get him tomorrow."

They went back into the bedroom then and made love anew, this time slowly, tenderly, lingering over caresses and wondrous sensations, savoring arousal, postponing fulfillment until it could no longer be delayed, basking in the afterglow of satiated passion.

"Have you eaten?"

"No, I don't think so."

He got up. "I'm a wizard with eggs." From his closet he retrieved his robe and handed it to her. Then he pulled on his pants.

She had not moved. He pulled her to her feet and helped her into the ridiculously large robe, even tying the belt for her. "Personally," he said, "I love the attire you just had on, but I can't cook in the dark, and I'm not ready to share you with the neighbors."

"I don't think I can eat."

"We'll see."

She followed him into the kitchen and sat in silence as he fried bacon, scrambled eggs, made toast. He was conscious of her eyes on him constantly, following his every movement, peering deep into his each time he turned to look at her. It was as if he were some unfathomable mystery she was trying to figure out. She did not speak, nor he. And the silence, the questioning search of her eyes, was not uncomfortable.

He served two plates of food, then poured two glasses of red wine. "Eat, drink," he said. "I have an idea you're not going to be merry, though."

He saw her bite at her lip. "I'm sorry. I shouldn't do this to you."

"Eat."

He watched her. She poked at the food, moving it around her plate with the fork, then raised a piece of toast and nibbled a corner. He saw her chew, swallow, take a larger bite. Then she raised a bit of egg, then a sliver of bacon and soon she was eating.

"It's delicious. I *was* hungry." She saw him nod, his mouth full of food. "I don't think I've hardly eaten all week. I don't remember it anyhow."

He swallowed. "You should always eat. It's the best tranquilizer I know. That's why people get fat."

Both ate a few moments, then she said. "Aren't you going to ask why I'm such a mess?"

"No." He scraped together the last crumbles of egg and pushed them on his fork with the last corner of toast. "Tell me if you want, but it is enough for me that you are here." He saw her look at him, eyes wide and unblinking. Again she bit her lip. "Unconditional positive regard, remember?"

Slowly she nodded her head. "I remember. Carl Rogers."

He hesitated, raising his fork halfway to his mouth, then he lowered it. "I'll tell you one thing, though. I knew that girl on the telephone wasn't you. I didn't like her very much."

"Oh, Hank, Hank, this is impossible. It's not right. I'm no good for you. If you knew about me, you'd. . . . Oh Lord, I shouldn't have come."

"Eat."

When she had finished—she ate everything—he put the dishes in the sink, refilled her wine glass and handed it to her, pulled her to her feet and led her into the living room, turning out the kitchen light as they went. In the darkened room, illuminated only by the lights from the street, they sat together on the couch, his arm around her, her head against his shoulder, their only movement to sip their wine.

They sat in silence for what seemed a very long time, each with his own thoughts. Finally, he spoke. "Tired?"

She sighed. "I guess so. I don't know."

"I've an idea I should put you to bed—to sleep, that is."

She was silent for a time. "That was nice," she said finally.

"What?"

"What you did."

"The eggs? I told you I'm a wizard."

"The last time we made love. I liked it."

She recalled all, the slow, deliberate discovery, the inexorable arousal, the cast of inevitability of hand within hand, mouth enmeshing mouth, flesh ensnaring sensitized flesh, so slowly, desires remembered, wanted anew, the pooling, the joining, satiation postponed, a renewing, effortless, taking effort, experimentation, old, new, so grand, triumph, longing not quite requited. So strange it had been. Just before her climax a quietness had come over her body, a stillness. It was as if the whole universe was centered in one spot deep within her vagina, a place known only to her, discoverable only by him. He did, again and again, creating contractions within the cylinder which went on and on, dissolving her quiet body. So strange. Hank, blessed Hank.

He said nothing for a time.

"Didn't you think so?"

"A masterpiece is its own commentary."

She turned her face up to him then and kissed him softly. "Do it again," she whispered, "exactly the same. Then I'll sleep."

"The marvel of it all is that it can never be the same, never repeated. A miracle it is."

Laura McGovern listened to the mechanical sound of the telephone ring into her fiance's apartment in Stamford. She had been dialing regularly all evening, both his home and his private number at his office. No answer. She even talked to his answering service. Yes, Dr. Randall was expecting to fly home this evening.

She hadn't heard from him all week, at least not since Monday. He didn't call her as he had promised to do, and he was never in when she phoned him. She could understand he was busy at the conference, but he must get back to his hotel room some time. Surely he received the messages she had called. Why didn't he phone her? Perhaps he was out late. With the time difference he might not want to wake her. But surely he knew she wouldn't mind. He must know how much she wanted to talk to him.

In mounting despair she listened to the ringing, so insistent, so demanding. She had dialed so often, listened to the sound so much, she was shocked when it ended. "Hello."

"Charles, oh Charles. Is that really you?" The silence on the line seemed strange to her, and she leaped to fill it. "I've been phoning and phoning. You're so late getting back. I thought maybe something had happened to you."

Again there was an empty sound over the phone, but finally he filled it. "You know Fridays at Kennedy. Planes never get down on time."

"I know. You can circle for hours." What on earth was she talking about airplanes for? "Oh Charles, it's so good to hear your voice. I called you a thousand times in San Francisco. I left dozens of messages." She laughed. "You were very naughty not to phone me, Charles."

"I was very busy, Laura."

"I'll bet you were." Again she laughed. "I think I'm going to be jealous." She heard a sound over the line, a sigh mostly, which she understood signaled annoyance. She responded with a chuckle. "I'm only teasing, Charles. I know you wouldn't even look at another woman—not twice anyway, you handsome brute."

"Laura, please. . . ."

"But you're home now. That's all that matters. When can I see you? Can you come over now—or would you rather I came there?"

The silence on the line was finally broken with a prolonged sigh. "Laura, it's very late."

"It's only a little past eleven, Charles. I do so want to see you."

Again a long pause. "I'm tired, Laura, been a long—"

"Of course, dear. You must be *exhausted*, the jet lag and everything."

"Yes, I am."

She pressed the receiver against her ear, waiting for him to say something more. There was nothing. The emptiness on the line seemed an abyss to her, a bottomless void in time. "Charles, is something wrong?" She could feel herself being drained into the silence. "You sound so strange, Charles, so—I don't know, so distant."

"I said I was tired, Laura."

Yes, that must be it. She laughed. "And all I'm doing is badgering you. I am sorry. When can I see you?"

It seemed forever before he spoke. "I've a lot of catching up to do. I've my rounds at the hospital. And I want to go to the office. I've been away a week. You can understand that."

"Of course." Again she laughed, but it was forced this time. "You poor overworked man. What you need is some TLC. We'll have dinner tomorrow night. Then you'll do nothing but put your feet up and relax. All right?"

She could feel the void growing. Stamford was receding from Westport at a terrifying pace. "I'm sorry, Laura. I'm very tired."

"And I'm keeping you up, you poor dear. All right, go to bed, I'll wait till tomorrow—somehow."

"Yes."

"Come as early as you can, Charles. Please."

Joanna awoke languidly, even deliciously, more relaxed and rested than she had been in a long time. When she opened her eyes she was disoriented for a moment, then she remembered, New York, Hank, his apartment, then all that had happened. When memories of the afternoon, Wofford, her hysteria, started to come, she shoved them away. Hank. They had made love. So beautifully. How many times! She sighed and stretched under the covers *Hank*. She shouldn't have come here. Abruptly, she threw back the covers and got up. She saw her clothes, the white pants suit she had worn, in a heap, Hank's robe across the foot of the bed.

Hank was working, or trying to, on the new book jacket commissioned yesterday when he heard the bedroom door creak open. He looked up and saw her in the hallway, in his robe, hair in disarray, sleep fogging her eyes. He had never seen her look lovelier. "Morning, sleepyhead."

"What time is it?" Her voice was husky, her vocal chords not yet taut. "My watch stopped."

"Well, it's still morning."

"C'mon, what time?"

"Eleven-twenty." He looked at his watch. "Twenty-two." He saw her grip her wrist, winding and setting the timepiece. Timmy came out of the kitchen, looking up at her. "Somebody here has been just dying with impatience for you to get up."

She turned and saw Timmy, his face somber, the big, lovely dark eyes upturned to hers. "Oh, Timmy." She knelt and hugged him. "Am I ever glad to see you."

Hank saw the robe fall away from her thighs. The whiteness, revealed from within his own robe, excited him. He guessed everything about her excited him.

She hugged Timmy tight a moment longer then held him away from herself. "I'f I'd known you were here, I'd have gotten up sooner."

"Daddy said you needed to sleep. I was real quiet."

"And so you were." Again she hugged him."

"Can we go swimming today?"

"I-I don't know." She stood up. "We'll have to see."

Hank had left his desk. "First things first. Like a Bloody Mary?" He saw her hesitation. "There's coffee if you prefer."

"Yes, coffee."

They went into the kitchen, Joanna being led by the hand by Timmy. "I've got the cards all dealt."

She saw the cards for gin on the table. "Wow, Timmy, I'm not sure I'm up to you this early in the morning."

"The kid's no dummy. Better keep the stakes low."

She forced herself to play, then strangely began to enjoy it, as the coffee began to work its wonders. She was smiling, she realized, and laughing, at Timmy, at Hank who stood above them, kibitzing. She lost easily and quickly, but that, too, seemed funny.

"Can we go swimming now?"

The question just stood there, awkward, unanswered. She didn't know what to say.

"Whoa, son, this is Joanna's holiday, remember? Maybe she doesn't fancy the beach."

"Sure she does, don't you, Joanna?"

She sighed. "I didn't think. I didn't bring my suit. I'm sorry." Indeed, she hadn't brought any clothes for a weekend.

Hank laughed. "I could loan you one of mine, only I think the lifeguards might trample themselves in trying to drown you so they could save you."

"Or I'd get arrested." She laughed. "Tell you what, Timmy. The beach sounds fine. I'll love it. I'll buy a suit somewhere. I need a new one anyway."

"Hooray. I'll go get ready."

"Can she have a little brunch?" But Hank's words were lost on his son's dash for his bedroom. To Joanna he said, "Sure you want to?"

She smiled. "Yes, it'll be fun."

He pulled her to her feet then and kissed her, warmly, longingly, feeling the heat and softness of her through the robe. He broke it off. "Don't buy too sexy a bathing suit," he whispered. "I don't think Timmy could take it."

"He'll just have to suffer."

17

She bought one of the new-style suits, one piece, sleek with a satiny finish, and so tight it fit like a second skin. Then on impulse she bought a sundress, hardly demure, and white sandals with stiletto heels, both on sale.

It was a nice day. They drove to Jones Beach, finding it too crowded, the sand not entirely clean. But they had fun. She worked with Timmy on his swimming, talking with Hank, or trying to, in between being pulled back repeatedly into the water by his son. She laughed. Yes, she had fun. But she was not carefree. Westport, Dillon, Wofford, her impossible situation with Hank, all nagged at her mind.

At one point he said, "Whatever your problems are, can't you set them aside for this weekend? You owe it to yourself."

And she looked at him. "Do you always notice everything?"

"About you, yes."

She looked down. "Hank, please," she said, her voice barely audible, "don't fall in love with me." He did not answer and she looked up. "I mean it."

"I know you do." He smiled. "Okay, I won't fall in love with you—if it isn't too late already."

Timmy ran up to them then. "Joanna, Joanna, come see my sand castle." They both went and Hank, with her help, applied his expertness to walls and turrets.

They stopped for dinner, leisurely enjoying it, and returned to his apartment. After showers and Timmy's bath, and a game of gin, she tucked him into bed, a very tired little boy. "Are you staying tonight?" he asked.

She said she was.

"With Daddy?"

The question startled her. "Yes," she said.

"He'll like that. Daddy likes you."

Wow! "Your daddy's a very nice man. Now go to sleep."

"That's what Daddy always tells me, too."

"You should always listen to him." She stood up to leave him.

"Thanks for tucking me in, Joanna."

"Thanks for asking me to."

When she came back into the living room, he had the lights low, soft music on the radio and a highball to give her. She laughed. "Is this a seduction scene?"

"No. This is thirst, saving electricity and playing music so Timmy won't listen to every word we say."

"Then I'm safe."

"Just like visiting the proctologist."

She grimaced. "That's a lousy simile."

"Not my best."

They sat on the couch again, his arm around her shoulder, her head on his, sipping their drinks, not talking. The song on the radio ended, another began, a third. He had such a sense of nearness of her. "Forgive me," he whispered. "I've been wanting to do this all evening." And he slid his left hand, the one that was around her shoulder, into the bodice of her sundress, cupping, lifting her breast.

She shuddered, but made no effort to stop him or remove his hand. "This is no good, Hank."

He felt her trembling. "Speak for yourself."

"Aren't you going to ask me what I do?"

"No."

"I can't stay a mystery woman forever. You must wonder about me."

"Everything about you is a wonder." He bent his head and kissed her, marveling at the softness of her lips, the instant passage they provided for her passion. Both their breaths quickened, mouths opened, tongues entwined. The fingers of his hand found and squeezed a small, hard nubbin.

She broke away. "Timmy?"

"He's asleep." Their mouths rejoined. Passion rose exponentially.

"Daddy, Joanna, I'm thirsty."

Both were laughing even before their lips separated. "Rotten kid," he said.

She moved to get up. "I'll go."

When she came out of the bedroom carrying the barely touched glass of water, he said, "I think I'll invent an old saying about anticipation being something or other." He took the glass from her, set it down and swept her into his arms, leaning against the doorway to the bedroom. As their mouths joined, so did their bodies, and she felt the length of him, his erection pressing firmly against her thighs. "Always did like to neck," he said.

They spent the night at the well of passion, dipping deep, filling up, pouring out, two young people with apparently unquenchable thirsts.

It was not so for Laura McGovern. Randall did not phone. He did not come. Dressed to the nines in a new gown calculated to show off her recently acquired cleavage, she stalked the house like a caged animal, looking at the phone as though it were an instrument of torture. The sound of a car sent her rushing to a window. It always drove by. She had planned everything, even giving her servants, Raphaela and Luigi Dicentes, a long weekend off. She and Charles would be alone. They'd drink champagne, go out for a quiet dinner, then return here. Plans to wait until the wedding would be abandoned.

Something was wrong, terribly wrong. She was certain of that. He had not phoned from San Francisco. He had been so cold, so aloof on the phone last night. He didn't want to talk to her, see her. Why? What had happened? In her stalking of the house she tried to think of everything. Another woman? He had met someone on the West Coast? Someone younger, prettier, sexier? It could be that. He was ashamed, embarrassed. He couldn't bring himself to tell her, so he avoided her. Yes, it had to be that. *Oh God*! The thought of Charles in bed with another woman—she envisioned her as young, large bosomed—corroded her mind.

She'd fight it. She wouldn't give up Charles without a fight. She might not be young and pretty, but she had maturity. She knew how to treat a man. And she had money, lots of money. Yes, she'd fight for her happiness. Fight whom? Why didn't Charles come? Why didn't he face her like a man, give her a chance? For the uncounted time she phoned him, listening to the torturous sound of the empty ringing. In the wee hours of the morning she took a sleeping pill, then a second before gaining the relief of unconsciousness.

Hank awoke first, unreasonably early as he usually did. But he was unwilling to accept it or to leave her. She was on her left side. He did the same, moving against her back, bending his knees inside her knees, his arm around her, her breasts filling his hand, bulging against his wrist, soft, heavenly soft. He felt her snuggle against him and moan in her sleep as his erection filled the crevice between her derriere and thighs. It all felt so good. He had been too long without a bed companion.

He heard nothing in particular. No sound, no warning reached him. But he knew to open his eyes. There was Timmy, looking down, watching them. Thank God for the sheet.

He smiled up at his son, then removed his hand from Joanna and put a finger to his lips for the boy to be quiet. Hank rolled out of bed, slipped on his pants and led Timmy out of the room, trying to ready himself for the inevitable questions, explanation, and disapproving and accusatory looks.

He closed the door, whispering, "We'll just let her sleep, okay?" In the kitchen he poured two glasses of orange juice, handing one to his son.

"Are you in love with Joanna, Daddy?"

He looked at him, those immense eyes, soft, alert, questioning. "I don't know, son. I think maybe."

"Are you going to marry her?"

"I don't know that either, son."

"I hope you do. I like Joanna."

He smiled. My son the matchmaker.

It was another nice day for Joanna, games with Timmy and Hank, a long walk in Central Park, ice cream cones, dinner and wine at a tiny Italian restaurant. Early on, Hank showed her some of his work, explaining details of technique, and she genuinely admired his paintings which filled the walls of the apartment. She didn't know much about art, but his paintings, some watercolors, many oils, were bright, airy, suffused with light and great feeling for his subject. "You're an impressionist," she said, "like

Cezanne, Van Gogh.''

"Which is probably the reason they don't sell."

"Have you tried?"

"Have you seen Timmy's pet turtle? He calls him Walter. Only maybe he's a her—or, he could be a transvestite.''

"Daddy, what's a trans—trans—whatever you said?''

He looked at Joanna, rolling his eyes, and she barely suppressed laughter. "Transvestite, Timmy. It's somebody who dresses up in girl's clothing.''

"That's silly. Walter doesn't do that.''

At the park he saw others, men and women both, looking at her. A few stopped and stared after her as she passed, holding Timmy's hand, animatedly talking with him. Hank couldn't fault people for staring. He had trouble keeping his own eyes off her, the delicate curve of her calf, the effortless way she walked in the ridiculous heels, the womanly slope of waist and hip. He was in trouble and knew it. This girl had him in a sexual turmoil. He was panting after her like a sixteen-year-old, and he'd already made love to her more often than any time since his honeymoon with Vicki. Hell, more than that. He ought to be bored with her, ready to get rid of her now that he was satiated. But he was not.

He bought cones, chocolate for Timmy, vanilla for her. They moved ahead as he paid, but he was in no hurry to catch up. She had good posture, he saw, despite those heels. Yes, posture, the way she carries herself, is a very sexy thing in a girl. Joanna was sexy all right. There was a style, élan to her. Look at the way her hair bounced as she walked. God, you are in trouble, Kraft. What are you going to do with her? Ask her to move in, live on peanut butter sandwiches, stand around bored stiff as Vicki had become while you work? Have you some tremendous yen for complications in your life? He saw her stick out a tiny, pink sliver of tongue and lick her ice cream cone. The sight wounded him.

Was it all sex? There was surely that. Never had he known anyone in bed like her. Vicki had been accommodating, even good, but this girl. God, what a turnon. What she did to him with her hands, her mouth, her body. And more than once. That's what got him. Vicki had been easily satisfied. Content, she had made him content. But this girl. Why did she seem to need it so? Was it just sex between them? He hoped so, because that was an eminently curable condition. It would go away in time. But watching her with Timmy, the natural, confidential way she had with him, he was not so sure. And his doubt worsened as he realized her beauty, style, natural reserve and grace appealed to the artist in him. Why the hell hadn't he become a plumber?

"Timmy wants to see the seals. I do, too."

"Okay, maybe they'll teach him to swim."

"I already know how, Daddy. Joanna taught me."

At the restaurant, she said she had to go back to Westport soon.

"Do you have to, Joanna? I want you to stay."

"I don't want to go either, Timmy, but—" she looked at Hank for assistance.

He had none. "Does there have to be a but? I could get you up early in time for work."

In time for work. "I-I don't have to be there till noon."

"Now that's what I call a job."

"Then you'll stay. Goody."

She reluctantly smiled acquiescence and Hank said, "That's what I like about you, a woman of conviction, so hard to change her mind."

If only he knew. "That's me, hard as jelly."

But she had come to a conviction. She was going to tell Hank the truth about herself. As soon as Timmy was asleep, she would tell him. This had gone on long enough.

Back in the apartment, Timmy, bathed and in his pajamas, asked her to read to him. He appeared at the couch and snuggled up next to her. Hank, at his table, trying or pretending to work, said, "Not that one, Timmy."

"I like it, Daddy. Joanna wants to see it."

She opened it. A photograph album. To Hank she said, "Have you something to hide?"

He turned back to his work. "Everything."

Timmy flipped pages, providing a running commentary on the photos. "That's Daddy when he was little."

She saw a boy about ten, in a baseball uniform, very stiff in his pose, a wide boyish grin on his face. She looked up at Hank. "So you were a baseball player."

"Yes, held the strikeout record in Little League, at bat eight times, struck out eight times. I only did it one year."

"You should have kept at it. Who knows? You might have been Joe Dimaggio."

"And you might have been Mrs. Robinson."

"That's Mommie."

She saw a snapshot of a slender, dark-haired woman in her late teens or early twenties.

"That's Mommie and Daddy at the beach before I was born."

She saw a young couple, the girl pregnant, Hank clowning, patting her stomach. Suddenly she had a feeling of invading privacy. She didn't want to see these photos. "Your mother's very pretty. She looks like you."

"No she doesn't. I look like her."

She avoided looking up at Hank, even though she knew he was watching her. "Could be. Let's see some pictures of you."

She did, forcing herself to give it a few minutes more, then tucked Timmy in bed.

When she returned, Hank said, "I tried to stop you from looking at that."

She smiled. "It was all right. It's just—you know, other lives, other times. You feel a little like a voyeur. That's silly of course." She had gone to stand beside him, her arm around his shoulder. She bent and kissed him lightly. "Does duty call? Or can we sit on the couch again and talk. I like that."

"I was afraid you'd never ask."

He turned down the lights, put on music and made drinks as before. And again they sat quietly for a time, enjoying warmth and nearness. Finally, she spoke. "Hank, this is all impossible."

"What is?"

"You and me, us."

"Is it?"

"Yes, you know nothing about me. Being a mystery woman was fun, but it has gone on long enough. There is something I must tell you."

"What d'you mean, I know nothing about you? I know a great deal—"

"Be serious, Hank."

"I am serious. You are twenty-five years old. Your name is Joanna Caldwell, which was your maiden name. You are divorced from a jock named Forbes."

"I told you all that."

"I know you did. You were born and raised in Zanesville, Ohio." He hesitated. "Zanesville, Ohio. Let's see. Small city, not over fifty thousand, I'd guess, nice place out in the Heartland of America, a regular depository of the eternal American verities. It's in the Bible Belt, isn't it?''

"Stop it, Hank.''

"You're an only child, or from a very small family. Your folks were—well, I don't know what they did, but they were busy. They loved you, but they were strict with you and, oh, sort of distant. Your father was particularly undemonstrative with you. I'd guess he was a small businessman, maybe a lawyer or doctor.''

She moved away from him and twisted herself to look at him, a most startled expression on her face.

"You were shy, withdrawn. You went to church regularly, but you spent most of that time daydreaming. You were very skinny, not much to look at.''

Finally, she was able to speak. "How do you know all that? My father is a minister, a Pentecostal preacher, Assembly of God.''

"And he disapproves of you now, the way you are.''

"Yes.''

"You weren't popular in school. You matured late and none of the guys would look at you and you were scared to death when they finally did. You were a good student, straight A's most likely.''

"Do you do palms and tea leaves? How do you know all this?''

"It's not hard. Everybody's lives are pretty much the same. Besides, an artist is paid to have insights.'' He hesitated, making use of the new information. "You went off to Ohio State. That made your father angry. It was a place of evil to him. He wanted you to go to Oral Roberts or some Bible college. But you were rebellious. There was a big world out there. You were scared of it, but still fascinated.''

"God, Hank, this is unreal.''

He smiled. "At the university some prof, taught

psychology most likely, brought you out of your shell, made you feel beautiful, talked to you about developing your potential. You went to bed with him.''

"No I didn't."

"But I bet he wanted to, tried hard."

"I suppose he wanted to."

"You forced yourself into athletics. Oh, yes, you tried out for cheerleader and were surprised when you were selected.''

"I'd always been athletic. It was one of my biggest quarrels with my parents.''

"Of course, I should have figured that. Anyway, as a cheerleader, all bouncy and pert, you attracted your jock Forbes. He was big man on campus. You were flattered. He finally married you. But you didn't live happily ever after.'' He leaned forward and kissed her lightly. "And for that I am most glad.''

"How can you know all this? You're awfully close to the truth.''

"It figures. How do I know? I'm just guessing, of course.''

"It's too good a guess. You're clairvoyant.''

"No. I can't explain it. You're with a person, you detect qualities about them. It isn't hard to guess the roots of these qualities. Want an example?''

"Yes.''

"Okay. You're a nice girl, really nice, with essentially decent values. You're generous, a giver. You reach out to people. You really want to help them. If you told me you were a nurse, I wouldn't be surprised. Despite everything, you're really a bit prim. Promiscuous is the last thing you are. Oh, I don't know, it's hard to explain. You're not prudish—oh hell, why don't I just say it? You really don't want to make love with me. It bothers you, but you do it—and so damnably well. It's as though you somehow need to, rather than really want to—deep down inside. Want and need are awfully close, but not quite the same thing." He saw her staring at him, mouth open, unable to speak. "You need me. You try to be modern about it all, but deep down a smalltown Pentecostal preacher's daughter can't quite accept it."

And then he saw the tears well in her eyes. He put his arm around her and sheltered her cheek against his shoulder. "See, I know an awful lot about you. You're no mystery woman to me."

"Oh God, Hank, you don't know. You—"

"Sh-h." And he silenced her with his lips, feeling again the saltiness of her tears and, again too, her sudden surge of passion. Before he led her into the bedroom, he whispered, "Preacher's daughter, it strikes me that it is difficult for anything so good to be too wrong."

"But it is wrong. You don't know—"

"Sh-h." He put his finger over her lips. "I just want you to know it has never been sex between you and me. If there is any such thing as lovemaking, then that's what we do."

Laura was waiting in the lobby of his apartment house Sunday night when Dr. Charles Randall entered. She stood up, her eyes fixed on him expectantly. He looked at her, then away. Finally, reluctantly, he met her gaze. "We need to talk, Charles."

His mouth firm, turned down, he nodded. "Yes."

He led the way to the elevator and she followed. They rode upwards in silence, her mind a cesspool of despair. With ingrained courtesy, he let her step from the elevator first. It was the same after he unlocked his apartment door. A step behind her, he flicked a switch lighting the large, familiar room. He walked past her.

She remained near the door, her body rigid, staring at his back.

"Would you like a drink?"

"I suppose." She remained there, clutching her purse, eyes wide, soaking up every nuance of his behavior. He wouldn't even look at her. He went to his bar and bent over the bottles. *Oh God*! "Who is she, Charles?"

The stony silence was finally broken. "Who is who?"

"The other woman. The one who's made you this way."

He turned and looked at her. "What're you talking about?"

"You met her in San Francisco, didn't you?"

He could only stare at her in disbelief.

"Didn't you?" Her voice was more strident now. "The least you can do is tell me something about her, give me some chance to fight back. What does she look like? Is she blonde? Redhead? Good figure?"

His anger broke through, enabling him to speak. "I don't believe you."

"Has she got big bosoms? Is she better in bed than I am?"

"Honest to God, you're *unreal*."

"Tell me *something* about her. It's an act of human kindness. Give me a chance."

He was moving toward her now, his anger flaring. He was only partially aware he was losing his temper. It hadn't happened for years, not since he was a child. "Jesus Christ, but you're something else. You come in here, accusing me of. . .of having another woman, when all the while it's you who— I don't believe it, Laura. You're unreal."

Staring, eyes wide, she heard him now. "What're you saying?"

"Don't pretend you don't know. You sleep with that

s.o.b. Then you come here accusing me. God, Laura—it's unbelievable.''

His language, his rage shocked her. "What. . .what are you saying?''

"I'm saying Lambert. You and him. How could you, Laura?''

He might as well have hit her. His words were like physical blows, knocking the breath out of her, causing pain. "I—I don't know what you're—''

"Don't give me that. Don't lie. Don't pretend.''

"But—'' It was the only sound she could get out.

"He called me in San Francisco. The s.o.b. wanted to congratulate me on my engagement.''

"He didn't!''

"Told me what a hot number you were. Bragged about. . .about fucking you.''

A long, low sound came out of her, half wail, half groan. "Oh, Charles, *God*! Please.''

"You've got your gall, accusing me, after you and he—''

"He didn't *say* that.'' She screamed the words at him.

"Of course the bastard didn't. He's too slick for that. He said you were his *patient*.'' The word was immersed in sarcasm. "He *treated* you. TREATED. That's the same as *fucking*, isn't it?''

"Charles, I—''

"ISN'T IT? Isn't it all the same thing?''

She could only stand there, eyes closed against his hatred, her face, her whole body beginning to crumble.

"How could you, Laura? I believed in you. I loved you. Then you went and—''

Another wail was rent from her. "Oh God, Charles. You don't understand. It wasn't like that. It wasn't. . .that word, what you said. It wasn't—''

"Exactly what was it, Laura?'' The words had a

savage, whiplike quality to them.

She stood there, sucking in air, chest rising and falling, trying to gain control of her mind. "After. . .after Ralph died, I was—I went. . . . Oh God, Charles, this is so *awful*."

Scorn rose in him. "I'll bet it was awful."

Again she tried, feeling as though she was teetering on the edge of a precipice, a terrible pit below. "I was frigid. For twenty years I was frigid. I had a horrible marriage. I—"

"So you went to see the good Dr. Lambert and he fixed you right up, made you as good as new, showed you what you had been missing all those years, made a new woman out of you, showed you how to FUCK."

"God!" She bent over, covering her face with her hands, trying to blot out his face, still his horrid words. In a moment she could say against her hands, her voice muffled, "It wasn't like that."

"It wasn't? Then tell me what it was like. You owe it to medical science to tell just what sort of *doctoring* that sonofabitch does."

Slowly she removed her hands from her face and stood up, looking at him. She wanted to tell him, explain, but no words would come out her open mouth.

"Go on, tell me all about it. He did *fuck* you, didn't he?" He was using the word like a club, beating her with it.

"God! PLEASE! Stop using that word."

He wheeled and went back to the bar and hurriedly poured himself a drink, whiskey neat, which he rarely drank. He turned back to her, his voice calmer. "I think it's the only word for it, Laura."

His actions had given her a respite. She gained some coherence. "I was ill, Charles. I was frigid. I'd never been able to do it. I needed help. I went to him. He's a doctor. What is so wrong with it?''

"Everything is wrong with it."

"But Charles, you're a doctor. You must understand."

His effort at self-control gave way before his anger. "I'll tell you what I understand. I understand there is no branch of medicine known as fucking. I understand the birds and the bees do it without any help from that goddamned quack. I understand even human beings manage without him—so much so we have an overpopulation problem. But you. You have to go to him to find out how to do it."

She could only stare at him now, defeated, bereft of thought or even feeling.

"How much did he charge you?"

She could only shake her head.

"He didn't charge you? Free medical care? You were a charity patient? I'll bet my ass."

Still she shook her head, gasping for breath now.

Abruptly he stopped. He raised his glass and drained it, shuddering against the sharp taste of the whiskey. For a moment he looked at the glass, squeezing his fingers around it. "You'd better go, Laura. I don't want to say any more."

She remained near the door, lost, bewildered. From some primitive place in her mind came words. "I thought you loved me."

"I did."

"You wanted to marry me."

"Yes."

"You knew I wasn't a virgin. I was married before."

"I knew that, yes. And it didn't matter." Again he looked at the glass, rolling it within his fingers. "I'm sorry. Lambert matters. I hate the bastard. I hate everything he does. He's a fraud. He ought to be locked up."

"I didn't know, Charles."

There was sorrow in his voice when he said, "I suppose you didn't. But you did go to him. You let him touch you. You let him put—" He pulled back his arm and threw the glass against the wall, shattering it. "After him? Never. My skin crawls at the thought of it."

Joanna awakened with a start, suddenly aware it was Monday. She opened her eyes and looked at her watch. Nine-thirty. Lord, she'd better get going. She slipped on Hank's robe and left the bedroom. The apartment was empty. Then she remembered. Hank had said he'd be taking Timmy to day nursery. He needed friends his own age.

Minutes later when she threw back the shower curtain and stepped from the tub to the bathmat, Hank was standing in the doorway looking at her. "Forgive me," he said, his voice a little husky, "if this is too big an invasion of your privacy."

She brought the towel to her face to dry it, not answering.

In a moment he was taking the towel from her, beginning to dry her. "God, but you're beautiful, Joanna."

"Don't rub, pat."

He dried her shoulders and arms, breasts, the rest of her torso, her back. She could hear his aroused breathing. When he knelt to dry her legs, she said, "This is impossible, Hank, all impossible."

"It is hard to believe. In all my life I've never been such a satyr."

He finished her toes, left foot then right, and hung the towel over the shower curtain. He held out the robe for her to slip her arms into. "Here's your modesty back."

"I'm not talking just about sex, Hank. There's—"

"Go get dressed. I'll warm the coffee."

She sighed, but obeyed, putting on the pants suit she'd worn an eon ago when she first came there. When she came into the kitchen, he reached to her. It seemed to him he was forever reacting to her. There was something about the suit, hard to describe, a sense of nakedness, although she was certainly well covered. He guessed it was his awareness she had nothing, no blouse, no bra, beneath the suit jacket. Lord, Kraft. You are sick, man, actually ill.

He handed her the cup and she stood there, leaning against the sink, sipping it, obviously keeping distance from where he sat in the chair. He sensed her impatience to be gone. The weekend was over. An idyll had been replaced by a week of work, affairs, business, humdrum, the ordinary. He understood. He had to get busy, too.

"I know you have to leave. I understand that. But can you understand I hate to see you go. It's difficult to let you." He saw her nod imperceptibly, her eyes on the cup held in both hands. "I have to see you again, Joanna. Can we do something together next weekend?"

He saw her revolve the coffee mug between her fingers. Then that movement stopped and her knuckles went white. "Hank, it's impossible. I shouldn't have come this weekend. I'm not being fair to you—to myself."

Suddenly she sat down the coffee, spilling some of it on the counter, snatched up her purse and ran out of the apartment. He sat there, brooding, too depressed even to drink his coffee.

He heard the buzzer for the front door. He arose and pressed the button. "Hank, open the door. Let me come up." He did, then opened the door to his apartment, hearing her feet rapid on the steps as she ran up them.

In a moment she was in the doorway, a little winded. He handed her a sack. "You forgot your new dress and shoes." She took it. "And that sexy bathing suit. Don't know how you got into it."

She nodded thanks.

They stood there a moment, her breathing quickly returning to normal. "Hank, I work for the Center for Human Potential in Westport."

"Whatever that is."

"It's a sex clinic, Hank. People come there who have problems doing it, married couples mostly. They need help."

"I know. Masters and Johnson. So?"

She forced herself to look at him, meeting his gaze. "Some patients are unmarried men." She felt herself shaking. "I'm a surrogate partner for them. I go to bed with men to help with their. . .their. . ." She swallowed hard. "Their sexual inadequacies." She saw him blink, once, twice. He was hearing her. "Last week I had two patients. One was a premature ejaculator. He was new. For two weeks I've also had a bad case of primary impotence. I-I worked very hard with him. He was finally able—"

She stopped, unable to say more. She couldn't help it. Her face began to screw up. She tried, but she couldn't hold back the tears. Choking, almost convulsive with sobs, she cried, "You see why it's impossible. Maybe you. . .you think you could. . .could live with it." She gasped, trying to hold on to air. "But could Timmy?"

Then she was gone, running down the stairs.

18

The couple across the desk from Dawson Lambert could not have been more routine, thirties, married nine years, two children, boy and girl. She was slender, attractive, well made up, attired with a certain flair. Her husband was also attractive, quite trim—golf or tennis, Lambert guessed—and Madison Avenue modish. Lambert glanced at the file folder on his desk. Yes, advertising, Young and Rubicam.

So typical, an attractive young couple, admired by their friends, living in a split-level in New Jersey, probably in hock up to their eyebrows to support the great American idea of having made it. But there was trouble in fantasy land. She was frigid. In nine years of marriage and probably a year of effort before that she had been orgasmic precisely twice, both times after cocktail parties. Twenty years ago, maybe only ten or even five, neither one would have thought much about it. But word had gotten out. She was supposed to enjoy sex. The big bang at the climax. She wanted everything that was supposed to happen to her as a woman. He wanted to feel he was a good lover. Welcome to the Center for Human Potential.

All this had flitted through Lambert's mind several minutes before. In truth he wasn't listening to them now, although a little green man from outer space with telepathic powers would have had difficulty knowing that, the way he looked at them, nodding his head in encouragement. They were relating a history of their marriage. Met at Swarthmore, didn't like each other at first, but, after the prom. . . . Garbage. All garbage.

His mind was on the telephone or, more accurately, Laura McGovern. He'd tried to phone her last evening, then again this morning. No answer. He had not thought too much of it last night, but this morning it was beginning to prey on his mind. He wasn't worried or anything. Mostly he was eager. Timing was everything in these cases.

Lambert felt sure he could visualize what happened. Randall had given her holy hell. The prig really laid it to her. There would be tears by the bucketful. Laura would go off into a blue funk of monumental proportions. That's why he wanted to talk to her. Now, the sooner the better, he had to give her the tea and sympathy bit, cheer her up, tell her what a shit Randall was anyway, let her know who her real friends were. Why didn't she answer the phone? Where had she gone?

"And so we came here, Doctor, hoping to make our marriage even better."

Lambert saw Mary Ann Pendleton reach out and pat James Pendleton's hand. How touching. "I have no doubt you'll be very glad you did, no doubt at all." He smiled his reassuring best and folded his fingers together over his desk top. "The problem you two have is quite common in marriage. I think it is important that you understand at the outset that you are not alone, not unusual in any way. You are simply intelligent in seeking a solution to what is a minor difficulty."

He saw the intense expression on their faces. They were eager for more pearls of wisdom. He had an abundance and slid into a much practiced discourse.

"As I tried to say in my book *In Search of Eros*—I encourage you to read it, if you haven't already."

"We have, both of us, every word. It's so wonderful."

What a nice lady. Sales had been dropping. "Then you know what I'm about to suggest. Coitus may be a simple exercise, yet there are certain difficulties. Complete success depends on intimate communication, much of it nonverbal, perceptions two human beings have of each other, mood, opportunity, the physical setting, thought, concentration, physical well-being and much, much more." He smiled. "When you think of all that can go wrong, the distractions, the human errors, it is only amazing sexual intercourse is as successful as often as it is. Indeed, there are those—Desmond Morris to name one, who believe coitus was made difficult to aid in creation of a lifelong pair bond, necessary of course for the care of offspring. A human child takes eighteen years to reach full maturity."

"That long?" It was Pendleton speaking.

"Yes, the body, certainly the brain remains in a state of growth, maturation at least that long." Lambert hesitated, as if waiting for questions, of which there were none. "Consider the difficulties. Two people of differing backgrounds and attitudes come together for sexual intercourse. You two went to college together. Your backgrounds may seem casually similar, but they are not. You grew up in different households geographically separated. You had different parents, a whole different environment." He chuckled. "At the very least you are a man and a woman—and, as the French say, *vive le difference*. Do you get what I'm trying to say? It is sometimes extraordinarily difficult for two people from radically different backgrounds, possessed of perhaps radically different physical, mental and emotional sets to suddenly declare they are going to have sexual intercourse and have that act be totally rewarding to both. It is unlikely for it to happen all the time. And it doesn't. Do you understand?''

They both spoke as one, she, "Yes, of course," and Pendelton, "We do."

"It is often people like yourself, intelligent, educated and aware, persons who are accustomed to success in all their activities who often have the most difficulties in sexual intercourse." He looked at their somber faces. "But enough. With your cooperation, we'll try to help you. No doubt it will be successful and rewarding for you both."

"What happens now?"

"Mr. Pendleton, I was just about to say that. I'm going to send you away with Miss Cromwell and Mr. Simms, two of our better counselors. They will take your history individually and then together. Later on today I will do a physical exam. I doubt if there is any problem, but we need to be certain, Mrs. Pendleton, there is no physical cause for your orgasmic difficulties, such as any sort of physical abnormality in your genital area, any vaginismus to make entry by your husband difficult or any dyspareunia that makes intercourse painful. Do you experience particular pain?''

"No, I-I—"

"Well, that's good." He smiled. "We'll check you out in any event." Now he chuckled. "We need to make sure the old plumbing is in good working order, no infection, that sort of thing." He pushed a button on his intercom, summoned his secretary and stood up. Conference over. Goodbye, Pendletons. At once he picked up the phone.

Unfamiliar with Manhattan, upset over Hank, Joanna missed the turn off the East Side Highway on to the Triborough Bridge and got lost. By the time she found her way back to the bridge, made the turn to Connecticut, she had wasted a half hour. There was no time to go home, and she went directly to her office.

There was a message that Lambert wanted to see her at four-thirty or whenever she was free. Good. She had to talk to him about Wofford. Memories of the Friday fiasco came back the moment she entered her office. How had it happened? Such a mess.

On the long drive to Connecticut she had gradually come to grips with her problem with Hank Kraft. Probably she should not have blurted the truth that way. There had to have been a better way, easier for him to take. But he wouldn't let her. She tried Sunday night, at least one other time, but no. He didn't want to know. He wouldn't let her.

It had to be. The charade couldn't go on. She couldn't let him fall in love with her. She couldn't go on, getting more and more involved with him. Yes, it was better this way, better for all. There was pain, yes, but it wouldn't last long. Better now than the suffering they were capable of inflicting on each other if the relationship continued. It was her fault. She shouldn't have gone. Never should have.

Joanna had calmed down, but she was still in no shape for Brad Dillon when he arrived. She wanted to be, and she tried. It wasn't fair to him to have her be so grim, withdrawn and depressed. But her efforts at cheerfulness and enthusiasm were mostly pathetic. The last thing she felt like doing was taking off her clothes and getting into bed with a man, any man, even one as handsome as. . . Lord, she and Hank had done it a lot. She hadn't known it was possible to—

"I'm fine, Brad, really."

"Forgive me, darling, but as they say in bad movies, you look used."

She saw him smiling. "I'm not sure I like that kind of

compliment.''

''Now who's being phony? It was not meant to be a compliment. You're still upset about something. That creep on Friday?''

''No—well, I—''

''What was that all about?''

''I don't think, really Brad, I've any right to go into it with you.''

He shrugged. ''Okay, I won't say a word.'' Suddenly he reached out and put cool fingers to her face, cupping her chin. ''I find myself thinking a lot about you. Been a long time since I had a girl on my mind so much.''

''Please, Brad, don't.''

''I don't like seeing you upset. For two cents, I'd quit this. It's too hard on you. You obviously don't like doing it.''

''Please, please.'' She took his hand from her chin so she could talk, then held it in both of hers. ''It's not you. It's nothing to do with you. It's not your fault. It's me. I had—'' She sighed. ''It was a bad weekend, that's all—oh, not really bad.'' Another sigh. ''I can't explain.''

''You don't have to, Joanna.'' He pulled his hand away. ''Do you want to call this off today?''

''No I don't want to do that.'' She stared at him. She sensed he was trying to help her. Ordinarily, she would have appreciated that, but not now, not after. . . . ''Brad, you are a very nice person, really thoughtful, very considerate. But, please, don't get involved with me. Don't think about me except when we're together. Don't—''

''That isn't easy to do.''

''But you must. The fellow who was here Friday. He's a patient. I've been seeing him. . .I was helping him, but. . .but he got emotionally involved with me. He came here—he wasn't supposed to come then, not till four-thirty. He saw you." She spread her hands, a gesture of desperation, a reaching out for help. "He became upset, very upset. It was a difficult scene." She stared at him. "Do you understand? Don't get involved with me. You're a patient, I'm—"

"I know. I thought maybe there was someone else—after me."

"Does that bother you?"

He shrugged. "I dunno, maybe." Then he smiled. "But it shouldn't. You do what you do—and very well. I hereby promise not to get—what's your term?"

"Emotionally involved."

"Never that." He grinned. "And I won't fall in love with you either. Your life is tough enough as it is."

"Thank you." She reached up and pecked at his cheek, but merely brushing it. "And don't make it worse than it is. The other fellow's gone now. I've just you. It'll be easier." She smiled. "You have my undivided attention." She began to unbutton her jacket. "I do want to help you, Brad. It's not all work, you know."

All things considered the session went well. Brad Dillon exhibited considerable control over ejaculation, even during intromission and containment.

Dawson Lambert greeted her cordially and motioned her to a seat. "I had a most unwelcome visitor at my home yesterday evening. Wofford."

"Lord!"

"That was very much my feeling. Want to tell me what happened?"

She sighed. "It happened again. The operation was a success, but the patient died."

"This is serious, Joanna. So am I."

She saw the severity in his face, his voice. "I'm not trying to be funny, Doctor. I was successful with

Wofford, more than I ever hoped. He was orgasmic on Tuesday, Wednesday and Thursday.''

"After intromission.''

"Yes.'' She saw his eyebrow raise in surprise. "I was surprised, too. Perhaps the success of treatment had something to do with what happened.''

"Which was?''

"I'm coming to it. I recognized that Jerry, I mean Wofford was becoming emotionally involved with me. I did everything I could to discourage him. But I also worried about losing him just at the point of success. It was a most difficult situation.'' She waited for him to say he recognized her problem. He said nothing. "He came to my home Thursday night.''

"Your house? You gave him your address?''

"Of course not. He had been following me for days. I hadn't realized it—oh, that's not quite true. I'd run into him, but I thought it was just an accident. I couldn't believe he would follow me.''

"He came to your house?''

"Yes. He'd been asking me out and I'd given excuses, said I was busy, that sort of thing. He arrived with food, Chinese food I think, and wine. I became, well, very upset. I told him it was an intolerable invasion of my privacy. I asked him to leave. It was difficult to get him to go. I guess words were said. I don't remember.''

Lambert waited, watching her, then he prodded her. "Go on.''

"He came to my office, quite early—over an hour early. He forced his way in.'' She hesitated, visions of the scene playing with her mind. "I was still with Dillon. He saw him.'' She sighed. "I'm sorry, but it was nasty.''

"He confronted Dillon?''

She saw the alarm in his face and heard it in his voice. "He saw him, but they did not speak. I wouldn't call it a confrontation.''

"Did he recognize Dillon?"

"I don't think so."

He sighed and shook his head. "What happened then?"

Joanna sucked in her breath, holding it, finally exhaling it slowly. "Wofford was most upset. He became angry. His language became most abusive. He called me a whore."

"He didn't."

"Much worse. He seemed to feel he'd paid a lot of money for me. Ten thousand dollars, he said. He objected to taking what he called seconds."

"Did he say ten thousand?" Lambert laughed. "If only it were true."

"That's what he said. He repeated it."

Again the laugh. "Obviously, he was as upset as you say, running off at the mouth." He laughed a moment longer than became serious, studying her closely. "It must have been difficult for you."

"Very." She bit her lip. "I tried to call you. You were gone for the day. I'm sorry, Doctor, but I don't think it was my fault. I don't really know what I could have done differently."

He smiled, most expansively. "Of course you couldn't. And I didn't ask you in here to upbraid you in any way. I just wanted to know what happened. I appreciate your candor—and I'm sorry you had these difficulties."

Greatly relieved, her voice barely audible, she thanked him.

"You may not believe this, but Wofford gave me much the same story yesterday."

"Really?"

"He blames himself. He said he was a possessive, jealous fool. What he really wants is your forgiveness, but he's afraid to approach you."

"I think he might well be."

Lambert hesitated, raising a hand to stroke back the hair over his left ear. "There is a lesson to be learned from all this. Clearly, all your patients must be cautioned in the future against becoming emotionally involved with you. I thought I was doing that, but—apparently not enough. I take full responsibility for what happened."

"It seems to me some involvement is unavoidable."

"That's not so. It doesn't have to be that way. Certainly it doesn't have to get out of hand, as in this unfortunate incident. In any event, I explained to Wofford what he did was intolerable. He had no right to go to your home—or mine for that matter. All matters are to be attended to in regular business hours. And, under no circumstances would I tolerate him being abusive to you—or anyone else in my employ. I just will not have it."

"Thank you, Doctor."

"I think he understood. He is quite contrite." He hesitated. "He wants very much to see you—to apologize personally."

"It isn't necessary. I don't want to see him."

Lambert again sensed the rock and the hard place. Most everything he said to Joanna had been the truth. He had leaned heavily on Wofford, a broken man, really. The fool was hopelessly in love with her, and just because she was the first woman to get his rocks off. Heavens! He couldn't face a new day if she hated him. He had to see her, be with her. He knew it was wrong to fall in love with her, but what was he to do about it now? Oh, chances are he'd never gain her forgiveness, make her love him, but he had to try, he just had to. He'd happily pay another ten thousand if he could just have a few more times with her.

"Joanna, my dear." He fastened his most sincere gaze upon her. "Believe me, I understand your attitude. Quite agree with it in fact. But such feelings are sometimes a luxury you and I cannot allow ourselves."

"What d'you mean?"

He sighed, shook his head as though it were a great weight and smiled his fondest. "I've told you again and again, Joanna, what you do is surely the practice of medicine. And you know I mean every word of it. In medicine, my dear, the patient and his welfare comes ahead of everything else, our needs, our feelings, even our time and comfort. Lord knows how many times I've gotten up at four a.m. to deliver a baby." His smile was positively sacrificial. "I'm trying to say, Joanna, your feelings about Wofford is my feeling. We both understand it. But is it best for Wofford? We do have to think of him. You treated him. You came such a long way with him. It would be, well, a sin to. . .to let him lapse back into impotence."

"You don't mean?"

"I'm afraid I do. That's exactly what will happen to him."

That's not what she meant at all. "You mean, you want me—" She looked at him, feeling dismay, almost horror. She had intended a question. Then she knew it wasn't even a question to him. "God, Doctor, you can't expect. . .you can't ask me to. . ." Clearly he did. "Not after what happened, what he said, after. . . ."

She looked away from him, down at her hands.

He let the silence hang there. "Of course, Joanna, if you insist—heavens, there's no way I'd force you to do anything. You know that. But I must ask. Are you prepared to just throw away this man, discard him again on the junkheap of life? Will you be able to live with yourself if you do?"

"It ought to be someone else. It would be better if it wasn't me."

"Hardly, Joanna. You must see that." He paused, looking at the top of her head. She seemed so small, delicate, vulnerable. He shrugged. "I think only a couple times will do it. It needn't be much." He chuckled. "Look at it as letting him down easy. You must have broken off a romance or two in your time."

She hadn't. Or had she? An image of Hank, her last minute with him, came to her.

"He's in my dining room. Why don't you talk to him. Hear his apology. You owe him that much, at least. If you still don't want to see him again, so be it. Is that too much to ask?"

She looked at him, his handsome face, his eyes so gentle and fatherly. She had seen him like this so many times. She was being enmeshed by him, ensnared, being pulled into a pit, unable to help herself. No! She wasn't going to let it happen. She pursed her lips and looked at Lambert levelly. "I think you're wrong, Doctor—very wrong."

"About what?"

"Wofford. I think it would be a gross mistake for me to attempt to treat him further." She hesitated, waiting for him to argue with her. He didn't. "Our relationship has sunk to a point of—where it's impossible. Too much has happened. Too much has been said. I can't stand the sight of him. His seeing me will only exacerbate his feelings about me. It would be a disaster, a total mistake. You are wrong to ask me to do it."

He just sat there, eyes fixed on hers. It seemed to go on a long time. "Okay. Perhaps you're right." He swiveled in his chair, his hand on his console. "But I think you should tell him that yourself. You at least owe the man a chance to apologize."

Then, at once, the door to the dining room was open. He was giving her no choice in the matter. As she stood up and walked toward the sunny room, she did not see Lambert smiling in triumph behind her.

The Jerry Wofford she went in to see was a familiar one, nervous, frightened, defeated. "Lord, Joanna," he cried, his voice choking, "thank you, thank you."

She said nothing.

"I don't know what I'd have done if you hadn't come in here. I have hardly slept. I—oh, Joanna, I'm so sorry. How can I tell you? Please forgive me. I didn't mean a word of it, not a word."

There was a lot more of it. He fell just short of falling to his knees and begging. He promised never to come to her house again. He swore he would not become emotionally involved. If only. . .if only she'd help him again.

Nothing in Joanna's life had prepared her to deny forgiveness, while everything in her life had prepared her to help those in need. She looked at him, shaking her head repeatedly in sadness. How could this have happened?

"Don't say no, Joanna. At least see me. At least talk to me."

She sighed. "All right. I guess we should talk. Perhaps I can convince you all this is a mistake."

He brightened at once. "Yes, yes, we'll just talk. That's all we'll do."

Her sigh was deeper now. "All right, Jerry. Come to my office tomorrow—usual time."

She did not have a pleasant evening. Hank called, saying he had to talk to her. She suspected the call might be from him. She didn't even say "Hello" when she answered. She hung up without ever uttering a syllable.

19

He was there, waiting for her, when she returned from running on the beach. She saw him from a distance, knew who he was. She wanted to stop, stay away, run somewhere else, hide, anything not to see him. But there was nothing to do but face Hank Kraft.

Panting, sweat gleaming on her face, streaming down her skin inside her sweat suit, she ran up to the apartment house entrance. "I have to talk to you, Joanna. You must listen to me." She heard the earnestness in his voice and she glanced at him, just fleetingly, then turned and went inside. He followed. She could not stop him.

She ran up the stairs, fast, and it finished off the last of her wind. She stood in the living room, not far from the kitchen, bent over, hands on her knees, desperate for breath, then in a moment, she went into the kitchen and poured a glass of orange juice. She did not offer him any. She did not want to see Hank Kraft. With great difficulty she had mustered the courage to finally tell him the truth about herself. She couldn't go through it again. She just couldn't. He had no right to ask it of her.

Carrying the orange juice, she went back into the living room, opening the zipper of her damp jacket a little. She longed to take it off, to feel cool, but she had worn nothing underneath.

He simply stood there, just inside the door, grossly uncomfortable, an unwanted intruder. "Aren't you going to say anything, Joanna?" He saw her chest rise and fall, the glass tilt to her lips. "All right. Have it your way. But I drove up here to tell you something, and I'm going to—regardless of how difficult you make it for me." He hesitated, hoping for encouragement. There was none. She wouldn't even look at him. He was a non-person.

Hank sighed, trying to relax. He had rehearsed what he wanted to say so many times, last night, on the drive up here. If he just said it, everything would be all right. He knew that. He wanted to believe that.

"I learned something about myself, Joanna—all day yesterday, last night. When you blurted out to me what you do, that you're a. . .a surrogate partner, I was—I'll admit it, I was hurt. The idea of you. . .in bed with guys. . .doing—yeah, I found it tough to take. You knew I would. That's why you laid it on me like you did. Anything to get rid of dumb old Hank Kraft. It almost worked—but not quite." He hesitated, looking for a sign she was listening. Nothing, just a tipped glass, blue eyes turned away, focusing on nothing. "I went to the library yesterday. The New York Public Library is a disaster. Files are a mess, half the books stolen. So I went down to Brentanos and bought the books, the one your guy Lambert wrote. What a chunk of baloney that is. I also bought Masters and Johnson. *Human Sexual Inadequacy.* I read it, at least the pertinent parts. That didn't help. Not much at all it didn't. The drawings, the descriptions. . .what you do as a surrogate partner. It wasn't easy to know, think about. . .visualize. . .you, them. . . . I had a bad afternoon." He smiled, even though she didn't see it. "The ugly green monster, no doubt of that."

He hesitated. "It would make it easier, Joanna, if you could bring yourself to at least look at me so I know you're listening." He waited. She busied her hands with the glass. She would not look at him. "Okay, so be it." He sighed. "I said I learned something about myself. I did. Last night. I learned I'm a big boy now. I may even be growing up a little. Joanna, I got over my jealousy or whatever it was. I can understand, really I can, the need for a surrogate partner. These men are in a Catch-22 situation. Because of impotency or whatever, they can't get a wife or partner who cares about them. Without a partner they can't get cured of their sexual problem. The only answer is a surrogate partner—someone like you. I can understand it. Really I can."

She looked at him for the first time, head high, gaze distant, as though he were a curiosity, some event noted within her range of vision, but unworthy of interest, emotion or reaction. She didn't want to hear any of this. She didn't know why. Her mind hadn't functioned that much. All she knew was his words were intolerable to her.

"Do you remember my telling you you were a giver, a compassionate person, a helper?" He smiled. "I said something about your being a nurse. That's pretty good, really. I was awfully close to the mark. Being a surrogate partner is sort of like being a nurse. And. . .and I've no doubt you're damn good at it."

Her mouth came open then, small, round, silent for a moment as the left cortex of her brain, always rational, problem solving, flashed a warning. But it was so fleeting, in milliseconds overridden by the impulsive, intuitive right hemisphere, and the words came out, sharp, staccato. "Don't say that. Don't you dare say that." She turned quickly back to the kitchen and set the glass down hard. Again she wheeled and came back to him. "I don't need any of this, Hank. I don't need your approval. I don't need your *okay*. I don't give a damn whether you've grown up or not. Just go. Just GET OUT OF HERE!"

He stared at her in shock.

"This stinks, Hank. I won't have it. Coming here, smiling, telling me it's okay." She mocked him. "It's all right, Joanna. I understand. You're a nurse. I can understand." She shuddered under her anger. "You don't understand at all, you fool. I'm not a nurse. I'm a surrogate partner. I sleep with guys for money. There are other words. Use them. For God's sake use them. Don't stand there simpering, cowering. I don't want your approval."

His anger flared, too, but he was less verbal about it. His voice hardly rose. "You really are something else. You really are. Do you know what your anger really means?"

"I don't care what it means."

"You're ashamed of what you do. You really are."

"All right, all right, so I'm ashamed." She was shouting now. "Just get out and LEAVE ME ALONE."

"Why are you ashamed? Why do it if you are?"

"GET OUT!"

"Joanna, please listen to me. It's no work for a pentecostal preacher's daughter from Zanesville, Ohio."

"Take your damned pop psychology out of here. Go before I call somebody and have you thrown out."

He moved toward the door, even put his hand on the knob, then he turned back to her. "I don't understand you. Probably never will. But I never thought you were dumb. This whole operation here, this Center for Human whatever it is, smells, smells to high heaven. And you're being used. God, are you being used."

"So I'm being used. It's none of your business. Just open that door and WALK THROUGH IT!"

"In a second." He glared at her, so angry, yet his voice remained level, controlled. "Masters and Johnson recruited surrogate partners and used them, but nothing like you're used. The women were all volunteers. Masters and Johnson used her no more than once a year, sometimes not that often. How often are you used? Every month, every week, constantly? Didn't you say you had two men last week? What was it? Oh yeah, a premature ejaculator and. . .and a bad case of primary impotence. That's what you said, isn't it? Answer me. For once in your life face the truth—even a little."

He had silenced her. Her mouth was open, eyes wide. He was getting to her. "Two men at once. It's madness. And you don't have to have written a stupid book on sex to figure that out. Joanna, hate me if you want, throw me out and never speak to me, wallow in your shame all you want. But Jesus Christ, be a little honest. This guy Lambert is using you. He's making a high priced call girl out of you. You're being sold for a buck."

"Get out, Hank." Her voice was mostly growl, coming from deep inner rage.

"How long are you going to let Lambert use you? How long are you going to play the fool? Hate me if you want. Don't ever see me again. But, for God's sake, don't throw your own life away. Go back to school. Have a career. Anything. Just make something out of yourself. You can, you know?"

She did something she had never done in her life. She wheeled to the kitchen, picked up the half empty glass of orange juice and threw it at him. It missed, breaking and splattering against the door. But it had an effect. Hank Kraft left. In her rage she growled again and picked up a glass figurine to throw. She was able to restrain herself in time.

With his leaving, her rage subsided to anger, eventually to unquiet seething. She picked up the broken glass and wiped up the orange juice. Then, in a fit of domesticity, did her dishes, straightened the apartment and made her bed. All the while her mind provided a litany of outrage: he had no right, no right at all, to come here, offering soft, self-serving words. What a phony. He'd learned a lot. He was a better man for having known her. He understood. He forgave. What a hypocrite. Yes, a hypocrite, the biggest hypocrite in the universe. Who did he think he was? God? Hank Kraft, Godalmighty God. She didn't need him. She didn't need him at all.

She showered and began making up her face. But with difficulty. Her hand was shaking. Hank Kraft was no different from other men. Not a speck. They were all alike, vain, preening, so sure of their goddamned peckers. It was a word known to her, but rarely admitted to her mind. He figured he was so special. *You don't want me but you need me.* God, the conceit, the colossal conceit of the man. She didn't need him, and she sure as hell didn't want him. He was nothing special. There were others. He had offered her nothing she couldn't—. She looked at the barebreasted girl in the mirror. *Half the girls in tinsel town would trade their souls for your figure.* Yes, Hank Kraft offered nothing special to her. She didn't need him. No, not at all. She didn't need him and she didn't need his approval. Above all, she didn't need his advice. You can make something out of yourself. The gall of the man. *It's all right. I understand.* What was there to understand? She was a surrogate partner. She did what she did. She was good at it. She had just cured a case of primary impotence. Let Hank Kraft try that.

Brad Dillon immediately saw the change in her. She had always worn suit jackets, concealing blouses and such. She wore the tank top, the thin one, mostly straps, her sexiest piece of attire. He looked at it, at her. "I like. You look good." She smiled at him, then on tiptoes raised her mouth and kissed him. He felt the heat of it. "Wow," he said against her lips, then pulled her against him, hands on the bare skin of her back, the kiss deepening, her head turning to fill the contours of his lips.

They were still in her office, just inside the door.

At last he could speak. "Wow, I say again." Still holding her, his arms folded across her back, he moved his head back to bring her upturned face into focus. "I don't know what's come over you, but I've no complaint."

She smiled. "It occurred to me," she whispered, "I've not been fair to you. You must be awfully sick of that moody girl."

"I've hardly minded her."

She reached up and kissed him, but lightly this time. "Come," she said, "we've got work to do."

He released her. "Such a slavedriver you are."

In the treatment room, she slid his silk shirt back from his shoulders, letting it whisper to the floor. "Lord, but you have a beautiful body, Brad." She slid her hands over his upper arms, feeling the powerful muscles, his shoulders, chest. "Have I told you that?"

"No."

"It's true."

He trembled under her touch. "I hope your fingers are in good shape. You're going to need all your strength."

"I know." The words were barely audible.

He felt her breasts through her shirt, kneading, squeezing. "How does this thing come off?" His breath was already shortening.

She showed him, removing the offending garment, and they stood there, hands on each other's upper bodies, the skin of their fingers and palms sensitized, breath quickening, eyes devouring each curve of body, each place discovered by hand, feeling, as they looked again and again into each other's eyes, the wonder of discovery, the acceleration of desire.

He unfastened her shirt and pulled down her briefs, and she stepped from the folds at her ankle. "You're so beautiful, Joanna."

And she knew she was. She felt his arms extend, the caressing fingers at her waist, hips. Then they came around her, and she felt him lean forward as his hands found, were filled with her derriere. "Yes," she whispered, "and so are you." Her fingers fumbled with his belt, the fastener on his pants, the zipper. She felt his erection straining for escape. He took his hands from her, helping her, bending, skinning off the pants, stepping out of them. She held him in both her hands, testicles in her left, the immense penis in her right, her fingers barely encircling the barrel, sliding up, embracing the glans. She felt him jerk spasmodically, and she knelt and held it, hot, throbbing, against her cheek. "I lied to you," she whispered. "It is special. It feels so good inside me I can hardly bear it." Her fingers, spread beside the coronal ridge, thumb hard against the fenalum, she squeezed him back.

Then she stood up and they were in each other's arms, bodies pressed together, she on tiptoes, almost off her feet, his hands on her derriere, cupping, kneading, his risen organ filling the space between her thighs, their mouths creating one large oval cavern.

He turned, still holding her, then lowered her to the bed on her back. He spread her thighs and came atop her. "No," she said, "the other way."

"The hell with that. I want you this way."

She took his penis in both her hands, squeezing him back.

"Stop that. Let me. . ."

She stroked him, once, twice, twisted her fingers hard, rapidly around the glans, then guided him into her, gasping, crying from the pain of it, the pleasure of being stretched, filled to bursting. "Oh God, Brad, it's so good." She felt him trembling. "Raise up," she moaned, and he obeyed. Again she squeezed him back, then aroused him by rubbing his glans between her vulva and labia, again and again over her clitoris, feeling the throbbing heat of him. When she guided him back into her and felt him crash full length into her, she cried out from the ecstasy of it. "Go, baby, go," was uttered against her ear. And she obeyed, bending her legs, gripping him, thrusting hard against his thrusts. And it was all at once, his groan, gasp, the splatter of hot liquid inside her, the explosion of her own orgasm, like dynamite in an enclosed canyon, deafening, paralyzing, then followed by aftershocks, reverberating repeatedly off the walls. It seemed to go on the longest time before the last echo disappeared.

He was beside her on the bed, looking at her. "Lady, you are something else."

Her breath still came out in a long sigh, making a "whew" sound. Finally, she was able to smile at him. "Pretty good, huh."

And he smiled back. "Not bad. You really go, don't you?"

"Sometimes." She smoothed her hair back from her face, feeling the perspiration on it. "You were almost too quick, though."

"I didn't try to hold off. I figured you would be quick."

"I won't always be."

He bent and kissed her and she quickly felt her passion rise again. She reached down and felt his penis, now soft. "Can you come again?"

"I don't know. I'm not sure."

She squirmed away from him then and off the bed, holding her hand between her legs as she ran into the bathroom for a towel.

He lay on the bed, utterly relaxed, and heard the sound of toilet flushing, then water running. He closed his eyes. What a woman she was. It was the first time he had ever made it together with a girl. God, it had been nice. Then, far away, he felt his penis being lifted, then wetness, heat. He opened his eyes. She was washing him, carefully, thoroughly with a cloth. He jerked from the sensations, then he saw her throw the washcloth away. She smiled, bent over and took him in her mouth. He gasped from surprise as much as sensation.

It was not something she did often. She couldn't help it, fellatio smacked of perversion to her. She knew better, rationally, but she couldn't quite shake her gut reaction. She did it now, to him. She wasn't finished. She had more to prove to herself. She felt him rise, rapidly, monstrously, pushing her head up from him, filling her mouth, forcing her jaws wider. There was almost no room for her tongue to move. She slid him out, then in, repeated that, heard him gasp. One moan was particularly loud. She raised her head and released him, moving up, taking him inside in the lateral position, moving against him, slowly at first, then harder, wanting, not caring, demanding, ever harder, quicker, until, shatteringly, she came again, a prolongation of pleasure for her because he remained hard within her and she didn't have to stop shuddering, writhing, crying out until at last his cry, a great groan really, ended it for them both.

As soon as she reasonably could, she sent him away,

then lay across the bed, dressed in her robe, staring up at the ceiling. Never in her life had she felt so degraded, and she had done it to herself. She had come in here, dressed like a slut, and deliberately provoked a man, a man supposedly her patient, into servicing her. Atop everything else, she had risked her whole treatment of him. She was simply lucky it had gone as well as it had.

With clarity she remembered her actions, shaking her head in disbelief. It was the first time she'd ever done that. She'd had plenty of sex, God knows, but never had she provoked it, not even with Judd Forbes. But just now she'd wanted it, gotten it, then gone down on a man to get more.

Revulsion, self-loathing stabbed at her. What on earth was she doing? Hank. She'd been angry at him. Had she been showing him, proving something to him? That made no sense. He didn't even know about it. Was she proving something to herself? Look at me, turning on a handsome, he-man movie star with a big penis. See how great I am. It couldn't be. Yet, what else was it? *Oh my God*! She was proving her self-worth in bed.

She thought of herself as smiling in bitterness. But it was more a grimace. So how worthy are you? Not very much. Aloud she said, "Welcome to the pits. Would you like a guided tour?" *God*! "Young lady, you're in trouble. I hope you know that." *Damn Hank Kraft. Damn him*.

In time she got up, showered, dressed and was ready for Wofford when he came. It was grossly difficult for her. She didn't want to see him, and she was massively ill at ease. He was also, standing before her, looking down at his feet, avoiding her eyes.

"This is no good, Jerry." She said it softly, with all the sympathy she could muster. "You're cured. You proved that last week. All you need to do is go out, meet women, fall in love. Please do it, Jerry. You owe it to yourself—'' She smiled, even though he wasn't watching. "—and to them. Believe me, there is a Miss Right for you—and she'll be far better than I.''

"There's no one like you.''

She sighed. "Jerry, you don't love me. You just think you do.'' She saw him raise his head to protest. "And even if you do, I can never be more than just fond of you. It isn't enough, Jerry. Can't you see that?''

He shook his head, an emphatic negative.

"You're a very loving man, Jerry. Your problem has been that you confuse sex and love. The girl you married was a model. You thought her beautiful. You wanted her. But you didn't love her. Find a nice girl, Jerry, who loves you and whom you can love. It doesn't matter what she looks like. If there's love, you won't have any sexual problems, believe me.'' Something in her words nagged at her, a basic truth was there, trying to reach her consciousness. But there was no time.

"It can't be you?''

She sighed, then smiled. "I'm sorry.''

She saw his chest fill up, then gradually shrink as air was torturously exhaled. "You're wrong. I'll make you love me—today, right now.'' He began to remove his sports jacket.

She had to stop him. This was impossible. "Listen to me, Jerry. You're well. There's nothing I can do for you.''

"But I'm entitled. I paid more money.''

He might have slapped her. "You didn't.''

"I did. I had to see you. I still want to. I still think if you give me. . .yourself a chance, we can—''

She turned away from him and looked out the window. There was no point in angering him. She couldn't take another scene with him. She sighed. "I was told two or three times with you. Will. . .will that make you feel you're. . .you're getting your. . .your money's worth?''

"Yes. Three. A total of three. Two more."

She tried. She really did. But nothing in her life had been so difficult. She suddenly hated him, his hairy body, his puppy dog ways. Touching him revolted her, and she had to will herself to do it. She faked her own arousal. It took a long time, much too long for her, but she finally propelled him into an erection. But in the brief time it took her to move into the female superior position, he lost it. And nothing she could do would enable him to regain it.

At last she said, "I'm sorry. We should have quit while we were ahead.''

"Yes.''

She climbed off the bed, put on her robe and from a vigil by the window watched him dress. There ought to be something to say, but she couldn't think of anything. When he had put his tie on and his coat, he looked at her a moment, then turned and walked out of the room, through her office. The door closed behind him. He didn't speak. Nor did she.

Joanna stood there a moment looking at the empty space where he had been. At last. He was gone. She could now surrender to total despair. She welcomed it. She had no idea what form it would take, nor did she care. She was just tired of fighting it.

The phone rang. Slowly, every step a special effort, she made her way to her office and picked up the receiver. "Yes.''

"Is this Miss Caldwell, Joanna Caldwell?''

"Yes.''

"I'm sorry to be so long in getting back to you. This is Julia Quennell.''

20

An hour and a half later, having stopped at home to change into more conservative attire, Joanna entered an office on East 56th Street in Manhattan. "I want to thank you for staying late to see me, Dr. Quennell."

"Julia. And it is I who should thank you for coming. I've been wanting to talk to you."

"Me?"

"Say, I'm famished. Have you had dinner?"

"No."

"Then let's. There's a little Italian place around the corner. We can let our hair down and have a nice chat."

Joanna liked her. She liked her casualness, the tinge of homeyness amid her sophistication. She liked her directness of speech, her obvious honesty, her intelligence, and before the ravioli and manicotti were ever served, she had concluded Julia Quennell was the most caring person she had ever met and one of the most beautiful. She had real beauty, the kind that comes from inside. It lit her face and made her beautiful. Most men probably wouldn't see it. All they'd notice was a lumpy figure, straight brown hair pulled back from her face into a bun, cheeks too full, lips too thin. Joanna knew better. This was a beautiful woman.

"Why did you want to talk to me, Dr. Quennell?"

"One last time, call me Julia." She smiled. "Because

you work for Dr. Lambert. You still do, don't you?"

"Yes. But I don't understand."

She smiled again, but a little nervously this time. "I was hoping you could tell me what goes on up there."

"What do you want to know?"

Julia Quennell looked at her hard for a moment, then made a production of buttering and eating a bit of bun, washing it down with Chianti. "Dr. Lambert is a very big name in the field, Joanna. And even if he weren't, one doesn't go around criticizing one's colleagues."

"I'm beginning to feel like a dunce. I still don't know what you want me to tell you. And if you're worried about my carrying tales back to Westport, don't. I won't."

This brought forth a broad smile. "I was worried about that." Again the knife and butter were applied to bread. "There are some questions being raised about Lambert's operation."

"What sort of questions?"

"Well, for example, two—no, three of his ex-patients have come to me. They spent a lot of money, went to Lambert's—what does he call that place?"

"The Center for Human Potential."

Julia laughed. "My, that does sound grand, doesn't it? Anyway, these patients were not helped and in one case were made worse. I know I'm not alone in discovering this. I fear Lambert is creating patients for many of us. I say fear, because it really is too bad—too bad for those who need help and too bad for a field of counseling which is still struggling to attain public acceptance. Do you understand now?"

"Yes, but I don't know if I can help you. I don't know what to tell you."

"What do you do there, Joanna?" Julia Quennell inserted a bite of bread in her mouth while she waited for an answer. When she saw only hesitation from Joanna, obvious distress on her face, she said, "I don't mean to pry. But are you a secretary or what? Do you have a title?"

"I'm a staff psychologist."

"Then you must know. Do you work with clients? Or does he call them patients?"

"Patients."

"I dislike the term. It makes them sound ill when they're not. But I suppose Lambert, coming from a medical background, is used to the term. Tell me what you do, Joanna?"

She bit at her lip. "Don' ask me, please."

Surprise registered on the older woman's face. "All right, but can you tell me how it operates up there?"

A deep sigh came from Joanna. She was beginning to wish she hadn't come. "I really can't. I just don't know. I know something is wrong in what we do, but I don't know what it is. I don't know what proper sex therapy is. That's why I came to you, to find out."

"All right. Sex therapy is a team endeavor, a man and a woman, both highly trained. They work with a couple, sometimes as individuals, often as a roundtable. A careful history of the relationship, the marriage, the sexual difficulty is taken until the exact nature of the problem is ascertained, including the underlying social and psychological causes, if any. Many, many hours are spent at this, as well as explaining it to the clients and making certain they fully understand it, emotionally as well as intellectually. As you must know, communication between the husband and wife, as well as with the therapists, is vital to any progress. Our central problem is to break down the barriers of lies, deceits, rationales and protective devices couples build up in a marriage. This can be very difficult, especially if the relationship has not been of the best and has had some duration. We often must spend a considerable amount of time just achieving the sort of frankness and honesty which can lead to the possible solution of the problem. Is this what you do, Joanna?''

"No." Again she bit her lip. "It's not."

"I was afraid of that." Another bite of bread, another swallow of wine. "From what I've been able to learn from those who've been to Lambert, he deals largely in what I call acrobatics. He sets his people to learning positions, performing certain routines which are to lead to sexual bliss. This may be enough for some. But it does not treat the underlying causes, the lack of communication, the stunted attitudes, the preconceived and wholly unrealistic expectations. For many people, I might say most, he is doing more harm than good. I may be wrong, but I fear that is the case." She now looked at Joanna intently. "Unfortunately, this is true of most so-called sex clinics. What ought to be, could be, but so rarely is a worthwhile and highly useful branch of psychology and medicine has become a racket. It is most distressing. I could weep over it."

There was what seemed to Joanna to be a prolonged silence, filled with the motions of eating, bread, wine, salad. She didn't know what to say. Then it just came out. "Dr. Quennell, I'm a surrogate."

Her fork in midpassage to her salad, Julia Quennell stopped, stared at her, quite startled. "Oh my dear, you're not."

"Yes I am. I know it's terrible. I'm so ashamed. I don't want to do it. But I don't know how to get out of it." She was near tears.

Julia Quennell put down her fork and reached across the table to squeeze her hand. "You misunderstand. There's nothing wrong or terrible about being a sex surrogate. It is a most worthy field. I employ surrogates myself—when I can find a good one." She withdrew her hand, resumed poking at her salad. When she spoke again, it was with less feeling. "I was just trying to suggest disbelief that *you* were doing it. You're all wrong for it."

Joanna gave a bitter smile. "You're telling me. But how do you know? Why am I wrong?"

"Just look in a mirror." She smiled. "I would never employ you, my dear. You're much too pretty, too feminine—face it, too sexy looking. You're every man's fantasy, the girl he's just dying to take to bed. And of course he never does. Never really wants to. No, I'd never use you, Joanna. Oh, I'm sure my clients would love it, but it would be a disaster for them."

Joanna waited for her to go on, to explain, then finally prompted her. "Why? I don't understand."

"Because the chances of a client ever finding a girl who looks like you, let alone developing a meaningful relationship with one, is positively remote. I don't mean to be unkind, Joanna—and I know you don't intend it and most certainly can't help it—but you're *fantasyland*. You're a first class example of what I call the *Playboy* syndrome. Hefner has all these girls in his magazine. He pretends they're the girl next door just dying to take her clothes off to please a man, any man, while making absolutely no demands upon him. Unreal. Fantasy. Not more than two or three percent of the population looks like those girls anyway. It drives women crazy because they don't. And it absolutely ruins men because they can't find such a girl. Joanna, you are a beautiful girl, really stunning. To send one of my clients to you, leading him to expect he's going to find someone like you—why I wouldn't dream of it."

"Then why does Dr. Lambert?"

Julia smiled. "That must be obvious to you, my dear. A person is often willing to pay a lot of money to live a fantasy." She smiled. "Isn't that the idea behind that television series?"

Joanna could only stare at her, not yet able to sort out her reactions to what she was hearing.

"How much does he pay you—if I may ask?"

"Six hundred a week. There are occasional bonuses."

"That's a great deal. How long have you been doing this—been a surrogate?"

"Nearly a year."

"And you're how old?"

"Twenty-five." Joanna saw her look at her a moment longer, raising an eyebrow in a quizzical expression, then turn back to her salad. "Am I too young?"

"Not *too* young. There are surrogates your age." She smiled. "Tell me about your work, your clients, what you do. Do you mind?"

"No." She hesitated, uncertain where to begin.

"Is it embarrassing for you?"

"It's all right. I want to talk about it." And she did, starting from the beginning, describing each patient, her methods of treatment, ending up with Wofford and Dillon, although she did not mention any names. She was interrupted frequently by questions. When she was finished, she was a bit unnerved to be greeted by rather strained silence. This was then filled by the waitress bringing their steaming pasta. Finally, Joanna could ask, "It is all wrong what I'm doing?"

"Oh terribly, my dear." Then she stopped, touched the corner of her mouth with her napkin. "I don't mean to disparage you. Actually, it sounds from what you tell me you are doing quite good work—under the circumstances. You have worked mostly with premature ejaculators. Thank God for that. It is a condition which does tend to respond to more mechanistic methods.''

"But you said I was terrible.''

"I meant to say what is going on is terrible—not that you are terrible.'' She smiled. "This food really does look delicious. Why don't we enjoy our dinner, then we'll go back to my office and talk.'' She glanced around the room. "It'll be a little more private there.''

Joanna tried to eat, but she mostly poked at her food, nibbling only a few bites. She knew she was upset by all she had heard, and there was more to come.

"Joanna, I don't mean to be unkind.''

"No, I want to know. It's why I came.''

She was rewarded with a smile. "Good. I like your attitude.'' A moment later, her fork filled with half a ravioli, the sex therapist said, "Since you're not exactly gobbling down your food as I am—pasta, indeed—I'll never improve my figure. Why don't you tell me about yourself? Where are you from? I know it's not New York or even the East.''

During the rest of the dinner, prompted with many questions, Joanna described her background, schooling, marriage, entry into the Center for Human Potential. Asked what she did for fun, Joanna mentioned jogging, tennis, swimming.

"And young men? Anyone you're serious with?''

Joanna hesitated. "No, not really.''

It was past nine o'clock when they returned to Julia Quennell's office. There was nothing lavish about it, just a desk, a couple of comfortable chairs, a table, items that were needed. Joanna remained standing while Julia checked with her answering service. There was nothing. Then she motioned her to a pair of Morris chairs, where they sat facing each other.

"What was so terrible, Dr. Quennell?''

She smiled. "You just can't call me, Julia, can you?

I'm afraid you are quite accustomed to authority figures."

"Yes, I suppose I am."

"And no doubt that makes it easy for Lambert to get you to do what he wants."

Joanna looked at her. She seemed so kind, yet rather sad somehow. This woman cared for her. She was trying to help her. "Please. Talk to me."

"All right." She took a moment to think. "To be a sex surrogate, Joanna, is the most difficult, demanding job I know. I'm only amazed there is anyone at all who can do it—do it well, I mean. A surrogate is working with desperate, extremely disturbed, emotionally stunted men. They must be handled with the greatest intelligence and sensitivity. Exorbitant patience is needed. My surrogates spend weeks, months, sometimes more than a year in the most painstaking work with a client."

She hesitated, letting what she'd just said sink in. For her part, Joanna was greatly affected by the directness and sincerity of Julia Quennell.

"A sex surrogate must be a truly extraordinary woman. Think of it. Here she is, involved with a client—patient if you will—on a protracted basis in the most emotionally and physically intimate way imaginable. Obviously, she cannot have the attitudes of a prostitute. She cannot be hard or cynical, in it only for money. She must be intelligent, caring, well schooled in counseling techniques. But a proper surrogate must be so much more. She must be, as near as humanly possible, secure about herself, her body, her own sexuality. She must have no hangups about what she is doing. There can be no guilt, remorse, doubts about the morality or propriety of her work. And, above all, she must have the inner strength to cope with the emotional and physical demands upon her and remain on an even keel. It is so difficult, so demanding, I am only amazed there are women able to perform as surrogates successfully. I know I could not." She hesitated. "Do you see what I'm saying, Joanna."

"Yes."

"I wonder if you do. You fail these criteria on nearly all counts, Joanna. You do not have the training, the knowledge even to do ordinary counseling, let alone be a surrogate partner. You are anything but a secure person. You are a bundle of hangups about yourself, your body, your sexuality. Your background can make you nothing else at this time in your life."

She stopped for a time, looking at Joanna carefully, seeing the hurt in her eyes. "I'm not saying this to bring you greater pain than you already know, Joanna. Actually, I think it criminal what Lambert has done to you. I'm sure there are no laws against it, but there ought to be. It's simply terrible. I'm aghast." Again she hesitated. "Would you like to know what my surrogates do?"

"Yes."

"All right. If I have a male patient who requires a surrogate, and if I know of one who might be suitable for him, and if she is interested and willing to undertake treatment, I bring them together with myself and perhaps a male member of my staff. The client is in regular weekly or biweekly conseling with me—more often if it seems necessary. The surrogate's work is closely supervised. We get constant feedback from the client—the surrogate, too—to determine not only the degree of progress, but to catch any errors, misjudgments, setbacks, fraudulent attitudes, that sort of thing.

"The surrogate, of course, works alone with the

client in her own office. In the case of a severely
inhibited man, she may do nothing for weeks but sit and
talk to him. Just getting him to look her in the eye may
be a great triumph. Getting him simply to laugh, be
comfortable with a woman, or touch her hand can
indicate great progress.

"Joanna, a surrogate does not take off her clothes
and jump into bed with a man. My dear, the sort of
thing Lambert has you do occurs—with my surrogates
at least—at the end of an extremely long road. And
often it does not occur at all. Unfortunately, some
clients abandon treatment before they ever reach it. But
many men come to an understanding of themselves,
their attitudes and enter into a satisfactory relationship
with a woman they know without ever having sex with
the surrogate."

The two women sat looking at each other, both ill at
ease. Joanna didn't know what to say. Julia wondered if
she'd said too much.

"I hope I haven't done the wrong thing, my dear. I've
given you a pretty strong dose. And I may be wrong.
Lambert is a big name in the field, right up there with
Masters and Johnson—but without their scholarship
and respectability. I'm sorry, but I can't help but believe
what he is having you do is debilitating to your clients
and an absolute disaster for you, Joanna. I don't know
how you've kept yourself together as well as you have.
You have great strength to have endured."

Joanna looked at her, questioning.

"I mean it. Two men at once, every day, in the most
intimate sexual acts. Why, the man should be horse-
whipped! I don't know how you've stood it. You have
no friends, no one to help you. It's unbelievable.
Joanna, even the best and strongest surrogates I know
are emotionally dependent on their friends, their

husbands and boyfriends, even their children. You have no one. You're estranged from your parents. You have no particular women friends to tell your problems to. You have no husband or lover or even male friend. How do you relieve your own sexual tensions? Who is there to make you feel loved, important, womanly—not in spite of, but *because* of what you do? Behind every successful sex surrogate there is a strong, masculine, understanding and supportive male—every bit as mature as she is. I would not employ her if it wasn't that way."

They sat in silence for a time. Finally, Julia Quennell said, "I suspect I've badgered you quite enough for now. It is late, and I'm tired. And you have to drive—"

"Yes." She smiled. I'd better go."

At the door, the sex therapist said, "Will you think about all this?"

"You know I will. I am now."

"Good. And please call me if you need to talk. Come and see me, if you wish." She saw Joanna hesitating, wanting to speak but afraid to. "What do you want to say, Joanna?"

"I-I. . .I just wish you'd tell me. . .what to do."

Dr. Julia Quennell smiled. "I can't. You know that. That is something you, I, everyone must decide for themselves."

21

Laura McGovern's suicide was not discovered until mid-afternoon on Tuesday, about the time Joanna was leaving for New York. Raphaela Dicentes, having had the long weekend off, followed her usual routine for a Monday. She shopped for groceries and household supplies, then busied herself with laundry, some kitchen work and downstairs cleaning. Indeed, she had a pleasant, relaxed morning, humming a Neapolitan tune while she worked. She and her husband Luigi, who was doing yard work, lunched in the kitchen. That Laura McGovern was not there caused her no concern. She assumed Laura had gone off with friends in their car, since Laura's vehicle was in the garage.

Thus, it was after three in the afternoon when Mrs. Dicentes, expanding her household chores to the upstairs, found the body of her employer. She lay peacefully in bed. Mrs. Dicentes thought her asleep. But when she touched her, she gasped, covered her mouth, called upon the mercy of the Mother of Christ, and ran from the room screaming for her husband, who was cleaning the pool.

Westport police, assisted by a medical examiner, spent some time investigating the death. They questioned the Dicentes—a difficult task because Mrs. Dicentes was nearly hysterical with grief—took photographs, went through the motions of dusting for prints, and had the body removed. There was no note, but there was no doubt in the minds of the detectives that Laura McGovern was a suicide. The open and empty bottle of barbituates indicated the cause of death. There were no signs of forced entry or foul play. Suicide. Probably popped the pills late Saturday night or early Sunday morning. Alcohol may have speeded the death. One detective shook his head. All that money and she takes her own life. Just goes to show you.

More time was consumed getting the next of kin out of the Dicentes. There were nephews, distant ones in Florida. Luigi Dicentes didn't know their names or how to reach them, and his wife was in no condition to even try to think. Mrs. McGovern was engaged to Dr. Charles Randall. Fine, only he wasn't a legal next of kin. Was there anyone else? Did she have a lawyer, perhaps? She did, George Heatherwood. The police knew him, of course. The bad news was broken to him. Yes, he knew how to contact the nephews. If the police wished, he would notify them. The detectives agreed, grateful to be rid of an onerous task.

Heatherwood picked up the phone and dialed the number of Henry Kraft in New York City. After identifying himself, Heatherwood said, "I'm calling to tell you your stepmother, Laura McGovern, is dead."

"Dead?"

"Yes, I don't have much information, but she was found dead in her bed this morning or maybe this afternoon. Today sometime, anyhow."

There was silence on the line. "You're not serious."

"I'm afraid I am, Mr. Kraft."

Again a pause. "Laura dead? It can't be. How on earth did it happen?"

"Apparently, Hank—" Heatherwood had never met Kraft, but they now would, and he leaped toward familiarity. "—she committed suicide. Hard to believe, I know, but police say she took sleeping pills."

"Suicide?"

"I can't imagine how or why, either, but that's what police say. We're just going to have to find out what happened."

"Yes."

Hank's immediate reaction to the news, aside from the shock of it, was one of regret. He had never been close to Laura. In fact, he'd been rather shitty toward her, putting her down, keeping her at arm's length, although she never showed him anything but kindness. "I really feel badly about this," he said finally. "I wasn't close to her, but—God, suicide? I saw her a few days ago. She seemed so happy. She'd had her face fixed. She was going to get married. You knew that?"

"Yes, Charles Randall. It doesn't make sense to me either."

There was a protracted silence. Neither man could go on repeating his disbelief.

"If it's all right with you, Hank, I'm going to arrange to have her body released by the authorities. Is that okay with you?"

"Yes, of cousre. Whatever you think best."

"I'll have to make arrangements with a local funeral director. Do you have a preference?"

"Preference? Oh, you mean for the funeral. No, I don't know Westport—hardly at all."

"All right, I'll make the choice. But you better come up tomorrow morning. There are certain details you really have to attend to, the casket, what to do about flowers—I imagine there'll be a ton of them. That sort of thing."

Hank was thoroughly confused. "Me? Come to Westport?"

"Yes."

Hank sighed. "Look, Mr—ah. . . ."

"Heatherwood, George Heatherwood."

"I'm sorry. Mr. Heatherwood, I'm sorry about Laura's death. I really am. She was a nice lady, always very kind to me—my son, too. But I hardly knew her. Ralph McGovern, her husband, was my father, that's true, but I was raised by my mother and legally adopted by my stepfather. I bear his name. I didn't even meet the McGoverns until a few years ago. I'm sorry Laura is dead, but—can you understand, Mr. Heatherwood?"

"She didn't tell you?"

"Tell me what?"

"I guess she didn't." There was a long pause on the line. "Hank, I think you'd better come up to Westport in the morning. Come right to my office. Can you do that?"

Hank sighed. "I guess so, sure, all right. If it's necessary, I can."

"Believe me, it's necessary."

"Can't you tell me whatever it is now?"

"Not really. I think it's better if we meet."

They arranged the time for eleven the next morning, then the lawyer hung up, leaving a mystified Hank Kraft standing with the receiver in his hand.

Heatherwood next called Lamont Dandridge at the Westport Bank & Trust to tell him, then almost as an afterthought dialed another number. The Center for Human Potential and Dawson Lambert had a vested interest in Laura McGovern's death. He might still be at his office.

The phone call stunned Lambert. It took all his aplomb to quell his panic long enough to talk decently on the phone with the lawyer. "Laura McGovern a suicide? I can't believe it. It can't be. She was so happy, so—"

"Yes, I know. It is very strange."

"Did she. . .did she give any reason—I mean, did she leave a note or anything?"

"I really know very little, Dr. Lambert. But my understanding is that the police have found nothing so far. The matter is still under investigation. Perhaps something will turn up. It is very strange."

"Yes." Lambert, his initial shock having passed, recognized a need to be careful. "I am terribly upset by this."

"I thought you might be. I know she worked with you. On your board, wasn't she?"

"Yes." He allowed a silence. The less said the better. "I do appreciate your calling me."

"I thought you'd want to know."

After hanging up the phone, Lambert stood there a moment, quivering with anxiety, then poured himself a drink. He forced himself to think rationally. There was no way to link him with Laura's suicide. Even if a note of some kind did show up, it would only be the rantings of an unstable woman. He had done nothing criminal. Nor was he involved, other than as her doctor and friend. Yes, that was so. He needn't worry.

Almost at once he began to feel better. Laura dead. He wondered if she'd left him anything in her will.

Joanna learned of Laura's death via radio the next morning, Wednesday. It was something more than just a news item to her. She knew Laura, even had a modicum of affection for her. The manner of her death, a suicide no less, was dismaying. She found it hard to believe Laura, who had been so happy only a week or ten days ago, had taken her life. But it would be an exaggeration to suggest that Joanna felt grief. She simply was not that close to Laura. Besides, Joanna's mind was very much on her own problems. That whole morning she was preoccupied with Julia Quennell and what she'd said.

Hank arranged for Timmy to remain over at the nursery school and for Vicki to pick him up. Then he took the train to Westport and a cab to Heatherwood's office on Imperial Avenue. He shook hands with a rather short, natty man in his fifties, mostly bald with a few strands of hair combed over the pate from just above his left ear in an affectation of hirsuteness.

"So you're Hank Kraft, Laura's stepson."

Hank looked at the man across the desk, trying to form some kind of impression of him. It was not easy. He couldn't deduce much other than the fact Heatherwood was a lawyer. From the furnishings, the office, the view of the Saugatuck River, Heatherwood's suit and two hundred dollar elevator shoes, Hank could figure only that he was a *rich* lawyer.

"I guess that's true, but as I tried to explain last night, it is difficult for me to think in terms of that relationship."

"And you have a son Timothy?"

"Yes, Timmy's my son."

"His mother?"

"We're divorced."

He smiled. "That's too bad—for her?"

Hank didn't like this cat and mouse game. "What are you getting at, Mr. Heatherwood?"

"George, please." He picked up a legal document from the top of his desk. "This may interest you, I think. It is the Last Will and Testament of Laura Wheeler McGovern. This was drawn up a few months ago, subsequent to the death of your father, Ralph McGovern. I know for a fact Laura planned a new will to reflect her approaching marriage. We discussed some of the terms, but, of course, that marriage never took place. This is the applicable will."

Hank stared at him, but said nothing.

Heatherwood put on reading glasses, half glasses which rested well down on his nose, giving him an owlish look. He flipped a page of the document. "I, Laura Wheeler McGovern, being of sound mind do hereby—" He looked at Hank over his glasses. "I guess there's no point in my actually reading the will. Let me tell you of its major provisions. Laura was a generous woman. She left five thousand each to William and—I guess their names won't matter to you. They are nephews, her only blood relatives. Both were rather—well, let's say not entirely kind to her. This bequest is a token intended to preclude their challenging the will. I told her a dollar would have sufficed, but, as I say, Laura was generous."

He read a moment longer. "She bequeathed twenty-five thousand each, a total of fifty thousand, to Raphaela Dicente, her longtime housekeeper and cook, and to her husband Luigi Dicente, the butler-chauffeur. Very generous of her, don't you think?"

Hank nodded. He suspected Heatherwood was being excessively theatrical, but did nothing to interfere.

"Laura also remembered various charities. Among the significant bequests are twenty-five thousand each to multiple sclerosis, mental retardation, the Red Cross and the library of her alma mater, Bennington College. I've an idea they'll all be pleased. She left fifty thousand to the Congregational Church here in Westport and—" Again he looked over his glasses at Hank. "—there is a bequest of one hundred thousand to the Center for Human Potential in Westport and its director Dawson Lambert. That's not two hundred thousand, just the one, but Lambert has the use of the money personally, if he wishes."

Hank finally reacted. "Really?"

"Yes. Most generous. Laura was active in the place. Served on some sort of board or citizen's council, something like that. She believed in the Center and its aims."

Hank shrugged. He wished to hell he could share her enthusiasm for the place. A painful vision of Joanna Caldwell flicked over his mind.

Heatherwood dropped the will on his desk and turned to face Hank, removing his glasses as he did so. "The remainder of Laura's estate was left to—" On impulse he picked up the will again and donned his glasses to read. "—and I quote, 'my esteemed stepson Henry Wadsworth Kraft and my esteemed step-grandson Timothy Fields Kraft, which is to be held in trust until he reaches age twenty-five.' There are technical provisions, but that's—" He smiled broadly. "As Walter Cronkite says, that's the way it is."

Hank didn't react. The words he had just heard had no meaning for him. He sensed he was expected to say something. All he could think of was, "What did you say?"

"I think you heard me. You have inherited the bulk of Laura McGovern's estate. She had set up the trust fund for your son on a permanent basis. That's to the good. But I don't believe Laura had any conception of dying so soon. I know she intended to provide for her future husband, greatly reducing the bequest to you. Thus, I fear the tax man is going to take a significant bite out of the estate. But no matter. You still remain a very wealthy man."

Hank reacted slowly. "Me? Timmy and me?"

"That's what I said." He smiled. "I think maybe congratulations are in order."

"But why? I hardly knew her."

"Apparently you made an impression on her." He

grew serious. "I've known Laura for a lot of years. I was her friend, as well as her counselor. She was a woman of strong loyalties. The great regret of her life was that she never had children. She wanted to adopt, but her husband, your father, would not hear of it. I think Laura thought of you and young Timothy as her family. This will can lead to no other conclusion."

"God!" Greatly agitated, Hank shook his head, crossed and recrossed his legs, then stood up and went to the window behind the lawyer's desk. "Forgive me, but I feel shitty. Absolutely rotten. I didn't care anything about her. I wasn't anything more than polite to her—and, hell, I'm not sure I was even that. This is awful!"

Heatherwood laughed. "Not too awful."

"Don't laugh. I don't care about the money."

"You will." He saw the anger rise in Hank's face. "I don't mean that the way it sounds. I do understand how you feel, what a shock this must be. But I'm sure you must have brought more happiness to Laura than you believe."

"Wow! It just goes to prove something. I don't know what right now. Maybe I never will. But I'm going to start watching how I treat people from now on."

"A good idea, I suspect."

Hank raised both hands and ran them through his hair. He sucked in air and exhaled deeply. "Wow, that's all I can say."

"Do you see now why I suggested you enter into the funeral arrangements. You are the next of kin."

Hank turned to face him. "Okay, I'll do that. And I'll do more. If I couldn't do right by her when she was living, I'm going to try in death. There's something fishy about this suicide. I'm going to get to the bottom of it."

The lawyer shrugged. "Fine. Go right ahead."

Hank went to the funeral home and met with an unctuous man who assumed a greater grief than Hank felt. Most of the arrangements had already been made by Heatherwood. There would be visitation that evening. Services and interment would take place on Wednesday. Hank asked if that wasn't a little soon, but accepted assurances it was all quite proper. Hank selected a casket, thinking it ridiculously extravagant. But then it was Laura's money. He knew of no special music. Yes, the arrangements seemed fine. He'd be there by eight o'clock.

After lunch, Hank met with Lamont Dandridge at the bank, as Heatherwood had arranged. Dandridge was a man in his forties, medium height, full head of dark hair, and a banker to the core. Seeing his dark, three-piece suit, Hank realized he was going to have to do something. Tweed jacket, suntans and loafers were hardly funereal.

"I'm pleased to meet you, Mr. Kraft. Laura spoke of you often."

Hank nodded. "This has been quite a morning for me. Mr. Heatherwood—George, told me about Laura's will. I had no idea. I'm still not able to accept it."

"I understand."

"And I'm certainly not able to cope with it. Whatever arrangements Laura had with you I want to continue."

"I think that's wise. The will has to be probated. That'll take some time. Meanwhile, you'll have expenses for the funeral. Then there's the upkeep on the house. I'm sure arrangements can be made to release some funds immediately."

"Thank you. I'm afraid all this is a bit out of my league—" He smiled. "—on the order of the difference between the Little League and the New York Yankees."

The smile was returned. "I quite understand. I'll take care of everything. Indeed, the bank did that for Laura in her lifetime. I might say Laura was more than just a customer, a client. I considered her a personal friend. Her death is a great loss to me."

"Yes."

"I can't really believe it—but never mind that for now. I think you should know Laura relied on us a great deal. After her husband died—that would have been your father—"

Hank nodded. He was not about to explain, however, unless he had to. He didn't.

"—We took—I think I can say I took great pains to see that she not do anything she might later regret. Widows sometimes do. I cautioned her against being foolish with her money. And mostly she listened to me. Oh, I thought her a bit overzealous sometimes. She did have a tendency to listen to a hard luck story."

"She gave money away?"

Dandridge laughed. "Not exactly that, but she did support a great many charities. If she believed in something, she was just naturally generous."

"What sort of charities?"

Again he laughed. "Oh, I'm sure the church will miss her, one or two others. I've an idea Dr. Lambert will be distraught at her passing."

"She gave him money?"

"Oh yes."

"How much?"

"I'm not sure. Have to look it up. The amounts were substantial I thought, but then perhaps they weren't. She was active in his place, really believed in it. Her gifts were not excessive, considering her wealth. I did not interfere."

"I'm not asking for an accounting. But I am curious.

What sort of money are we talking about?''

"To Dr. Lambert? Oh, there were several gifts over the last couple years. I should guess they didn't exceed two hundred thousand.''

From the bank Hank went to Laura's house, comforting the weeping housekeeper and asking her and Luigi to stay on. He borrowed Laura's car, then went downtown and purchased suitable funeral attire. After that he found a watering hole and made several trips to the trough.

22

Joanna knew one thing. Nothing in her life had hurt as much as Julia Quennell's words. They had not been said in anger, but in sorrow, with compassion. But the effect was to strip her bare. She did not cry or emote in any way. She did something far worse. She saw herself with terrible clarity.

She had had sex, prolonged sex, with all these men, believing they needed her, that she was helping them. It simply was not so. She was not aiding them. She was harming them. They did not need *her*, but rather someone qualified, someone who knew what she was doing. Perhaps hardest to take was the pitiless self-knowledge that she had deluded herself into believing she was a "staff psychologist" qualified to do counseling of any sort, let alone work with seriously disturbed men. She was not a psychologist. Her qualifications consisted of being pretty, well-built, orgasmic and gullible. She was not even a surrogate partner. She was fantasyland. *And,* she was a very mixed up, if not greatly unbalanced person herself. How could she not have seen it? How could she have thought otherwise?

Lambert had deluded her, used her. She was in reality a whore, a call girl, albeit a high priced one. Quickly she did some mental arithmetic. Jerry Wofford had paid ten thousand dollars for two weeks with her. She made six hundred a week, twelve hundred in two weeks. That left Lambert with eighty-eight hundred. Not a bad profit at all. Then she realized. She had Dillon at the same time. He must be paying at least ten thousand. *My God*! Such greed.

She visualized Lambert behind his desk, his blue-violet eyes trained on her, the kindly smile, the exaggerated interest. *You are so very good at what you do. It is precisely because you are such a caring individual. . . . Oh Lord*! She loathed him. She hated him. He had used her. He had—

No. It wasn't Lambert. It was herself. She was to blame. From the start she had known, really known, deep down, that she was being a whore. Nasty word. Use it. Whore. Whore, whore, whore. She had known. But she hadn't wanted to believe it. She listened to anybody or anything that told her otherwise. Lambert had done only what she wanted him to. *If this isn't the practice of medicine*. . . . Yes, she wanted to hear that.

And she wanted the sex. Face it, she liked it. She liked having men admire her. She liked turning men on. She liked being in control, telling them what to do. It made her feel important. She liked the variety. If Judd Forbes could see me now. Does he know what he missed? Yes, oh yes. True, all true.

Joanna did not shield her inner vision from the harsh light in which she now saw herself. She was being burned by a laser of self-knowledge, but she made no effort to protect herself from the pain. She simply absorbed it. Perhaps the pain would make her a new and better person.

The real problem, she knew, was not the past, but the future. What was she going to do now? She would quit this business immediately. She would go to the office, pick up her things, walk out, never come back. She wouldn't speak to Lambert. His was one face she never wanted to see again.

And do what? Go back to Ohio? No, not that. It was impossible. She'd go somewhere, New York maybe, get some kind of a job, go back to school. And study what? Psychology. Why not? She obviously had a lot to learn.

Grateful to have made some kind of plan, however hazy, she went to her office for what she thought would be her final appearance. But once there she realized it couldn't be. Dillon. Yesteday she had seduced him. She couldn't now just disappear. It would be too destructive. She might not be helping him, but she just couldn't stab him in the back. She had at least to see him, talk to him, try to explain. She could do no less. And Wofford. Oh God, poor, pitiful Jerry.

When Dillon came, she said, "I shouldn't have done that yesterday. I could have set you back. I'm sorry for it."

He grinned at her. "Maybe you're sorry, but I'm not. You were something else."

"But the success was mostly accidental."

"So, who said all accidents are bad?"

From her office she watched in dismay as he entered the treatment room and began to strip off his shirt. This couldn't be happening. She wasn't going to do it anymore.

"Are you coming?"

Slowly she got up from her chair and went to the other room. She just stood there, watching him disrobe, hesitant, uncertain what to say to him.

"Brad, stop." He did, standing there, bent slightly, his pants half rolled from his hips. "I'm not doing this anymore. I can't." He was looking at her, questioning, doubting. "I'm only here to quit. I just wanted to tell you that and say I'm sorry."

He pulled up his pants, fastened them and snugged up the zipper. Then he turned to her and smiled broadly. "I sure am glad to hear that."

She was surprised. "You are?"

"Sure. This is no job for you. Anybody can see that. You can be so much more."

It was the second time she'd heard that. Hank had used almost the same words. "I-I thought you'd be angry with me."

"Naw. Why would I be angry?"

"You paid for two weeks. You. . .you're entitled to today. . .two more. . .until Friday."

"Forget it. I got my money's worth."

Then she was able to smile, if only wanly. "Thank you, Brad. You don't know what this means to me." Impulsively, she leaned forward and quickly brushed his cheek with her lips. "But you really should finish your treatment—but somewhere else I think."

"Naw, I'm okay. I think I've got the hang of it. Just a matter of doing it. I'll work on it." He grinned. "I didn't do too bad yesterday, did I?"

"No." She smiled. "You were quite good—almost too good."

There was a moment of awkwardness which he ended. "Say, let's have a drink—celebrate your coming to your senses."

She brought ice, he made drinks, they toasted her future. "What're you gonna do, Joanna?"

"I don't know. Go somewhere, get a job, maybe go back to school."

He swallowed from his glass. "Can I make a suggestion?"

"Of course. I can certainly use one."

He hesitated, but only momentarily. "Come to California with me."

She stared at him. "California?"

"Why not? The whole world goes to California—land of orange trees, movie moguls and sunlit smog. You'll love it."

Still she stared. "Live with you?"

He lifted his glass, swallowed. "I wouldn't mind, Joanna. It musta occurred to you—after yesterday. We'd make quite a team, you and I."

Her surprise at his suggestion was wearing off. "I don't love you, Brad."

"Who needs love these days. Just think of it as a place to hang your hat." He laughed. "Or in the case of California, your bikini." The laugh faded. He became serious. "Look, there's no harm in trying it. If it doesn't work out, it's see ya 'round and lots o' luck. If something happens—why fight it?"

"What if we just end up hurting each other in the end?"

He laughed. "I thought it didn't hurt?"

"I'm serious. I was married to Judd Forbes, remember? I'm just not masochistic enough to want to go through it again."

"What's that word mean?"

"I'm not going to deliberately put my hand in the wringer."

"I get it. But you won't be. You're not in love with me. You won't be some starry-eyed kid. It's a relationship of convenience. If it becomes more than that—or less, so be it."

"Why me? You could have anyone."

"That's a dumb question."

She looked down at her drink, shaking the cubes in the liquid.

"You're at loose ends, Joanna. You don't know what you're going to do. You got no place to go. Why not

California? Call it a vacation. Have a good rest. Lie in the sun. Give yourself a chance to regroup, make up your mind, plan.''

She looked at him and smiled. ''A strategic advance to the rear.''

''Is there anything wrong with that?''

She saw him, really saw him, the blond hair, handsome face, the muscular body now shirtless. ''No, there's nothing wrong with it. I'll probably have to go back and start over anyway.''

''Why not in California? You said you wanted a job. We got jobs. You mentioned school. We got Southern Cal, UCLA. Name a college, we got it.''

''I know that.''

''Then why not, Joanna?''

She pursed her lips in her characteristic gesture. ''I'm not sure. I-I just know it wouldn't be fair—to either of us. If I went to California—with you—it would be just escape, escape from here, from my life, myself.'' An image of Hank reached her mind. She acknowledged it, then ignored it. ''It's not a very good reason.''

''What's wrong with it?''

''I've been running all my life, Brad, escaping. I escaped my parents by going to college. I escaped having to decide what to do with my life by marrying Judd Forbes. I escaped Judd Forbes by taking this job here. Going off with you will just be another escape.'' Again an image of Hank. ''Don't you think it's about time I faced up to myself, my life?''

''That's all crap, Joanna. You said you were quitting this job. If you make one step out the door—that's escape. Anything you do, anywhere you go is escape. Look. You gotta go somewhere. What's wrong in my offering you California—'' He smiled. ''—particularly if you're escaping in some style. And, hell, Joanna, you might even find yourself having fun.''

She rendered her wan smile. "Where do you live?''

He told her, Malibu, beach house. He described the house, the life they would lead, his friends. He told of his car, how far they were from the studio, Rodeo Drive, downtown LA. She only half listened, her mind on him, his handsome face, the broad shoulders, what they had done yesterday. He was so big. Yes, it had been good, could get much better. She could visualize life with him, companion to a movie star, lots of money, celebrity friends. She'd be the most envied and talked about girl in the world. It would be a good life.

"I know it would work, Joanna. And if it doesn't—what's the harm?''

"None, Brad. None at all." Again she made the pursing motion, biting the inner surface of her lip. She forced a smile. "I'll think about it, okay?''

"Sure.''

"Just don't pressure me.''

He laughed. "You know I'd never do anything like that. Say, since you've quit, why don't we get the hell outta here, go to the beach, have a drink somewhere?''

"Thank you, Brad, but I can't.''

"Why not?''

She sighed. "Someone's coming—another patient.'' She saw him react and smiled. "Don't worry. I'm just going to tell him I've quit." His doubt was visible on his face. "I have to, Brad. I owe it to him, just as I did to you. I just didn't show up for you. I can't for him.''

"Okay, I understand. How about tonight? You gotta give me a chance to not pressure you." He saw her already shaking her head. "I'm not talking sex, Joanna. I won't even touch you.''

"A friend of mine died—suicide. I have to go to the funeral home.''

"How about afterwards?"

She sighed. "All right. Come to my place about ten. I'll buy you a nightcap." She told him where she lived.

Joanna waited for Jerry Wofford with unparalleled dread, but she busied herself collecting her things and putting them in a box. She started to take the robe, then thought better of it. She never wanted to put that garment on again. In fact, she'd never be able to wear a terry robe again. She went through her files, selecting what honestly belonged to her. Lambert and his files. Guarded them like they were the crown jewels. Should she write him a farewell note? Tell him what a rotten fraud he was? How she was wise to him? How she would never forgive him for taking advantage of her? The idea appealed to her, but no. There was no point. Just leave, forget him.

Jerry Wofford didn't come. That surprised her, but she was relieved not to have to see him. He must have come to his senses. Maybe she had helped him—a little.

The rituals of American funerals turned out to be grossly difficult for Hank. He felt like an intruder, standing there near the closed casket amid a bank of flowers and a havoc of sickly sweet odors, greeting people he did not know or ever expected to meet again. Half of Westport must have answered the call for bereavement. His hand wearied of shaking other hands and his mind boggled at the incessant repetition of "Yes, she was a fine, fine woman." "What a loss," "Such a pity." The only thing that saved him, he felt, was his invitation to Charles Randall, George Heatherwood and the Dicentes to join him. Thus he was able to take a break from time to time.

The appearance of two people broke his ennui. One was a tall, middle-aged man with startling blue-violet eyes. "I cannot express to you," he said, his voice somber as a viola, "my deep sense of personal loss. Your stepmother was one of the finest women it has been my honor to know."

Hank nodded his thanks. "Forgive me," he said, "But I'm not from Westport. May I know your name?"

"Dawson Lambert. Laura was—I like to think of her as a benefactor. . .no, a co-worker."

So this was Dawson Lambert, *the* Dawson Lambert. Hank took an instant dislike to him. He told himself that even if he did not know of Lambert's misuse of Joanna Caldwell, he would still have felt antipathy toward him. The man was too handsome, too suave, too calculated. He was a phony. And Hank applied a personal yardstick to judge him. No, he would not buy a used car from Dawson Lambert.

Joanna came. He had been expecting her, looking for her, but that did not prepare him for the inner excitement he felt as he saw her. She wore a summer dress, light blue in color, simply cut, her fragile arms bare to the shoulders. He saw—in what order?—bare arms, lightly tanned, her skin so thin, luminescent, the tender fold of flesh, lighter colored, at her armpit, the small mouth, in repose, the lips, lightly painted, turned out, the big shielding glasses, the hair combed back, tied behind her head. His first thought was that he'd never seen her wear her hair that way. Then he remembered. On the tennis court when he'd first met her. Her hair had been tied back with an orange ribbon. Lord, she was lovely then. She was lovely now.

She was surprised to see him, momentarily taken aback by his dark suit, his standing beside the casket, shaking hands. Then she remembered. Laura was his stepmother.

Joanna let him take her hand, the smooth coolness

enveloping hers, producing again the special sensation, the drawing together, the special intimacy. "I'm sorry," she said, her voice little above a whisper. "I forgot Laura was your stepmother till just now. I should have called you."

"Can we go somewhere and talk a minute?"

She didn't want to. She had resolved never to see him again. She knew what he did to her. Over and over she had told herself it was all just physical. The only way to get over it was to not see him again. If she had realized he would be here, she would not have come. But she was here. There was no way to avoid being alone with him. She felt his hand on her arm, high, near the armpit, leading her to another, larger room.

"I am sorry about Laura, Hank."

"Strangely, I am too."

"Why is that strange?"

"Because I was cruel to her. I hardly ever thought of her. Mostly she annoyed me. I resented her fussing over Timmy."

Timmy was someone else she didn't want to think about. But she had to ask. "How is he?"

"Okay. Vicki has him. I'll bring him to the funeral tomorrow. He'll want to see you. I'm trying to say that I had no stepmotherly feelings toward Laura, whatever they might be."

"You're here now."

He grimaced. "Yeah, and I don't like the reason. Joanna, she left damn near all her money, the house, everything to Timmy and me."

"You're kidding." Her surprise was genuine and showed in her face.

" 'Fraid not. Lots of money, Joanna. I'm going to have a hard time carrying on the poor starving artist bit."

She smiled. "You won't have to."

He looked at her intently, holding her eyes with his. "I won't change. Nothing about me has changed. Never will."

She let him hold her with his eyes, slowly biting at her lip, then looked away. At that instant, she resolved never to see him again. She'd never get over him if she kept seeing him.

"If I neglected her in life, I'm not now. Her suicide doesn't wash. I'm going to find out what happened."

"What d'you mean?"

"Did you think she was despondent? I'd personally never seen her happier than at that tennis party."

"That's true."

"I want to find out what happened. I figure I owe it to her. Do you know of any trouble she was in?"

"No."

"Any reason for her to kill herself?"

She shook her head. "I can't think of anything. She looked so well. She was going to be married." A thought came to her. "Anything happen with Dr. Randall?"

"No. I just talked to him a little while ago. He said he saw Laura Saturday night. They had a drink at his place in Stamford. She was fine when she left. He seems in a state of shock to me. I've no doubt he's extremely upset.

She looked at him. "I can't think of any other explanation, Hank. I'm sorry."

"I can. I've an idea your friend Lambert—"

"He's not my friend."

"Really?" He raised an eyebrow in doubt. "Anyway, whatever he is to you, I've an idea he's the key to Laura's death. Something was going on."

"Look, Hank, just because you don't like him. Just because I—" Abruptly she stopped. Why was she defending Lambert?

"You're right. I don't like him—and for the reasons you were about to say. He's a phony if I ever saw one."

"Have you ever met him?"

"I just did." Another couple entered the room. Hank took her arm and led her further into a corner. "Joanna, for the last couple of years, Laura paid him money. Big bucks, as far as I'm concerned. In the neighborhood of two hundred grand."

"You're kidding!"

"No. I don't know the exact amount, but I can get it—from the bank. I think he was blackmailing her."

"That's silly, Hank. Why would he?"

"I don't know, but I intend to find out—with your help."

"Me?"

"Yes. You work there. You've the run of the place. You can—"

"I can't, Hank."

He looked at her, his eyes hard. "You mean you won't. He's your great benefactor, sex therapist to the Western world."

She heard the sarcasm, but let it run off her. "I can't, because I've quit my job—as of today." She saw his eyes start to brighten, his lips begin to smile. "I'm thinking of going to California."

His smile died aborning. "Good news, bad news, uh?"

They stood searching out each other with their eyes. "I've got to be going, Hank. I am sorry about Laura. I wish I could help." She saw him looking at her, his eyes trying to penetrate. To escape, she turned, started to walk away.

"Anyone I know?"

She stopped, but did not turn around. "No."

The silence seemed so heavy to her, then she heard, "I

only loved you, Joanna. You didn't have to tell me what you did. I never wanted to know."

She stood there, back to him, waiting for more. When it didn't come, she moved a foot forward, then another, and soon she was walking away from him, out of the funeral home, out of his life.

Her hand was shaking as she inserted the key in the ignition, and she had trouble breathing. She felt that only simple actions, long practiced, walking, unlocking the car, starting it, turning the wheel, putting on the headlights, driving, the simple, humdrum activities by which one person gets from place to place in America kept her dry eyed and in one piece.

Oh, how he could get to her. And she knew why. She loved Hank Kraft. That knowledge had always been there, but not until this moment had she given it the finality afforded by mental articulation in the left cortex. She loved Hank Kraft, and the realization made her eyes smart. But it also didn't make a particle of difference. Hank Kraft was still an impossibility. Her love for Hank Kraft was something to be gotten over, like an illness, hopefully not chronic, measles, the flu, at most mononucleosis. She had had it in college. Took a couple of weeks.

23

Dillon was waiting for her when she got home. He entered with her, stopping by the door as she turned on the lights. "Nice place."

"Not really. I'll be glad to leave it." She headed for the kitchen. "The drinks are in here." He followed and she showed him where the liquor was. How long ago had she showed Hank how to make drinks? She went into the bedroom, deposited her purse, glanced at herself in the mirror, then returned to stand in the kitchen doorway. That's where he she had stood when Hank made drinks. *Stop it. It's all over.*

"Bourbon, isn't it?"

She always drank bourbon. Hank had fixed her that. "No, I think I'd like a Scotch."

"You've just named your poison."

In a moment he turned, handed her the drink, then he bent and gently kissed her. Memory stabbed at her, standing in this spot, Hank kissing her, her drink spilling down his back. She shuddered.

"You sure do turn on fast."

He had misunderstood her trembling. Or had he? It was a nice kiss. Brad Dillon had a divine mouth. Yes. Apparently she could do it with anyone.

She slid past him into the living room and sat on the couch. He followed to sit beside her. At once, he bent to kiss her again. "You promised, remember."

He smiled. "So I did." He sat back on the couch, imitating a prim and proper boy. "And I was going to not pressure you about California."

"I'll never be able to hear the word without thinking of you."

"You're not coming?"

"I don't know. I said I had to think about it."

"Then think."

She smiled at him. "It's some offer. I'd be the most envied girl in America."

"Naw. I'd be envied—as a guy, that is."

He sat forward then, turned and kissed her. It was so sweet, tender, so soft and enveloping. She did not oppose it, but let her head fall back against the back of the cushion, responding, letting her lips mirror the motions of his. In a moment, he moved away, put his glass on the table, then took hers, placing it beside his. He returned to her, mouth hot, moist, welcome. She felt the smooth entry of his tongue, her own sharp upsurge of sensation and passion. His hand gripped her breast through her dress. She did not oppose. Again he moved away from her, this time to unbutton her dress, reach inside, as he reunited their mouths. It felt so good, his touch, his mouth, to be desired, needed, to enjoy sensations, to want it to happen, to know she was a fully functioning woman, to surrender, as only a woman can, giving up all her problems, letting someone else take care of her. *Tell me what to do?* I can't. *Everyone must decide for themselves.*

It took her a moment to extricate herself from him, stand up, button her dress. He did not try to stop her. He just sat there, looking up at her.

"I'm sorry. I can't, Brad."

"But you wanted it."

"I know. But if I do it, I'll be lost. I'll be in the pits. I'll wander around there forever, never able to get out."

"Nonsense. It's only sex."

"I know that, too. It would be nice. I want to, really want to. But I can't. Not now." She reached for her drink and took a large swallow. "I met a woman in New York. She made me see what a mess I am. There are women in this world who've come to grips with their bodies, their sexuality, themselves. I want to do that—at least try. Probably won't make it. But I've got to try—for awhile at least. It's something I have to do alone."

Still he looked at her. "Then it's no to California."

"I'm sorry." She bit her lip. "For now anyway. Maybe later. . .after I've—?"

He laughed. "Learned about your body, your sexuality, your—"

"Don't make fun of me."

"I'm not." He stood up, looking at her a long moment. "One thing every actor learns is when the scene ends get off the stage."

She watched him stride for the door. "I'm sorry, Brad. You're a nice person, really you are. You deserve more than this."

Hand on the knob, he turned. "Can I ask a question?"

"Of course."

"Are you sure this is what you want to do?"

"No. I'm not at all sure." She smiled. "Does that make you feel better?"

"Sure. Just like a second broken leg makes you forget the first one."

She shook her head. "God, Brad, you must be sorry you ever came here, ever met me."

"Don't be silly. I owe you a great deal."

"That's not so. Whatever you spent was too much."

He laughed. "Okay, you win. It was too much."

"Yes, and I am sorry."

He was going out the door when she said—she didn't know why, "Brad, how much did you pay?"

"You really want to know?"

"Yes. Will you tell me?"

"Sure. Twenty grand. You were worth every penny."

The door closed behind him, and she went and bolted it, an automatic action she had long ago trained herself to do. She leaned her back against the door. Twenty thousand dollars! He had paid twenty thousand dollars! Great God, twenty thousand dollars! Her disbelief gave way to anger. "Why the slimy bastard. Twenty thousand dollars and I did all the work." *You're just mad because you only got six hundred a week.* No! Lambert was running a racket and he *used* me. I was part of his racket. "By God, he'll hang. I'll have him behind bars. I'll get on the stand and tell everything. What do I care—just so long as he pays? Oh-h, is he going to pay."

Greatly agitated, she stalked through the apartment, vowing over and over to get Lambert, make him pay for what he'd done, to her, to all these patients. She remembered. Hank thought Lambert was connected to Laura McGovern's death. Probably was. Nothing was past him. Lambert would walk over his grandmother for a buck, the greedy weirdo. Hank wanted her to help. Yes, she'd help. She'd do anything. Lambert had to be stopped—and right away.

She went to the phone and dialed Hank's number in New York. She let it ring and ring, visualizing the apartment, the location of the phone. No answer. He wasn't home. Then she remembered. He was in Westport. The funeral was tomorrow. He probably stayed over. Hurriedly, she looked up Laura McGovern's number and dialed it.

There was an answer on the third ring. "Mrs. McGovern's residence." Then there was a moaning sound. "Oh-h, that's not right. She's not here. . .any more."

Joanna heard the sounds of crying. Must be the maid. What was her name? Then she remembered. "Mrs. Dicentes, this is Joanna Caldwell. Is Hank Kraft there?"

"Mr. Kraft? You want. . .to speak to. . .Mr. Kraft?" Her words were broken by sobs.

"Yes, I'd like to very much."

"He's not here. He. . .he stopped. . .down town."

"But you're expecting him?"

"There was a pause, then a voice more controlled. "Yes, he said he was going to sleep here."

"Would you ask him to call me, Joanna Caldwell. I'm at home. Tell him it's urgent."

"Yes, I'll tell him. Joanna Caldwell."

Then she remembered her unlisted phone. She gave her number to Mrs. Dicentes, making her write it down. When she hung up the receiver, Joanna was calmer, more lucid. Hank would call. She'd tell him everything. He'd know what to do. Together they'd get Lambert. He had to be stopped. He had used her, used everyone. Stopping him, putting him behind bars was the most important thing she could do in life. Somehow it would make right all she had done wrong. Yes, it would do that.

She walked across the room and picked up her drink. No, she didn't need alcohol. She had to be right when Hank phoned. Food. That's what she needed. She hadn't had any dinner. She hadn't eaten all day. She went into the kitchen, opening the refrigerator. Almost empty, orange juice, half a carton of milk, eggs in a carton another half dozen she had hardboiled a few days ago. She opened the freezer compartment. A couple of TV dinners. She thought about it. No, nothing appealed to her. You've got to eat. She slowly closed the refrigerator, stood there a moment, then wandered back into the living room. Why didn't Hank call? Give the man a chance. It's only been five minutes. She looked at her watch. Eleven o'clock. Might as well listen to the news while she waited. She flicked on the TV, Channel 2. The news was already on. Another OPEC price increase. Price of gas going up. That was news?

She wandered back into the kitchen. She really ought to eat. Her weight was down from 104 to 96. This could get serious. What was that disease? *Anorexia nervosa*. Yeah, bad stuff. She opened the refrigerator and took out a hardboiled egg. She closed the door and began to tap the egg on the front, cracking the shell in many places.

"Another subway death in the news tonight, this one an apparent suicide."

She stripped the shell from the egg, dropping the pieces on the counter. She reached for the salt, then saw the pieces of shell. She had to begin to be neater, really she did. She started to sweep the offending trash into her left hand.

"Witnesses told Manhattan police the victim was standing alone on the Fifty-seventh Street IRT. There was no one around him. Police conclude he simply leaped to his death just as the express roared into the station."

Clutching the fragments of eggshell, she went over to the trash can, opening the lid, intending to throw them inside.

"The victim has been identified as Gerald T. Wofford, owner of a chain of fabric shops in Manhattan. No cause for the apparent suicide has been determined. Police are investigating. In other news. . . ."

She was bent over the open trash can, clutching the fragments of shell, as though frozen. Her only movement at first was to clench her fist, crushing further the shell in her hand. Slowly, unbelieving, she stood erect and turned to look at the television. It gave no denial of what she had just heard. Slowly, so slowly, she walked to the set and turned it off. *God, Jerry, no*! Her face began to distort, her stomach to cramp, and she bent over, elbows on her thighs, hands covering her face, the egg shells being pulverized against her cheek, falling eventually to the rug.

No coherent thought would come to her. She could only scream, once, twice, in great pain, then to stop that noise, she ran and threw herself across her bed, burying her face in the pillow to choke back the screams. The tears came then, great sobs shaking her body, and she pounded the mattress with her fists as though there was someway to beat this anguish out of herself.

She heard ringing, far away, repetitious. Then she knew. The phone. Slowly, painfully, she pushed herself from the bed and, staggering a little, made her way to the wall phone in the kitchen.

"Joanna, this is Hank. What's up?"

The voice was so cheerful. "Oh-h Hank. Something. . .awful. . .has happened."

He heard the hysteria in her voice. "What's wrong?" She didn't answer. He heard only a strange noise. She was crying, sobbing actually. "Joanna, what happened? Tell me."

"The man. . .in the subway. I killed him."

"What?"

"The man. . .Jerry Wofford, I-I. . .killed him."

Hank heard the rise in pitch of her voice, the ragged edge and tried to calm his own. "Joanna, you're talking nonsense."

"Jerry. . .God, Jerry. . .I killed him."

He listened, trying to make sense of it, but he could detect only meaningless words. . .subway. . .patient . . .suicide. . .all her fault. All he knew for certain was that she was coming apart. "Joanna, I'm coming over there." Still her torrent of incoherent words raced on. He couldn't stop them. "Joanna, listen to me." She didn't. "*Joanna*, stop, listen to me." He heard a pause and leaped into it. "Do you hear me, Joanna? I'm coming over there. I'll be there as soon as I can." He hung up without knowing whether she heard him or not.

The girl who opened the door looked terrible, at least as terrible as it was possible for her to look to him, hair disheveled, eyes red, cheeks tear stained. And that look in her eyes, wild, slightly demented, teetering toward hysteria. He said nothing, just swept her in his arms, holding her close, trying to comfort her. He could feel her sobs shaking her body. "I'm here now. Everything will be all right."

Against his shoulder he heard sounds, muffled, distorted, then he realized she was saying, "awful. . .so awful." Another word sounded like "terrible."

He abandoned trying to say anything. She couldn't hear him. He just held her, patted her back, stroked her hair. It was not at all unpleasant for him. Ultimately, the bursting of sobs slackened, and he was able to lead her to the couch and sit down with her, still clutching her in his arms, her head against his shoulder.

"It's. . .it's so. . .awful. . .so terrible."

"I know." He had no idea what she was talking about. All he wanted to do was comfort her, somehow get her back together. "But everything's all right now. I'm here."

"No it. . .isn't." There was more timbre to her voice now. "Jerry's. . .dead. I. . .I. . .killed him."

He patted her back. "You didn't kill anyone."

"I-I did so. . .in the. . .subway."

At least she was arguing with him. It made her more coherent. He laughed. "Okay, have it your way. You killed somebody."

She raised her head from his shoulder. "God, Hank. . .don't laugh. It's. . .not funny. A man. . .is dead."

He knew he was getting to her. "I'm not laughing at a dead man—but at you." He brushed her cheek with his finger. "You look awful. What did you do? Go over Niagara Falls without a barrel?"

Her anger burst through her sobs. "Damnit, Hank, don't patronize me. What's it matter. . .how I look? Can't. . .can't you understand a man is dead?"

"What do you want me to do? I haven't had too much practice coping with hysterical women."

Angrily she moved away from him. "I am not hysterical."

He smiled at her. "Not now, anyway. Can you tell me now what happened?"

She stared at him, slowly recognizing that he had tricked her. She was calmer now, her breath more orderly. "Oh Hank, it's so. . .terrible. I killed him. . .the man in the subway."

He shook his head slowly. "You've said that six times. What subway? What man? Who did you kill? I don't know what you're talking about."

She pointed to the TV. "On the news. A man. . .

jumped in front of the subway. He's dead."

"That's a start. Who's dead?"

"Jerry Wofford. He-he was my. . .my patient. I-I killed him."

He could sense her starting to edge toward hysteria again. "Nonsense. You killed no one."

"But I did. . .I did."

"Were you in New York? Were you in the subway? Did you push him?"

"No, no, but. . .but don't you see, I-I made him jump."

"How did you? Did you say, Jerry Whatsisname, please go jump in front of a subway train?"

"Damnit, don't patronize me. I told you not to."

"I'm not patronizing you. I'm just trying to find out what you think happened. And you're doing a lousy job of telling me."

She did then. Prompted by questions from Hank, she got out the story of Jerry Wofford, her treatment of him, his falling in love with her, the dismal failure of yesterday. It was not easy for Hank to hear. Mental images of her in bed with this guy sped across his brain.

"Do you see now? I killed him."

"No you didn't. You didn't push—"

"All right, so I didn't actually kill him. But I'm the reason he killed himself. Can't you understand that?"

"I can understand you think that's what happened, but it's just not so. If anyone's to blame, it's Lambert." He saw her startled expression. "Yes, it's Lambert. I don't know anything about this sex therapy crap. But I don't see how anybody can expect a guy to be in bed with a beautiful girl every day and *not* have him fall for her." Still she stared at him. He knew he was making progress. "What did you say this guy had? Primary impotence?"

She nodded.

"There you have it. You were probably the first girl he'd ever had. Guys always fall for the first girl. I know I did."

She looked at him a moment longer, then got up from the couch and began to pace the room, thinking. He watched her a moment, then saw the two glasses, half full of booze, on the table. She'd had someone else here earlier. At least she'd called him when she got in trouble.

"That's too easy, Hank, blaming it all on Lambert."

"You're still defending him?"

"No. I know what he's done, to me, to others, to lots of people. Believe me I know. I even know he's the root cause of Jerry's death. But I'm to blame, too. I'm the one he got in bed with. I'm the one who—"

"And I'm probably to blame, too. No man is an island. The bell tolls for me. All that sort of thing."

She stopped and turned to him. "I know what you're trying to do, Hank. You have made me feel better. But the simple fact is I am partially to blame for Jerry's death—not partially, a whole lot. I allowed Lambert to use me. I got in bed with a seriously disturbed man, a man who was suicidal. I thought I was a hotshot sex therapist. I wasn't. I was playing games with a man's life." She saw Hank opening his mouth to speak. "Don't you see? If Lambert was the gun, I was the trigger."

Slowly he closed his mouth, then shrugged in resignation. He picked up a whiskey glass from the table. "Got any more of this stuff?"

The question interrupted her thoughts, startling her. "What? Oh that. Yes, in the kitchen."

He went there, leaving her alone, slowly, painstakingly making them both a drink. When he returned, handing one to her, he said, "Okay, I guess a little guilt is good for the soul. The question is—what are you going to do about it now? He's dead."

She looked at him sharply. "I'm going to get Lambert, that's what. I called you earlier to tell you that. I want to get Lambert. I want to close him up. I want you to help me do it. More than ever he's got to be stopped."

A smile spread his face. "Have you eaten?"

"What?"

"When was the last time you ate?"

"I-I don't know."

"I thought so. You look terrible. You're too thin—and that's fact, not patronization."

He wheeled, went to the kitchen, found some half-dried bacon, eggs and a half loaf of hardly fresh bread. At once he began the business of cooking for her. "Tell me everything you know about Lambert."

She did. As he fried the late night breakfast for two and as they sat in the living room eating it around the coffee table, he sitting on the couch, she on the floor, she told him of her visit to Dr. Quennell and what she'd learned. She told him of Lambert's immense fees and heard Hank make a whistling sound and refer to greed.

"What do you know about Lambert and Laura?"

Joanna shrugged. "Not much. She was on his advisory board. I think she was around there a good bit. I think she helped him with community relations."

"He sure as hell needs it. But she did more than that—two hundred grand more."

"Yes, you told me."

"If a guy's got the gall to charge twenty grand for two weeks of phony treatment, he sure as hell would have no trouble getting ten times that much from a lonely, middle-aged widow."

"Hank, I know your interest is in Laura, but I think that's a side track. Can't Lambert be arrested, charged or something in Wofford's death?"

"There you go again. I doubt if Lambert pushed him."

"I know that. But Lord, Hank, there must be some laws against what he did."

"Don't ask me. I draw ads and book covers for a living. All I know about the law is that if you drive too fast somebody blinks red lights at you from behind."

"Can't we find out, ask somebody?"

"Sure, and we will—tomorrow. I've an appointment with a police detective to talk about Laura's suicide."

She brightened. "Can I go along?"

"Sure. I'll bet Detective Rosetti would love to meet a pretty girl with a tearstained face."

She touched her cheeks. "Do I look that ghastly?"

"I refuse to answer on the grounds I might patronize you."

"And you were, too." But she got up, went to her bedroom and washed and fixed her face. When she came out, she said, "Now will you stop badgering me?"

He seemed not to have heard. "You know, Joanna, I think you're wrong. Laura isn't a side track. On consecutive days two people who knew Lambert, went to his place, have committed suicide. There's got to be some connection, don't you think?"

"I suppose so."

"We have to find out what it is—or rather you do. When you go to work tomorrow, nose around, see what you can find out about Laura."

"No I won't." She saw him look at her, startled. "I've quit, Hank. I'm never going to set foot in there again. All I want is never to lay eyes on Dawson Lambert again."

24

Hank arose early and made a quick trip to New York to get some clothes and bring Timmy back to Westport. Vicki asked him if he thought it wise to take Timmy to the funeral. Hank said it was part of life. He ought to experience it. She also asked him if he was going to move to Westport with Timmy. He said he didn't know. There were advantages to life in the posh suburbs, but he'd do nothing without consulting her.

Hank drove too fast back to Westport. He knew he wasn't hurrying to make the eleven o'clock funeral. He was eager to see Joanna. Lord he was happy just to see her and be with her. He'd thought it was over. He had accepted her loss. Now he had another chance. If it took Laura's death and that other guy's death to do it, so be it. He wouldn't muff this opportunity.

"Hank, let's get one thing straight," she said last night. "I want to close up Lambert if I can. But I don't want to get re-involved with you."

"I know. You got some other guy. You're going to California."

She considered saying there was no one else and she was not going to California, then decided not to. "It's just—Hank, it's no good, you and I. There've been too many Jerry Woffords, too many other guys for you and me ever to make it. Do you understand? We'd just end up hurting each other. We'd be miserable."

"Whatever you say, Joanna."

Now, driving up the Connecticut Thruway, he smiled. Hope springs eternal in some part of the human anatomy.

"What're you smiling at, Daddy?"

"Was I smiling? I guess I'm just happy to be with you, son."

"Me, too, Daddy. Will I be able to swim in Grandma Laura's pool?"

"Later today? I don't see why not." Maybe he could bribe Joanna to come.

The funeral, while very well attended, was mercifully brief. Joanna was there in a black summer suit he considered most fetching. God, the woman excited him. He watched as she squatted and hugged Timmy. Lucky kid. When she stood up, the boy was holding her hand.

Joanna didn't want to sit with Timmy and Hank. She wasn't part of the family. But she didn't know how to get out of it without hurting Timmy. She saw Lambert. She tried to avoid looking at him, but failed in that. For his part, Lambert was surprised to see Joanna sitting up front. The red-haired guy was the stepson. He got the money. Maybe that's why Joanna was sitting with him and the kid. Couldn't blame her.

After the interment, Joanna spoke to Charles Randall, expressing her condolences. The man seemed genuinely bereaved, quite unnerved. "Could I come and talk to you, Doctor?"

He seemed surprised. "Of course, do you want an appointment?"

"It's not medical, doctor—something personal. I-I need some advice."

"About what?"

She looked around. "I can't go into it here, Doctor, but it has to do with. . .with medical ethics. You are on that committee, aren't you?"

"Yes." They arranged to meet that evening. He offered to take her to dinner and she accepted.

Hank hadn't realized the ladies of the Congregational Church were having a potluck lunch after the funeral. He could think of no graceful way out of it, and he forced himself to tolerate what he considered a massive intrusion into his day. He didn't know any of these people and didn't want to. It was past two-thirty before Hank and Joanna could leave, drop Timmy off with Mrs. Dicentes, and go to the police station.

Detective Al Rosetti left no doubt of his ancestry. He was short, dark, with lots of curly black hair and a slightly swarthy complexion. Looking around the station, Hank saw many others of Italian descent. Then he remembered Laura's telling him that with all the exurbanites moving in and out of Westport, it was the indigenous Italian population which kept the town running. They manned the police and fire departments, city offices, postal service.

"I really don't have much to tell you, Mr. Kraft."

He and Joanna sat across Rosetti's desk. He was in shirt sleeves, tie at half mast, obviously not thrilled by what he considered an intrusion into police affairs. "Have you investigated Laura's death—I mean Mrs. McGovern's?"

"Yes, and we really have come up with nothing. I simply don't know why your stepmother took her life."

"There's no doubt it was suicide?"

"None at all. The coroner's report says barbituate poisoning. She took enough pills to kill six people—even without the alcohol."

She left no note."

"I know." He sighed and picked up a pencil and began to play with it, sliding it through his fingers, point down against his desktop. "Most suicides are accidents, Mr. Kraft—or miscalculations. They're angry, hurt.

They're going to show someone, make them sorry for being mean to them. I think this is particularly true with sleeping pills. The victim swallows a handful and waits. Maybe they write a note. They plan to call up whoever they're mad at and tell them what an awful thing they've done. They know damn good and well the person will rush over, save them and be sorry. They'll get a lot of attention. But sometimes they miscalculate. They wait too long. The pills have taken effect too much. Or, the person they're calling isn't home." He shrugged. "Marilyn Monroe was found with the phone in her hand."

"Was Laura on the phone?"

"No, and that's the point. Sometimes, suicides really want to do it. They want to be dead. No notes, no phone calls. Nothing but death. I think that's the case with Mrs. McGovern."

"But why?" It was Joanna speaking. "She was so happy. She was going to be married."

The detective nodded. "I know. There just is no reason for it I can find—except. . . ." He put down the pencil and leaned over his desk. "Her lawyer, her doctor, a couple people who knew her well tell me Mrs. McGovern was. . .well, moody. She had her ups and downs. Nothing too serious. She wasn't under any medication for it. But she'd get depressed sometimes. Apparently she was a sensitive lady, feelings easily hurt, that kind of thing. I can only figure she got in the dumps and decided to end it all. I'm sorry. That's all I can tell you." He wanted to end this discussion. "We're still investigating. If anything turns up, I'll call you."

Hank was not about to be dismissed. "Did you know she gave two hundred thousand dollars to Lambert—the Center for Human Potential or whatever it's called?"

Rosetti raised an eyebrow. "Yes, I knew that. Two hundred eighteen and change, to be exact."

"There you have it. That's a lot of money. Don't you think it strange?"

"What's strange about it? You and I might think two hundred and eighteen grand a lot of money. Was it to her? I understand she was loaded. Old money. Two hundred and eighteen might have been pocket money to her."

"Don't BS me, Lieutenant."

"Sergeant."

"That's a lot of money to anybody. Was Lambert blackmailing her?"

Rosetti looked at Hank sharply, his eyes squinting a bit. "Was he?"

"I don't know. I'm asking you."

Rosetti smiled. "We have no reason to believe Dr. Dawson Lambert blackmailed your mother or anyone else. We don't deal in speculations around here."

"Then how come you know about the two hundred grand?"

Again the detective smiled. "Let's just say we try to know what goes on in our town."

"Sergeant Rosetti, I work at the Center."

"I know."

She hesitated, then went ahead. "Last night, in New York, a man. . .jumped in front of a subway. The TV said it was suicide."

"Yes."

Again she hesitated, watching the detective's black eyes, hard, intent, questioning. "He—he was my patient."

"At the Center?"

"Yes."

"You were treating him for some kind of. . .of sexual hangup?"

"Yes. He was impotent."

Rosetti smiled, just a little. "Exactly what do you do

at the Center for Human Potential, Miss Caldwell?''

He seemed to be all eyes. "I-I'd rather not say." She saw him raise an eyebrow.

Hank came to her rescue. "That's what we're trying to get at. Two suicides from people at the Center on consecutive days, one Tuesday, the other Wednesday."

"We figure Mrs. McGovern died Saturday night or early Sunday."

"All right, Saturday, but you're quibbling. You must get my point."

He acted like Hank was a nuisance. His gaze returned to Joanna. "I gather you think there was some link between this man's treatment and his suicide in New York."

"I don't think—I know there was."

"And what was that?"

Joanna bit at her lip and looked away from him. "This is very difficult for me, Sergeant."

"Will it help if I say you are not being recorded? Everything you tell me will remain confidential unless you tell me otherwise."

Joanna again looked at him, feeling the penetration of his eyes. Yes, this was what she had come here to do. "Jerry Wofford was at the Center for two weeks of treatment, which is customary. During that time he. . .he became. . .emotionally involved with me. He became jealous of my other patients. He followed me, came to my house. He became very. . .difficult."

"Were you. . .*emotionally involved* with him?"

"No, not at all—except as the treatment required."

"And what exactly does this treatment consist of?" Rosetti saw the acute distress on her face. He watched it a long moment then said, "I'll withdraw that question. I gather what you are saying is that this Wofford fell in love with you and—"

"He only thought he was in love. It was just an

infatuation—solely on his part. I told him that."

"In any event, you believe his love for you, his infatuation, whatever it was, led him to jump in front of a subway train."

"Yes. That's what I believe happened."

There now came a long pause. Rosetti was obviously deep in thought, staring off, leaning back in his chair. Finally he leaned over his desk and fastened his gaze on Joanna. "Miss Caldwell, why are you telling me this? After all, you work at the Center. You're employed by Dr.—"

"Not any more. I quit yesterday."

That news obviously startled the detective. "I see. May I ask why you quit?"

"I found out—I mean to say I came to realize the methods of treatment Dr. Lambert uses were not. . .proper. They were not in the best interests of the patients. They certainly were not in my best interest. I discovered Dr. Lambert is only in it for money. He is charging outrageous fees—and only harming the patients. Jerry Wofford's death is proof of that."

"And Laura McGovern's death, too."

Rosetti glanced at Hank. "Was she a patient there?"

"I don't know. Not that I know of."

Rosetti looked at Joanna questioningly, and she shook her head that she didn't know either. "What sort of fees are you talking about, Miss Caldwell—the outrageous ones?"

"I know Jerry Wofford paid ten thousand dollars—twice the usual fee. Then he paid an additional amount for extra treatments. . .which were interrupted with his death. I don't know how much more he paid. I know of another patient who paid twenty thousand."

The detective whistled. "That much."

"He was a celebrity. I guess he could afford it."

"Did he object to paying so much?"

"No, not at all. But I think it's terrible, Sergeant. I think Dr. Lambert should be put behind bars for ripping people off this way."

Rosetti laughed. "Miss Caldwell, if we locked up everyone who overcharged, this country would be one vast prison. I'm sorry. Greed is not a crime in the United States."

"It ought to be."

He laughed a moment longer, but it quickly faded. "Miss Caldwell, I get the impression you are, shall we say angry at your former employer. I gather you would like to—"

"Close him up? Yes indeed. I want to see him run out of town at the least and behind bars if possible."

"Why? Because he overcharges? Because someone jumped in front of a subway train?"

"That, yes—and more. I think he's running a racket, taking money under false pretenses." She stopped, staring at the dark eyes. "And I have. . .personal reasons. I don't want to go into them. Just say he took advantage of me."

"I see." He smiled. "No, actually I don't see. But that's all right." He hesitated, looking at her, then at Hank Kraft, then back to Joanna. "I said a minute ago anything you said to me would be confidential. If I were sure you would afford me the same privilege, I might tell you something."

He watched the two heads nod, saw expectant looks. "I think I can tell you this department—there are other agencies interested, too, but we are the primary ones at the moment—well, we're, shall we say, *interested* in Dr. Lambert and his dandy little sex clinic. We have had some complaints. A couple of things you mention, Miss Caldwell, excessive fees, prolonged treatment, what seems to be less than satisfactory treatment, have been brought to our attention—not just locally, but from other police agencies around the country. We have undertaken a little investigation to see if there are any *irregularities* up there at the Center."

Hank spoke. "There are. Believe me there are."

Rosetti glanced at him. "Perhaps. But these cases are difficult. We have need to be careful. We must work in the framework of the law. We must determine if any laws have been broken first of all." He hesitated, again fixing his eyes on Joanna. "Miss Caldwell, I have an idea you might be useful to us, if you'd like to be."

"I'll do anything."

He looked at her a long moment as though assessing her, her words. Then he smiled and looked at both of them. "Miss Caldwell, Mr. Kraft, as a sergeant I get to boss patrolmen. Unfortunately I get bossed by lieutenants, captains and others. What I'd like to do is have a little chat with my superiors. Then, if you're agreeable and things work out as I expect they will, I'd like to see you both later today."

"Of course." The words came in unison. Hank added, "Any time."

"How about six o'clock or so?"

Joanna looked pensive. "Will it take long?"

"It might."

"Then I can't." She looked at Hank. "I made an appointment to see Dr. Randall. I want to ask him something."

Hank wanted to ask what, but the detective spoke first. "How about afterwards. Sometimes the days get long around here." Arrangements were made for Rosetti to come to Hank's house—really Laura McGovern's place.

Hank was disappointed not to take Joanna to dinner—and a little miffed that she didn't invite him along to talk to Randall. But he tried not to show it.

25

Joanna met Dr. Charles Randall at the Showboat, a large, popular restaurant and nightclub below Stamford. It was in Greenwich actually. She thought it a strange choice of meeting place—she did not have dancing in mind—but the dining room was relatively peaceful and the view of the water was nice.

There was the usual business of drinks, ordering of food, various items of small talk. Joanna measured him carefully. This choice of restaurant made her wary, but she could detect no sign he was trying to come on to her. Indeed, he seemed quite depressed, exactly as a man would who had buried his fiancee that day. He had picked the Showboat, she decided, simply because it was well known and easy to find at a Thruway exit.

As soon as she could, she got to the point. "Dr. Randall, what constitutes medical ethics—I mean, I guess, lack of medical ethics."

"What does a physician do that violates medical ethics? Is that what you're asking?" She nodded. "A great many things, actually. In simplest terms, you could say anything that violates the Hippocratic oath."

"Could you be more specific? Isn't unnecessary surgery one thing?"

"Yes. We watch that carefully. Any tissue removed is examined to determine if it was diseased."

"What else?"

"Oh, any violations of the law, of course. Gross incompetence. Improper medical treatment. Improper use of drugs. Careless writing of prescriptions for narcotics or harmful drugs. Gross neglect of patients. Any sort of gross misuse of patients. Improper keeping of medical records. Violating rules of confidentiality. That sort of thing. As I said, there are many ways to violate the AMA code of ethics."

"I see. And how do you prove it?"

He smiled for the first time. "Not very easily, I'm afraid. Most physicians—nearly all—are scrupulously ethical. And those who aren't are extremely knowledgeable. They know the law, the code of ethics, and are in most cases extremely adept in concealing their actions. It is simply very difficult to prove the difference between an honest mistake or misjudgment and deliberate unethical conduct."

"But you do prove it sometimes?"

"Yes."

"What do you do then?"

"To the offending physician? It depends upon the seriousness of the violation. We may, in the case of a minor matter or first offense, merely speak to the man, tell him what's he's doing wrong and ask him to stop it. Indeed, this takes care of the matter in most cases. In more serious matters involving repeated offenses, we may censure a physician. This is extremely serious for him. He'll lose patients. Word will get around. Other doctors will stop making referrals to him."

"Censure. That is the worst that can happen?"

A second smile came to him. "That is extremely harsh, I assure you. But there are other recourses. We can recommend that he be removed from the medical staff of a hospital. As a last resort, we can ask the state to revoke a physician's license. It's happened a few times."

Joanna smiled broadly. "Good."

"Why are you asking me all this? Do you have someone in mind? Do you wish to make a complaint?"

"I do. Dr. Dawson Lambert." She saw him react, but she couldn't read it. Was it surprise? Yes, but something else. "Dr. Randall, until yesterday I worked for Dr. Lambert. I am familiar with his methods, what he does. He charges outrageous fees, for example."

"My dear, the AMA tries to control the fees charged by physicians. But we can only recommend. In the last analysis, a doctor's fee structure is a matter between himself and his patients. Whatever we might think privately, a high fee is not unethical."

"But what if his treatments are harming people? Isn't that unethical?"

"Of course—if it can be proven. In the case of Lambert—and believe me no one disapproves of what he does more than I do—it is impossible to prove anything he does is improper or unethical. There are no standards for sex therapists. If a doctor does improper or unnecessary surgery or gives incorrect or dangerous medication, if, in short, he violates standard, accepted medical practice, we can detect that. But there are no standards for treating impotence or other alleged sexual disorders. I'd like to help you, believe me, but I don't know how."

"Doctor, a patient committed suicide yesterday. Doesn't that mean something?"

She saw him turn pale and look at her in shock. "You mean Laura?"

"No, not Laura—Jerry Wofford. He was under treatment for impotence. Last night he jumped in front of a subway in New York."

He looked at her a moment, a pained expression on his face. "I'm sorry. I'm sorry for him. I'm sorry for you. And I'm sorry I cannot help you when I want to. But the plain fact is Lambert cannot be held accountable for the man's death. Dr. Lambert is operating in a gray area between medicine and psychiatry. A psychiatrist is not responsible because one of his patients turns suicidal or homicidal. The same applies to Lambert, I fear."

She looked at him. "Then you can't help me."

"I'm afraid not." He sighed. "And I would like to—believe me I would. I personally feel Lambert's so-called sex therapy is improper. I don't know what to do about it."

She looked at him. As emphatically as she could, she said, "Believe me, Doctor. I'm going to get him. I'm going to close him up, put him behind bars if I can."

He watched her for a moment. "I think I should warn you. It won't be easy."

"I don't care how hard it is."

"You may be inviting more trouble than you want."

"What sort of trouble?"

"If you make any charges against Lambert, it is certain to make the press. It seems anything involving sex does. Are you sure you want the notoriety, the scandal? It might make life difficult for you."

"I don't care, Doctor. Sometimes we have to take a stand."

He seemed to be studying her intently. "You mean that, don't you?"

Their dinner came and the process of eating consumed their attention. Conversation stopped. It seemed to Joanna he was preoccupied. There was distance between them, but she felt no need to try to breach it. She cared nothing about Charles Randall. He was of no help to her. This meal was the playing out of a string for a kite which had not flown. But why was he so nervous? Something had upset him. What? She didn't know.

Finally it came. "Joanna, I cannot sit here in silence. You shame me." It was obviously true. He wasn't looking at her, but down at his food, at nothing. "I have lied. I have hidden behind silence. You make me know—I'm not very happy about it—that I lack courage. I have too much to lose in attacking a colleague. I am unwilling to pay the price."

She didn't understand. His silence seemed to stretch to infinity. But she sensed she should not break it. Just let him be.

"Laura was a patient of Lambert's. I know it to be true, although I can't prove it. I found out about it. I berated her. I lost control of myself. I said awful things. Terrible words came out of my mouth. That is why she committed suicide."

Joanna gave no reaction. Indeed, she continued eating. Why, she didn't know. Randall was not even looking at her. Finally, when he did not speak, she said, "How do you know she was his patient?"

"He told me. Oh, not in so many words. He's too smart for that. But I knew. I became jealous—a jealous fool. A madman." Now he looked at Joanna. "I loved Laura. I really did. The idea of Lambert. . .and her. . . . I couldn't stand it."

"And that's why you haven't told the police?"

"Yes. What good would it do? Would it bring her back?" She saw the agony in his face. "It's something I'll just have to live with. It's punishment enough."

She filled her fork, lifted it, chewed, swallowed. "You said violating a patient's confidence constituted unethical conduct."

"I know. I want to get him, too. But I can't. I had no

recording device. It's his word against mine. And even if I had, all he said was that she was his patient. I knew. He knew I knew. The actual words—in court—could mean anything, just that he took a pap smear.''

"Why are you telling me this?"

"To help you do what I haven't the guts to do."

Sergeant Rosetti was at Laura's house when Joanna arrived. A drink was made for her. There was some small talk. Then Timmy got out of bed and came to see her. She hugged him, then tucked him in. He asked her to come and swim with him tomorrow. She was non-committal. She'd try. Yes, she wanted to. But she'd just have to see.

When she rejoined Hank and Rosetti, the three of them sat in a small, book-lined room which must have once been Ralph McGovern's study. Hank asked, "What did you find out from Randall?"

Joanna had been expecting this. She would tell Hank about Randall's confession—why Laura had killed herself—but she didn't want Rosetti to know. There was no sense in having the police hammer on Randall. He was suffering enough. "I learned an ethics charge is so difficult to substantiate as to be impossible."

"But they happen all the time."

"Not that often, Hank. But when they do a lot of publicity results. It just seems there are a lot of them. Usually they involve unnecessary surgery, writing prescriptions for drugs, cheating Medicare. To prove Lambert is unethical is virtually impossible. As Dr. Randall explains, Lambert's working in a gray area between medicine and psychiatry. Just about anything he does can be construed as proper treatment. There are no standard medical practices in treating sexual disorders.''

Her words just lay there, creating a sort of large, un-

pleasant lump between them. Finally Rosetti spoke.
"It's much the same with a criminal investigation.
Lambert is a licensed gynecologist. His business is
women's bodies. He treats sexual disorders. The
operative word is *sex*. That it goes on at his so-called
clinic is only to be expected."

These words were added to the lump created by
Joanna, forming a significant mound of unpleasant
reality. "Then there's nothing that can be done to stop
him?"

"I didn't say that, Miss Caldwell. There is—or I
should say there may be. It is just extremely difficult.
For one thing, any investigation of Lambert is hardly a
high priority for our department. We may not be the
South Bronx, but Westport has its crime and its
criminals. We just don't have the time or manpower to
launch any serious investigation of Lambert. I'm afraid
a significant attitude in the department is that if people
are dumb enough to spend a lot of money learning to do
what comes natural, then so be it. We have a lot more
serious crime to worry about."

"Two suicides are not serious?"

"Yes they are, Mr. Kraft, and that's why I'm here.
There is something fishy up there. We'd like to find out
what it is. But it's difficult." He paused, swallowing
from his highball. "Police work involves specific crimes
that lead to specific charges. If a man shoots somebody
it's murder or maybe felonious assault. If he sticks up a
liquor store, it's armed robbery. The police gather
evidence that leads to the charge." He sighed. "The
problem with this Lambert thing is that it is so
amorphous. We have no charge. Indeed, we don't even
know if there's a crime. Do you understand what I'm
saying?"

Both Hank and Laura nodded.

"We have at the moment only the vaguest idea of

possible charges. His high fees, his apparently inept treatment suggests a charge of conspiracy to defraud. But that's extraordinarily difficult to prove under the best of circumstances. In this case, it is virtually impossible."

"How about blackmail?"

Rosetti smiled at Hank. "Still on that, are you? Yes, of course, it's a crime. Have you any evidence?" He saw Hank shake his head. "When you do, please let me have it."

There was silence then, which Joanna broke. "Sergeant, you've said what charges are hard to prove. I have a feeling there is something else—something you view with a more positive attitude."

Again Rosetti smiled. "Yes, Miss Caldwell, there is. The very nature of the Center makes a police officer think of a charge of gross sexual imposition. It's an interesting charge. It was used a couple of times out west recently—Ohio I think. A psychiatrist was convicted for—you know, with his patients. A judge was convicted for demanding sex from some female defendants." The detective paused, looking at Joanna sharply. "Miss Caldwell, has this guy Lambert ever put his hands on you. . .has he tried to. . .to force himself on you?"

"No."

"Not once?"

"I'm sorry, Sergeant, but he hasn't. Oh, he's touched my hand, my arm maybe, but nothing. . .nothing sexual at all." She watched him frown, then swallow deeply from his glass. "I gather that's disappointing to you."

"Yes. It would have made everything much easier. Too easy, I suppose."

"I don't know, Sergeant, but I've an idea he treats female patients. There must be lots of women he's—"

"A patient's no good. He's a gynecologist. He's supposed to examine women. Even if he goes to bed with them, he's treating their sexual disorders. A patient won't work. Now if he'd done it with you—an employee —that would be gross sexual imposition. Do you know of any other employees he's—"

"No."

That word led to another bout of silence. The mound of frustration was now a small mountain. "Is there nothing we can do?"

The detective looked at Joanna. "I guess I can level with you two. We've sent in a ringer, a nice looking policewoman. She's posing as a divorcee. She's supposed to be scared of sex. I don't know the technical term."

"Orgasmic dysfunction."

"Whatever. We thought maybe something might happen. At least we'd know how the bastard operates. She's gone a few times. I'm not gonna tell you who she is. Nothing much has happened. There's been a lot of palaver. He hasn't so much as touched her. He didn't even try to get her out of her clothes."

Joanna smiled. "He will, Sergeant. That comes later."

"Yeah, I can imagine. There was only one thing. Lambert showed her a bunch of dirty pictures—video tape on a television set. It looked to. . .to the policewoman as though they were home movies made there at the Center. Now, if that is the case, and if he's showing movies of people naked and in bed without their permission, then we might be getting someplace. Unfortunately—" He sighed. "Unfortunately, the policewoman couldn't *borrow* the film." He raised his glass, drained it, and gave it to Hank who was reaching out for it. "Miss Caldwell, do you suppose you could get hold of that film long enough for us to take a look, maybe copy it?''

"No." She saw his surprise. "I told you I'd quit. I'm never going back there.''

"But just for a few minutes, just long enough to—"

"Even if I were willing to do it, which I'm not, it would still be impossible." She explained Lambert's security system. "That film is probably kept in those files, his desk or somewhere. I have no way to get into his office when he's not there. No one does.''

"There are ways of opening locked doors, Miss Caldwell. I could give you a device called a Quick Key which would—''

"No, Sergeant. I'm not going back there.''

He shrugged. "Then that's it." He took his highball from Hank and drank deeply from it. "We're all wasting our time.''

Joanna knew he was annoyed with her. But she didn't care. No one could ask her to go back there. These thoughts filled the silence until she said, "Sergeant Rosetti, isn't there a charge called procuring?''

"Yes, what about it?''

"I know you think I'm not serious about stopping Lambert. I know you think I don't want to help you. I'll prove to you I do." She hesitated. There was an expectant look on Rosetti's face. She glanced at Hank. He seemed puzzled, worried. A moment longer she hesitated. This was difficult. "Sergeant Rosetti, I couldn't tell you this afternoon. It isn't easy now, believe me. But I do want Lambert stopped. I-I was a. . .a surrogate partner. I. . .I went to bed with men. . .to cure their sexual disorders." She smiled bitterly. "—or supposedly cure them. How well I did it Jerry Wofford proves.''

Rosetti's gaze was level. "I'm not at all surprised,

Miss Caldwell. I figured as much."

"Isn't that procuring? He fixed me up with men."

"It could be. Were these guys sick? Did they have. . .whatever you call 'em—sexual disorders?"

She had been avoiding it. But now she glanced at Hank. She saw—what was it? Pain? Not exactly. There was something else. She looked back at the policeman. "They were not normal."

She saw his shrug. "There you have it—square one. If he'd fixed you up with. . .with normal guys, with men who had nothing wrong with them. If he was collecting money under false pretenses, taking dough just to let you. . .service them—then we might be getting somewhere. As it is. . . ." Again he shrugged. "I'm sorry." He stood up. "It's late. My wife might like to see somebody besides a TV set."

When he had gone and Hank had returned from showing him out, the two of them stood there, just looking at each other. "I'm sorry," she said softly. "I know you didn't want to hear that. I felt I had to."

He crossed in front of her, picked up her glass and made them both a fresh drink. "It wasn't too bad. I guess I already knew it." He handed her a glass, smiling. "Besides, it's supposedly all over with us, isn't it?"

"Yes." She met his gaze, hoping her determination showed. "I have something to tell you, Hank."

He misread her, figuring she was going to admit she cared about him. "Yes?"

"I learned something else from Randall. I couldn't tell Rosetti. Randall has suffered enough." Then she told of Randall's admission, Lambert's phone call, the fight which caused Laura's suicide.

Hank could not help but react with delight. "Then she was Lambert's patient. He was going to bed with her."

"It looks that way."

"Why would he call Randall—tell him about it?"

"Randall thinks he was trying to break up the marriage. He feels badly, not only for Laura's death, but because he played into Lambert's hands."

"Why would he care who Laura married?"

"I don't know."

Hank smiled. "Yes, you do. Laura had given Lambert two hundred grand—two hundred eighteen, to be exact. He knew if Laura married Randall, there wouldn't be any more."

Joanna hesitated. "I suppose. It makes sense."

He turned, pacing the small room, thinking. "Joanna, if Laura was his patient, there has to be some kind of record of it."

She glared at him. "Those damn files again. You want me to—"

"Wouldn't there be a record, something?"

"I suppose. He's very methodical, very orderly. But I'm not about to—"

"Would he keep a record of the money Laura gave him?"

"I don't know, Hank. All I can tell you is he is a stickler about those damn files. Everything had to be written down, times of appointment, what happened. He's very—well, methodical, as I said." Hank said nothing, just looked at her. She saw, understood. "No, Hank, don't ask me."

"But just a few minutes, no more than an hour, long enough to get into his office. Just a little while. Can't you do that—for Laura, for me?"

26

Going to Lambert's office on Monday morning was the hardest thing Joanna had ever done in her life, or so she believed. She never did make a conscious decision to go. It just happened.

Perhaps the main instigation was the phone call from Lambert on Friday. He asked why she wasn't at work. She hated hearing his voice. She wanted absolutely nothing to do with him. "Dillon had to go back to California early. I took the day off." Why didn't she tell him the truth? Why didn't she tell him off? Tell him she'd quit?

"Two days—but it's all right. Were you finished with Dillon? Was he—"

"Yes, he's all right."

"Good. I'm glad you have some time off. You've earned it. Just enjoy yourself and I'll see you on Monday."

No you won't. Why didn't she say it? The man thought he could get her to do anything. Why didn't she tell him she was wise to him? Why didn't she—yes, why didn't she?

She slept a lot over the weekend. She ran on the beach, engaged in her pampering exercises—anything to keep from thinking about what she knew she ought to do. Timmy phoned on Saturday, begging her to swim with him. Reluctantly she gave in, went there. She even stayed to eat with Hank and Timmy. *You have to eat. You know you won't at home.* She was nice to Timmy, talking with him, playing cards. But she was little more than civil to Hank. She refused to do anything that smacked of a special relationship. Shortly after Timmy was in bed, she insisted on going home. Hank walked her to her car, closed the door behind her and stood leaning over the open window.

"I think I erred."

She looked at him, saying nothing, maintaining her distance.

"I told you I had forgiven you. I know now what's important is that you forgive yourself."

She stared at him, blinked, then started the car and drove home. She did not see him on Sunday. She did call Rosetti. He brought her the gadget for opening the office door and showed her how to use it.

As she approached Lambert's office, Joanna had made up her mind to tell him she was quitting—and why. Oh, not the real reasons. Somehow she couldn't face a scene with him, the recriminations, the angry words. No, she'd tell him she'd decided to go back to school. Nothing he would say—and would he ever!—would affect her. She would not listen. She would look at him as little as possible.

Outside his door she glanced down at the lock, mentally rehearsing in her mind what she was supposed to do. The Quick Key, shaped something like a small pistol, was heavy in her purse. Yes, she'd wait around till Lambert was gone. Then she'd come and do it. Wouldn't take long.

It took courage to rap on the door and to open it when she heard the lock buzz. To her surprise he was not alone. Another man stood up as she entered, and she was introduced to Edward Mueller of Philadelphia. Lambert's next words stunned her. "Miss Caldwell will

be working with you, Ed. You'll find her one of our
most competent people.''

Joanna stared at Lambert in disbelief. What was he
up to? She saw Lambert smile at her, warmly, as if this
was the most routine of situations, then say, "This is the
Ed Mueller I mentioned to you the other day." He had
mentioned no such thing. She was to have no more
patients. He had promised to let her counsel married
couples. What was he doing to her? All other thoughts,
even her reason for coming here, fled her mind.

"I'm pleased to meet you, Miss Caldwell."

She turned to the voice and saw a man of perhaps
forty-five, maybe fifty, medium height, a little pudgy,
balding, wearing a shiny suit. He was smiling nervously
and extending his hand toward her. From long
ingrained habits of courtesy, she took it, nodded to him,
but did not speak. Rather she turned to look at
Lambert, wide-eyed, unrestrained dismay on her face.
She was so surprised she was momentarily paralyzed.
All the things she might have said were never uttered.
Lambert moved quickly to make use of the void.

"I'm sorry to do this, but I really have to be off. I'm
part of an HEW seminar in Washington on government
funding of sex education. If I don't go now, I'll miss my
flight." It was the truth. He did have to go to
Washington and he was in a hurry. He had no time to
argue with Joanna, convince her to take his new patient.
So he just stuck her with him. She'd be angry. She'd
scream and holler—no, she'd cry. But all that would be
later—after the fact. He came from around his desk and
thrust a file folder into Joanna's hand. "Now you two
stay right here, get acquainted. Order some lunch,
Joanna." He chuckled. "You know where the dining
room is." He was across the room now, pushing the
button which opened his liquor cabinet. "Make

yourselves a drink if you like."

"When will I see you again, Doctor?"

"Tomorrow—no, Wednesday. This seminar is a two-day affair. Might as well stay over. But don't worry. You'll be in good hands with Joanna." He was chuckling as he went out the door.

It seemed to Joanna the whole exercise took only seconds. What a rotten dirty trick for him to pull. How could he do this to her?

"That drink sounds good. Can I fix you one, Miss Caldwell?"

She only half heard. Still in shock, her mind on anything but her new patient, she could only manage to shake her head no. What was he doing to her? He knew she wouldn't accept another patient. The bastard, he'd cooked up this scheme to force one on her. Well, it wouldn't work. She just wasn't going to do it.

"I have to tell you, Joanna—may I call you Joanna?—it took a lot of guts for me to come here." The voice came from behind her at Lambert's bar. "But I read about Dr. Lambert and the Center for Human Potential. I knew there was nothing else for me to do but button up my courage and come here."

How was she going to tell him? It was all a mistake, a dreadful mistake. She couldn't. She wouldn't. Suddenly, she saw him standing opposite her, drink in his hand, mouth open, words tumbling out.

"I hope you'll help me, Joanna. Ever since my wife. . .my wife left me for. . .for someone else, I. . . I need help. I can't go on this way."

She saw the sincerity in his face, heard it in his voice.

"I know you can't cure me, Joanna. I know I have to do it myself. But—no buts. I will—with your help."

She stared at him. "Mr.—" She didn't even know his name.

"Mueller. Edward Mueller. It's a little hard."

"Please, Mr. Mueller, I—"

"Please let me make you a drink. You seem awfully tense." He turned and went back to the bar.

Panic welled within Joanna. She could feel a trap closing in on her. Damn Dawson Lambert. He was doing it to her again. Frantically she looked around for a means of escape. Then she realized. She was inside Lambert's office. He wasn't there. She was alone, except for this guy, this Mueller. What did he know. It was what she wanted. Everyone wanted it. She wouldn't have to force the lock.

She glanced at Mueller. His back was to her, bent over the bar. Yes, do it now. She stood up, forcing herself to be calm, not to hurry. She went behind Lambert's desk, looking for his console. There was a switch marked FILES. She flicked it and saw the panel slide away from the room. She'd done it. There were the files.

Again suppressing her excitement, she went to the files, opened a drawer, looked, closed it. Then a second drawer. A third. M's. There it was—McGovern, Laura W. She pulled the file out, laid it open over the drawer and read. She knew what she was looking for. Yes. Laura McGovern had been his patient. There were pages of notes. Over a year. My God, almost two years. She read with a praticed eye, knowing what she wanted to find. Orgasmic dysfunction. Of long standing. Lateral position. Orgasmic. Her eye swept down the page. Orgasmic. Always orgasmic. Yet, he saw her once, sometimes twice a week. He'd kept her in treatment when there was nothing wrong with her.

"I've got your drink now, Joanna. May I call you Joanna?"

Mueller's voice intruded. She glanced at him. He was

standing to her left, a few paces away, two drinks in his hand, looking at her expectantly. "I'll be right there. I just have to check something first."

She'd best hurry. She turned back to the file and dug deeper into it. Receipts. Laura McGovern. Gift of thirty-five thousand dollars. . . . Gift of fifty-seven thousand dollars to create the Laura W. McGovern Fund for charity patients. There were no charity patients that she knew of. Quickly she turned more pages. Her eye caught a drawing, an artist's sketch of a building. She read the name at the bottom. THE LAURA W. MCGOVERN PAVILION. Below that was printed, CENTER FOR POTENTIAL, CALIFORNIA BRANCH. She picked up the next page. It was full of numbers. The heading read ESTIMATED COSTS, CALIFORNIA BRANCH. Quickly she read—land, building, equipment. Total: $5,700,000. Quickly, her eyes scanned the page. One line leaped out: "Gift of Laura W. McGovern—$1,000,000."

She tried to think what all this meant. But she couldn't. Suddenly she was aware of Mueller in the room. She looked at him. He was just standing there, watching her. She didn't want him to notice what she was doing. He shouldn't think what she was doing was unusual.

She forced a smile. "I'm sorry to keep you waiting." Leaving the file on top of the drawer, she went to Mueller and accepted the drink he had made. She had to distract him, keep him from paying too much attention. "What's the nature of your. . .your problem, Mr. Mueller? You were saying something about your—" She remembered. "—your wife."

"Yes, it was a big blow to me when my wife left me. I took it very hard. I won't deny it. I think I've gotten over her—wouldn't take her back now if she begged me,

Charlotte Mallory

and she almost has. I've seen her. She's hinted. No, I'll not take her back. I've gotten over Marcia, I know I have." He exhaled deeply. "But my problem persists. I. . . I know Marcia's the cause of it. I read Masters and Johnson, you see. I know the cause, but that doesn't seem to help much."

She glanced down at his file folder, open on the chair. "Ejaculatory Incompetence." God! She'd never had a case of it. Indeed, it was not a common sexual dysfunction. The male seems normal. He reacts to a woman. He is easily erective, can, in fact, maintain it sometimes for hours. But he simply cannot ejaculate, certainly intravaginally, occasionally not at all. What a dirty trick, Lambert. What a goddamned dirty trick.

"I guess you'll want to know when my problem started. My wife—her name was Marcia—left me four years ago. She had been seeing my best friend—now a former friend as you can imagine—for a long time. I had no idea. We were celebrating our twentieth wedding anniversary when she told me the jolly news she was leaving me for Mark. A great buddy, Mark. I don't know why I never suspected anything. She said they were tired of lies. *They* were tired. They'd tried to break it up, stop seeing each other. But they couldn't. The sex was too good. They couldn't live without it, each other." Again he exhaled slowly, painfully. "I guess it's a familiar story. But I assure you it wasn't to me."

She was only half listening, her mind on the files. "Mr. Mueller—"

"Ed, Please."

"All right, Ed. Would you mind? I still need to check something in the files." She moved away from him. "You keep on talking. I'll be listening."

She was at the files now, trying to think. A million dollars. A California branch. What did it mean? She couldn't think. She remembered Mueller. He wasn't talking. She turned. "Go ahead, I'm listening."

"I don't know what you want me to say."

She couldn't remember what he'd been talking about. Oh yes. "When did your ejaculatory incompetence start? Right after your wife left you?" She turned back to the file. She didn't have to figure it out—not now anyway. It had to be important. Rosetti would want to see it. She closed the file and put it on top the cabinet to take with her.

"I-I suppose it did. I was upset. I wasn't interested in seeing other women. It was a long time before I did—almost a year I suppose. Then when I tried, I-I couldn't. Haven't been able since."

What else was she to get? Yes, the film. The dirty pictures. It must be here somewhere. "Have you tried recently, Ed?"

"I don't know what you mean by recently."

"How long since you've been with a woman?"

"A couple months. At least that long."

She was opening and closing drawers. It had to be here. But where? Did she have to look in all these drawers?

The silence from Mueller weighed on her. "Do you masturbate?" More silence. She turned to look at him. "These things have to be asked, Ed."

"I suppose. I have—but not for a long time. It's easier if I don't."

She was opening drawers now, trying to be more systematic about it. "How is that?"

"Oh, the tension, the need, builds up for a few days. Then it seems to recede. If I-I relieve myself, I have to go through the whole process again."

"I see. Do you have nocturnal emissions?"

She found it, in the bottom drawer on the right.

"No, not since I was a kid. I always wake up before. . .before anything happens."

She squatted before the open drawer. So many reels. Which one did they want. A little desperately she knew she had no time to find out. Quickly she picked up three of them to take with her. On impulse she added a fourth, closed the drawer, stood up and placed the reels on Laura McGovern's file.

She picked up her stash of stolen materials and turned back to Mueller. What was she going to do with him? "Are you sure you have ejaculatory incompetence? It's rare. Who diagnosed it?"

"My family doctor."

She looked at him, squinting a little. She didn't believe him. She'd heard of ejaculatory incompetence, but she'd never really believed it. There was no such thing as a man who couldn't do it if he wanted to. "Mr. Mueller, has it ever occurred to you that you just might not have met a woman who appeals to you? If you circulate more, met more—"

"I've tried, lots of times, Joanna. And please call me Ed."

"I'm just trying to suggest perhaps you don't need treatment. I'd like to save—" she remembered. "How much are you paying, Mr.—Ed?"

"I paid by check just now. Twelve thousand five."

God! The greedy bastard. She wasn't going to be a party to it. Never again would she. . . . "Ed, I'm sorry you paid so much money. I can't help you. I just can't."

There was a wounded look to him. "But why? Dr. Lambert said. . ."

She couldn't tell him the truth. What would it mean to him anyway? "Mr. Mueller, I know it's in the literature. Masters and Johnson described it. But, honestly, I don't believe there is any such thing as ejaculatory incompetence. I think—"

"Then why can't I—"

"Dr. Lambert is just taking advantage of you, getting you to pay a great deal of money for something you can—"

"I don't care about the money. It's worth anything to me to. . .to be normal, to. . . ."

She sighed. "Mr. Mueller, there really is nothing wrong with you, believe me. I tried to tell you, if—"

"You don't know. How do you know?"

"—you just circulate, go out with women. Just go out on dates, dinner, movies or something. Just enjoy yourself. Your problem is you worry too much. You feel pressured. Just relax and it will happen naturally. You don't need—" She made an expansive gesture. "—all this—me."

He wasn't even listening. "You don't know. There's no way for you to know."

"*All right*, I don't know. I probably don't know anything. But I'm trying to do you a favor. Go home, stop payment on your check. This is no place for you. It's no good, believe me."

Annoyance, stubbornness was in his face. "I'm not going to go. I paid my money. I want what's coming to me. It's my right. I know what's wrong with me."

She looked away from him, sighing deeply. Insufferable. This man was insufferable. This whole situation was insufferable. Why wouldn't he believe her? Once again she tried to reason with him, making her voice as calm as she could. "Mr. Mueller, believe me, you are being taken advantage of. Dr. Lambert is just taking your money. He's—"

"Why won't you believe me? What do I have to do to prove it to you? I can't do it. I haven't been able to since my wife left me."

so. "Mr. Mueller, did you read *all* of Masters and Johnson?" She saw him shaking his head. "Did you read the early chapters in which Masters and Johnson talk about the people who need sex therapy, the history taking, the counseling, the screening, the attitudes they encourage? Did you read any of that?"

"No."

"Mr. Mueller, Masters and Johnson—no reputable sex therapist brings a patient in and throws him in bed with a woman and expects anything to happen—other than a few cheap thrills. Ed, do you want to be cured?"

"Yes, of course. That's why I'm here."

She nodded, unaware it was affirmation of her own realization she was doing the right thing. "All right, then sit down. You and I are going to have a nice long talk." He looked around for a place to sit. "There, on the bed is okay." He sat and she came around to the far side of the bed, standing over him. "Tell me about your wife, Ed."

"My wife? What about her?"

"What did she look like? Was she pretty?"

He hesitated, thinking, obviously forming a visual image. "No, not really. She was short, about your size I guess, but heavier. She wasn't fat but—" He gave a bitter laugh. "Why am I protecting her. Yeah, she was fat, thick in the waist, big breasts."

"You liked that?"

"Yeah, I guess so. Sure, why not?"

"Was she blonde, brunette?"

"Brunette, sort of dark brown. She dyed it to hide the gray."

"Pretty?"

"No, not really, not nearly as beautiful as you. She didn't have nearly as good a figure. You're a hundred times better than her."

"I'm also a lot younger, Ed." She turned, wanting a chair. She should sit, not tower over him. But she didn't want to sit on the bed beside him. The chair from the office.

She went to get it, then saw Lambert's files, the reels of film on her desk. Lord, she should get that to Rosetti now. She turned to Mueller. "Ed, do you mind coming with me? I've got to run an errand, then we'll talk."

Mueller beside her in the Karmann Ghia, she drove downtown to the police station, leaving him in the car while she ran inside. Rosetti wasn't there. She felt a moment of panic, then left the material with the desk sergeant to give to the detective. "He'll know what it is."

"Who'll I say left this?"

"Joanna Caldwell. Tell him to phone me."

More deliberately now, she returned to the car and Ed Mueller. As she backed the car and started away, she realized she didn't want to return to the Center, couldn't. But where? A bar was no place to talk to him. Her home. Why not? If she were a full-fledged psychologist, she might have an office in her home.

As she drove down Imperial Avenue toward the beach, she tried to remember the causes of ejaculatory incompetence. There is nothing wrong with the man. His failure is entirely psychological. Some event, something he's seen, knows about or fears has traumatized him so badly he cannot release his semen. An unfaithful wife has caused more than a few of them. The knowledge his wife was cheating on him behind his back, laying with his best friend. . . . Yes, it would explain Mueller.

At almost that precise moment, someone else was deep in thought while driving a car. Only this one was

being driven at a higher rate of speed, for Dawson
Lambert felt great urgency to get back to Westport.

Going the other way, from Westport to LaGuardia
Airport to catch the shuttle for Washington, he had felt
exhilarated. The look on Joanna Caldwell's face
amused him greatly. He had simply stuck her with
another patient, and had she been mad! If looks could
kill. But he knew her—better than she knew herself.
She was a sucker for a hardluck story. Any man could
get her to do anything—if she felt sorry for him. And
she'd feel sorry for Mueller all right. She'd protest,
swear to herself she wasn't going to do it, but she
would. Mueller would tell about his wife, how he
couldn't do it—oh yes, it'd be easy. They were probably
at it right now. His mind visualized the scene, Joanna
pumping away, maybe going down on him. The images
excited Lambert. Lucky man Mueller. Maybe he should
have asked for fifteen grand.

Yes, things were going well now. Laura McGovern's
death had been a worry, but no note had turned up.
Nothing pointed to him. So, the million was gone.
Wasn't it anyway if she married Randall, the prick?
This way he got a hundred grand. Not bad. He'd earned
it. And there was another good thing. He wouldn't have
to get it up with her anymore. This new one would be
more fun. Younger. Nice tits. Just this morning he'd
stuck his hand down her bra, up her skirt. Driving his
Cadillac into the airport parking lot, he laughed. God,
the way she'd jumped. Such a struggle. You'd think
he'd raped her. Now that didn't hurt, did it, Helen?
You're no worse off because someone touched you.
Yeah, Helen Wexler would be fun. She wanted it
bad—every protesting step of the way.

Yes, everything was going just fine. Laura
McGovern's death had paved the way for Helen Wexler.
That creep Wofford's kicking the bucket had freed

Joanna for Mueller. Poor Joanna. Back in the sack.
There'd be hell to pay when he got back to
Westport—only there wouldn't be. He wasn't going to
take any more crap from her. He'd humored her long
enough. She'd do what she was told. What she needed
was a little authority in her life.

Lambert really did believe this—he knew he could
control Joanna Caldwell—yet, something bothered
him. She was acting strangely, staying away from the
office, acting so distant on the phone. She wanted to
quit, he knew. Only she couldn't. The video tape he had
with her and a half dozen guys would assure that. She
was probably getting uppity because she was going out
with that guy Kraft, America's newest millionaire.
Wonder how Kraft would like to see some home
movies? Too bad he wasn't taping her going down on
Mueller.

Lambert was standing in line waiting to board the
shuttle when it came to him. That Joanna was angry,
wanted to quit wasn't what bothered him. He had left
her alone in his office with Mueller. Dumb. How could
he have been so stupid? She wouldn't. It wasn't
possible. He even shook his head, told himself not to
worry. With Mueller there, Joanna wouldn't look
around. And what would she hope to find if she did? At
once he left the line at the gate and headed for his car.
Joanna was seeing Kraft. He was Laura McGovern's
stepson.

Inside her apartment with Mueller, Joanna was
momentarily flustered. Thank God she had cleaned the
place over the weekend. She pointed to the couch. "Sit
there, Ed." She pulled over the other stuffed chair,
closer to him, so she was facing him over the coffee
table.

"There's nothing physically wrong with you, Ed.

It seemed to snap in her mind. If she was right, and she knew she was, it would prove something. Procuring, certainly. Lambert was taking money, soliciting men for her. And it was unethical. Taking money, lots of money, for unnecessary medical treatments. Yes. Then a vision of what she would be doing came to her. She recoiled inwardly. She shuddered. But it had happened so often already. She had said she would do anything to get Lambert.

She looked at him a moment, her eyes squinting. "All right. Come with me. You'll get your proof."

She led him to the door, opened it, waited for him to pass through, then suddenly stopped. She had forgotten to close the door on the files. "Excuse me," she said again to Mueller. "I'll be with you in a minute."

She went back inside, leaving him standing in the hallway outside the door. Behind Lambert's desk she reached to push the button, then stopped, an idea beginning to form. Lambert had left her alone in here. She might as well use it. If Lambert had kept Laura McGovern in extended treatment, he must have done it with others.

It turned out to be more time consuming than she figured, searching through files for women's names, checking the records. She was aghast when fifteen minutes had passed. She had to go. Couldn't take any more time. She had pilfered three files. It would have to do. As she closed the files and hurried out of the office, profusely apologizing to Mueller for keeping him waiting, she heard the door lock shut. No one could enter that room now. Not even Lambert's secretary. It gave her savage glee to think that maybe, just maybe, with any luck at all, Lambert's dirty trick on her, trying to stick her with another patient, might backfire on him.

27

In the passage to her office with Mueller, Joanna steeled herself. It had to be done. She had to prove there was nothing wrong with Mueller. She had done it with so many guys. What would one more matter? She could do it. It would be worth it to get Lambert.

She let him into her office and deposited her stolen materials on her desk. She had to get these to Rosetti as soon as she could. Had to get this over with quick. She looked at Mueller. He was standing there, expectant, perhaps even a little apprehensive. He might have been visiting the doctor for a checkup.

Suddenly, it seemed to Joanna the walls of the office were closing in on her. She felt hot. She stepped past Mueller, opened the door and entered the treatment room. Yes, that was better, more space, sunlight through the windows. But the bed, God, the bed.

Get it over with. Just get it over with.

She turned to Mueller behind her. "All right, Mr. Mueller—Ed. Take off your clothes and we'll find out what's the matter with you." The abruptness of her words shocked her. No discussion, no preliminaries, just take off your clothes. She saw he was surprised, too. Then he began to remove his jacket, his tie. He started to unbutton his shirt.

She watched him, hesitating, not wanting to do this.

Just get it over with. Yes. It meant a procuring charge against Lambert. She brought her hands to her blouse and began to work the buttons. Strange. Her fingers didn't seem to work right. She managed the first, then the second, all of them. She pulled the blouse out of her skirt, conscious of a flash of bare breast as she did so. She looked at him. He was watching, pupils of his eyes wide. There was nothing wrong with the man but lust. Still she looked at him. He was waiting for her to remove her blouse, eager, wanting, excited, and she was aware of her hands gripping the front of the open fabric, ready to remove it. *Oh my dear, you're not. I'd never allow you near one of my clients.*

She turned, went to the bathroom and closed the door, standing before the mirror over the sink, looking at herself. Would she be able to look in a mirror after this? She remembered the little she knew about treatment of ejaculatory incompetence—and shuddered. As a sex surrogate she would masturbate him. No matter his difficulty, she should get him to ejaculate, prove to him he could, that there was nothing wrong with him. Even if she had to do fellatio, she was to get him to ejaculate. Again she shuddered. She was to keep doing it until finally she gained intromission while he was still ejaculating. If only a single drop came inside her, it would prove to him he could ejaculate within a woman. Mental images of what she would be doing flicked over her mind.

"I can't. I just can't." You wanted to prove there was nothing wrong with him, prove Lambert was only procuring. "I can't." You must. Anything to stop Lambert. "I can't." She looked at the image in the mirror, saw the lips moving. "There'll be nothing left of me."

She returned to the treatment room. "Are you sure

you have ejaculatory incompetence, Ed?''

He seemed fascinated by the strip of skin showing through the front of her open blouse, but then he raised his eyes to look at her. "Yes. I told you I did."

"You can't. . .ejaculate within a woman?"

"No."

"You get an erection, achieve penetration, all that, and you still can't?"

"I told you I couldn't."

"And how long has this been going on?"

"I told you that, too—almost four years—since Marcia left me."

"Yes, I'm sorry. You did tell me that." She began to button her blouse. It was an almost involuntary act. She never made a conscious decision not to get into bed with him. She simply buttoned her blouse.

"I thought you. . .we. . .were going to. . . ."

She saw his disappointment. "No, Ed, we're not." She finished the buttons, opened her skirt and refastened it around the tail of the blouse. "How old are you, Ed?"

"Forty-eight."

Lord, a year older than her father. *You're fantasyland. I'd never let you near one of my patients.* "Ed, you said you read Masters and Johnson. That's how you learned about your condition."

"Yes."

"And you know what the treatment is. You have an idea what. . .what was going to happen. . .what you expected me to do."

"Yes."

"Is that what you expected to happen when you came here—paid your twelve and a half thousand?"

"Yes."

She shook her head, sucking in her breath as she did

Your problem is in your mind—related, I think, to your wife, the breakup of your marriage. To cure you, we must get at this problem. My getting in bed with you and. . .and performing some. . .some tricks—'' Why did she use that word? "—it's just not going to help you. Do you understand?''

"I don't know. I guess so.'' He was disappointed, she knew. He wanted what he had come for.

Haltingly at first, then more facilely, she got out of Mueller the story of his courtship with his wife, their marriage, an account—prompted by many questions from her—of their sex life. She got him to tell about his friend Mark, what he now knew about the clandestine romance between Mark and Marcia, the discovery of the affair and Marcia's infidelity.

"How did you feel?''

"How do you think I felt?''

"I know what I think you felt, but I want to hear you say it, Ed.''

"I wanted to kill her. I wanted to kill him. I wanted to go over there and shoot them both—right there in bed.''

"But you didn't.''

"Of course I didn't. They aren't worth going to prison for.''

Joanna hesitated, searching him out with her eyes. "When you are with other women, what do you think about?''

"What do you suppose? What does any man think about?''

"No, no, Ed. You're not just any man, an ordinary fellow. If I'd gone to bed with you when I started to, you'd have been thinking about whether you were going to make it. I understand that. What I want to know is what was on your mind in the beginning—right after Maria left you.''

He looked away from her. "I dunno."

"Yes you do. Weren't you thinking about your wife? Weren't you showing her how much she missed, how great you were in bed, how much other women liked you?"

"Yeah, I suppose."

Joanna knew that was wrong. The thought flitted across her mind that she was projecting herself, her attitude toward Judd Forbes. "Or were you thinking of your friend Mark with Marcia, her thighs spread, his body atop hers?" She watched him, saw pain. "Did you think of his big, powerful penis in her, where you had been so many years? Did you hear sounds, groans, moans, screams maybe? Then he pulled away. You looked. . .saw. . .his semen running out of—"

"Stop!"

Joanna saw his twisted face. "You still love her, don't you?"

"No." He looked at her. "How could I—after what she did."

"What did she do, Ed?"

"How can you ask that? What did she do? I'll tell you. I trusted Marcia. I thought we were happy. I thought we were good in bed. But it wasn't good enough. She had to have another man. She's nothing but a whore—a goddamn whore. Who can love a whore?"

Ed Mueller was a reasonably empathetic man, but he missed the effect of his words on Joanna, either that or he didn't know her well enough to read the expression on her face or, in letting out his bitterness toward his wife, he forgot all semblance of tact.

"She wants me back. I know she does, but never. When a woman's been with another man, behind my back, giving herself to him, I'll not take her back, no,

never." Then, his vehemence stopped as easily as it had
begun. He looked at Joanna, an expression almost of
horror on his face. "God, Joanna. I'm sorry. I didn't
mean—"

"It's all right. She struggled to submerge her feelings,
to somehow survive the hurt. And she made it. "I
understand. Your wife hurt you. You're angry at her."

"Yes."

"And you can't forgive her—or forget what
happened?"

"No. Once she did what she did—Oh God, there I go
again. I'm sorry. I shouldn't say things like this. I don't
know what I think. I'm just confused."

Joanna could feel her eyes beginning to smart. None
of this was what she wanted. But she was stuck, and she
grasped at the only straw she knew—to try to help the
man. "None of us is perfect, Ed. We all make mistakes.
We all do things we're. . .we're sorry for."

"He who is without sin may—"

"—cast the first stone. Yes. Maybe you should stop
picking up stones."

Then suddenly she knew. Except for Lambert's greed,
this man should never have come here for a surrogate
partner. His wife wanted to come back to him. They
could have been brought in for counseling. They could
have done this therapy together. Lambert was simply
selling her for a dollar, twelve and a half thousand of
them.

"Is there such a difference, Ed? You've gone to bed
with other women. You came today, expecting to do it
with me. What would it have been?" She saw him shake
his head. "Just sex, Ed. There would have been no love
in it. Nice, enjoyable, even useful, but what would it
have meant? Hardly anything. I don't know your wife,
but I'll bet it was the same with her, just sex with your
friend, not love."

"She said he. . .it was great, the best ever, better than me."

"So she said it. She may have even thought she meant it. But I'll bet she didn't. If she wants you back, she must love you. And I'll bet she's sorry."

She looked at him, as deeply as she could, mustering all the compassion she could find. "Just sex, Ed. Nothing much really. Everybody does it—one way or another. It's not that important. It isn't worth ruining your life over."

Silence spread between them. She didn't fight it. She just let her words sink in. Finally she asked, "When you and your wife talked the last time, what did she say?"

"Nothin'. Just the kids and stuff."

"I don't mean that. When you get the idea she wanted to come back to you, what did she say?"

He looked down at his feet. "She said she was sorry, that it had all been a terrible mistake on her part." He paused, seemingly fascinated by his shoes.

"And what else?"

"She said she wouldn't blame me if I never forgave her." Then he looked up at Joanna. "She said lots of things."

"Including the fact she still loves you, I'll bet."

He returned her smile. "Yeah, she said that."

"And you? How do you feel about it?"

"I don't know. When you nurse a grudge for a long time. . ." He smiled boyishly. "You get used to it. It's hard to give it up."

"I know. But isn't love so much better than hate? Why not give love a chance. See her, talk to her." She saw him shaking his head vigorously. "Yes, Ed, talk, talk it all out. Don't hold back. Don't worry about her feelings. Let all your hurt out, tell her everything, including your ejaculatory incompetence. Even tell her about me."

"Really?"

"Yes. Start off on a whole new foot. I have a sense of you, Ed. Maybe I'm wrong, but I've an idea you're too kind. You're too sensitive to the feelings of others. You hold back rather than deliberately hurt another person. That may be all right some of the time, but not now. Lay it all on her—guilt I mean. Tell her how you feel, what she's done to your life, how hard it's been."

"I don't think I could do that."

"Yes you can. It'll never work if you keep it bottled inside you. It'll just come out in some other, nastier way." She smiled. "Besides, she wants you to. Believe me, it'll make it easier for her."

"Easier?"

"I can't explain. But when we do something wrong. . ." Suddenly, she realized her eyes were smarting, her voice choking up. ". . .we can recover. . .if we feel. . .our guilt. . .our sorrow. . . . Then—" And suddenly the tears came, and amid the sobs she just managed the words, "—then, if we are. . .granted. . .absolution. . ." She couldn't finish.

He had no idea why she was crying, but he handed her his handkerchief. She cried a moment, dabbing at her eyes. "I'm—I'm sorry. I—I don't know. . .where. . . that. . .came from." She smiled and wiped at her face, then handed him back his handkerchief. "I'm all right now," she sighed, "—except I could use a drink."

She stood up, intending to go to the kitchen, but she stopped, looking at him. She told him again he ought to see his wife, give his marriage a chance. She predicted they would patch it up, saying twenty years of marriage had to mean something. Suddenly, she had a thought. "I know. Maybe the two of you should have counseling. If you still have difficulties, sexual difficulties, the two of you could work together on it. Believe me, Ed, it will make your marriage better, so much stronger.''

He laughed. "Whoa. I haven't even said I'd talk to her.''

"But you're going to and it's going to work out. I know it is. I suppose I could speak to Dr. Lambert about having your fee applied to joint counseling. He might agree." She looked at him. "Will you try, Ed?''

"I don't know.''

"At least think about it?''

He sighed. "Okay.''

"While you do, I'll make us a drink.''

She never did. There was a knock at the door.

28

"Dr. Lambert! What are you doing here?"

"A better question is what *you're* doing here?" Then he saw Mueller. "Don't you think this is better confined to the office?"

Joanna could only stammer.

"I guess it really doesn't matter." He smiled at Mueller who had stood up. "I'm glad to see she is dedicated to her work."

"We were just talking doctor."

Joanna found her voice. "I thought you were going to Washington."

"I was. I got all the way to the airport, then realized there was something I needed to speak to you about. I came back. You were not in your office. I hoped you might be here."

"Wh-what did you want to see me about?"

He smiled. "Later. We'll discuss it later." He turned to Mueller. "So how did your treatment progress, Mr. Mueller?"

"Fine—I guess. Joanna thinks I should try to patch it up with my wife—my ex-wife, then both of us come for. . .for—"

"Counseling. I think there's hope for the marriage, doctor." Joanna was being her most emphatic. "His wife seems to want a reconciliation. I think the effort should be made."

"You do, do you?"

Joanna heard the coldness in his voice. He might have been a teacher speaking to a recalcitrant child. She stood her ground. "Yes, I do. If a reconciliation is possible—or even just an attempted one, there is no need for a surrogate partner."

"It is Mr. Mueller who has complained of ejaculatory incompetence. I don't believe his former wife has been having this trouble."

"Yes, but Doctor, I—"

He cut her off, smiling condescendingly. "But never mind." He turned to Mueller. "If Miss Caldwell thinks a reconciliation is wise, then it is. I just wish she had consulted with me, that's all. If you and Mrs. Mueller—or whatever her name is now, want to come for counseling, I will of course apply your fee toward that." There was no way he was going to return the money.

Mueller was looking at Joanna. "If you don't think I should, Doctor, I'll—"

"No, by all means, try for a reconciliation. Talk to your wife. Why don't you go now and call her." All Lambert wanted was to get him out of there. He moved to open the door. "By all means, Mr. Mueller, go now. Let us know what happens."

In a moment Joanna was alone with Lambert. She looked at him warily. He seemed all right, yet different. She couldn't help but feel afraid of him. "I'm sorry, Doctor, but I felt Mueller—"

"Hang Mueller. I don't care what you did with him. Above all, I don't care if he ever gets his rocks off."

She was shocked by his language, his tone of voice, and her fear rose exponentially.

"I want those files, Joanna."

Her mouth came open. "What files?"

"You know very well which files." His voice was

level, but with a glint of hardness to it. "Unfortunately I don't—not yet. I know Laura McGovern's file is missing. Others are gone, but I didn't take the time to figure out which."

"I-I don't know what you're talking about." She was unaware of stepping backwards, away from him.

He smiled. "You are a very poor liar, Joanna. I suspect it comes from your pentecostal upbringing. No matter. Where are those files?"

"I don't have them."

He made a quick search of the apartment, upturning the couch cushions, opening drawers and closets. When he returned to her his voice still had the same controlled but hard tone. "Where are those files?"

Joanna had been trying desperately to think, but her fear—she couldn't seem to stem it—paralyzed her mind. "I don't have them."

She was standing near the middle of the living room, between the doorways to the kitchen and her bedroom. Lambert came to her, a slight smile twisting his mouth, his eyes intent upon her. He reached out and gently clasped her upper arms. "Those files are my personal property, Joanna. You had no right to take them. Now I want them back."

She felt enmeshed by those eyes, by him. Always it was so with him. She looked away, determined to fight him. "I'm not going to tell you."

"Oh yes you are, Joanna." His fingers began to bite into her upper arms. "You're going to tell me and right now." The voice was not loud, but firm, demanding.

"His fingers were digging into her now. She felt the pain. "No." She winced. "You're hurting me."

"I don't want to hurt you, Joanna, but I will. I intend to get those files back."

The pain was sharp then and she cried out. She didn't

think it was possible for anyone's fingers to be so strong. "I-I gave them. . .to the police."

Slowly he lessened his grip, finally releasing her, surprise, disbelief on his face. "You gave them to the police?"

"Yes."

"Why did you do that?"

"To stop you, to put you out of business." Her fear was making her voice rise. "You're not running a clinic. You're operating a racket. You're just in it for money—as much of it as you can get." Her voice was becoming ragged now. "Money. That's all you want. Twenty thousand from Dillon. Ten thousand from poor Jerry Wofford. Twelve and a half thousand from this man—this Mueller. It's outrageous. I had to stop you." She saw the anger in his face. "You weren't helping people. You were *milking* them. Laura McGovern is dead. Poor Jerry Wofford jumped in front of a subway. How many lives do you want?" Her anger was cold fury now. "You made a whore of me. You *sold* me to men. I'll get you for that."

He seemed not to have heard her. "You gave them to the police?"

He hit her, with his right hand, palm flat against her left cheek, hard, jerking her head backwards and sideways. It happened so quickly she didn't even see the blow coming. "You turned me in to the police?" Again he hit her, harder this time. The third blow, hard against her other cheek, came as she was screaming with pain.

"Go ahead. Beat me up. Isn't that what pimps do?" The word seemed to stop him. "Yes, pimp. That's what you are. I'm your whore and you're just a pimp. Beat me up. Go ahead. Be a pimp."

The ugly word, repeated so often, seemed to stop him. He slowly lowered his head. His fury remained, but he had it under control now. Turning from her he strode over to stand before the front door. She thought he might be leaving, but he turned back to her, the strange, twisted smile on his lips.

"I believe you, Joanna. It's just the sort of cockeyed, do-gooding thing you'd do. Where did you come up with these idiotic notions?" He waited for an answer. She gave none. "Who did you talk to?"

"I'm not going to tell you."

He sighed. "All right. I guess it doesn't matter. What matters is that the police have my files." He hesitated, obviously thinking.

"Yes, and you're going to jail. There's nothing you can do about it."

He looked at her, his fury again rising. "Miss Caldwell, if you value your skin, you will go over there—" He pointed toward the couch. "—sit down and KEEP YOUR MOUTH SHUT." It was the first time he'd raised his voice. "I have to think."

She obeyed, sitting on the couch, watching him warily as he paced the floor, arms folded across his chest, deep in thought. It seemed to go on interminably. Once he asked if she had any whiskey. She motioned toward the kitchen, and he went there, opening and banging cupboard drawers. She thought about escape. She could get to the door and run. She knew he couldn't catch her. But the thought took too long. He was in the kitchen doorway, bottle in his hand, pouring into a glass, watching her as he did so. He set the bottle on the coffee table, then continued his pacing, carrying and upturning the glass.

Again she thought of escape. If she moved fast enough, she could get away. No. It wouldn't work. He would grab her at the door. And she knew he was too strong for her. Then she remembered. When she left the files at the police station, she left word for Rosetti to call her. He would. She'd find a way to let him know she was in trouble. Inwardly, she smiled. Everything was going to be all right.

"What files did you take beside Laura McGovern's?"

"I don't remember. And if I did I wouldn't tell you."

He glared at her a moment, but said nothing more, just resumed his pacing.

It seemed to Joanna many minutes passed, perhaps close to a half hour before he stopped. She saw him smile. He even laughed as he picked up the whiskey bottle and poured into his glass. "Fine bourbon, Miss Caldwell. You have good taste."

"Thank you." She didn't know what he was up to, but she was going along.

He tilted the glass and swallowed generously. "Yes, indeed, fine sour mash." He looked at her, a bright, almost kindly expression on his face. "I'm sorry you went to all this trouble, Joanna—stealing my files. It won't do you a particle of good."

"That's what you think."

"It's what I know. You've wasted your time."

"I looked at those files, Doctor, at least enough to know the charges the police will bring. You kept Laura McGovern, those other women in treatment long after they needed to be—if they ever did. I saw the reports. Orgasmic, orgasmic. They didn't need you. But you kept them, just to get their money."

"True, my dear, all true."

"That's conspiracy to defraud. And it's unethical. You'll lose your license—if you don't go to jail. And you took a million dollars from Laura McGovern. That's more conspiracy."

He laughed. "I didn't get it, Joanna. I merely hoped to—and would have except for Cupid's arrow and that prick Randall."

"That's another thing, you—"

"No more. I'm sick of your juvenile rantings. The simple fact is the law cannot touch me. The police now hold stolen evidence. No court in the land will allow them to use it."

His words stunned her, but she vaguely knew he was right. "But what's in those files will enable them to get you. They're already investigating you. Those files will—"

"Will do nothing. Even the fruits of stolen evidence is inadmissible." He laughed. "Our esteemed Supreme Court justices are sometimes extremely wise."

She gaped at him, unwilling to let him get away with his crimes. "Then I'll testify. I'll tell everything I know about you, everything you've done, to me, to the patients, to. . . ." She stopped, realizing what she was saying. The look on his face, cunning, triumphant, hard, told her he was thinking the same thing.

"You're not going to testify, Joanna. That must be obvious to you."

She watched him, warily, suddenly frightened. "You wouldn't. You haven't the guts."

He laughed. "We'll see, Joanna, we'll see." Casually, he drained his glass. "Really fine whiskey." He helped himself to some more. "The question is how is best to dispose of you. It shouldn't be difficult. As a physician I ought to be able to think of something." He sipped some whiskey, then began his pacing again. When he spoke it was as much to himself as to her. "The easiest, safest way would be to drop a hair dryer in the bathwater."

"I—I don't. . .have a hair dryer."

"I'm sure you do. All pretty girls have them. But no. I can't do it here. Somebody will have seen me come in or my car outside. I'm going to have to take you somewhere. Then what?"

Joanna watched him in undisguised horror. He was plotting how to kill her.

"An overdose. Needle marks." He stopped and looked at her. "You don't take drugs, do you?" He waited a moment for an answer. "No, you wouldn't. You're a pentecostal preacher's daughter—saving humanity from a horrid sex doctor." He made a sound of derision, then resumed his pacing.

When he again turned to her, he was smiling. "Would you like some of your excellent sour mash, Joanna?" She shook her head, not once looking away from him. "Too bad. We're going to have to wait, you and I. Can't leave here till dark. We might as well make ourselves comfortable."

"What're you going to do?" The words were hardly audible.

"You and I have gone out for a drive. We've been discussing business affairs. I'm taking you out to dinner. There's a terrible accident. A fiery one, I think. The gasoline tank explodes on impact. I'm thrown clear. Just manage to survive." He saw her reaction. "I think we'll use my car. I could use a new one."

She ran for the door, but he was too quick. In three strides his hand was planting against it. "I've been expecting that, Joanna. Just sit down. It will make everything easier." She fought him, screaming, kicking, flailing with her arms. Calmly, he transferred his whiskey glass to his left hand, leaned against the door and belted her as hard as he could in the face. She fell backwards against the back of the chair, then slid slowly to the floor. She was stunned but not knocked out.

"I told you to sit. You have a choice of the floor or the sofa."

She saw him raising his glass to his lips. "You pimp. That's what you are, a PIMP!"

"Whatever you say, Joanna. You should know."

Slowly she got off the floor, glaring at him, feeling the pain in her jaw.

"If you're bruised, I'm sure it will be attributed to the accident."

She was glaring at him when the phone rang. Rosetti. He was calling her back. She'd find a way to alert him.

"Don't answer it. Let it ring."

"But I have to. I'm expecting a call. If I don't answer, he'll wonder. . .come looking for me."

"Who will?"

"Hank Kraft—my boyfriend."

"Oh yes." He glanced at the ringing phone, then her. "All right, answer it. But if you try anything, I'll wring your neck right here. That can be attributed to the accident, too."

He grabbed her arm and pulled her toward the wall phone in the kitchen. He lifted the receiver off the hook and handed it to her. The warning in his eyes was clear. As she put the receiver to her ear, he leaned closer to her, listening. "Hello," she said.

"Joanna, is that you?" Nothing had prepared her for such a disappointment. "Joanna, this is Timmy Kraft."

"Oh, Timmy." God, Timmy. Why wasn't it Rosetti? Timmy couldn't help her. Or could he? She forced herself to brighten her voice. "How nice of you to call, Timmy. I didn't know you could use the phone."

"Oh, it's easy, Joanna. You just push the buttons."

"Yes, you're a very smart boy."

"Can you come and swim with me, Joanna?"

"Now?"

"Yes. The water's nice."

She saw Lambert shaking his head. "Timmy, I'm sorry, I can't—"

"But there's nobody to swim with me."

"Where's Hank, your daddy?"

"He went to New York to talk to Mommy. Then he's bringing his drawing board and stuff out. He won't be home till later."

"Are you alone?"

"Mrs. Dicentes is watching me, but she don't swim. I want to swim, Joanna. Can't you come and swim with me?"

Lambert jerked the phone from her ear. Covering the receiver, he hissed, "Get rid of the brat. Right now. And I mean it." He handed the phone back to her, but as she raised it to her ear, he gripped her wrist, his fingers biting in hard.

"I can't Timmy. Not today."

"Please, Joanna. I wanna swim."

Lambert slid his palm over the phone. "Get rid of him—NOW."

When his hand was gone, she blurted, "You're a nasty boy, Timmy. I don't want to swim with you. I don't ever want to see you again. Goodbye." Hurriedly she reached and hung up the phone with a bang. "Is that what you wanted?"

"Fine." He smiled. "So Kraft was going to call, was he? From New York, I suppose."

"He said he'd call."

"You're a lousy liar, Joanna."

She watched in dismay as he took the receiver off the hook and let it fall to the floor. "I think we'll have no more of these calls." Seemingly as punctuation, he shoved her hard toward the living room. "Now you sit, over there on the couch. And there'll be no more bolting for the door. I hate to hit a woman."

"I'll bet." But even as she spoke, she was obeying him, sitting where he pointed.

"You misjudge me, Joanna, always have. I'm the one person who did the most for you. All you've done is turn against me." He strode to the coffee table, bent to the bottle and poured generously in his glass, raised it, drank. "Yes, Joanna, very fine sour mash. Who enabled you to afford it? I did. I paid you well. I gave you opportunity—to learn—didn't I teach you all I know?—to improve yourself, to meet—" He snickered. "—*interesting* people, rich men. Why, look at all the fun you had with that actor. Surely you could have made something out of that."

She never took her eyes off him, just watched as he bent the glass again to his lips. The whiskey was making him expansive, voluble. She had never seen him drunk, but it had to be possible. Maybe if she kept talking, got him drunk. . . . "Dillon wanted me to go to California with him."

"And?"

"I refused."

He smiled. "Of course you did. A pentecostal preacher's daughter couldn't live in sin, could she?" His smile broadened and he shook his head in a parody of sadness. "Such a waste, Joanna, looking like you do, your face, your body. You were the best damn surrogate partner a man could have. I always said that—and I meant it. What a team we were. We had the world by the tail—" He laughed. "—no pun intended. Dillon was only the beginning. You and I could've made a ton of money."

She tuned him out, thinking about the phone now off the hook. Rosetti couldn't call her. Nor Hank. Would they know where she was? Would they think to come here? God, no. Hank was in New York. Rosetti was out on some case. He might not return for hours—until it was too late.

Lambert's words entered her consciousness. He was rendering a spirited defense of himself, his work, the sex clinic. She prodded him with arguments, questions—"What about Jerry Wofford? Was he a success?"—"Why did you keep those women in therapy when they were orgasmic?"—"Why such high fees? You were just milking them." She had to keep him talking, and it worked. He emptied his glass, refilled it, drained that in three swallows. When the glass again came to the table, she quickly grabbed the bottle and poured.

"Thank you, Joanna. It is good whiskey." He raised the glass, then hesitated, smiling at her. "Don't think you're going to get me drunk Joanna. It's never been known to happen. I've got a steel head and a cast iron liver."

Her optimism plummeted. It was probably true. All the liquor was doing was giving him courage. She half listened to a long harangue about all he'd done for Laura McGovern, describing the unhappy, frigid woman who had first come to him, how he had made her over. Joanna glanced at her watch. Five after five. God, how much longer could she keep this up?

When she looked back at him, she sensed the change at once. He had stopped talking and was looking at her, eyes bright, mouth open, a strange expression on his face. Only it wasn't strange. She knew what it meant and that knowledge frightened her more than his hitting her.

"Do you know what's been so hard for me the last few months, Joanna?" There was a low, liquid sound to his voice.

She shook her head.

He hesitated, his violet eyes fixed on her, his lips twisted into a slight smile. "Having you around, sending you off with other men, humoring you and your stupid virtue, denying myself.'' The smile widened. "We have a long time till dark. I think we should make use of it, don't you?''

"No," she said in disbelief.

"You are a sexpot, Joanna. And I've denied myself long enough. It's only fair and right that I—" He laughed. "—see what the customers are getting." A longer laugh this time. "I'd hate for them not to get their money's worth."

She tried to run then, thrusting from the couch, hoping to dart past him, into the bedroom, the bath. She could lock herself in there. It didn't work. Laughing, he reached out a hand, grabbed her forearm and held her, pulling her back toward him as though she were a rag doll. She struggled, digging in her heels, but it was useless. He was too strong.

"I do so like a woman who struggles." Casually he dropped his whiskey glass to the rug and seized her with both hands. She kicked, flailed at him with her fists and screamed, but her struggles were as nothing and her screams were lost in his laughter.

It came as one, the movement of his hands, the ripping sound, the sudden violent action, and she was shocked into ceasing her struggles. He had ripped open her blouse, pulled it back from her shoulders and she was naked to the waist. "God, Joanna," he said. "I should have raised the fee."

"Don't you touch me."

His hand came toward her and she backed away, although he still held her right arm.

"You really are lovely, Joanna."

She felt his hand on her breast. Amid her fear and revulsion she found a momentarily island of calm. "You really are a pimp, Lambert, a real pimp. You beat me, then you rape me. Isn't that what pimps do?"

"Probably. I wouldn't know. But does it matter now?"

She was pulled against him and he was trying to find her mouth with his. She twisted away, shaking her head, biting, scratching, trying to kick. It was to little avail, but somehow she had to fight him. She couldn't surrender. She knew she was screaming. She felt the pain of the slaps as he tried to silence her, heard him curse and laugh, felt her skirt being ripped away, herself being lifted, carried. Still she fought him and screamed and screamed. So loudly did she scream, she did not hear the noise of the front door being broken open.

29

Joanna awakened hard, sleep tugging at her repeatedly. Finally, after she had lain on her side, then tried to roll to her stomach, a sharp twinge of pain in her jaw sparked her awake. She remembered. Lambert had hit her.

Abruptly she sat up, pain, fear remaining even after she opened her eyes. Where was she? Groggy, confused, her fear mounted a little. Then she remembered. Hank. He said he wasn't about to let her be alone. He'd brought her to Laura's house. Then it all came back to her, Lambert planning to kill her, trying to rape her, Hank and Rosetti bursting in to stop him, her shaking in his arms, crying against his shoulder, his patting her back, saying silly yet comforting words. Yes, she remembered. Lambert in handcuffs, being led away, a jacket being wrapped around her shoulders, sitting in a police cruiser with Hank. They'd wanted to take her to the hospital. She said no, she was all right. Over Hank's protests, she'd gone to the station, given a brief statement, then she'd let him take her here. A doctor. He'd insisted on a doctor. A shot. Yes the doctor had given her a needle.

She moved to get up, sitting on the edge of the bed. Absently, she picked up her terry robe from the foot of the bed, not reacting to it until she saw her clothes on a chair, her pink suit, a stack of panties, the sundress, shoes and bathing suit she'd bought in New York. She smiled and then did get up, wrapping herself in the robe.

Laura's house was unfamiliar to her and she had trouble finding him. He was not in the living room or kitchen, even the study. Finally, she found him, leaning over his drawing board, in a bright, sunny room, obviously a converted porch at the rear of the house.

He heard her and looked up smiling. "Good morning."

"What time is it? My watch stopped."

He glanced at his. "Quarter to eleven—about." He got up and came to her, putting his arm casually around her shoulders. "How do you feel?"

"Okay. Not quite awake, but otherwise. . . ." For the first time she smiled. "Glad to be alive. Glad to be able to say good morning to you."

He squeezed her shoulders tighter. "How about breakfast?" With gentle pressure he moved her in the direction of the kitchen. "To prove my talents extend beyond eggs, I've made pancakes. Sound good? You must be starved."

She laughed. "Even if I'm not, I'm sure you'll make me eat."

In the kitchen, he sat her at a dinette and turned on the electric grill. "Coffee?"

"Yes, please." Two cups were poured, sipped, tasted, then set down. "My clothes. How'd you get them?"

"I borrowed your key and went to your place. Didn't know what to get. Picked out the things I'd seen you wear and liked. Hope it's all right."

"Fine, but I've got to go home. Can't stay here."

"I know. A little later, okay? Rosetti called. When you feel like it, the police want you to come down to the station, give a statement."

"Okay." She looked up at him as he stirred a pitcher of batter. "Is there any way I can thank you enough. . .for—"

"I didn't do anything, Joanna. It was Rosetti mostly—and Timmy. He's the one you have to thank."

"Oh Hank, I hated being mean to him. Will he ever forgive me?"

"Already has. You were smart to do it. Only trouble was, I was slow to catch on. Nearly blew it. I came back from New York. Timmy was moping around, saying you didn't like him any more. I was disgusted with him. I kept saying he had misunderstood. You wouldn't talk like that to him. But he insisted. Then I tried to tell him you were just upset about something, didn't mean what you'd said. But he wouldn't believe me." Hank laughed. "The kid was inconsolable."

"I am sorry. But I couldn't think of what to do."

"Then Rosetti called. He wanted your unlisted phone number. That was another good thing—your not being in the phone book. Awhile later he called back. Your line had been busy for a half hour. He wanted to leave. What was your address? He'd stop there on his way home. I told him where you lived. Then he asked if I'd talked to you. Did I know how you'd gotten the files? After he hung up, I got to thinking. Something was wrong. I decided to go to your place myself. You know the rest."

"Thank God you came—both of you."

"It was too close for comfort. We were almost too late."

She shuddered. "I know."

He reached out and gripped her hand. "Forget it, Joanna. It's over." Suddenly aware of touching her, he took his hand away. Then to fill the awkwardness, he said, "Rosetti thinks they've got a helluva case on

Lambert—assault, attempted kidnapping, attempted murder.''

He didn't say rape. She was glad for that.

"Then they figure to get him for extortion, conspiracy, even that gross imposition charge." He smiled. "Seems Lambert forced himself on the police-woman. That's one reason Rosetti wanted to talk to you, to tell you that bit of good news."

"It is good news."

"Lambert's finished, Joanna. You've closed him up."

She nodded. "Good riddance."

"My thought, too." The griddle hot, he poured out four medium sized pancakes on the surface. "You'll have to testify against him. That all right?"

"Yes."

"Shouldn't keep you from going to California. You can always return for the trial."

"California?" Then she remembered telling Hank she might be going there. How long ago it was.

Pancakes were turned, then served, a pat of butter on top, syrup offered, accepted, poured. She sat there, looking at the food. "They look delicious, Hank."

"They are. Eat."

She picked up her knife and fork, then, holding them, looked at him. "I'm not going to California, Hank. I decided that long ago. It seems eons—but I guess it's only a few days."

"Eat." He saw her purse her lips, then bend to the stack of pancakes, cutting a small wedge, inserting it in her mouth. "What made you change your mind?"

She chewed, swallowed. "I never really thought seriously of going. I just said I was—to hurt you."

He said nothing for a time, watching her eat. "More syrup?"

"No, this is fine."

"What *are* you going to do?"

"I don't know. I'm not sure."

He watched her handle the knife and fork, continental style, fork in her left hand. "You want to talk about it?"

She had just stabbed a wedge of pancake with her fork. She stopped the motion of her hands. "Yes." She placed the knife and fork carefully on her plate, dropped her hands to her lap and looked down at them. "When you think you're going to die, it does something to you."

"I should imagine."

She looked up at him, great intensity showing in her face. "I thought of you, Hank—and Timmy. Really I did. But mostly I thought of me. I felt so badly. It's—it's hard to explain. I didn't want to die. I'm sure of that. But I felt so awful—really terrible that I was going to die without ever having done anything with my life. Can you understand that?" She looked up at him, saw him nod, then looked down again. "I felt—I knew I hadn't accomplished anything. There just had to be some purpose to my life. It couldn't just—*end*. It was all such a horrible *waste*." Her shoulders slumped and she sighed. "I'm not explaining it very well, am I?"

"I think you're doing beautifully, Joanna."

Again she looked up at him, intensity on her face. "I don't know how or what, but I've got to do something with my life. It all has to mean something. If I'd gone to California. It would have been just—" She shrugged. "—more of the same, waste, emptiness, escape."

He let the words sit there a moment. There was no hurry. "So what're you going to do?"

"I don't know." She sighed. "I want to be something more than I've been."

"You were never cut out for that surrogate partner nonsense."

"I know. But it's not just that. All my life there's been a man—my father, teachers, then Judd Forbes. After that there was Lambert, all those men—you. I threw myself at Dillon. I—"

"Was he the one you were going to California with?"

"Yes. Don't you see, Hank? All I've been is a. . .a companion—a seminal vessel. I'd like for once to try to find me, who I am, what I can do." Suddenly she stopped, seeing the hurt on his face. But he spoke before she could.

"You weren't a seminal vessel to me, Joanna."

"I know. I'm sorry I said that. You loved me—I know that. But wouldn't it be more of the same? I'd be leaning on you, depending on you, never knowing myself."

He nodded. "I suppose. So what are you going to do? Go back to school? Get a degree?"

"Psychology, you mean?" She saw him nod, which led to another deep sigh from her. "I've never known what to do in psychology." She spread her lips into a bitter smile. "I'm hardly going to do what I've been doing."

"You're marvelous with Timmy, you know. Ever think about child psychology?"

"No." She looked at him. "Might be an idea. I'll think about it."

"Good. No hurry. You've lots of time."

She nodded. Then she looked at him, a long time, intently, biting at her lips as she did so. "I love you, Hank. Yesterday, last night, when he was. . .when I thought I was—God, Hank, I've been so stupid. I do love you—and Timmy." She looked at him, waiting for him to speak. But he did not, merely returning her gaze.

"I had a patient—was that only yesterday? He was an incompetent ejaculator. Couldn't do it because all he could think about was his wife in the arms of his best friend. I felt so sorry for him, tried to help him. And I did—but not the way I—Lambert wanted me to. I talked to him, about forgiving his wife, about the absolute unimportance of loveless sex, the mistakes we all make." She felt her eyes beginning to burn and she hesitated, trying to get control of herself. She had only small success in that. "While I talked to him, I-I kept tearing up, starting to cry. I didn't. . .know why. I do—now." She felt the tear rolling down her cheek. She couldn't help it, nor did she make any effort to wipe it away. "It's what you said, Hank. I have to forgive myself."

He smiled at her. "Have you?"

"I don't know. . .I guess so, yes. I know I'm glad it's over. I'm sorry I ever got into it. I know. . ." Through her tears she managed a smile. "I know I'm tired of using a whip on myself."

He laughed. "Good. Eat." He watched her pick up the fork and take a bite, begin to chew. "Did you mean what you just said about loving me?"

"Yes. Very much so."

"Can I say thanks?"

"For loving you?"

"Yes—and for giving me another chance. I love you, Joanna—really love you. I won't make the mistake I made before—with Vicki. Because I love you, I want you to be you—your own person, independent, feeling useful, valuable, accomplished. It's the only way anyone can live a life—and everyone has to do it for himself, herself. I want you to."

"Will there be a you and me, an us?"

He laughed. "And Timmy makes three. The little

matchmaker's practically got us married already. But we'll resist him. You get your act together, decide what you want to do. I suspect you'll be going back to school. You're a career girl at heart."

"And you? Won't I see you?"

"Try to keep me away." He smiled. "Eat your pancakes before they get cold."